BROKEN INNOCENCE:

ALPHA BILLIONAIRE ROMANCE ENTIRE SERIES (BOOKS 1-5)

By Bridget Taylor

© 2018

COPYRIGHT

Broken Alpha Billionaire Romance Entire Series (Books 1-5)

By Bridget Taylor

Copyright @2018 by Bridget Taylor.

THIS SERIES INCLUDES THE FOLLOWING BOOKS:

BROKEN INNOCENCE

BOOK ONE

BROKEN PURITY BOOK TWO

BROKEN CHASITY BOOK THREE

BROKEN DESIRE BOOK FOUR

BROKEN LUST BOOK FIVE

TABLE OF CONTENTS

BROKEN INNOCENCE
BOOK ONE

ONE

Opulence.

That was the first word that came to my mind as I walked into the Lennox. The large, fifteen-foot tall fountain greeted me with a rush of water jetting into the air and its soft mist touching my nose. I turned my head to the left to see the Bluepointe Lounge, where a young man in a crisp white shirt and black slacks opened the doors from the lobby into the restaurant. To my right stood the passageway to the parking deck. It was exclusive to the Lennox Building, even though three other buildings sat adjacent to us on this block.

Tomorrow I would be walking through that passageway. Today, I had been too nervous about my first day to consider driving as an option. With the rotating glass doors behind me and the elevator lobby ahead of me, I walked forward. I was taking a new step into a bright and energetic future. My next step would be –

"Oh, excuse me."

I stopped and turned my head, averting my eyes for the tall, blonde woman I had nearly blundered into. "I am so sorry."

"That's quite all right." She extended one long, narrow hand out to me. I noticed that her nails were perfectly sculpted and felt a twinge of envy and intimidation as I took her hand to shake. "You must be new. Everyone is thrown off by the lobby the first day."

"Thank you." I hesitated and looked up to meet the bright blue eyes that studied me carefully. I thought this woman was as intelligent as she was beautiful. Every feature seemed perfectly in place, from the curve of her eyebrows to the small smile that accentuated her lips. "I'm Stacy Caldwell."

Her smile broadened. "Then it's fortuitous that we almost ran into each other. We can take the elevator up together. I'm Ana Golde."

I dropped her hand, trying to be casual about it. I was hoping to have a few minutes to collect myself, maybe fidget with my hair in the bathroom before meeting Ms. Golde. She was the Human Resources Manager for Lennox Advertising, and would be the one responsible for the orientation process of my first week.

"It's a pleasure to meet you, Ms. Golde," I said. I was proud of myself for keeping my voice even and remembering my manners.

"Please, call me Ana. We like to keep on a first name basis in the office. It helps to foster and maintain a creative atmosphere. Save the 'Mister' and 'Missus' for the meetings with clients." Ana gestured around the fountain and I followed her through the lobby and to the elevators. Six total waited to take us and other employees of the different Lennox Enterprise subsidiaries up to their offices.

Everyone appeared tailored and groomed, perfect in their appearance. I looked down at my own clothes, a simple, modest pantsuit, and open jacket with a white button down blouse underneath. It and the seven similar outfits I had were all very nice, probably the nicest clothes I had ever owned, bought with the very generous sign-on advance that I received.

My brown hair was pulled back neatly into a wrapped bun, and I had spent an hour in front of the mirror to make sure that my makeup was as smooth and flawless as I could make it.

Next to Ana and the other beautiful men and women I saw waiting on the elevators, I felt plain and simple. I kept my mind focused on the qualifications that had won me the coveted

Creative Assistant position and tried to keep my nerves calm. As the elevator doors opened, Ana's words caught up to me.

"I'm going to be meeting with clients?" I watched Ana step onto the elevator. Around me, others moved in as well.

"Yes," Ana said, giving me another of her warm smiles and gesturing inside, "and if you want to meet your team, you should probably get in the elevator now."

I nodded and stepped in, easing between Ana and another young woman as the doors to the crowded elevator closed. I was not expecting client meetings. I thought that I would simply be in the background, one of the many cogs working to make the creative team function and flow. Mr. Cavanaugh had certainly not mentioned client meetings.

My center of gravity moved down as the elevator jetted upward, as though caught in a sudden draft. The sensation was dizzying and I felt disoriented as the elevator arrived at the first of its floors. I inched around as others began to move out of the elevator car and onto their floor.

Ana gave me a sympathetic look. "It took me a year to get used to them. I still hate these elevators. It is worse going down."

I swallowed hard. Another young woman nodded in agreement with Ana as the elevator began its rapid ascent again. I would be in here for another fifteen floors. Lennox Advertising was the crown of Lennox Enterprises, and as such, it was on the top suite of floors and a part of Mr. Lennox's own offices.

We finished the nightmarish elevator ride with three other passengers, all women, all as beautifully sculpted as Ana. They chatted together happily, as we walked off the elevator and onto our floor. I followed Ana quietly to her office, taking note of the different people that I saw as I walked through the halls.

Everyone here was beautiful. Most of the staff were women, though I noticed a few men. Of the women, most were blonde sprinkled by a few vibrant redheads and dark brunettes, the deep almost black color that I wished my hair had managed to attain. I was stuck with a light, dull color that passed as brown, if you were very kind and generous. The men were as chiseled as the women were and carried themselves with natural confidence.

Even the woman working in the mailroom, diligently separating sealed envelopes and sorting them, was beautiful. She was shapelier than most of the women I saw with a generous hourglass figure. She smiled as I passed, her cheeks dimpling, and I could not help but return it. I wondered if she offered that smile to everyone, and if anyone could resist its charm.

Ana guided me into her office and to one of the very comfortable chairs in front of her desk. She took her own and, on cue, her secretary entered with two cups of steaming coffee and a plate of sweeteners and cream. I thanked her and turned my attention to Ana.

We spent the morning sipping coffee as she briefed me on the same boring corporate details that I had heard while I was an intern at Lellman& White. Ana was thorough and her voice was even and pleasant, making listening to her easy. We went over the basic office protocols, dress codes, appropriate behaviors, and the importance of attendance and punctuality. She gave me an overview of emergency procedures and showed me how to access the business continuity site both in the office and from home. She provided me her card – I was to keep it as my first number in my rolodex – in case I ever needed to speak to her about anything at all. She then went over the benefits package and when everything would kick in.

"There is one more thing." Ana leaned her elbows on her desk and fixed me with an even look. "Henry Lennox."

"I won't bother Mr. Lennox," I said. I supposed that working in the same office as Henry Lennox had to have an appeal. It seemed that every few months he was on the cover of a magazine or featured in an exclusive spread. "I assume he has a pretty busy day, managing the different companies he owns."

Ana smirked. "You would be surprised." She straightened in her chair. "Henry is known to wander the floor. The advertising wing of his company is his favorite. This is where he began and where he spends most of his time. It is his pride."

I nodded, understanding. "I will make sure I'm focused and working, so that I -"

Ana shook her head. I was missing something, something that Ana thought should have been apparent. I thought back to my interview with Mr. Cavanaugh and the discussions that we had about my role on his team and in the company. I could not think of what I had missed or overlooked from the conversation. Ana's eyes softened and she smiled.

"Henry is always *available*," Ana said. The gentle and straightforward way she said the word *available* told me its meaning right away. "Affairs between him and staff in this office are not unusual. They are brief, casual affairs – as casual as such a thing can be. It is important that you understand right away that they are not for personal advancement. They are only pleasure and nothing more. No raises or promotions follow his attention. If at any point you had in your mind to use an affair for that, please just turn your attention elsewhere."

With my hands in my lap, I fidgeted, dancing my fingers together. "It never crossed my mind." I searched for a way to say this and be polite. I sensed protectiveness in Ana's words, as if she was looking out for Mr. Lennox as much as looking out for me. Was it a friendship between them, or perhaps another young woman who did once think an affair would get her special favors? I realized it could be both. A direct approach would probably be the best. "Men like Mr. Lennox are not my type."

Ana laughed and her eyes shone bright. "Of course he is your type." Her laugh stopped, but the amusement did not leave her eyes. "Henry is every woman's type. That is exactly the point of men like him."

A knock sounded at the door. It opened, and Mr. Cavanaugh peered in. He was a handsome man, in his mid-thirties with neatly trimmed brown hair that was beginning to see visits by flecks of grey. He gave me a smile and turned his attention to Ana.

"Are we ready to meet the team?" he asked as he stepped into the office.

Ana looked at me. "Do you have any other questions for me?"

I shook my head. "No, I think I'm ready to get started."

Ana offered me her hand again and we stood. "Perfect. Then welcome to Lennox Advertising. I know you are going to make a wonderful addition to Michael's team."

Ana walked me out of her office and left me with Mr. Cavanaugh. He asked me about my morning, and if I had questions for him before I met the team. I gave him a brief overview of my conversation with Ana, and that I felt confident and ready – that was partly true. I was nervous, but there was no point delaying anything. I did not tell him about the part of the conversation about Mr. Lennox. I was not sure if it would be appropriate to discuss with him and decided not to take that chance. I thought about Ana's words, that Mr. Lennox was every woman's type. As I looked at Mr. Cavanaugh, I could not disagree more. He was more the type of man that I would be attracted to, were he not my direct manager anyway.

"My first rule is to please call me Michael, not Mr. Cavanaugh." Michael smiled and led me up a flight of stairs to the second level of the office suite. "My second is to feel free to socialize with your team. If you can laugh together, you can create together. As long as deadlines are met, I am flexible about your lunches, but I do ask that you come in on time in the mornings. We have a quick creative meeting every morning and it is important that you attend."

"Be on time in the mornings. Meet my deadlines so that I can take a longer lunch, and call you Michael." I smiled at him as he looked back at me from the stairway. He returned the smile and I felt a small warmth in the center of my stomach. Definitely, the kind of man I could fall for. "I can handle that."

"Good." As we reached the top of the stairs, he gestured to a set of double doors. "Let's go and meet your new team. I did take the liberty of showing them your internship portfolio from Lellman& White, so they are really excited to meet you."

My nervousness returned, but I kept my shoulders back and my head straight as he led me through the double doors. My work at Lellman&White had been good, but part of that was because I was inspired by the chance opportunity to hear something the client had said, something that had sparked a creative fire. I was proud of my work and terrified that it was the expectation of all my future endeavors. It was going to be hard to live up to it.

He led me into the team office, and I was struck by the layout. On one side of the room, desks were situated perpendicular to the wall, each with a lamp and wide enough for papers and sketches to be strewn about, which they were. On the other side of the room was a round table with several chairs around it. Here the team was gathered, all women and all beautiful. Of the five, four were blonde. One sported deep red hair, the kind that only comes from a box that looked incredible against her creamy skin. They leaned over papers, chatting happily, as we entered the room.

Between the table and the desks, situated against the back wall of this open office was one final desk, which I assumed to be Michael's desk. It was neat and tidy, a complete contrast to the other desks in the room.

Michael led me up to the table and cleared his throat in order to get everyone's attention. The women turned, and each one of them was as beautiful as every other face I had seen in the office so far. Perfectly symmetrical faces, soft lines; they each had a graceful smile that broadened at the sight of me. Under their gaze, I felt frumpy and self-conscious.

"Ladies, please meet Stacy Caldwell." He paused and waited for everyone to utter their hellos to me. Then, gesturing around the table starting with the redhead and working his way around the blondes, he introduced them. "Lillian White, Tina Abernathy, Karla Levin, Michelle Gordon, and Wendy Smith. This is going to be the ad team you will be working with."

"It's nice to meet you all." I felt stupid for saying such canned words, but before my self-consciousness could grow, they pulled me into their group and conversation erupted.

My attention was drawn from them to the pictures covering the tables, models in various outdoor action-wear, hiking clothes, climbing gear, and even yoga outfits. Any worry about the possibility of a perceived faux pas was quickly discarded as I was bombarded with questions about terminology, target market interest, and if it was important to highlight color choice in the sportswear line.

"It's not like we haven't written ad copy for a clothing line before," Lillian said, looking up at me. "It's just that this is the first line we have had to do that was not born for a Paris runway."

I liked these women. I could not be more different from them. I was the new girl in a big office, fresh from college. Yet here they were, turning to me for guidance. Suddenly I felt confident in recreating my work from my intern portfolio. It was not inspiration that they needed. If the mess on their desks was any indication – and it usually was when it came to creative talent – they had inspiration in droves. What they needed was my experience working with outdoor clothing. Between my portfolio and my hobbies, I had that in spades.

"You just have to think of the outdoors as the Paris runway," I said, gesturing to the photo of the yoga gear. "High fashion belongs in New York and Paris. This belongs in the gym." I pulled over the hiking gear. "This belongs on the Appalachian trail. That belongs on a mountain." I pointed to the climbing outfit.

"We could have a model suspended on a cliff face." Karla's eyes widened. "In profile, we could show off the model's curves very nicely."

I laughed as we began brainstorming ideas over the pictures. Lunch came in to us, trays of Chinese and Sushi to mix and match. We balanced plates on our hands as we discussed the different products of the clothing line and what ways we could bring them to life. By the time our plates were emptied of food, I realized that these women had completely welcomed me. I was part of their team.

By the afternoon, as work was winding down and we were preparing for our rush-hour trips home, I understood with that welcome came inclusion, something I was not used to from women as attractive as they were.

"Have you met Mr. Lennox yet?" Wendy asked as she began gathering up photographs.

"I haven't had the pleasure," I said.

Michelle's eyes glazed over, and I realized my double entendre.

"Expect to be flirted with," Karla said.

"In the office?" I tried to imagine that. When I was in high school, I worked part time at a fast food restaurant. Another high school student was in the habit of flirting with the girls from his place at the fry cook station. None of us minded the flirtation. He was cute and he never said anything crass. Our shift manager, on the other hand, took it upon himself to educate him with three hours of sexual harassment videos.

Of course, who would be pulling aside Mr. Lennox for education? I tried to picture Ana doing so, but that idea quickly faded as her warnings and advice came to mind. Obviously, HR did not mind.

"It's flattering," Michelle said. "You get a compliment on your work, and a reminder that you're a beautiful woman."

Michelle's lashes fluttered over her blue eyes and I wondered why in the world she would need the reminder. She had to have a mirror she dressed in front of every day. None of these women carried themselves in a way that would suggest they doubted their attractiveness. Perhaps, I thought, it was just a matter of getting away from the cold, sterile behavior expected in an office.

Tina glanced back to Michael as he sat at his desk. "We can tell you stories if you want to join us for drinks downstairs."

Normally office gossip was something I would ignore, but I felt caught up in the inclusion. I nodded happily. We finished cleaning up the planning table. I familiarized myself with my desk, realizing that I had not even looked at it since walking into the office. Tomorrow, I would take a little time to arrange myself, since this would be my workspace once brainstorming was finished. It would have to wait until then. The girls were chattering away for me to join them. I waved back to Michael as we walked out and followed them downstairs.

TWO

The Bluepointelounge was crowded, but somehow we managed to secure a large high top near the bar. I was starting to suspect that a drink and appetizers here was a common way to wait out rush hour traffic. We each ordered a round of drinks and a sampler to share. Before any stories began, I was bombarded with questions about myself. My team seemed genuinely interested in me and I found it easy to answer their questions.

Half way through our drinks, Tina decided to start the stories.

"It was my first week here," Tina tapped her chin. "It was when I was on Angela's team. Mr. Lennox came by to see us and it started with his smile. He might have had my underwear down by the time he was leaning on my desk."

"Oh shut up!" Michelle tapped Tina playfully on the arm. "He doesn't do anything but flirt in the office."

"In the office maybe," Wendy said. "His elevator is another matter. We were halfway down and he was halfway up my skirt."

Lillian shook her head, a twisted smile on her lips. "He told me he wanted strawberry lemonade. I thought at first, he just wanted a drink. Then he brought Linda and me..." Lillian paused and leaned closer to the table. "She's got this thick, golden hair. She's on maternity leave now. She got married last year. Anyway, he brought us to his condo so that he could have us both at the same time. He would take turns going down on us, and then I realized what he meant by strawberry lemonade."

I found myself wondering if she took the time to dye the hair between her legs, or if she was a natural shade of red as well, and started blushing.

Karla laughed and patted me gently on the back of the hand. "You can stop us any time we make you uncomfortable."

The idea of admitting what brought on my blush only made my face feel hotter. I shook my head, took a sip of my drink, and let the alcohol warm and calm me. "It's okay. If this really is a regular thing, I'm going to have to get used to hearing the stories."

Tina nodded. "When it's your turn, just be frank with him about what you are okay with. Mr. Lennox likes it rough, tie you up and whip you with a flogger. I got so caught up in what was going on, I ended up with a welt on my ass that would not go away for a week."

I winced, trying to picture how hard a strike would have to be to do that. I remembered my grandmother spanking me with a switch when I was a child. It left a mark that was gone the next morning. I could not imagine having a mark that lasted a week.

"She couldn't sit down," Michelle said. "I felt really bad for her."

Tina shrugged her shoulders. "It's what safe words are for. My fault for not using it."

"You weren't upset that you got hurt?" I asked.

"You don't leave a night with Mr. Lennox upset," Michelle said. Tina nodded in agreement. "It can get rough and sometimes it hurts. He doesn't do anything you don't want him to, and everything you want to feel."

As we finished our drinks and nibbled at the plate of appetizers, I listened to them exchange their stories. Every woman at the table had an encounter with Mr. Lennox at some point, typically soon after joining the company. Lillian and Karla had the opportunity for repeat encounters, something that everyone acknowledged was rare. For Lillian, it was her willingness to take part in a threesome. Karla was a masochist who was happy to let him flog her for a few hours.

The stories entranced me. Mr. Lennox seemed to balance his dark desires for pain with their need for pleasure, taking them to limits, and pulling back. I had heard of stories like that, but never with the kind of detail that they shared. In college, those stories were always, "I read this," or "Did you hear what happened to So-and-so after Friday's party?" They were offering me firsthand accounts of situations that I wanted to find revolting. Instead, I felt tantalized.

Then there were their reactions to each other. I was so used to girls like them – or at least girls who were attractive like them – shooting daggers at each other, even at me on occasion. It marked my experiences through high school and college. If two girls so much as looked at the same boy, the daggers were out. For them, the experience was a rite of passage or a badge of pride. There was no jealousy. They did not compare stories to one up each other.

Their expectation that I would accept Mr. Lennox's advances was not odd to me. I thought of Ana's words. He was "every woman's type." What amazed me was the expectation that he would as quickly and easily make the offer to a girl like me as any of them. Sure, I could stand toe to toe with them at the brainstorming table. Beauty was not the only thing these women had. They had talent and mine was a match for them, but my looks were not, and I could not imagine Mr. Lennox singling me out in a room of any of them, except as someone to pass over.

THREE

The week passed quickly and any thoughts of meeting Mr. Lennox, or how I would react if he did decide to flirt with me were pushed from my mind. My focus was on the project, since the client would be in on Friday to see our initial ideas. Between the constant brainstorming sessions and my growing nerves at having to stand face to face with a client, I could not think about him.

Friday morning, I decided that my nerves would simply have to go. I had suggested, quietly, that I could sit out the meeting and get a head start on concept art. That was quickly hushed. My presence was expected because I was part of the team, and it was just something that I was going to have to accept.

As I came into the office, Michael gathered everyone together for the morning brainstorm and pep talk. He was as nervous about the meeting with the client as I was and that was a relief. He gave me a smile that made me feel warm and I could not help but return it. Was it flirting or just reassurance? I decided either one was good.

Michael focused us on preparing for the meeting and retired to his own desk to review projects and plan. The rest of us exchanged ideas on how best to present the ad proposal to our client in order to bring him in. I was hardly aware of the door to our office opening until I saw the wistful look on Michelle's face.

I turned around to see Mr. Henry Lennox enter the office, his head high, his shoulders back, and a slight but strong swagger in his step. His black hair was brushed neatly black and his green eyes sparkled. This was a man who knew just what he owned. He was at the top of the world and the top of his game. At eighteen, he was recognized as one of the advertising geniuses. At twenty-four, he had turned that genius into one of the most successful advertising start-ups in the country. Twenty years later, he was sitting at the top of a multi-national media conglomerate.

I turned back to the work at hand and realized that while Mr. Lennox was here, my teammates were not going to be completely focused. Each of them seemed to take turns noticing him, offering him almost worshipful doe-eyes. I would have sighed and rolled my eyes, except for my knowledge that their infatuation came, in part, from their experiences with him.

"How are my loveliest ladies this morning?" Mr. Lennox walked up to our table and stood between Lillian and me.

"We're doing wonderful, Mr. Lennox," Tina cooed.

At that, I did roll my eyes and Karla giggled at me.

"You must be Ms. Caldwell." Mr. Lennox reached down and took my hand in his. Before I could say anything, he kissed the back softly and released it. The gesture was courteous and quick. It was also possessive and assuming. It was just the kind of flirtation that I imagined a man like him making.

"It's nice to meet you," I said. I tried to meet his eyes and found that I could not manage it. I realized a girl could get lost in them, and I did not want to be that girl. I turned my attention back to the pages of concept art on the table.

"Beautiful," Mr. Lennox said as he leaned in next to me.

I smiled. His attention was drawn to the art, good. "Thank you. This one is Karla's idea for the climb shot and the accompanying sportswear. We've all been working really hard on these."

I glanced up at Karla to see her smiling at me.

"I wasn't talking about the pictures," Mr. Lennox said evenly.

I could feel his eyes on me and felt perplexed by Karla's smile. Did she think his flirting was cute? I quickly moved around the table, putting Tina and Wendy between us. When I glanced back up at Mr. Lennox, his green eyes darkened and I could tell that he understood the rejection he just received. I braced myself for what would follow.

"Yes, these pictures are great too. Michael has shown me the work; I think our client will be impressed." Mr. Lennox's eyes captured mine and would not let go. I felt terrified. "You've been a real asset to the team. You should be proud of your work so far."

His eyes released me and he turned his attention to Michael, walking over to his desk. As the two men discussed the upcoming afternoon visit, my teammates drew me back to them. When I turned back, Michelle's eyes were wide and Lillian looked amazed.

"I have never seen anyone do that before," Tina leaned in over the table and whispered.

"Do what?" I felt strange and confused.

"Turn down Mr. Lennox," Karla said. "Everyone fawns over him."

I swallowed hard and glanced back at Mr. Lennox as he leaned over Michael's desk to look at something. "He seemed to take it well."

I turned back to the girls to see Lillian smiling. "For now, but I doubt he will give up the chase. Men like to go after what they can't get."

I shook the encounter off and decided to refocus, bringing the team back with me. Talk of flirtations and turndowns could wait for after dinner drinks. We finished talking about plans until lunch, where they regaled me with more stories of Henry Lennox's conquests. Somehow, the stories helped me relax from the office flirtation and I was able to put it from my mind by the time we met with the client.

Joseph Stafford was not an easy man to please. He had a reputation for chewing up ad proposals. He looked for organic concepts. He wanted campaigns that would feature his clothing before gimmicks. Fashion, in his philosophy, sold itself. If an article of clothing required a catchy line to be pulled off the rack, then it should not be there in the first place.

We presented the proposal to him, focusing on the concept art first, what we envisioned for model photos featuring different articles from the clothing line. When Mr. Stafford looked pleased – that is to say, he did not throw anything down in disgust – we introduced the text to go with the print ads or as voice over for television spots. He listened carefully, comparing words to pictures to get the full idea.

By the end of the meeting, we were all relaxed and I was amazed. Mr. Stafford pulled out three pictures from the concept art. He wanted to see changes, incorporating more elements from them. They were my contributions, and I felt elated that my work had been singled out by someone known to be so picky about his ad campaigns. Michael took final notes of the changes Mr. Stafford wanted to see, and after he left, we all celebrated a successful meeting.

I was elated. As we wrapped up our afternoon, I received congratulations around the table that my work was singled out by Mr. Stafford. Even though my professors had told me to expect success if I applied my talents, I never dreamed my first assignment at my first job would go like this. My head was spinning and I felt dizzy with the excitement of it all.

Tonight there would not be drinks. Everyone had plans with family or significant others. It seemed I was alone in having my Friday night free, but I had wanted it that way. I knew I would be too tired to attempt anything. Tomorrow night, I would be going out with my friends from college. I straightened my desk, tossing discarded ideas into the garbage and waving to everyone as they left. Lillian was the last out, wishing me a good weekend.

"You had a good day today." Michael walked up to my desk.

"Thank you." I took hold of my purse and turned off my desk lamp. "We all worked really hard."

"You especially. You really put everything into this proposal, which is why I wanted to talk to you." Michael paused and rubbed his hands together. I felt like a shoe was about to drop, but I could not fathom what could possibly be going wrong. The team was welcoming. They were proud that my work had been singled out and seemed excited about making the changes Mr. Stafford had requested. "I noticed that you turned away Mr. Lennox's advances earlier today and that is, worrisome."

My blood ran cold. I thought of Ana's warnings to me about trying to use Mr. Lennox's attention for my own personal gain. She had mentioned nothing about consequences if I turned him down.

"Mr. Lennox takes his business very seriously. This is his life, built from the ground up by his hands. Even the building we are standing in was erected just for him. Now, I would never tell you what to do with your personal life, but

I know that Mr. Stafford wants you having a more active, up front role in the project. Now the girls seem happy to let you shine in the spotlight, which I think is great. For me, I have to look at more than just teammates sharing glory. You're new and I'm happy to let you shoulder that responsibility, but I need to know that you're a team player."

I couldn't move. I wanted to. I wanted to bolt right out of the office, screaming down the hall. My feet felt like weights, and no part of my body seemed to work. I could not believe what I was hearing from Michael. I got his point, as plain as if he told me flat out that I should invite Mr. Lennox into my bed. I wanted to slap him, and that seemed to give my body the ability to move again.

"I hope we're both on the same page." Michael gave me the same smile I saw from him every day. Only now, it did not seem kind and subtly flirtatious. It was hungry and demanding.

"We are," I said.

I turned and walked out of the office. I did not want stand in there with him for another moment. I stormed down the stairs and through the hall to the elevator lobby, thankful that most of the rest of the staff had cleared out for an early Friday. I pressed the button and waited. I had never in my life wanted to hear the ding of an elevator so badly.

I heard footsteps move from hardwood to the stone tile floor of the lobby. I turned, daggers in my eyes, to see Mr. Lennox walking with his slight, confident swagger. When he saw me, his eyes grew wide and he stopped abruptly. I realized what I had just done and softened my expression, stammering out a greeting.

"You look like someone who could use a drink before she takes on Friday traffic." Mr. Lennox seemed to ignore my clumsy attempts at pleasantries and I found myself thankful.

"Maybe," I said.

Mr. Lennox nodded. "Why don't you join me down there? You can relax and I can get to know a little something about Lennox Advertising's newest member."

I sighed. A drink would not hurt. I needed to relax. I thought about the traffic waiting for me and cringed at the thought of having to listen to the horns of impatient drivers. "Thank you. That would be nice."

Mr. Lennox gave me a smile and gestured for me to follow him away from the elevator lobby. "I have a personal elevator I use. Follow me."

I did as he asked, walking back the way I had come. I looked up at the stairway to see Michael halfway down it. As we passed, I did not miss his smile. My stomach turned, but I decided to focus. The big boss wanted to get to know me, and I somehow had to balance my desire not to be another Henry Lennox conquest with my desire to not have another awkward encounter with Michael or jeopardize my place on the team.

We took his private elevator down to the main lobby, and walked through the rapidly thinning crowd of Lennox Enterprises employees to the Bluepointe Lounge. The host led us through to a small, semi-private table. I thought this one probably remained reserved for Mr. Lennox on a daily basis. He waited for me to sit down before taking the chair across from me. We ordered drinks and an appetizer for a snack between small talk and pleasantries, and I felt myself begin to relax from my stressful end-of-day.

"By the way," Mr. Lennox said as drinks and our snack arrived to our table. "Mr. Stafford stopped by my office this afternoon. He was incredibly pleased with the work your team did. I understand your work had especially drawn his attention. Congratulations."

The compliment left me dizzy and pleased, and I felt a smile come to my lips. I had expected flirting. It seemed the natural thing to follow the small talk that we started with. Instead, he was showing genuine interest in an employee.

"Thank you, Mr. Lennox." The elation of the afternoon was returning.

"You can call me Henry. We're not in the office." He took a potato skin from the appetizer tray. "Your team has been sending me emails about your progress this week. It's something I like the teams to do when a new member comes on. Everyone has been impressed. It's good to see you getting along with them and really making an impact."

"The team has been great. Everyone welcomed me right away and started asking me for input on the proposal. I couldn't have asked for a more ideal team."

As we finished our drinks and the appetizer, Henry kept me talking about my first week, asking me questions about how I liked the team environment or what I thought about the office layout. Was it comfortable? Did I think it helped to add to an inclusive environment? He asked me about my personal experiences as well, if I felt like I was able to get to know my co-workers.

Henry asked me to stay for dinner, and without thought, I accepted. This man had me intrigued. I had come down expecting one thing. What I found was completely different. I found genuine interest, not a road to conquest. By the time dinner arrived, our conversation moved to my college years, and I found myself talking about professors and the aggressive course work I had taken on.

The conversation stayed focused on me. Every time I tried to ask Henry a question about himself, he turned it back into another question. I wanted to think that he was just being secretive, but I sensed something else and it had me curious.

No, more than curious. As I tried to pry and he spun the conversation back to me, I felt a strange attraction. Beneath the playboy exterior was just a man. He was as real as I was, and like me, he had his own insecurities. I continued throughout dinner to try to get something from him, a hint of the inner person. I thought it made him smile, as though he were playing a game by turning my questions away.

Dinner wrapped up and I felt relaxed. Michael and our "talk" were far from my mind. I was enjoying the dinner with Henry and reluctant to see it end. I knew that I had to get home at some point, though, and I was not going to presume that Henry had nothing at all to do on a Friday night.

"Thank you again for dinner," I said as the ticket arrived and Henry kept it securely on his side of the table. "I should get home now, though."

"My pleasure. Are you sure, you're okay to drive home? I can have someone take you."

Henry's concern was touching and I could not help but smile in response. "I'm sure. Not even feeling buzzed, I promise."

Henry's eyes locked mine in place again. I felt powerless under his gaze as he carefully evaluated me. He finally nodded his head. "I wanted to be sure. No point in taking unnecessary risks."

"Thank you." I could not think of anything else to say. I said my good night and headed out of the restaurant and through the lobby to the parking deck. My mind was full of Henry and our dinner, and the strange and inescapable feeling that his mind was elsewhere by now.

FOUR

With the Friday rush hour traffic well and truly gone, I made it to my apartment quickly. Inside, I locked the door, walked the five steps to my couch, and collapsed. The entirety of the day flooded over me. I felt elated and stirred by my dinner with Henry. I told myself to be calm. It should not be that big of a deal. It certainly would not be to him. I was just Stacy Caldwell. Sure, I had impressed a client, but I could not be the first person in his office to do that. I was certainly not one of the angelic, model like creatures that made up the rest of his staff.

A knock sounded at my door, drawing me out of my self-defeatist reverie. I stood up and walked over, looking through the peephole. Henry stood there, waiting patiently for me to answer. I stood back and pondered the door, thinking that it was a strange thing, capable of creating illusions.

I left something at the restaurant.

I was not sure what I would have left, but it was an easy explanation for him being outside my apartment. I unlocked and opened the door, offering him a smile.

"Is everything okay?"

I noticed he had nothing in his hands, except for his car keys.

"Everything's fine. May I come in?" Henry asked.

No reason to refuse popped into my head. I opened the door wider and gestured. "Come in."

I was curious now. What would bring Henry Lennox to my little apartment on the edge of the city? He lived in an uptown condo. This was not exactly on his way home.

"I'm sorry about showing up like this. I'm not the kind of person that would follow a woman home uninvited. I told myself the entire drive that I was just concerned about our safety. Two drinks, even with dinner, can impair you." He paused and once more locked me with those eyes. In them, I saw all of my insecure doubts dashed. He had not followed me home for my safety. "The truth is I could not get you out of my mind, and I've not obsessed about a woman like this in a long time."

I had no words. It was not as if I had never had crushes, or boyfriends. I had never had a man approach me like this before, though, so eager and hungry. Standing next to my door, he seemed at once larger than life, and small and insecure. My mind tried to rationalize the two things, and only seemed to spin in response.

"Would you like to sit down?" I could not seem to form any other cogent words.

"I like you."

My world moved suddenly, down becoming up. I was dizzy and I felt hands around my waist and at the small of my back. I looked up to see Henry holding me as I leaned forward. A man told me that he wanted me and I fainted. My face burned with embarrassment.

"I'm sorry." Henry's words were gentle.

"Yes." The word pushed through my lips.

"What?"

I met his eyes again. "Yes."

Henry pressed his mouth to mine. He was eager and searching, and I opened to him, feeling his tongue press into mine and dance. He tasted sweet and desire pushed all thought from my mind. I wanted more of him.

He pulled away and looked at me, his green eyes becoming dark. Behind them were things that I could not imagine. I thought of the stories that Lillian and the others told, and the muscles in my stomach twitched with excitement. Why did I want to see more of that darkness?

"I have peculiar tastes," he said.

"I've heard the stories." I expected the admission to embarrass him, but he simply smiled.

"I have so many things I would like to do to you." That darkness pushed forward in his eyes. I felt the instinct to flee it and found myself wanting to drown there instead.

Henry nodded. He backed away from me slowly, his hands moving to my arms to make sure that I was standing steady. I took one of his hands in mine and led him back to the tiny room that served as my bedroom.

There was little space here. I had my queen-sized bed, a small dresser with a mirror over it, and a nightstand. Henry did not seem concerned. He kissed me again, unbuttoning my shirt as he took me in. The muscles of my stomach twitched as his fingers trailed down to push down my skirt, my panties with it. When he saw my thigh high stockings beneath, held up by their own adhesive since I could never manage a garter belt, he smiled.

I stood naked before him, feeling once more insecure. He looked over my body and smiled, taking my breasts into his hands and squeezing them firmly. I sighed at his touch and he danced his tongue lightly over each nipple.

"I want to blindfold you."

"Okay," I said nervously.

"Then I want to tie your hands to your headboard."

I nodded.

He took off his tie and wrapped the soft silk around my head, blocking my vision. Sound and touch came to life, and when he took hold of my body to guide me to my bed, I gasped. He laid me down and brought my hands up above my head, bidding me to hold onto the metal headboard. I felt the bed shake and could feel him moving next to me. The cotton of his shirt brushed by arms and wrapped around each of them, tying tight enough to secure me. I pulled and realized that he had threated his shirt through the bars of my headboard and used it to secure me in place.

Bound, I felt a strange release. I was almost helpless to him and alive, craving his touch. Henry parted my legs and I felt his mouth between them, his tongue pushing into the folds of my labia and up to dance at my clit. I gasped as his lips closed around me and he began to suck. I wanted to close my legs around him, to pull him close, but he held them firmly apart with his hands. When I struggled to close them, he grew more intense with his mouth, drawing passion out of me. I arched my back and cried out as I felt it swirl at his touch and come to a head, spilling across my body with a tremor.

He pulled away and I relaxed my back onto the bed, breathless and excited. I heard the ripping of foil and knew what was next. He moved between my legs again and I felt him sheathed and hard, pushing into me slowly. I wanted to feel him fast and hard, as brutal as the stories made him sound, but he inched in, filling me with agonizing care. I wanted to cry out for him to go harder and held back, only to hear him laugh as he inched in.

"You shouldn't hesitate to ask for what you want," he said. His voice was warm and cruel, gentle and taunting.

"I want you to go harder," I said.

He pulled out and pushed in again, slow and gentle. He was taunting me. I thought of our conversation at dinner, the way he spun questions back. He was doing it to me again with his body this time, and I tensed around him to express my want and need. Still he moved slowly, pushing in deep before pulling out to move in again. He reached down and took hold of my breasts, gripping them firmly and squeezing the nipples between the fingers of each hand.

I raised up my hips to meet him, to make his thrust harder, and he pulled back. I whimpered and he squeezed my nipples harder. He was enjoying my want, taking it in as much as my body took in him. In easy strokes, he began to increase his speed, but never the pressure. My frustration and want built up until I felt another swell of pleasure, this time from the denial. I cried out as it moved through my body and he pressed into me firmly, moaning as he pulsed inside me.

Henry pulled out slowly, kissing my lips and allowing me to taste myself on them. He moved down to kiss my breasts, then down my stomach to the top of my sex. There he left one last kiss before coming up to rest beside me. I breathed slowly, feeling spent and warm.

"You are so beautiful when you want to be." Henry kissed my lips again, lingering this time to dance with my tongue. When he broke away, he removed his tie from around my eyes. He removed his shirt next, smoothing the wrinkles as he sat up.

I watched him dress, my thoughts blurred by the pleasure I experienced. He would not be staying the night, but I did not expect him to. I wanted him to, but felt a strange warmth at watching him prepare to leave.

Once he was dressed, he pulled the covers of my bed under my body and brought them over me. "I'll lock the door as I leave. You sleep well."

He kissed me once more and walked out of the room. I heard the door to my apartment open and close, and I was alone with my spinning thoughts. The night perplexed me. Being bound was exciting. I was at his mercy, and he was gentle with me, even when I pleaded for him to go rougher. I could have taken it as the gentleness of a first time encounter, except that he had taken a joy in withholding it from me, and that excited me as much as everything else had.

I rolled over and chased my thoughts until they finally led me into sleep.

******

Saturday I felt that I had had a one-night stand, one of the many that Henry Lennox had in his office. I tried to tell myself that I should feel bad for it. I was even tempted to call my mother and tell her, just so I could get the "tsk-

tsk." Somehow, I could not muster the emotion. The only other man I had ever had sex with was someone I had dated for two years beforehand. It did not make sense to me that I had this sense of – of being fine with it. Of all the things that I got down on myself about and felt bad for – eating a whole half-gallon of chocolate ice cream in one sitting, skipping the gym because I had been out drinking with friends and telling my trainer it was my period, getting caught reading a Harry Potter book on the train at twenty-one – the one thing that I should be ashamed of, a one-night stand, I could not muster.

Then I asked myself, why should I feel bad about it? Every other woman on my team had slept with him. None of them seemed to judge each other or be ashamed. At least one woman in the office had come out of her brief fling, got married and had a kid. Obviously, she was not ruined by the experience. I would not be either.

Resolving in my head that I did not have to make myself feel something I did not really feel left me open to navigate the rest of my weekend of clubbing with friends and listening to Mom ask me why I had not introduced her to a new boy yet.

"Lewis was so nice. I never understood why you broke up with him."

That was because I had never told her. How could I explain to a woman who was married to the same man for almost thirty years that I just was not feeling it anymore, that I thought I had outgrown the boy who still thought fart jokes were funny and the most important news of the month was the announcement of a new video game?

My weekend passed in its typical fashion with no word from Henry, not that I had expected it. He was a playboy and I was just another girl in his office. When Monday morning came, I drove to work wondering if I was going to have the nerve to tell my teammates about my encounter with Henry. How would it sound? Their tales were steamy adventures, full of spankings and rough sex. He tied up my hands and was no rougher than pinching my nipples. Comparatively, my encounter did not seem nearly as tantalizing.

When I arrived at the office, the girls were gathered around my desk. Michael sat at his own, giving me a smile as I walked in. As I made it up to my desk, Lillian turned around, a broad smile on her face. Behind her, I saw deep red roses and a glass vase.

Someone had a dozen red roses delivered to my desk before I arrived for work.

"Lillian wouldn't let us peek," Karla pouted at me. "Who are they from?"

Lillian moved aside so that I had access to my desk. The roses were beautiful, their blooms thick and partially opened, and smelled rich. I reached down for the envelope that hung neatly over the lip of the vase. I opened it and pulled out the small card. A stylized L was on one side, which drew gasps from everyone around my desk. Michelle threw her hand up to her face. On the other was a simple note.

Thank you,

HL

"Are those really from Mr. Lennox?" Michelle asked from behind her hand.

I nodded. I was not expecting this. The thank you note could be innocent enough, but not with red roses. They sent a very clear message.

"I knew you would end up saying yes to him," Tina said. "Every girl does."

Beside me, Lillian shook her head. "No. A grounded girl like Stacy, she doesn't fall for a man like Henry Lennox. A girl like her teaches a man like him how to settle down."

Michelle let out a light squeal. Tina flashed Lillian a skeptical look. "How do you know?"

"Because she is the first one to get flowers." Lillian's voice was calm and even.

Around us, the other girls let out squeals and gave me smiles. It did not seem to matter to them that none of them had flowers from their encounters. In their minds, romance was in bloom on my desk. As we moved over to the planning table, Wendy and Michelle exchanged their own ideas of how a Stacy Caldwell and Henry Lennox romance would play out. Michael had to clear this throat three times before the chatter finally settled.

"Thank you so much for finally letting me get a word in," he said, once everyone was quiet. He fixed me with a knowing look. "Stacy, it's good to know you're part of the team."

Around me, the girls nodded, the innuendo of his statement missed. I looked back at the flowers on my desk and felt a knot form in my stomach. Henry had given me red roses. I had done what, slept with him to secure my role on the team? Suddenly the guilt that I refused to feel over the weekend pushed its way up from the knot in my stomach and into my chest. I pushed it down and tried to concentrate on the project at hand. The client accepted the proposal. Now we had to turn it into a full campaign.

Still, I could not get the question out of my head. Was that the reason I had slept with Henry, because of what Michael had said? I played through the night. It did not feel that way at the time. Henry had enthralled me. He had somehow managed to come to life, to go from simple rich playboy to a real person, and that was enough.

I felt satisfied about my own intentions. What if Michael happened to say something to him or to someone else and it reached Henry's ears? I pictured him looking at me, hurt, his pride wounded. That feeling of guilt that had lodged in my chest and died a moment ago surged to life again and pushed itself upward. I wanted to cry and was amazed that I somehow managed to keep it all back. Behind it was a very simple question for myself: why did I feel so strongly about that?

We wrapped up the morning planning session and the real work began. Everyone kept their questions about my weekend to themselves until lunch. We adjourned downstairs, where they bombarded me with questions. I kept the details of the evening to myself, but thought admitting to drinks and then dinner could not hurt. I decided to leave out the detail that his following me home had been unexpected.

After lunch, we headed back up to the office. As we stepped off the elevator, I saw Henry walking down the hall, toward the elevator lobby with purpose in his footsteps. The girls offered their "oohs" as he walked up to me and he looked at me curiously. I waved them on toward the office, feeling the heat rushing to my cheeks. I offered Henry an apologetic smile.

"The roses," I said.

He smiled and I felt a warmth surge through my body. "I hope I didn't embarrass you with them."

"No. They were unexpected, but they're beautiful."

Henry tilted his head to one side, and I braced myself for the uncomfortable question. "What are you doing Wednesday night?"

Not the question I expected. I blinked my eyes, my head trying to process the meaning of his words so that I could form the proper answer.

"Wednesday?"

Henry's smile broadened and his eyes turned dark and playful. I remembered the dance of words over dinner and the way he denied me Friday night. Between my legs, a new heat was growing. "It's that day that follows Tuesday, but comes before Thursday."

"I know what Wednesday is." My words did not seem to deter the playfulness; they only seemed to encourage it. That excited me and I had no idea why. "I don't have plans."

"Would you like to go to the opera with me?"

The world around me froze and I was stunned. Henry Lennox was going to take me to the opera. I had a strong suspicion that like the flowers, this was not something that the other girls in the office received. My mind began to spin, trying to piece together what this meant and make sense of it.

"An opera is a dramatic work set to –" Henry started and I held up my hand to hush him.

"I know what an opera is too." I looked into his eyes to see them still playful, but darker now. My act of defiance had excited him. I pictured him pushing me up against the wall behind me and had to remember to breathe slowly. "I would love to go."

The darkness in his eyes eased. Around me, the world became motion again. The elevator doors opened and more people stepped off to make their way to their offices.

"I do need to ask a personal question," he said. I nodded and he continued. "What size dress do you wear?"

Also not the question I expected. I breathed in and out slowly before answering him. "Size eight."

"Perfect. Meet me Wednesday after work in my office."

Henry did not wait for me to respond. He moved and walked past me, to whatever destination he had in mind before I chanced to walk off the elevator. I watched him turn the corner and decided it was best to make my way to my own desk. The girls, I realized, would have many questions for me.

FIVE

Wednesday was a busy day, one that left my head spinning. We paired off to work on moving proposal concepts to real plans. I worked with Wendy, who relieved me by asking few questions and kept herself focused on the task. That was more of a relief than I thought it would be. I had not missed the looks from Michael. The light smiles that I had gotten the week before were replaced by darker looks.

He was unhappy with me about something, though when I asked if everything was okay with my work, it was perfect. I had a growing suspicion as to what those darker looks meant, and they only heightened my unease.

By the end of the day, however, I had other thoughts to occupy my mind. I wrapped up my work, bid goodnight to everyone, and headed down the hall to Henry's office. His office suite was dark and warm, rich wood tones against which his secretary Hillary, another beautiful blonde, stood out. She ushered me into his office with a smile and Henry stood to greet me as the doors closed behind me.

Henry's office was as rich and warm as the rest of the suite. Two oversized chairs sat in front of his desk, doubtless to meet clients. To my right, a small couch sat against the wall with bookshelves on either side. On the other stood a waist-high cabinet featuring a small, angular sculpture that captured the diffused light in the room and a decanter half-full of a rich brown liquid. Next to it, two crystal glasses sat upside down.

"I took the liberty of buying you a dress for tonight's show." Henry walked over to a large cabinet that stood next to one of the bookshelves. He opened it to reveal a coat closet and pulled out a garment bag. "I hope you don't mind."

"Thank you."

He smiled and unzipped the bag. As he opened it, I could see that he had purchased more than the dress. Around the neck of the hanger, the clear stones of a necklace sparkled in the light. I could not imagine Henry Lennox buying anything that was not diamonds. He laid the dress along the couch and walked up to me.

"We should get you ready for the show." His eyes held mine.

"Okay."

Slowly his fingers moved up to my shirt and began removing the buttons. I trembled as his fingers brushed my breasts and he smiled. He removed my shirt without a word and tossed it over to the couch. He reached around my body and unfastened my skirt, slipping it down my body and kneeling as he did. When he tapped my leg, I stepped out of it. He slid his hands up the smooth silk of my stockings and the skin of my bare thighs. He hooked his fingers into my panties and lowered them as well.

"You won't need those." He tapped my leg again and I stepped out of the panties. He tossed the skirt and panties onto the couch and stood, reaching his hand between my legs and touching me softly. "I want easy access tonight."

He pressed his fingers into me, sliding them up to my clitoris. I held in a gasp as he pushed into it gently. I wanted to feel more than his touch, but he withdrew his hand and turned his attention to the dress instead. He unzipped the back and took it off the hanger. I raised my hands and he brought the dress over my head. I felt the smooth satin underlining brush my skin as he pulled it down. It fell to my knees and the faceted beads sewn into the lace caught the light. It hugged my body and felt luxurious on me.

Henry walked around me and zipped up the dress. Then he stepped back to the couch and picked up the necklace. He walked behind me once more and brought it around and fastened it behind my neck.

"It's a good thing you always wear black shoes. I forgot to ask what size," he said.

"I guess so," I said as he walked around me. I looked up into his eyes again and tried to read what was there. I felt elegant in this dress and necklace, so unlike myself. "Thank you."

"The dress and the necklace are yours. I would love it if you wore them again sometime."

I nodded. I could not speak. My head was spinning at the implication of that. Henry planned on more dates. Somehow, I had managed to snag one of the most sought after, eligible bachelors in the world. After one night, he was buying me expensive dresses and jewelry, and I still had not figured out exactly what I had done. Was it something I said?

"You shouldn't do that," Henry said.

"Do what?" I blinked. Was I fidgeting?

"You shouldn't doubt yourself." Henry brought his hand up to my cheek and caressed it softly. "You are beautiful."

I wanted to fall into his arms. Instead, he lifted one and offered it to me. "Now, if we may, dinner and the show."

I put my arm in his and he led me out of the office. Hillary gave me an appreciative smile and I felt as though the world were made for me.

Dinner was a different occasion tonight than Friday. The casual atmosphere of the Bluepointe was abandoned for much nicer faire, a five-star French restaurant with a menu that I could barely decipher with my rudimentary knowledge of the language. I cursed myself silently for my lax attitude about my foreign language courses and Henry helped me to select something.

We enjoyed dinner with a peppering of light conversation. He wanted to know more about me, and before I could try to turn the conversation to him, he moved onto the opera. Everything would be in Italian, which I admitted I did not know. He explained the basic premise of the opera itself, breaking it down by acts as we finished our main course and waved off desert. I was amazed by his knowledge and the passion with which he spoke about it. He was not taking me some place to impress me. He was sharing something intimate with me.

In a sense, he was talking about himself, and I listened carefully to each word, looking for what I needed to decode to learn more about this man.

After dinner, we walked down the street to the theatre, enjoying the cool night air. He led me past the box office and we were ushered quickly inside as flashes erupted from cameras. This was Henry Lennox; naturally, he would have photographers following him. I wondered if my mother would see the pictures on TMZ. She watched the show religiously. I wondered if she would even recognize me. I felt so different from myself.

Henry had a private box for the opera, giving us a clear view of the stage and the crowd below. As the music started, I realized that this box was probably one of the best areas for sound in the theatre as well. The lights dimmed and the stage came to life, the actors entering, their songs coming to life around me. As I remembered Henry's explanation of the opera and what to expect at each point, I found myself inching forward on my seat, gripped by a plot I knew and the words I did not understand.

Next to me, Henry gently pushed up my dress. He brought his hand between my legs and pressed into the folds of skin there, drawing new excitement from me. I gasped quietly as his finger slipped up and began to dance around my clitoris. As the music climaxed toward the end of the first act, I felt my own pleasure swell and push over me. I clenched my teeth to keep from crying out and leaned back against the chair, breathing slowly.

"This next act is the romance," Henry whispered into my ear. His breath sent shivers down my body. He took my hands and pulled, drawing me to move in front of him and down to my knees. My stomach tightened in anticipation and my mind began to spin. I knew what he wanted and felt eager to give it to him. He released my hands. I brought them up to his pants and unfastened them. He shifted as I brought him out, hard and erect.

What if someone enters the booth?

I pushed the thought away as I moved forward, taking him into my mouth. He sighed as he brought his hands up to my head, pushing his fingers through my hair and gripping, guiding my head as I took the length of him in and sucked, pressing my tongue against him. I questioned what I was doing, and when I answered that he had given me a silent command and I obeyed, I began to go more eagerly. I wanted to taste him, even as I felt insane and prurient for doing this. He inhaled suddenly and began to pulse in my mouth. I felt his pleasure spill out over my tongue and I swallowed as he held my head firm.

He pulled me back gently and I looked up him. In the darkness of the box, I could just make out his expression, appreciation, followed by something darker, something that I feared and wanted to reach out for at once. In my mind, I heard *bad girl* and felt a thrill run up my spine at the thought of what actions might follow. Henry gestured for me to move back to my chair and I obeyed, licking my lips and still tasting him in my mouth. I wanted more, but as he fastened his pants back, he turned my attention back to the opera, filling me in on what I had missed, catching me up to the action at hand. Fearing that his grip had ruined my normally neat bun, I slowly pulled my hair down and combed my fingers through it, hoping to smooth it into something neat.

We watched the rest of the opera in silence, save for a few moments of clarifications from Henry, reminding me of a key point in the drama. I was entranced by the show, elated by our boldness in the booth, and intrigued by the man beside me. His ability to be refined and carnal in the same moment, containing both parts as though they were perfect compliments, seemed so odd to me and so attractive at the same time.

Once the opera concluded, we left. He offered to drive me home and I said yes. I could always take a taxi into work in the morning and drive home tomorrow night. I did not want to leave his side. I was aroused and elated, feeling on top of the world next to him. Even the flashing cameras as we exited the theatre were of no consequence to me. We walked back up the block toward the restaurant and the private parking deck next to it where he had parked.

The parking deck was almost empty now. We walked up the two flights of stairs to the level he was parked on to see it devoid of anyone else. He let me into the passenger side and walked around to climb into the driver's side next to me. I watched him place the key in the ignition and felt my own desire swirling. I did not want to go home. I wanted to be here, and that was all.

Henry placed his hand on my cheek and turned my face to him. He kissed me, passionate and long. I melted into his kiss, letting my own desire feed it. He brought his arm behind my back and pulled me to him, guiding me across the center console, and moving the seat back as I crossed over him, sitting astride his body. As he pushed up my skirt my hands rushed down, unfastening his pants and gripping onto him. He was firm and hard, and I wanted him so badly that my body ached.

He broke the kiss and I felt a moment of panic. Was he prepared? His hands moved to his sides and then behind me. I heard the crack of foil and smiled, leaning down to kiss him again. As he brought the condom around, I took it from him, taking his cock into my hands again and slowly easing the sheath down over him. He brought his hands up to me and moaned in delight as he slipped his fingers over and inside of me.

I raised up my hips and he brought his hands around my waist, guiding me down onto him. He pierced me and I gasped to feel him enter. My hips tightened and I shuddered, feeling my arousal and want building up. I broke the kiss and pulled back as he pushed me down further onto him. His eyes were dark and full of lust and I wanted to drown in them.

"Beautiful," he whispered and I shuddered again under the compliment, feeling every inch of him as he guided me up and down. I brought my arms up and he released my waist and took hold of them, bringing them back behind my back and holding them there, using them to guide my body. I was his prisoner now, helpless to struggle or break free and my mind soared. My hips relaxed again and I pressed against him, trying to bring him deeper into me, to feel some part of him that I wanted to touch and was afraid to.

I trembled and moaned, feeling my pleasure build up beyond the point I could take. It washed over me and I felt alive, sitting astride him in his car, feeling him pulse into me and hearing him moan as his own pleasure overtook his body. When I felt him spent, I stopped rocking, leaning forward against his body, my arms stretching as he held me firm. I did not want him to stop, and felt my heart drop when he released my arms, letting them fall to my sides.

"It is nice to see you let go," he said. I sat up and looked down at him again. His eyes still danced with desire and darkness. A resolution was in them as well. I realized that in a moment, I would be moving back to the passenger seat and he would be taking me home. My beautiful evening would be finished. "The next time we are together, would you wear your hair down?"

I smiled. Everything that he said had a musical quality. He could have been singing the opera. "Yes."

He tapped my hip and I moved back to the passenger side. I looked back to see him, still sheathed, erect, though not as hard. I fought the temptation to try for more and instead fished through my purse for tissues. He took them with thanks and deposited the used sheath in the center console's small garbage can.

"You need to work on that," he said as he started the engine.

I turned my head to him as he turned his body back and pulled out of the parking space. I felt as though I had fallen into the middle of a conversation and I was not sure where we had left off. "What?"

Henry gave me a smile as he turned back to face the front. "When you want something, you need to let me know."

I focused my eyes forward on the road ahead, heat rushing to my face. One moment he could have me feeling released and elated, the next shy and awkward. The shift left me dizzy and confused. I wanted to buck against it and felt energized doing so. I finally turned my face back to him as the street passed by around us. "I knew we both needed to get home."

He looked at me from the corner of his eye. Darkness and delight looked back at me. Once again, I found myself drawn to it, wanting to see more, terrified by what I would find, and yet craving it all the same.

SIX

The next day was a flurry of activity. I walked into the office feeling the smile that drew curious glances from my teammates, and it would have easily carried me through the day were it not for Michael. I told myself that I was imagining it. His looks grew darker each time his eyes happened upon me. If the others noticed it, they said nothing to me. I carried on through my day, throwing myself into the project and letting the passion of the previous evening spill over into my work.

In the back of my mind, the same worry still plagued me. I had to do something about the conversation with Michael and battled with myself on what I should do. I still feared what would happen if word of it somehow reached Henry. It was secret I was harboring and I found I did not want to keep things from him. I knew so little about him and yet I was eager to share. I shared my life when he asked about it. I shared my body when he wanted it.

I had to tell him.

The workday ended and I made my way quietly back to Henry's office. Hillary smiled as I walked up.

"Is Mr. Lennox available?" I asked. I felt strange and nervous.

She offered me a kind smile. "He's in his office. You can go in if you'd like."

"Thank you." I turned from her to the doors and opened them slowly. Henry looked up and seeing me, smiled. My nervousness grew and as I closed the doors behind me, I saw his look darken and his face become drawn. He sensed something was wrong and I saw worry crease his brow.

"Stacy, what's the matter?" He stood and walked around his desk.

I walked forward and stopped at one of the oversized chairs, placing my hands on its back and using it to keep myself steady. I met his eyes and felt some of the nervousness ease. The worry that I saw there outstripped anything that I had to say.

"I need to tell you about something," I said. "It's important."

He nodded and listened as I told him about the conversation. I tried to recall it word for word. Though I knew I missed one or two points, the meaning of what Michael had said, the implication was as clear to Henry as it had been to me that evening. In his eyes, I saw something dark there, frightening and tantalizing. This time I sensed that darkness directed somewhere not at me, and yet I still felt drawn to it and wondered at its power to entice me.

"I'm sorry I didn't tell you sooner," I said. "When you took me down for a drink, I think that was because of what he had said. Not because I was doing what I was told. Because I was so angry with him. I knew he was pleased to see me following you, I knew that he would take it as my compliance, but I need you to know, that's not why I've done anything."

Henry placed his hands on my shoulders and kissed my forehead. It was a gentle and warm touch, and the rest of the nervousness faded away under it.

"I know," he said. "If you were the kind of person who would use me for her own advancement, you would not be working here. Ana screens all of the new hires very well." He kissed me again, on the lips this time. It was a shorter kiss, but still full of his longing and passion. When he broke away, he looked down at me. "You also do not have anything to be sorry about."

He placed his hand on my cheek and I rested against it.

"I wish I wasn't going out of town now," he said. "I want to be with you, even if just tonight."

"You have no time at all?" The idea that he wanted to be there, to comfort and reassure me made me feel warm.

"I have to leave for the airport in a half an hour. You came in as I was just wrapping things up." He kissed me again, quicker this time. "Don't worry about any of it. I'll get everything straightened out with Michael, okay?"

I nodded. "No worries then."

Henry let go of me and walked back around his desk. "Would you like to have dinner with me on Monday?"

I breathed out, not realizing I had been holding it in. "Yes."

"I'm thinking that we will order in and I'll take you to my condo. I have something I want to show you." That darkness returned, directed at me once more, and I felt my stomach flutter. My worries were gone, consumed by my desire.

"I look forward to it."

Before I could become lost in that darkness and risk Henry being late for his flight, I said goodnight and left. I was at the elevator before I realized that I still had not gotten my clothes back from him and wondered what had become of them.

I spent my weekend with friends, telling them only the barest of details about my newfound love life. I had no idea how to explain what I was feeling or what was happening to me. I had no frame of reference for any of it. On Sunday, I decided to sit down at the computer and begin exploring on my own, to try to understand a little bit of what might be behind Henry and why I hungered so much for what he offered, even when it terrified me.

The day passed under the tutelage of BDSM websites as I sought to understand something about bondage and discipline. I tried to make sense of what I read, about the desires of sadists and masochists, about the inner workings of submission and domination. So much of it swirled in my head, but one thing became clear. They were dichotomies that spoke to each other. What one gave, the other received in dark harmony.

I could not make sense of all of it, but it gave me a place to start. On Monday, I thought, I would be able to talk to Henry about some of this. I made notes and jotted down questions that I had. One particular one plagued me. Was Henry turning me into his submissive? I thought of the balcony at the opera and of how I followed his silent cues. He did not ask and I did not say no. The thought of not doing as he bid was impossible, even though what he wanted was so out of character for me.

By Monday morning, I was ready to face the new week. I drove to the office with my mind split between the project and Henry. Everything was categorized. I knew the questions that I had. I had an idea of the things I wanted to explore. As I entered the building, I thought of Michael and wondered if Henry had the chance to speak to him yet. Would I be greeted with more dark looks, or would things begin to balance out with him?

I stepped off the elevator and walked up the stairs. I passed bits of conversation. Something in the office had everyone buzzing. A promotion had happened, one that everyone thought was long overdue. I walked into the office and stopped as the door closed behind me. Lillian, Tina, Karla, Michelle, and Wendy were all gathered around the planning table. Michael was not at his desk. Someone else sat there instead, a severe, though beautiful blonde woman. She stood as I entered and a smile warmed her face.

"Our prodigy," she said, walking around her desk. Her voice lacked any hint of mockery and I looked to the rest of the team. They all smiled as I dropped my purse at my desk and walked up to the table. The woman walked up last, taking the place that Michael always took. She looked around the table before speaking again. "Everyone knows me – almost everyone. I will do this formal and quick."

"As always," Lillian quipped. I looked at her startled. When Michael spoke, Lillian always kept quiet. Everyone did. I looked back at the woman in Michael's place. She gave Lillian a brief look that was both impatient and resigned. The two women, I decided, had a history, and quips from Lillian were to be expected.

"I am Nora Jameson. I am your new team manager. I've had a chance to look over everything this weekend. I'm happy with the progress and the way that the six of you are working together as a team. So, no changes. Business as usual."

I looked around the table. Everyone nodded and I did the same. Nora smiled and gave us our marching orders for the day. We continued to work through the proposal, fleshing out the ad campaign and turning it from an idea into something real. By the end of the week, I thought, it would be ready for Nora to review and pick through. By the end of next week, it would be in front of the client and the only thing left would be to hand it over to our production team.

Curiosity ate at me the entire day. In whispered tones, we all spoke to each other, asking about Michael and the sudden ascension of Nora. Nora had been like the rest of them, working on creative teams, though often taking supervisory roles when projects required coordination between multiple teams. I thought of the comments that I had heard as I came into the office. It was no wonder, then that people were saying the promotion was past due. It sounded as though Nora had long since earned it.

Michael was more of a mystery. No one on the team knew what had happened to him, only that Ana had brought Nora in and informed those in early that she was taking Michael's place. If Nora had the weekend to read over the project, the changeover had obviously happened sometime after Friday. I knew that it had to be related to my conversation with Henry. The timing was too perfect.

If that were the case, no one else indicated it. I also noticed that no one seemed to mind Michael's absence. The relationships seemed amiable, but I noticed traits coming out among everyone over the course of the day. Lillian had a playful sharpness to her attitude that Nora responded to with what I realized was only half-hearted exasperation. Wendy told jokes. Michelle hummed. Karla engaged anyone who would participate in discussions about soccer. The only person who did not seem to undergo a huge metamorphosis was Tina. She was simply more relaxed.

It made me wonder about what the relationship between Michael and the team had been prior to my joining. What had his leaving actually saved me from? He was not a taskmaster. The team worked too efficiently to need it. Then again, that efficiency could have been brought on by his attitude. I simply fit into the team before he had a chance to show it.

The day ended and I made my way back to Henry's office. As I approached, he stood at his secretary's desk, discussing work with her. Both of them smiled as he approached. He said his goodnight to Hillary and walked up to meet me.

"Your hair is up," he said.

I reached back and touched my bun. "I don't like hair in my face when I work."

Henry said nothing. He gestured and I followed him to his private elevator. We stepped inside and he turned to look at me. His eyes were bright, but that darkness swirled deep inside, waiting to spiral out.

"I would like you to follow me to my place," he said. "I was hoping you would stay the night."

My heart leapt at the request, but my mind, still working analytically from my day, stopped it and pushed it back down. "I don't have a change of clothes."

"I took the liberty of having your outfit from Wednesday cleaned. It's waiting for you at my condo."

The consideration and the presumption both struck me. I tilted my head as I tried to measure how much of each was present. "There wasn't even the option for me to say no, was there?"

Henry brought his hand up and behind my head. He reached his fingers into the twist of hair until he found the clip that held the bun in place. "No is always an option."

Warmth flooded my body at his words. I thought about everything that had been done so far. Henry might gesture and command. He may, I thought, even demand. He assumed compliance was consent. If I did not want to, then I should simply say so. I knew that. The girls had told me the first time they spoke of their own exploits. He had told me that as well. That it never occurred to me to say no – that was on me after all. The idea of that made me giddy and afraid all at once. It was easy just to go along, to say yes because yes was easier; that was not what Henry wanted.

"Understood," I said. I nodded slightly and he removed the clip from the bun, letting my hair fall loose down my neck and across my shoulders.

He smiled and held up the clip for me to take. I put it into my purse and took out my keys. I would be spending the night with him. That meant that this was not just a fling. I was not merely a girl in the office who would spin to him and then spin away. The thought brought something else to mind. I had a question and I wanted it out of the way before anything else happened.

"Michael?" I said, looking up at him again.

Henry's eyes grew dark. "I let him go."

I frowned. What Michael said was out of line, but I was not sure if it was worthy of him being fired. Henry seemed to catch onto my discomfort and offered me a smile.

"I gave him a nice severance package and high recommendations. He will be with another company by the end of next week." Henry's smile faded again. "He and I took a different outlook on my affairs. For me, they are strictly personal. I do not play favorites in the office. Michael did not see it that way. He seemed to think I was favoring him because of the affairs I had with girls on his team." He paused and fixed me with an even look. I felt as though something important was about to follow, something he needed me to understand. "I take this company very seriously, most especially Lennox Advertising. It is important to me that everyone is on the same page, that we all understand what things mean and where limits are. For me, the limit is carrying my personal affairs into office politics. It is dangerous and people get hurt."

I thought of the team, of how everyone changed as soon as Michael was replaced. I wondered now if Michael had conversations with them similar to the one he had with me. The idea shed new light on the changes and how no one missed him.

"Personal stays personal, work stays work," I said. I remembered Ana's speech to me. "I can live with that."

Henry leaned down and kissed me, pushing me back against the side of the elevator and holding me in place. His tongue danced over mine and I let thoughts of Michael and the office float away. Work was work. This was personal.

SEVEN

Henry's condominium was uptown in one of the many high rises that lined the cityscape. I followed his car into the private parking deck and received my guest pass from the guard at the gate. My Ford felt small and out of place next to line of luxury vehicles. I parked next to him and followed him to the elevators and up to the building.

His condo was as immense as I imagined it would be. He occupied the top floor of the building, and as we entered, I was greeted by the city unfolding below me out of the large windows that dominated the room. The space was open, the foyer becoming the living area, flowing to the dining room and onto a gourmet kitchen. A single hall denoted any breaking of the space, and I suspected it led to the bedrooms.

Where his office was warm woods and gentle curves, everything here was about clean lines and open space. Four or five dozen people could move through this space without touching elbows. Functional furniture dotted areas of the room. A large TV sat on one wall with a couch and chairs set up beneath it. The dining room table with its chair set that part of the room apart while a bar near the windows

80

and three discreet, comfortable chairs created another lounge.

I stepped in and felt swallowed up by the space, alone and exposed. I thought of my little apartment and how the space embraced me. This was luxurious, but it was also cold and distant. I turned to look at Henry as he closed the door and walked into the room and wondered how he could live here.

"You don't like it." His voice was even. He did not sound surprised or hurt. He was simply stating a fact.

"It's beautiful." I tried to focus on the positive aspects. "It would be great for parties."

"It is not personal, though." He walked up to me and kissed me, a short one that was full of passion and want. When he pulled away, he brought his hands up to my shirt and began to unbutton it.

I placed my hand on his and looked at the enormous windows that made up one wall.

He brought his hand up to my chin and turned me to face him with one finger. "Someone would have to have a helicopter to see us."

I thought of the photographers greedily snapping shots of us at the opera. "Someone might."

Henry sighed. He stepped away from me and walked to the kitchen. There, he picked up a small remote and pressed a button. Slowly black blinds between the panes of glass lowered and closed, shutting out the rest of the world. It made the room seem colder and I suddenly regretted my need for privacy. He stepped up to me again and returned to the work of removing my blouse.

"Dinner?" I asked.

He did not stop this time.

"I have sushi waiting for us in the refrigerator. It was brought up this afternoon."

"We're eating sushi naked?" I asked.

Henry smiled at me and the darkness in his eyes began to swirl outward. "You will be."

I stood still has he removed my blouse and my skirt slowly, and then my stockings, collecting the clothes and taking them to the kitchen and a door beyond it. Clothes for the next time I spent the night, I thought. My bra and panties remained on, and as he walked to the refrigerator, I realized that I would not be completely naked for dinner. I felt strange and sexy wearing only lingerie for the meal. I walked up to the counter that separated the kitchen from the rest of the room. Three stools stood here and I decided to sit down on one of them.

We ate sushi and drank cactus water. It was sweet and blended well with the small wraps of fish and vegetables. I wondered at the lack of wine and what that meant for the rest of the night. In my research, I saw cautions about mixing BDSM and alcohol. Was that why we did not have wine, then, to keep our minds clear for things later? As we ate, I decided it was a good time to bring up my questions. I was just not sure how to begin.

"What is it?" Henry held his chopsticks and looked at me. "You've been quiet and you keep looking at me."

"No one looks at you?" I was not sure if I was sensing insecurity or curiosity from him.

"You want to know something," Henry said.

I put down my chopsticks. "I want to know about BDSM."

He smiled and placed his bite of sushi in his mouth. I waited patiently for him to chew and swallow. "What do you want to know?"

I sighed. "I've been reading up on the basics. I want to know – what do you want from me?"

"That's a fair question."Henry placed his own chopsticks down and folded his hands together. "I know that I want to show you things, but I don't know the extent of what I want from you yet. It's – too soon for me to decide that."

That seemed fair to me. "What do you want to show me?"

"Pleasure and pain, the height of ecstasy and the lowest points of humiliation."

"You are a sadist," I said.

The darkness in Henry's eyes stirred and swirled. My stomach twitched and the muscles between my legs clenched. Why did I want that darkness? What was in it that I craved?

"You are drawn to it," Henry said. His words made me tremble. "I want to learn why."

"You don't know?"

Henry gave a small laugh. "Everyone is drawn for their own reasons. You waited. You wanted nothing to do with me until we had drinks. Why?"

I did not want to have this conversation with him, but his eyes held me. In them, I saw a command, but this was different than anything else I experienced from him. This was not a desire to sate himself. This was something that he needed to know.

"You were more than just a playboy," I said. "In the office, you may as well have been a picture in a magazine profile. You flirt, but it is shallow and I don't like shallow. At dinner, you were someone else. You became – human."

Henry nodded and picked up another bite of sushi. "Finish eating."

I did. We peppered our food with more conversation. He asked me about what I had learned already. I told him about the sites I had found, and what I learned about the dichotomy between sadism and masochism and dominance and submission. I knew little about the specific activities that happened. I had been too interested in the higher-level discussions about philosophy and psychology. That seemed to spark something else in him. The darkness moved aside and fire replaced it. I thought of the opera and the passion with which he had discussed it. He showed the same passion now.

We finished our water and let our meal settle. We talked about bondage and release, and I told him how I had felt when he tied me to my bed and held my hands behind me in his car. He talked about processing pain, about taking it in and finding pleasure from it. As he did, his eyes grew darker and I found myself once again drawn to it. I was a moth. I knew the darkness was fire and it would burn, but I wanted to reach out.

"What is that?" I asked.

Henry tilted his head to one side and studied me carefully. "What is what?"

"In your eyes. You have this darkness that comes into them sometimes when you look at me."

"Does it scare you?" The question was a taunt, but it was more. In that darkness I saw want. He wanted me to fear it.

"Yes. I also want it, and I don't understand why."

Henry nodded. "It is all of the things that I want to do to you." That darkness swirled as he spoke. "It excites me that you are afraid of it. I want you to fear it." Henry paused, and I saw the darkness settle. My breath caught in my chest. Suddenly, I was more afraid. "That you want it balances me. That keeps me in my place and gives me discipline. I could do anything to you, and I would. But when you want it, you will only let me do what *you* want. While my spirit lashes out and roars, I can keep it still because you *let* me do them to you."

I wanted to run. I wanted to hide. His words carried a weight that I did not know if I could carry. I knew what he was telling me. His words permeated my bones. He would hurt me; he would not harm me. It would not be because of some sense of morality. It would not be because of some off switch within himself. It would simply be because I did not want to be harmed.

Somehow, that would be enough to keep that darkness at bay. I believed his words. I had the stories from five other women to testify to it. I imagined that I could speak to every woman in the office and their stories would back up his words.

I did not want to run from him. I wanted to run from me. I needed to run from me because when I looked into that darkness I did not want to stop him. I wanted to see how far that darkness could go. I needed to see how far I could take it.

"A safe word," Henry said. The words startled me back into myself. I stared at him, not really understanding what he was saying. "You need to choose a safe word. It will allow you to push yourself and warn me when it is too far. It will also tell me when you need to pause or stop."

I felt grounded again. The fear began to subside. "A safe word, right." I thought about what I had read. So many people had opinions about them, a few even claiming not to need them. "Red?"

"If you will remember it and use it when you need it, it's perfect." Henry stood and offered me his hand. I took it and he brought me to my feet. I felt spellbound. My fears were calmed, but beneath them, my body buzzed. I understood why he avoided wine tonight. I did not need it. My mind felt light and aware. I followed him to the hall and into his bedroom.

The room was sparsely decorated. An oversized king bed dominated the center of the room. Its iron frame was menacing, but right now, it was like the darkness in his eyes. It called to me. He did not lead me to it, however. Instead, he brought me to the center of the room, so that I stood a few feet from the foot of the bed. I looked around to see his dresser, a wardrobe, and large black chest.

He slid my panties down my body, discarding them to the side, and walked to the chest and opened it. On the inside of the lid, I saw various tools situated. I could not name some of them. One looked like an oversized electric screwdriver with no tip. Others I did not need a name, for their purpose was apparent. I saw several hooks, the hilt of a knife, and other metal objects.

Henry brought black rope from the chest and a flogger, its handle wrapped in leather and its long, narrow tails trailing down. I shivered and looked up, noticing for the first time the eye hook situated in the ceiling.

"I want to tie your hands together and tether you to that hook." Henry's voice was even. "Then I want to use this flogger on you. I will avoid any part that will harm you, but I will hurt you, as much as you can take."

I looked down and met the darkness in his eyes. It swirled and I nodded. I was too afraid to use my voice. He hung the flogger by its wrist strap from the iron bed and held up the rope. I lifted my arms and he took my right hand. I watched fascinated as he wrapped one end of the rope, forming it into a cuff. It was tight, but comfortable, and when he pulled, it did not slip or tighten.

"This lets you struggle if you need to." He took my other hand and with the other end of the rope formed another cuff on my left wrist.

"Should I struggle?" I felt as though I were embarking on some new adventure. I watched him work, fascinated by the careful way he manipulated the rope.

"I would like it if you did."

I looked up at Henry again and my knees felt weak. He tightened the rope and the cuff held firm. He found the center of the rope and brought it above his head, threading it through the eyehook. Slowly he pulled, lifting my arms above my head until he drew me up off my heels, pulling me up the balls of my feet.

"Can you breathe normally?" he asked.

"A little." I could feel the strain on my chest. He lowered the rope back a touch, and I rested the balls of my feet flat. Now, I felt the strain in my chest lessen. "Much better."

Henry tied the middle of the rope off on the iron footboard of his bed. I tested my bonds and found that I could not pull any slack. The eyehook was anchored securely and the bed was heavy. Solid iron, I thought, probably purchased just for this purpose. I could squirm, but the way that he had me tethered left me little room to move. I would have a few inches if I tried to move one way or another, and then I would lose footing.

Though my feet were free, I was well and truly bound. That feeling of release began to rush through my body and I smiled. It was stronger now, tethered as I was, and I wanted to laugh with delight.

I heard the crack of leather on skin before I registered the impact and the pain. Across my right thigh, a bright red pain shot up my spine and into my head. Henry followed it with another strike to the same place and I cried out, trying to stifle the sound. I did not want to alarm anyone that lived downstairs.

"Scream as loud as you need to," Henry said. "I own all the units on this floor and below. Downstairs, they are full of soundproof insulation."

No one can hear me scream. I thought of Henry beating me, harder until I began to bruise and then bleed. He could do anything to me and no one would know. My fear rose and chased those thoughts, chasing his darkness. Adrenaline flooded through my body and I wanted to chase them further.

"Red," I cried out and felt the tips of the flogger brush my thigh lightly.

"What's wrong?" Henry sounded afraid and I realized my eyes were shut tightly. I opened them slowly and looked at him. The concern in his eyes faded and a smile broadened his lips and touched his eyes. He was touched, and I felt confused.

"My head," I said. "It was racing to dark places."

"Memories?" Concern touched his eyes again. I shook my head and it receded.

"Fear."

"I will only do what you want me to do," Henry said. "When you need me to stop, I *will* stop."

"What if I don't let you?" I could still feel my mind trying to chase his darkness, falling into the thoughts my mind conjured.

His eyes became calm and serious. "I need you to."

I nodded my head. "I will."

"Can you go on?"

"Yes."

Henry returned behind me and brought the flogger around again, striking my left thigh this time, harder, sending sharper, heavier pain through my body. I cried out as he struck again over the same spot. He moved then, up to the buttocks and brought the flogger against them harder still. The pain was excruciating, and as the flogger pulled away, I wanted more.

He continued the strikes and my mind began to swim. Nothing seemed to exist but the tails of the flogger smacking my skin and the burn left behind in their wake. He alternated his strikes between my thighs and my ass, each one building up pressure through my body until it released with a scream, louder than the others. My body trembled and with confusion, I realized that I had an orgasm.

The strikes stopped. My head buzzed and spun. I felt dizzy and elated, even as my body ached from the strikes he delivered to it. He loosened the rope and eased the tension slowly, supporting my body as I fell limp. I did not want to move. I did not want him to stop either, but when I looked up into his eyes, I saw the darkness there quelled. He had not forced it down like before.

The darkness was sated.

He laid me down on my stomach and I sighed as the soft rope caressed my skin. He loosened the cuffs and removed the rope. I stretched my arms out and let the softness of his bed soothe me. Around me, I sensed movement, and then something cool and soothing over the warm pain. I breathed slowly as he gently rubbed the ache and then laid down beside me.

I rolled onto my side, hurting, but seeing that the pain eased. I looked into Henry's eyes to see them still calm, gentle now, more so than I had ever seen them.

"You were beautiful under my flogger." He moved the hair from my eyes.

I did not have words for what he was. Beautiful was too simple a word. It did not encompass everything. He smiled and kissed me, long and passionate, pushing his tongue between my lips. I brought my hands up and began unbuttoning his shirt. I could not think, I could only want, and I wanted him. I wanted him inside me and all around me. I wanted to be consumed by passion. As I unfastened his pants and felt his hardness in my hands, I knew he was only too happy to fulfill my wishes.

EIGHT

Tuesday at work was interesting, and I was thankful that most of the work for the day required me to stand. Sitting had been painful, but the pain reminded me of the night before. The experience had been beyond anything I imagined. Intoxicating was only the beginning of it. Making love to him after - I had no other name for it, no one had ever been so gentle in touching me before - served to bring me down from the high he had brought me to and somehow seal the pleasure I derived from it.

I did not get to see Henry that night, which I hated. Every part of me craved him, but I reminded myself that this was just starting. I could not expect to dominate his time, especially times like this when meetings popped up from nowhere. Still, I felt like a schoolgirl who had been kissed by her crush. I could not escape it.

On Wednesday morning, the pain from Henry's strikes was almost gone. It was enough that I could sit, which was good. I had to focus on designs and layouts for the portion of the ad campaign I was in charge of. It was grueling and tedious work, and I reveled in it. In the back of my mind, my night with Henry played on as I was plotting and notating.

After lunch, I had a message from Ana that she needed to see me. I walked down to her office, confident and paying little attention to the hushed tones around me. I knocked on her door and she called me in, turning off her small television as I entered.

"Stacy," Ana gave me a smile that wore away my confidence quickly. It was a smile meant to reassure me. "Have a seat."

I sat down in one of the chairs in front of her desk and waited. I tried to run through my mind what could be wrong, and came up with a blank.

"First, I want to tell you that you are fine," Ana began. I did not feel it, even less so with her reassurances. "A complaint has been made and a lawsuit has been filed."

"By whom?" I was numb. I knew the answer to my own question and I did not want to hear it. I needed to know, though. I also thought I knew the cause of Henry's sudden meetings – lawyers.

"Michael. He has filed a complaint of sexual harassment and a suit over the circumstances of his termination."

"He's not saying that I –"

Ana shook her head. I breathed out and waited for her to explain just what was going on. "Michael is making the complaint against Henry, stating that his affairs with his team members created an uncomfortable work environment. You are named by him in the complaint and in the lawsuit, since your relationship with Henry is the last one prior to his termination."

Ana paused and opened one of her desk drawers. I did not miss how she used relationship to describe Henry and me, and not affair. That word had to come from him. What normally would have made me feel warm made me nervous instead. Ana pulled out a sheet of paper and turned it around, placing it in front of me.

Statement of Response filled the top margin of the form. Below it asked several questions before giving me a place to write information. I wondered if the complaint was made against Henry, why I had to complete this.

"Henry told me what Michael said to you." I looked up at Ana. She fixed me with a stern look before continuing, her voice softer than her eyes. "I wish you had come to me right away. What he said was beyond inappropriate, and I would have handled it immediately."

"I'm sorry." Suddenly everything was more complicated than it should have been. "I was caught off guard."

Ana nodded her head and the sternness left her eyes. "I understand. I do. But it is my job to remind you that any time something like this happens, I am here to help you. Now I need you to answer that and write down everything that you recall of what Michael told you. Be as exact as you can and sign the form. I will witness it."

I began answering the questions and writing. Michael's words played in my head and I captured as much as I could. This seemed surreal, and I wondered what it would mean for me, for the team, for Henry, and for us. When I finished, I signed it and watched as Ana placed her witness signature below mine. This was an official document, then. I wondered if it would stay within the confines of HR, or if it would go to court.

"That's all I need," Ana said. She looked at me evenly again. "This will all be okay. You and Henry did nothing wrong – well, he should have come to me when you told him, but Henry is stubborn. He likes to solve his own problems and does not accept help easily. Do not worry about this. Do your job, enjoy your free time, have fun with Henry when he has time to see you. I will get this taken care of. That is my job."

"Thank you." I wanted to hug Ana, but I was not sure if she was the kind of person who would accept it. She was kind and personable, but that level of warmth felt beyond her.

"Now, get back to work. I understand that Nora wants to see the campaign by the end of the week."

I smiled. "She's a slave driver, that one."

Ana laughed. I stood and walked out of her office. The weight of the situation lifted with Ana's words. She sounded confident. I doubted that this would be the first time something like this happened. Ana would take care of the complaint and file it away. She might even take care of the lawsuit. Everything would return to normal.

I opened the door to my office and stepped inside. The team was gathered around Nora's television, a new addition. As I walked up, Karla turned, her face a ball of excitement.

"I think you're on television," she said.

I felt my stomach drop. I stepped up and Karla and Tina parted so that I could see the television. The commercial spot ended and the cable news returned, opening their society segment with a picture of Henry and me in front of the theatre. My face was partially obscured, but I knew exactly what this was. I knew the dress and my shoes.

"Media Mogul Henry Lennox is the target of a new lawsuit from a previous employee." The news anchor read her lines smoothly, as though the people involved were merely actors in a show. To the world, perhaps we were. "The former employee is claiming sexual harassment over the affairs that Mr. Lennox is rumored to have had over the years. The lawsuit mentions specifically a woman, a direct report to the plaintiff. The name of the woman has been blocked from the media; however, this may be the woman at the heart of this lawsuit. If it goes to court, it could result –"

I stopped listening. I turned and walked to my desk, sitting down in my chair and placing my head in my hands. I heard footsteps behind me and hands touched my back and shoulders, offering me reassurances. Their voices were kind and supportive, but could not drown out the anchor as she talked about how this could be the scandal to finally lay low the media "ice king."

Nora insisted that I take the rest of the day off, but I could not. As the shock of the report wore off and it set into a dull, aching fear, I poured myself into my work, letting it absorb me so that I could ignore the world for a little while. I did not stop until five o'clock came with Nora's insistence that I at least had to go home now. I did so, reluctantly.

I sent Henry a text message, hoping that tonight he might have free time, but I was not so lucky. I did get to talk to him that night, but it would not be until next week that I would see him; between meetings, a trip during the weekend, and, as he admitted, lawyers, he had no free time at all. From the sound of it, I wondered if he had time to sleep.

I waded through to the weekend. Nora had the ad campaign in hand to review. I had my weekend to try to sort out my fears. All week my mother called and I avoided talking to her. Even though she left no message, I knew what it was about. I put it off until the weekend, only to be bombarded with questions.

Why didn't I tell her that I was dating Henry Lennox?

Was I okay?

The questions came in that order, but it didn't bother me. What bothered me was how the whole controversy had grabbed her attention. She turned on TMZ every night to follow the story. When it came to media scandals, my mother was typical. I could only imagine how many people were following this and wondering who I was.

That idea mortified me, but not as much as the idea that this would harm Henry. I knew that this could get so much worse for him. The media was his business and his image in it was everything. What if this scandal started to shake up his clients?

On Sunday, Henry sent me a text message. He wanted me to come to his condo. I felt elated and terrified. I knew what had to follow, and I wonder how it would play out in his sanctum.

I arrived at seven o'clock. While paparazzi lined the sidewalk in front of the building, none of them were allowed near the parking deck. I entered unmolested and unnoticed by them. Why should I be noticed? A woman driving a beat up old Ford would hardly be worth Henry Lennox's attention.

Henry waited in his apartment. When I entered, I could tell that he had been pacing, though he stood still and smiled. That smile faded when he saw me. I knew I was not smiling and I suspected that all of my worry was clear on my face. I walked into his living room and he came up to me, putting his arms around me and holding me. I let the warmth of his embrace feed me.

When he stepped away, he looked at me, holding my shoulders with his hands. "I'm sorry. I should have cancelled appointments. I didn't realize how much this would affect you."

"It's okay." I took a deep breath. I had to be strong. "It isn't your fault, but Henry…"

I looked up at him. His eyes turned dark and his mouth drew down. He knew what was coming, as surely as I knew I had to say it.

"Stacy." Henry brought his hand up to my cheek. I wanted to keep it there, but knew better. I removed his hand from my face and held onto it. He at least had to know this was not his fault.

"I have to end things. I've listened to the reports, but more than that, I've heard people's reactions. I cannot be the one responsible for ruining you. I won't be. If the media does not see me with you, then they don't have something to chirp about. It just becomes another corporate lawsuit."

The darkness in Henry's eyes swirled. I waited for the shouts, for the tirade that was his right to launch. I was being afraid and I was being irrational. I was also right and I knew he saw that too.

"The company," Henry said.

I shook my head. "I'm staying. My team is important to me. Besides you told me, business and personal is separate. I can at least respect you in that."

Henry gripped my hand tightly. "This will all be fine." His grip lessened and he breathed in and out slowly. "I will take care of this whole mess, I promise you. When it is done, I hope that you will reconsider things."

My heart jumped up into my throat. I wanted to kiss him, to throw my arms around him and tell him I was sorry. He could stripe me with his flogger for my insolence. That idea warmed me. Instead, I brought his hand up to my lips and kissed it.

"Good bye, Henry."

He let go of my hand. I turned and walked out of the condo. I picked up my steps to the elevator. Downstairs I ran to the parking deck and my car. I needed to get away before I grew weak.

As I started my engine, one thing plagued me.

I will take care of this whole mess, I promise you.

I did not miss how the darkness stirred in his eyes. I felt afraid, not for myself and not in a way that I wanted to run to it.

Thanks for reading! I hope you enjoyed Book 1 of the series. ☺

Make sure you get a copy of the next book in the Alpha Billionaire Series Book 2: Broken Purity

BROKEN PURITY BOOK

TWO

ONE

I walked past the mob of reporters in the lobby of the Lennox Building and made my way to the elevators. The cacophony of their voices as they murmured and shouted questions drowned out the relaxing sound of the enormous fountain. I smiled to myself, knowing that I really should not take so much joy in this. I turned to look at the reporters and photographers. One of them spotted me and then turned back to her partner to watch the Bluepointe Lounge. I just shook my head. Their mystery girl was standing right there, and none of them saw her.

I was beneath their notice, especially compared to the angelic creatures that populated Lennox Enterprises, beautiful women for Henry Lennox to adore and seduce. As the elevator doors opened behind me, the throng of reports jumped excitedly and began to shout. Ana walked out of the Bluepointe Lounge and began to make her way through the press of people.

I stepped into the elevator and held the *door open* button as others joined me. Ana squeezed past the last of the reporters and dashed to join us. I released the button and offered her a smile.

"Slow news day?" I hoped a little levity would help her. She looked aggravated by the assault.

Ana stared at me evenly and then smiled. "Apparently." She sighed. "Did you enjoy your long weekend?"

I shrugged my shoulders. "The extra day off is always nice."

In truth, I hated it. I spent the day alone, cleaning my apartment. I still had the diamond necklace that Henry gave to me sitting on my dresser. As much as it pained me to look at it, I could not put it away. That seemed like a finality to me, an end. I thought about his words, *when it is done, I hope that you will reconsider things.* Oh how I wanted all of this to be done.

"I hid in my house with a megaphone and told reporters if they did not get off of my lawn that I would shoot them." One of the other girls in the elevator giggled, and I noticed that Ana seemed to brighten at the sound. "My neighbor asked me this morning if I had taken to aging over the weekend."

"It can't last much longer, can it?" I wanted her to say that it would be over soon.

Ana shook her head. "Ternion Communications has been looking for a chink in Mr. Lennox's armor for years. Our media arm is a direct competitor, and we have slowly been gaining traction in cable and online media."

"Actually," one of the other young women spoke up. I did not recognize her, so I thought she must be from another floor. "We're out performing Ternion in online media. Our Lennox News Online has more subscribers and we are receiving about fifty percent more hits per day."

Ana nodded. "These are the things I miss." Ana gave me another smile as the elevator stopped for the first floor. I looked out to see Lennox Communications on the wall, and the young woman who spoke up and three others stepped off the elevator. We ascended again, stopping at two more floors to let the rest of our co-passengers disembark.

When the doors closed, Ana leaned against one wall and looked at me. "Your co-workers are worried about you."

I felt my blood run cold. Why was my team going to Ana about me? I was performing well, active in each meeting and brainstorming session. Our first campaign with me on the team was a success; the client loved everything that we put together.

"Nothing bad," Ana said. "You've been throwing yourself into your work and you haven't been cheerful. They were worried that it had to do with the whole media circus, so they asked me to give you reassurances."

The elevator door opened for our floor. I decided to follow Ana, sensing that our conversation was not finished. When we arrived to her office, she gestured for me to sit down and took her own chair.

"I know that you ended things with Henry. I also understand why." Ana let out an exasperated sigh. "Believe me, I do. It is so much easier to deflect questions about their 'mystery girl' when I point out that she's not been seen with him in two weeks."

I smiled. At least it did something. I imagined an even thicker throng of reporters if they were still spotting me out with him.

"The circus will get better. It is already lessening. I am seeing less mention of it on news segments. Even Ternion is easing up. They will probably be the last sharks to leave. Then life can get back to normal." Ana leaned forward and placed her elbows on her desk. "You need to focus on you. You've lost weight since this all started. You're still letting it take a toll on you."

"I know. I –" I struggled with what to say. I hardly knew Ana. Did I want to confide my emotional turmoil in her?

"Henry is an addictive person," Ana said. "It's fine to miss him, but you still have you and your life. I don't want to see you burn yourself out because of this. If I have to, I will make you join the gym and yoga classes downstairs. You need to let yourself relax and let go."

Ana was right. I thought of the necklace at home. I had to let him go to preserve him. I needed to let my feelings go to preserve me as well.

"Thank you." I seemed to say that a lot to Ana.

"You're welcome. Now get to your office. Nora will be waiting."

I stood. "Yes, ma'am."

I turned and walked out of her office. I crossed through the elevator lobby and up the stairs to the second level of the suite. In the office, the team waited at the planning table. I dropped my purse at my desk and walked over with apologies for my tardiness. Nora waved it off and started the morning planning session. We were being given a second project to work on, and this client was extremely meticulous.

I listened through Nora's debriefing and she handed each of us a folder with pictures from the fashion photo shoots and the instructions from the client. I glanced over it and winced. When she said *meticulous*, she apparently meant anal-retentive. I shook my head at the sheer detail in the notes, wondering exactly how we were supposed to get creative with this. It seemed that the client already had a proposal written. We would be doing little more than parroting his ideas back to him.

"I've worked on one other project for Mr. Braedon," Nora said. "He's exacting, but he does appreciate a job well done. I have absolute confidence in all of you."

I looked around at the rest of the team. No one else seemed buoyed by her vote of confidence either. Nora left us to our creative planning and returned to her desk. I began laying out photos and notes, wondering how to turn all of this into something spectacular. His notes were exhaustive. He left little room for interpretation.

"You're doing it again," Michelle whispered, drawing me out of my thoughts. I looked up at her. Around me, everyone had the same serious and concerned look.

"You've been like this forever now," Tina said. "We're worried about you."

"I know," I said. "I talked to Ana this morning, and I appreciate the concern. I just need time."

"The media attention will stop," Lillian said. "It's not like they've found out who you are."

They didn't realize I broke things off with Henry, and I smiled in spite of my own feelings.

"I'm not seeing him anymore." I kept my voice low. I was greeted by startled looks from around the table. I held up my hand before anyone could say anything. "I broke it off. I didn't want to make things worse for Henry. I couldn't."

Michelle pouted and looked on the verge of tears.

Tina placed her hand on my shoulder. "You didn't have to do that. It's not like anyone in this building is going to blab to the media. The moment we do, it opens all kinds of floodgates. No one wants to see their face all over the news."

Lillian slapped Tina lightly on the shoulder. "Hello."

Tina frowned at her.

"It's okay," I said. "I didn't think about it like that. I didn't realize just how disciplined the office was."

Lillian glared at Tina and then turned to me, her expression turning gentle. "We all look out for each other, even when we say stupid things to people who do have their faces all over the news."

I laughed as Tina rolled her eyes. "It's okay. It really is. I'll be okay too. I'm just getting over having to do what I did."

"You're so strong," Michelle said.

I wished I felt it, but I offered her the best "strong" smile I could. I turned my attention back to the pictures and notes, inviting my teammates to join me in contemplation this time. I wanted to find a pattern, something we could take and twist. I had a feeling that everyone simply regurgitated his ideas back to him. What if we offered him something original?

TWO

By midweek, we had solid ideas for the Braedon project. We would have a proposal together within two weeks easily and I was confident the client would like it. Our other project was simpler, the client more willing to work with us on ideas. Work was going well and it was leaving me more time for contemplation. Even though I put the necklace away in a jewelry box, I could not escape the feeling of longing. I missed Henry and had no idea when that would ease.

Another thought came to my mind – Michael. Henry's promise to "take care of this whole mess" still haunted me. I had no idea what a man like him would do. I knew his darkness stretched deep. Would he try to hurt Michael or threaten him? I wanted to reach out to him; I still had his cell number in my phone's contact list, put there in case I needed to reach him for an emergency. I had no idea what I would say to him. *Henry had said something that could be a threat, but might not be.* I had a feeling that would just add more fuel to the fire.

As I walked into the Lennox Advertising offices on Friday, I felt good about work, confused about Michael, and depressed about Henry. I made my way up the stairway and paused, hearing Henry's voice. I did not hear what he said, but a giggle followed it. I looked down to see him pass by the stairway, an attractive blonde walking with him, blushing at something that he said. I rolled my eyes and finished my ascent up the stairs.

My depression was starting to shift into something else.

After our morning brainstorming session, I decided that some hot tea was in order. I made my way to the break room and paused at the doorway. Two women were talking inside and their conversation made me hesitant to enter.

"Nipple clamps?" One sounded astounded. I could not place a name to the voice and hated that I knew so few people here.

"Yes. Hard too. Then he kept thumping them. It drove me crazy," the other said.

"Sounds like you had a hard night."

I turned to walk back to the office. Tea could wait. I thought I might enjoy something a little stronger at lunch anyway. It seemed that Henry had decided to move on. I pulled my phone from my pocket and flipped through until I found Michael's number. I selected text message.

Busy this weekend?

I walked into the office and to my desk. I needed to work on projects. I started going over notes and designs as my phone buzzed.

I'm surprised to hear from you. I'm not busy.

I smiled.

Coffee Sunday?

I continued working on notes. Michael's message came back, *Sure*. I sent him a time and location and put my phone away. I would be able to make sure that he was okay. I told myself that was all that it was, and not some immature ploy to "move on" myself.

I decided to spend my Friday and Saturday out with friends from college. It allowed me to put work and the drama tied to it out of my mind. It was also nice simply to be young again, not a woman chasing a career, but a young woman just enjoying life. I could be that girl again, whose biggest worry was getting a homework assignment in on time, not if the paparazzi was going to show up on her doorstep.

That my friends had not pieced together that I was the "mysterious woman" on Henry Lennox's arm did not surprise me. I was the girl who studied hard all week and let her hair down on the weekend. I was not the kind of person who would accompany a playboy to a show. I also noticed that most of them simply didn't care. The news was big to people like my mother, who watched Henry Lennox rise through the media ranks like a rocket ship. For my friends, there was always a Henry Lennox, and rich people always got into trouble.

It was refreshing to be in a crowd that was not concerned with what was happening among the elite of society. We were just kids again, hopping between clubs and enjoying the simplest part of life. We were having fun.

By Sunday, I was calm and ready to meet with Michael. I arrived early to the Starbucks I told him to meet me at, ordered my Chai Latte, and sat down at a table. He joined me a few minutes after five, with his own purchased coffee in hand. He looked casual in blue jeans and a button down shirt. His brown hair was combed back neatly and his face was clean-shaven. In my mind, I had expected to see the stereotypical unemployed job seeker, sweatpants, t-shirt, and eternal five o'clock shadow. It seemed that he too was moving on.

Except for the whole lawsuit thing, of course.

"You're looking well," Michael said as he sat down. He offered me a relaxed smile. I saw something in his eyes, but I wasn't sure just what to make of it. It was curiosity and something else. "I wasn't really expecting you to message me, all things considered."

"You left suddenly," I said. "I wanted to make sure that everything was okay."

That something else in his eyes became more prominent. It made me think of the exchanged glances before our conversation. I was not sure what to make of Michael. He seemed attracted to me, interested. If he was, then why push me to Henry?

"I'm sorry that you got mixed up in everything." Michael sipped his coffee. "It wasn't my intention."

"What did you expect would happen?" I said it harsher than I meant to, but the point had to be made. "You named me in the complaint. You practically pointed at Henry and said 'if you want your place on the project, you need to sleep with him.'"

Michael almost choked on his sip of coffee. He coughed a few times and shook his head. "You didn't have to do that. I only meant for you not to give him the cold shoulder."

I glared at Michael. Innocent was not the same as stupid, but he didn't seem to be getting it.

"I didn't mean for you to get played by him." Michael was still trying to recover.

I picked up my own drink. "Henry wasn't playing me."

Michael sat back. "That's what men like Henry do. It's all they know how to do."

I shrugged my shoulders and tried to ignore the jealousy that I saw in Michael's eyes as he spoke. It was hard to tell if he was jealous of Henry in general or jealous over me. I didn't want to chase it right now. I was willing to accept that Michael didn't mean for me to be hurt or pulled into a media whirlwind. I didn't buy his back peddling, however. I wished that he would just be honest with me about his intentions.

I decided to change the subject to something else. I wasn't there to talk to him about the past. I was there to make sure that he was okay. I asked what he was doing now, and learned he was working with Lellman& White. I was not sure what to make of that. There were dozens of other advertising agencies in town who would be happy to hire a midlevel executive fresh from Lennox Advertising. Then I remembered that Lellman& White had been bought out by Ternion Communications about three years ago. I wondered if they smelled a controversy when they saw Michael on the market or just hoped for inside information. In either case, the thought that Michael was just a pawn in a larger game softened me to his situation.

"So, I have a question." We had been talking for over an hour, sipping our drinks as they slowly cooled. He was moving on, but I still did not have an answer to my main question coming here. "This lawsuit, do you ever worry about going after someone like Henry Lennox?"

Michael laughed and shook his head. "It's intimidating, sure. He's a media giant. Henry may be a womanizer of the worst kind, but when it comes to business, he has a set of principles. They are strange principles, but they are his and he follows them to the letter. At the end of the day, this is all just business."

I nodded. Michael moved on to talking about other things, not even blinking at my question. I felt a sense of relief and shame. Had I allowed the image of Henry Lennox to cloud my judgment of the man? In the end, it really didn't matter. For now, at least, Henry was behind me. I focused on the conversation until I decided it was about time to go home. The sun was down and clouds were in the sky. I wanted to get home before the rain started.

Michael walked me to my car to finish off our conversation. I unlocked my door and as I turned to say goodbye to him, he kissed me. His lips touched mine, passionate and firm, and my questions about his attraction were answered. When he pulled away, he smiled.

"Drive careful on your way home." With that, he turned and walked to his own car.

I got into my car and sat down, feeling excited and dizzy from the kiss. My own attraction to Michael leapt up, and I breathed in and out slowly. Michael was the kind of man I could fall for so easily. Even with those feelings stirring, I still could not get Henry out of my mind. I started the engine and pulled out of the parking space slowly. I was going to have to find some way to resolve this, for my sanity's sake at least.

I pulled into the parking lot of my apartment building, finding a space near my apartment and cut the engine. I felt strange. It was more than just the kiss from Michael and my unsettled feelings for Henry. I had this feeling, as though someone were following me. I mentally played back through my drive. I remembered the car Michael walked to and I did not think I saw it on the drive home.

I stepped out of my car and looked around cautiously. Michael's car was not here. Were there other cars that I didn't recognize? I spotted one, a black sedan with a person seated behind the wheel. This, I thought, was the source of the feeling.

The occupant could be anyone, from a private investigator to a mad man. I thought more likely it was a reporter, someone who finally managed to sniff out who I was. Did someone from college finally take notice and recognize me? Had Michael decided to disclose my identity? The thought that he would do something so invasive and then kiss me in the parking lot seemed counter intuitive.

Placing my keys between my fingers, I walked up to the car slowly. If this were some pervert, I would be ready. If this was a reporter, I would give him a piece of my mind. The driver's side window lowered and Henry looked up at me. I stepped back, not sure what I should do.

"Are you following me?" I looked around to see if there was anyone else in the parking lot, someone who might call for help if he jumped out of the car.

"Tonight I was," Henry said. "By chance."

He did not sound convincing, and I did not believe his words.

"You're spying on me." My fear gave way to indignation. How dare he spy on me and invade my privacy.

Henry let out a long sigh. "It's not like that. It's not something I can really explain out here. Can I come inside?"

My heart leapt to a yes, but I hesitated. Everything screamed that I should just turn around and walk inside now. I studied Henry carefully. He looked forlorn and as lost as I felt. I sighed. Henry would not hurt me any more than he would hurt Michael. "Come in."

Henry opened the door and stepped out of his car slowly. I walked to my apartment, not waiting for him to follow and knowing he was right behind me. I opened the door and let him in as the first drops of rain started to fall.

Inside, my apartment felt small and cramped, while the world between Henry and I felt enormous. He stood silent in my living room and looked at me, his eyes full of me. I wanted to run to him and hold him, and I felt unsure. I realized that I didn't even know what I was to him – a conquest, a girlfriend, or just a friend he could play with. I did not know where I stood, and I did not understand why he looked so pained.

"I miss you." He spoke the words as if he had more to say. I thought of the office, of the giggling girl and the overheard conversation.

"If you miss me, why bother with other women?" I asked. I felt silly. I had no claim over him, but the question seemed right to ask. He couldn't be a jilted lover and a playboy at the same time. He had to choose.

"Why did you have coffee with Michael?"

I frowned. "You are spying on me."

Henry shrugged his shoulders. "I've been watching out for you, to make sure that reporters stay away from you. This has been hard enough on you without having your name and every detail of your life in the papers."

"Someone told you I was having coffee with him and you decided you would, what? Waltz in and break it up?"

Henry placed his hands in the pocket of his pants. "I was making sure you were okay."

I leaned against the back of my couch. "I was making sure he was okay. When we talked about it, you sounded," I struggled for the right words. I thought about him just showing up in my parking lot, sending people to watch me. It was best, I thought, to let him see exactly what it looked like from outside of his grand tower. "You sounded like you wanted to hurt someone."

I braced myself. Henry stared at me and then he laughed. His shoulders relaxed and he seemed to actually be feeling the amusement behind the sound. When he stopped, he fixed me with another serious look.

"I wouldn't harm Michael. I know how it sounded. I guess I know how all of this looks to you. I know people. I have contacts that are helping me control the media storm. When I said that I would take care of it, I just meant that I would get things quiet again and keep the media from finding you, that's all."

I stared at Henry, trying to sort him out. I had two men in my life and I was not certain that either one was good for me. One was a manipulator. Even if I believed his good intentions, he turned too easily. The other – I realized I had no idea what Henry was.

"The girls," he continued. "They were a way to try to get past you, to get over you leaving."

"Did it work?" I asked.

Henry shrugged his shoulders. "The media storm is starting to die down, slowly. They've moved from my condo to my office, hoping that some employee will talk to them. No one does. I noticed fewer on Friday. I won't be surprised if the number continues to trickle down this week."

I felt a twinge in my chest. Did he not pick up on the jealousy? Did it not occur to him someone could feel that way about him? He was being adorable, and I thought as I watched him that he had no idea how. "I meant the girls."

Henry took a step forward, shortening the divide between us. "I followed you from the coffee shop to your apartment." He took another step closer to me. "I think I wanted you to see me. I wanted you to challenge me. You have from the moment I saw you. You don't just smile coyly and follow along. You want a reason, a purpose."

To hell with misery and worry. I pushed myself off the couch and threw my arms around him, bringing my lips to his and kissing him. He brought one arm around my waist and the other to the back of my head, wrapping his fingers in my hair, gripping and pulling as he held me against him and pushed his tongue between my lips. This was what I wanted.

We broke the kiss and Henry pulled my head back by my hair. I gasped at the pain of the pull and he kissed my neck down to my collar bone. My body was on fire for wanting him. I brought my hands up to his shirt and began to unbutton it, my fingers sliding down the soft cotton. Beneath, his skin was hot and smooth and I wanted to feel him pressed against me.

He released my hair gently and brought my shirt over my head, discarding it on the couch behind me. My stomach twitched as he moved his fingers down to my jeans to unfasten them and then he moved to his knees. He pushed down my jeans and panties in one motion and his mouth was there between my legs, hungry and eager to taste me. His lips sucked at me, his tongue danced over my clit and I cried out. My want, my weeks of denial swelled up into an orgasm and I laced my fingers through his hair, relishing the feel of it.

He did not stop and my head began to spin and hum with the pleasure he was bringing me. He brought my legs up, one at a time, out of my pants. He draped one leg over his shoulder, opening me wider for him. His hands came up, exploring my body. Fingers pressed inside me as others slid back. I gasped as he teased and danced around the tender hole behind me. I wanted to give him all of me, that as well. As he eased his finger inside, I let out another cry and clenched my fingers, pulling his hair. He sucked harder in response, taking my pleasure from my body as it swelled up again.

His ministrations eased. Henry pulled his fingers from me. I loosened my grip on his hair and looked down as he kissed me softly and lowered my leg. He sat back and looked up at me, his eyes still full of lust. "I want to tie you down to your bed."

In his eyes, I saw the darkness stir. Mixed with his longing, I saw something deeper there. Yes, the bondage was about control, but the control had a purpose. He could not control if I walked out of his life or back into it. In the moment I let him tie me up, however, he could. In that moment, all power was given to him if I stayed or if I left.

"I have scarves in my dresser," I said.

Henry stood. He took my hand and led me back to my bedroom. I opened the dresser and pulled out a pile of soft, satin scarves. Most of them had never been worn. I bought them on impulse, just liking the look and feel of them. He chose one and brought it up to my eyes. I smiled as he wrapped it around my head and tied it gently at the side.

He guided me to lie down and brought my hands and feet out above and below my body.

Shivers ran down my spine as the smooth material of the scarves danced across my skin, first my left wrist and then my right. He tied my ankles and pulled the scarves tight to the foot of my bed. I pulled against my bonds and could not move. I could not see Henry, but I could hear his breathing. I heard the shuffle of clothes as they fell to the floor.

Henry pulled the cup of my bra down and folded it under my breasts, making them stand from my chest. Then he was over me, sitting astride my hips. I felt his warm flesh against mine and let out my breath. I wanted to feel him inside me. Instead, his fingers gripped my nipples and pinched, pulling them. I stifled a cry. My walls were thin.

"Do you remember your safe word?" His voice was calm and even. Under that even tone, though, I could hear the darkness that swirled in his eyes. It was taunting me, begging me not to use it.

"I remember." I marveled at the internal struggle of the man over me. To be driven by something so deep and powerful inside, to accept the control I handed over, and to still be willing to heed a simple word. Nothing stopped him from ignoring it except for – for what?

He needs me to trust him.

He pinched harder at my nipples and I clenched my teeth. It hurt as he pulled them, but the pain signals turned warm, moving into my shoulder blades, to my spine, and up to my head. There the pain became a pool into which my consciousness dove. He twisted and I grunted, pressing up against him, inviting him to enter me.

"So hungry." He laced his words with delicious venom. As they bit into me, I felt them mingle with the pain.

"Please." Between my legs, I was on fire. I wanted to feel him thrust into me, hard and fast, with no regard for anything except to fill me and take me.

"So polite. I have to be gentle." He taunted me. I grunted as he moved off me. I heard the rip of foil and he was down again, pressing against me.

"Please." I remembered his words. I needed to say what I wanted. "I want it rough."

He eased into me slowly. He felt wonderful there, and I wanted to feel more of him. "Rough? But you're so sweet and polite."

I moaned and he laughed. He was torturing me and he loved it. I realized that through my frustration, I loved it too. He pulled out slowly and back in again, the motion so wonderful, even as it taunted me.

"Are you mine?" he asked.

The question tossed my mind into the pool that the pain, still throbbing in my nipples, had formed. There I was surrounded by him. I wanted to drown there. He took hold of one nipple and squeezed, demanding an answer from me. It created waves over my body and I clenched around him, feeling an orgasm overtaking me, as slow and steady as his pace. It eased through my body, stirring the pool in my head.

He pinched harder and twisted. I let out a weak cry as the last of the orgasm shook through my body. From the pool in my mind, I saw everything laid out: Henry, the lawsuit, my fears, and his insecurities. I saw Ana at her desk, managing complaints and damage control with the media. I saw his contacts, shadows, keeping rabid photographers at bay with misdirection and coercion. I saw him and me, standing in the pool of my pain, brought by him, carried by me. Here both of us were exposed and I felt safe and complete.

"Yes." I was relieved when he did not ease his grip on my nipple. He pulled out and thrust in, hard and fast. I gasped and felt the surge of pleasure move up through my body, stirring all the images in my head back into a jumble. He pulled out and thrust, repeatedly and harder each time. Each impact of his body against mine, hard and painful, was completion.

I gave over to the sensation and to him. There was no point in denying myself or what I wanted. Damage control would manage with me there as much as without.

THREE

I was surprised on Monday morning when I could walk normally. As Henry massaged my inner thighs and pelvis after, he had said it was to manage the effects of the rough sex. I was bruised and sitting down hurt. Like the stripes from his flogger, however, it left me feeling warm. They were marks, asked for and given. As I walked into the office, I could not help but smile, and the others noticed right away.

"Someone had a good weekend," Karla remarked as I walked over to the planning table.

"It's about time." Lillian gave me a smile.

I said nothing about my night. I just let them state their guesses and theories around me. Nora silenced everyone with a cough. As she was about to start the session, the office door opened. A courier stepped in with a dozen red roses in hand.

"Ms. Caldwell?" He looked nervous under Nora's annoyed gaze.

The appearance of the flowers stunned me. I raised my hand and he brought them over with a quick apology for the interruption. I took them with thanks and the courier quickly vacated. I took in the scent of the flowers and looked at my team and Nora.

"We won't get anything done until you say who they're from," Nora said.

I smiled. She was not as annoyed as she played and I saw the curiosity in her eyes as well. I opened the envelope and pulled out the card with the embossed L. On the other side was a simple message that sent a thrill down my spine and between my legs.

For Mine,

Henry

I didn't need to say anything for the girls to know who sent the roses. The L on the card was unmistakable. Around me, squeals of delight sounded and I saw a hint of satisfaction in Nora's eyes as well. Everyone, it seemed, was invested in the success of my strange romance. I wondered if they had an idea of how dark it was, if they would be so excited. Then I remembered that each of them had been with Henry at some point. They knew his proclivities.

I took the roses to my desk and set them neatly. The card I turned so that I would see the message when I worked. As I walked back, I was bombarded by questions. I held up my hands and smiled. My mind was swimming, but I wanted to get to work on the project as much as I knew Nora wanted.

"Yes, we're back together."

Squeals erupted again. Karla promised that we would all celebrate over lunch. Nora reminded us that would only come after the noon deadline she set for us. Everyone quieted and we focused on the task, a proposal to put together for a very demanding client.

I was surprised by my focus through the morning, and everyone seemed to fall in line with the quick pace that I set. The first part of our proposal was complete before noon. Our first hurdle for this project was behind us. At lunch, I shared an abridged version of my Sunday, sans mention of Michael or Henry following me home. I did not go into too much detail. They might all be familiar with Henry's appetites, but I was not comfortable discussing such intimate details.

When we arrived back at the office, a second set of roses sat on my desk. These were a bright yellow. The girls oohed as we each walked to our desks. They thought the flowers had come from Henry, but I was not so sure. I opened the envelope and pulled out the card.

M

I put the card back into the envelope and contemplated the flowers on my desk. This, I thought, could get very messy.

At the end of the day, I walked down to Henry's office. He had sent me an email shortly before five o'clock. Both sets of flowers were still on my desk, though Henry's card was in my purse. I wanted to keep his message on me. His secretary, Hillary, her soft blonde hair neatly pulled back, gestured for me to enter. I walked into his office as he was hanging up the phone. He stood and walked around his desk as I came in.

"Everyone in the office is buzzing about the flowers you received today," he said.

Heat rushed to my cheeks. "Your card is kind of obvious."

He walked up to me and smiled. He brought his hand behind my head and removed the clip holding my bun in place, letting my hair fall down. I sighed at the sensation of my hair touching my neck and took the clip that he offered me. "So, who was the second set from?"

I coughed as I put the clip into my purse, surprised by the question. I looked up at him. "Michael."

Henry tilted his head to one side and smiled. "Two suitors."

He placed his hand behind my back and guided me to the door. I saw no jealousy in his eyes and marveled. I knew better than to question whether he cared. It made me wonder, then, why he was not concerned. Was it trust, or was it simply that he didn't see Michael as a threat?

We left the building separately. I remembered Ana's comment at how easy it was to divert questions about me when reporters did not see me with Henry. I wasn't eager to add to her workload and the reporters were not showing any signs of thinning their ranks in the lobby, not yet. I walked up to my car and started down the parking deck. Henry pulled out behind me and we drove to his condominium.

I hated the idea of hiding and I hoped that it would not bother him. I was happy to be with him again, but I didn't relish the idea of reporters in my face. At the opera, they had been polite enough to stay back so that we could walk. I remembered the way they had engulfed Ana and didn't expect to fare any better.

When I arrived at his condo, I was relieved to see that he was right. The reporters had abandoned it completely. I pulled into the parking deck and was surprised when the attendant gave me a guest pass without question. I wondered if he recognized me or if Henry had called ahead on the drive. The latter seemed more likely and I felt warmed by the forethought. Life had so many little intricacies, and Henry noted each one and accounted for them. Such meticulousness had to be exhausting.

I found a place to park and waited for him inside the lobby of the building. He led me up with the promise of a hot meal waiting for us upstairs. When he opened the door, the smell of rosemary and roast beef greeted me. I followed him to the dining room table, where two places were set and a meal of beef, diced potatoes, and fresh vegetables waited for us. It was surprisingly warm and homey compared to the cool opulence around me.

As I sat down, I thought the meal was perfect.

Henry closed the blinds of the windows and brought out sparkling water for us to drink. I waited for him to sit down and we began to serve ourselves from the offering left for us.

"I want to ask you about something," Henry said as he placed slices of the roast onto his plate. "I wasn't sure about it, but this afternoon told me that I could discuss this with you."

I looked at him curiously. What about this afternoon would have told him anything?

"It was your honesty about the flowers and your discretion about leaving," Henry said, seeming to sense my confusion. "Both of those things are very important to what I want to ask you."

A shiver moved down my body and I sipped my water to try to ground myself. I knew what was coming, and the idea was exciting and terrifying. It was one thing for him to tie me up. That was limited control, one thing for a short time.

"I want to train you to be my submissive," Henry said.

I studied him carefully, measuring his expression. Once again, he was suppressing the darkness in his eyes. Whatever internal struggle he fought, he was battling it now to control himself. I wondered at that, at why he would only show it at certain times, when I welcomed it so eagerly.

"That's a big commitment," I said. "What would be involved?"

I took a bite of my food and waited for him to answer. The beef melted in my mouth and I fought the urge to give up the conversation and simply indulge in the food.

"I want to explore that with you. I want to start small and add to it as you feel comfortable giving me power. This is all new for you. I could give you a list of things, but it would be meaningless. Even if you know them, you won't have a basis of comparison to know if it is something you can or want to explore. If I introduce them over time, then you can decide based on what you've experienced and how much you trust me."

I swallowed my bite of food. "What if you bring up something that I just don't want to try? I want to talk about things before we add them in."

Henry nodded. "Communication is key in this. So is consent. If it is something that you look at and know it is just not something you can do, tell me and we won't do it. If it is something that just scares you, though, I want to try."

I saw the darkness rise up in his eyes. This was my chance to learn something new. "Why?"

Henry pulled the darkness down again and I was afraid he would not tell me. "Fear is the power that other things have over you. I would like it if you gave that power to me."

Another shiver moved through my body. I took a bite of the rosemary potatoes and chewed them. Dominance and submission was a power exchange on a deeper level than just being tied up and smacked with paddles and floggers. I was also understanding that it was more than just giving commands. He wanted power over my fears as well. Would he use them or help me overcome them? I could see Henry delighting from either one. I could see myself giving over to both as well.

"I can do that." I knew my voice didn't sound confident, but Henry nodded all the same. This was new to me, but not to him. I supposed that he knew how hard it could be to be subjected to a fear.

"I want to start simple, rituals for when we are together and the commands that I want you to obey. I want to explore more pain with you. You're my submissive, but you still have your own power. If something is too much, you have your safe word. If you need to step back, if things become too intense, use it."

I finished my meal in silence, contemplating what he said. He did not push me to talk. He simply ate his meal and waited. He did not look uncomfortable with the silence, and the patience that I saw in his eyes was reassuring. I could do this, I realized. In a way, it was the game we were already playing, but in small measure. Now, we were going to be moving it to another level.

When we finished our meal, he brought me to the middle of the enormous room that dominated his condo. He told me to strip and I removed my clothes, folding them neatly for him to take away. I remembered that I still had a change of clothes here from the last time I had spent the night. I wondered if I would be staying tonight as well.

I stood naked, exposed to him. Henry walked around me and I could not help but look down. I felt strange standing here and his manner seemed so odd, powerful, appraising, and cold.

"Is it comfortable to look down?" His voice had an inquiring tone.

"Yes."

"Then look up. I want your head even, your eyes forward. You may not raise them to look in my eyes, but if I engage your eyes, you will not look away." I raised my head up and looked straight ahead, my eyes focused on the kitchen. To make his point, Henry stopped his pacing and fixed his eyes on me. I did not look up to his eyes until he brought his head down to meet mine. He straightened again and I followed him with my eyes, careful not to break contact.

"Very good. Understanding when to make eye contact and when to look away is important. Averting your eyes can be a sign of respect or a signal for deception. I want you always open and honest with me. I will signal you when I want eye contact by meeting your line of sight. You will always keep your head even in my presence so that I do not have to be below you to look into your eyes. You should always be willing to let your Dominant come down to your level, but you should never make Him lower Himself beneath you."

I nodded, keeping my eyes on his.

"You may look away," he said. When I did, he continued. "When I bring you here, you are to immediately remove your clothing. I want you naked before me. At any time, I want to enjoy your body. You will stay naked until you leave or we go out somewhere. Sometimes people will come into the condo. Servants will be here shortly to clear our dinner away. I sometimes have guests come up. They are always close friends, people that I trust. I never bring strangers or mere business associates here. You will not hide your nakedness from the servants or the guests." I darted my eyes up to him with a gasp. His eyes narrowed and I turned them back quickly to look ahead. "Servants are beneath your notice as my submissive. Their role is to simply do their work and leave, heedless of what takes place around them. My guests are to see what is mine. I won't lie. I like to boast. I will not be sharing you with them and they will not be allowed to touch you."

The thought of others seeing me naked in his apartment made me shiver. I clenched my fists and tried to control it. I focused on the idea. Was I just scared or was it something I simply could not do? I decided it was fear. That, I could give to him. I nodded, keeping my eyes focused forward.

"This is how we will begin then," Henry said. "I will delight in your body and use it. We will explore sensations of pleasure and pain. You will submit to me by being open."

He walked to the kitchen counter and picked up the small black remote that controlled the blinds. He pressed a button and I watched as they opened and lifted. I closed my eyes and clenched my fists tightly. Tears rolled down my cheeks as my nakedness was exposed to the city. It was foolish, I knew. We were several stories above the closest building; no one could see us. That still did not change the way that it felt.

Henry walked up to me and placed a finger on my cheek, lifting away a tear. I opened my eyes to see him at eye level. I followed him as he straightened up again. His eyes swirled and I understood that this was a fear he was enjoying. As I kept my eyes focused on his, I began to feel warm and safe. I was not merely a naked woman before an open window. I was His naked woman before His open window.

"On your knees." His voice was steady. I lowered myself to my knees, still keeping my eyes on his and tucking my heels under my buttocks to support myself. "Very good. Place your hands behind your back. Keep the palms out, but overlap the wrists."

I did as he told me. He unfastened his pants and bid me to look down. I watched as he pushed his pants open and pulled out his cock, hard and erect. My breathing quickened. I knew what he wanted, but I held myself back, waiting for his command. He did not use words this time. He brought himself closer and pressed into my lips. I opened my mouth and welcomed him, sucking him and rolling my tongue around to taste him. He was rich and I savored him as he gently pushed deeper, forcing me to widen my throat to take him. When he came, I sucked harder, feeling him issue onto my tongue and the back of my throat. When he did not pull out after, I continued, relishing the taste of him and bringing him back to his hardness and pleasure once more.

When he finished, he pulled out of my mouth. I licked my lips, looking at him still wet. Henry guided me to stand up and I did, lifting by one knee and then the other, keeping my hands behind me. Henry led me to the bedroom and I followed, wondering what he would do next. He led me to stand under the eyehook and I watched as he opened his black trunk and looked through his tools.

He took out the black rope and brought it over. Behind my back, he tied my hands together at the wrist, forming a wide cuff around them. He tightened it and brought the rope up through the eyehook. I watched as he tied it off to the iron footboard, pulling so that my arms pulled up behind my back and forced me to lean forward.

"Very beautiful," Henry said. He brought his hand between my legs and pushed them apart until I was standing flat on the balls of my feet. "Can you breathe okay?"

"Yes." I was surprised at the complexity of this binding. I balanced on my feet and pulled with my arms to hold myself up. It was tiring, but the strain was all in my arms and legs. With time, I would spread, but I doubted I would be restrained long enough for that to happen.

Henry turned to his chest and brought out a new toy. I recognized a riding crop immediately and felt afraid. He brought it around and struck gently along my left buttock, using only the tip. I sighed and he struck hard, the resounding pop of the cracker accentuating the quick, sharp pain. It was not as severe as the flogger was. He struck again in the same location and again. Each impact added to the one before. I cried out as the sharp pain began to intensify and shuddered as it began to warm through my body. He moved to the other buttock, striking softly at first and then hard, repeatedly over the same spot. I cried out again as the pain grew and spread warmth over my body. It was bliss striking my skin.

He struck between my legs, the impact moving over my labia and teasing my clitoris. My eyes flew open wide and I gasped loudly. He struck again and I moaned. The pain and the pressure of impact combined. I wanted to feel him drive inside me and he struck again, a little harder this time. My knees wanted to buckle and I struggled to keep them straight. My arms could not take all of my weight. He struck me again and I groaned, wanting more.

"Harder please." I uttered the words before I realized what I was saying.

"As you wish." His voice was even, deep and cruel. I imagined the darkness filling his eyes and he struck between my legs, harder than before. I screamed and my body shuddered. He struck me again and again. The pain and the pleasure filled my head until I was drowning in them. Another strike and another and I felt the tremors of my orgasm overtake me. One more strike pushed it through, a red wave of pleasure and pain that drew out a loud, long scream from my lips.

Then he was easing me back. The rope was untied and I realized that I had blacked out on my feet. Henry held onto my waist as he threaded the rope back through the eyehook and loosened the cuffs around my wrists. The rope fell onto the floor and he picked me up, carrying me to the bed and laying me down gently.

My head still swam. I tried to say something but could not get the words out. I watched him as he moved to his nightstand and pulled out a tube of something clear. He dabbed it on his fingers and brought it between my legs. It felt cool and soothing, and the throbbing there slowly eased into a light and steady pulse.

He kissed my lips and I felt the tide in my head recede. He met my eyes and once again I saw the darkness receded, sated and chased away. Gently he eased the blankets beneath my body and brought them over me. I tried to speak again, to ask him to lay down. He undressed and climbed under the covers next to me. He picked up a remote and clicked it, lowering the lights around us. Then he brought me close to him, draping my body over him, and cooing softly in my ear, bringing me back into my mind.

I wanted him inside me, but as he brushed my hair slowly, I felt exhaustion overtake me. I listened to him breathe and closed my eyes, the waves of sleep slowly carrying me away.

FOUR

My week was divided between work and Henry. Wednesday and Thursday night, he wanted me at his condo to continue my training. By Thursday, I was comfortable standing naked in front of his windows. No servants had yet appeared while I was naked. On Monday, they had not come in until he had taken me to the bedroom. I knew it would only be a matter of time before it happened, or he had a guest over. He was easing me into it, allowing me time to be comfortable, and for that I was thankful.

I was enjoying this role so far. On Thursday, I felt giddy as I stripped for him, ready to stand and allow him to inspect me. He walked around me, quietly observing my body, just as he had the night before. I wanted him to touch me, but I knew this was not the time to ask. That would come later, when we discussed the evening. He was experienced; all of this was new for me. I quickly understood that this was a learning experience for him as well. He knew what it was to be Dominant, but he had to learn what it was to be my Dominant as much as I had to learn to be his submissive.

I did not see him for the weekend, even though he was in town. There were still parts of his life that were kept apart from me. Even though he was bringing me into this deep and intimate role, there were things that I was not privy to. I knew some of it was the lawsuit and I wished that he would open up to me about it. Other times, it was whatever he did socially, and I had no idea what that was. I was beginning to develop strong feelings for him. I dared to tell myself that I was falling in love and my submission to him was only heightening it.

I enjoyed time with my friends on Saturday. I noticed that our group was thinning. Typically, anywhere from seven to fourteen of us would get together to wander the clubs downtown. Two were gone for good, it seemed. One was moving out of state, the other had picked up a job that required evenings and weekends. As nine of us managed Saturday night together, I wondered who would be next to leave our little group.

On Sunday, Michael invited me to lunch. I accepted. I saw no reason not to. The flowers didn't bother Henry, and if I were around Michael, I could keep things friendly. As we enjoyed our lunch, I wondered if that was going to be so easy. He was not shy about his intentions, even when I gently discouraged. I liked where things were going with Henry and I did not want to change it or give it up. At the same time, I saw something with Michael that Henry was not offering. Michael was willing to share. He talked eagerly about his life and about himself.

It was night and day between him and Henry. I could see how Michael and I could work. He was sincere and simple in his tastes. There were no complex rituals, no rules of obedience and punishment. No safe words, no wondering if neighbors might hear. The simplicity was in its own way as tempting as the darkness that stirred Henry.

By Monday, the confusion that stirred my emotions was calmed. I focused on work and was happy to see the message from Henry that he wanted to see me that night. I would be spending the night with him again, which meant more training. I decided that I would tell him about my lunch with Michael and what each of our intentions was. He had told me that my honesty was part of what made him decide that I could be his submissive. I did not want to shatter that.

The reporters were thinned out by the time I left the building and I was surprised by that. The crowd this morning had been just as thick and energetic as the crowd last week. I doubted, however, that it was a sign of lessened media interest. Most likely, they were looking for other avenues to get their scoops and stories.

I drove to Henry's condominium and found him ready to greet me. When I arrived, I stripped obediently and waited for him to inspect me. This time he touched me, lifting my breasts and examining my nipples. He reached between my legs and parted the lips of my labia gently, and then parted my buttocks to examine me there as well. The whole exercise was erotic and it left me flustered and aroused. When he was finished, he guided me to the table where sushi waited for us.

"I saw Michael yesterday," I said as the small talk that started our dinner dissipated. He looked up at me and cocked an eyebrow. "It was just lunch, but I thought after the flowers I should tell you."

Henry nodded his head and swallowed his bite of sushi. "I appreciate that. He's doing well, I take it?"

"He's enjoying his position at Lellman& White," I said. I picked up another bite of sushi with my chopsticks.

"Interesting choice in employers." Henry's eyes stirred and I thought I saw a hint of something there.

It did not look like jealousy, though it was close. Protectiveness? I thought so. I hoped that his caution was more about the current ownership of Lellman& White, and not about Lellman& White being the company where I interned. To me, the former was of greater concern.

"He's not talking to the media about you, though," Henry said. "That at least shows that his intentions are honorable."

I smiled. "You don't mind me having lunch or something similar to that with him from time to time?"

Henry placed his hands on the table and looked at me evenly. Once more, the darkness in his eyes looked suppressed to me. "Stacy, you are my submissive and that requires us both to be committed to that relationship. I will ask if you want to give me more control as we go along. You may even ask me if you can give over more control. One thing I will not do is tell you who you can socialize with or who you can be friends with. That is your decision."

I felt warm from his answer. A simple "no" would have sufficed, but this was so much better. This told me so many things, about how serious he was about this relationship and a little more of what he expected of me.

"How would you like to go to a party with me this weekend?" Henry's tone changed as the conversation changed. My ears perked up at the question. This was finally a chance to see into the rest of Henry Lennox's world.

"I would like that."

"This is my kind of party," Henry's voice took on an air of caution. "That is, everyone who is attending the party is involved in the lifestyle in some way. Most people will be Dominants and their submissives or slaves. We have a few people who are professional fetishists, models, exhibitionist, that sort of thing."

The idea sounded intriguing. I tried to imagine what this type of party would be like. "What do I do there?"

"Mostly, you stay by my side. You will be expected to keep your eyes averted downward. Only address a Dominant if they address you first, and they should not do so without addressing me. You can speak to other submissives freely, of course. Protocol at parties like this is strict and you will be able to tell quickly who is what. You can address me freely. You can just call me Henry; you don't have to address me as any specific title. I want that to come naturally from you."

I nodded, understanding, and swallowed another bite of sushi. "Will I be wearing a collar?"

The idea of a collar was exciting to me. I had been studying more about Dominance and submission and reading books at home. Collars were not uncommon at parties and denoted who was owned and who was not.

"No. I'm not ready to give you a collar yet. That is another level of commitment." My expression dropped. I wondered why I was not worthy yet to have a collar. He claimed me as his already. He loved to refer to me that way, and I loved hearing the words. He touched my hand gently as he spoke again. "Giving and receiving a collar is like a marriage. I don't do training collars either. I have only ever collared one woman, and I want to be sure that when I collar another, she does not decide later to give it back."

I met Henry's eyes and felt my confidence return. It was me, but it was him as well. It was not a matter of worth. It was whether or not we would both stay committed to this relationship. We continued eating, Henry telling me more about the party and what to expect. I listened as best as I could and hoped that I would be able to remember everything for him.

I pulled at the hem of my skirt and fidgeted in my heels. I was nervous. I was excited while Henry was dressing me. I felt sexy, wearing a skirt that came down mid-thigh and flared out.

I wore a black lace halter over it and sheer thigh highs underneath. I was not allowed to wear panties, and Henry warned me that at any time during the party, he might touch me. I was not to act startled or ashamed when he did, and that I needed to tell him then if I was not comfortable with the idea. As I stared at myself in the mirror, I thought the idea was wonderful.

Now I was beginning to doubt my convictions.

"You will be fine," Henry said as the elevator doors closed. He turned me around and tilted my face up to him. "You need to stop pulling at your skirt. Keep your shoulders straight, your head tilted down slightly, and relax. I'm not going to embarrass you and I know you will not embarrass me."

I breathed in and out slowly to relax. The elevator doors opened and I waited for Henry to step off the elevator. I stepped off behind him. I would be expected to stand just behind and to his left, and so I wanted to practice that now. The side, he told me, was a preference. He preferred to turn to his left to see me, and being right handed, he wanted that hand closest to him, as a sign of my readiness to serve him.

I followed him down the hall and to the suite that waited for us. The hotel was incredible and I expected the suite would be breathtaking. He knocked on the door and Ana answered. I was startled to see her. She smiled at Henry, keeping her head high. She was a Dominant then. I wondered if that explained the type of discipline I sensed in the office. Was she responsible for those hints that I picked up? I kept my head tilted slightly and my eyes averted.

"Stacy, it's wonderful to see you." Her voice sounded sincere and I smiled. It made me glad to know that she was not displeased that Henry and I were together again.

Henry coughed. I peeked up under my eyelashes to see Ana give him a sheepish look.

"Please forgive me," Ana said to him.

Henry gave her a warm smile. "*You* can address Stacy any time you like."

Ana gave Henry a smirk and turned her attention back to me. I quickly averted my eyes again. "Welcome."

She stepped aside and we entered the room. I raised my head a little so that I could look around. I saw several men and women, a few alone but most in pairs. Some women held their heads high, others slightly downturned. From them, I noticed that I only needed to tilt mine slightly and adjusted my posture accordingly. Some men kept the same posture as well, and I marveled. Intellectually, I knew male submissives existed, but I could not imagine how it worked. Most men I knew were aggressive and boisterous. These were as quiet as the women were.

I followed Henry as he walked around the room, mingling with other guests. He was relaxed here and I marveled at the change in his demeanor. The protocol and formality that had me so nervous was second nature to him. As he spoke to people, he introduced me as his submissive. I felt goose bumps each time he spoke the word. No one asked about a collar and no one mentioned the lawsuit or the media frenzy. Everyone was courteous and respectful of Henry and of me.

After a while, a few of the submissives pulled me away from him gently. I was nervous, ready for a thousand questions about Henry. Instead, they were curious about me. I relaxed and talked. As they shared their experiences, I listened. One offered tips on how she remembered party protocols. Another discussed sub-space with me, something that I realized I had experienced often with Henry, even though I did not have a name for it at the time.

A couple of hours into the party, I was relaxed. I could have been clubbing with my friends from college, though in a way, this felt more natural. Even with the rules and the expectations, I felt more myself here than anywhere else, except perhaps in the office. When I asked one of the submissives a question about thoughts or an emotion I experienced, she understood right away.

"I call it the dragon," Cheryl said. She was a cute strawberry blonde with luscious curves and an infectious smile. "When I see it in my Sir's eyes, I get weak in the knees. I look for ways to draw it out because it's dangerous."

I felt so relieved that I was not alone in noticing that something deep, that something worthy of being feared, and wanting to touch it. I was strange, but I was starting to understand that we were all strange in this room. We were strange for the kinks and fetishes that we enjoyed. We were strange for the way that we saw this lifestyle as a dark reflection of the rest of the world. We were strange, different, and unique. We were not alone, and that was a relief to me.

Henry came around to me and politely excused me from the company of the other submissives. I followed, asking how he was enjoying the party.

"I felt bad that I was not with you," he said. "You look like you were enjoying yourself, though, so that's good."

Now I felt like I had abandoned him. "I'm sorry. I should have come back over."

Henry stopped and looked down at me. I glanced up, feeling that I was supposed to meet his eyes and he smiled. "I'm here; I'm fine. It's you that I wanted to make sure enjoyed herself."

He started walking again and I followed. He walked up to a tall woman with long, straight, deep brown hair and piercing ice-blue eyes. She was a little taller than Henry and strikingly beautiful. As we approached her, I was sure to avert my eyes. She had a fierce bearing and I realized that I didn't want to see her displeasure.

"Mistress Aevia." Henry offered her a slight bow, "I would like to present my submissive, Stacy."

I stood still, my head tilted slightly, my hands open and behind my back. I felt her eyes burn into me and understood one thing very quickly, even without having to look up to her. She tapped her finger against her hip in a quick, rhythmic motion.

"Isn't she precious?" I could hear the venom in Mistress Aevia's voice and I did not want to chase it. She did not approve of me. I looked down to see Henry's fist tighten. She must have seen something in his face. When she spoke again, her voice softened, for him at least. "Still, you have always had the penchant for picking up strays and nurturing them. I hope that she's worth all of the trouble she has been."

"She already is." Henry's words were a comfort, but I did not miss the hint of deference in his voice. He respected Mistress Aevia, which meant that her opinion would matter to him. I felt my heart sink and wanted to be anywhere else.

"So you say. Ah, there is dear Ana." Mistress Aevia stepped aside. "Enjoy your pet."

She walked away and I felt relieved. Henry walked to the balcony and I followed him outside and onto the quiet porch. He leaned against the railing, looking out over the city. I took my place next to him, letting my gaze follow his.

"Did I do something wrong?" I asked at last.

Henry turned to look at me. I saw him bring his face down and turned to meet his eyes.

"You did nothing wrong, but I should have defended you better."

I thought about the exchange. I was new to this lifestyle, but I was not new to women like Mistress Aevia. They existed everywhere. They had an inflated sense of their own importance. It did not matter if it was deserved or not. They believed that it gave them the right to pass judgment on anyone, and woe if anyone challenged them. No, what he had said was fine. Anything more would have caused a scene, one that she would likely spin to prove her point.

"You defended me perfectly," I said.

"I hoped she would be nicer to you. Mistress Aevia is the one who trained me when I first found the lifestyle. She's a professional fetishist, respected here and in many other cities. I should have remembered that she is also exacting and hard to please." Henry took my hands in his and kissed the back of them.

I remembered that he told me once that he had only been obsessed with one other woman. It was obvious to me that Mistress Aevia had been that one. I felt something strange stir in my gut. As I thought that she did not deserve his obsession, I realized what it was. I had almost forgotten what it felt like, even though for much of my young life it plagued me like an ill begotten friend.

Jealousy.

I followed Henry back inside and we rejoined the party. While the protocol of the evening was still in place, the atmosphere seemed more relaxed. I did not know if it was because Mistress Aevia had apparently found another part of the suite to entertain herself in, or because some of the guests were giving small demonstrations within their groups. One Dominant had her submissive down on his hands and knees. Her legs rested comfortably across his back. Another had a paddle and was using it to show a young couple proper striking areas on the bare and exposed backside of his submissive.

Henry sat down in a chair and bid me to stand to his right. Another man joined him. I did not miss the look that he gave me as he sat down and was happy to avert my eyes. The lust there was clear. He looked familiar and my mind struggled to place the face. I chanced a glance down at Henry as the two began to speak, talking like old friends and saw darkness stirring in his eyes. As they talked about their different business conquests, Henry's hand rose slowly up my leg. I steadied my breathing as it moved up between them and found its place, warm, wet, and eagerly waiting for him.

This, I understood, was Henry's demonstration, his ownership of my body. As his fingers slipped easily into me, emotions flooded me. My heartbeat raced. I kept calm and focused on his voice as he spoke, even and confident. He pushed his finger forward, and I could feel my knees want to buckle. His touch was delicious and I wanted to give over to it. I also knew that was something I could not do. I counted in my head, focused on the tone of his words, anything to keep the swelling pleasure at his fingers from overtaking me.

Then I felt it, warmth moving over my body slow and smooth. I flexed my fingers and clenched my teeth to keep from moaning or crying out. He slipped his finger out of me and up toward my clit. Every part of me seemed alive from the orgasm he had brought on and I struggled to keep myself still and calm. He stopped before he reached my clitoris and pulled his finger back down, his touch fire and ice on my skin, before slipping his finger back inside me. I felt a tremble begin and took a slow, deep breath.

Their conversation ended. The other man started to stand and paused. "May I address your submissive?"

"Of course." Henry kept his fingers inside of me. I felt terrified. I knew that I would be expect to answer or to say something. I had no idea if my voice would work.

"Miss Stacy, it is a pleasure to meet you." The man gave a slight bow, and when he did, he met my eyes for only a moment. When he rose again, I did not raise my eyes with him. I was not sure if it would be appropriate. Henry pushed his fingers deeper into me and I fought to keep myself steady. "You are a credit to Henry and I hope that he appreciates you."

With that, he turned and walked away, not waiting for me to reply to him. Slowly, Henry removed his fingers, sliding them through the inner layers of my skirt. He stood and with his right hand took mine.

"Are you ready to go?" he asked me gently. I could hear want in his voice.

"Yes." My heart pounded in my chest at his display. I knew that I should be embarrassed by it, indignant at the casual way he played with my body. I also knew that it was exciting. Some part of me wanted to do it again. I thought of his promise that he would have guests while I was with him. I wondered what things he would have me do as he spoke to them.

Henry led me out, giving a few goodbyes as we walked past people. He was silent as we walked to the elevator and I wondered if everything was okay. He pressed the button and when the elevator door opened, I followed him inside.

When the door closed, my world was full of him. He brought his arms around me, gripping my hair and holding me in place as he kissed me, pressing his body against me and pushing me into the wall of the elevator. I welcomed his tongue and the passion with which his body tried to absorb mine. I wanted to unfasten his pants, to push them down and have him take me here, and hesitated. I thought of all the shots of elevator footage. The last thing he needed was the hotel selling a sex video to one of the tabloids.

He released me when the elevator dinged for the lobby. I straightened my hair as the doors opened and pushed down my skirt. He walked out quietly and I followed him. I was eager for more of him. He felt wild in the elevator, alive in a way that I had not experienced before. We walked quietly to the car and he opened the passenger door for me. I climbed in and sat down. He closed it and walked around to his own.

When he sat down and closed the door, I started to move toward him. I wanted him now. I needed to feel that fire again. He placed his hand on my arm and eased me back down into my seat. "Not here." He turned to me. His eyes swirled, the green of his eyes so dark that I could barely make that out as the color now. "What I want to do to you, I can't do here."

My heart leapt into my throat and I could not push out words. I sat back in my chair and fastened my seatbelt. Henry pulled out of the parking lot and started the drive home. When we were out of the deck and onto the road, he moved his hand and placed it between my legs, holding it there, touching, but not playing.

The drive uptown seemed to take forever tonight. When we finally pulled into the parking deck of his building, I felt as though I had been in the car forever, drowning in my frustration and desire. I followed Henry out and up to his condominium on the top floor of the building. When he opened the door and I walked inside, I did not wait. I began removing my clothing, careful for the delicate material of the halter and the skirt. Henry took them from me as I removed them and walked through the door from the kitchen. I walked to the center of the room and waited for my inspection.

Henry walked up to me and invited my eyes up to him. "You've already had your inspection this evening." His eyes were still deep and dark. I was so afraid of him pushing it down. "You were lovely at the party, so much more that I could have asked. What you let me do to you was daring and naughty, and I have a punishment that I want to use for it."

Now I understood his desire to wait. I nodded.

"It is called Bastinado. It is very painful. I can use many different implements, but I prefer a narrow paddle that I own. It is light, swift, and sharp. I will use it to strike the soles of your feet, between your arches, while I have your feet bound."

I said nothing. I thought of what he described. He did not warn me about pain often. It was usually to be assumed. I imagined, then, that it had to be severe. He took my hand and I stepped forward to follow him to the bedroom. He laid me down on the bed and went to his trunk of tools. He pulled out cuffs, a narrow bar with more cuffs on both ends, and a thin, narrow black paddle lined with leather.

He brought the loose cuffs to my wrists and bound them securely. He then pulled my arms straight up and clipped the cuffs together by their short chains behind one of the posts of his iron bed. He brought the bar to my feet and slipped the cuffs around my ankles, tightening them carefully. The bar kept my legs apart. He had told me about this device, and the many ways it could be used, but this was the first time he had decided to use it.

Henry raised my legs by the bar and picked up the thin paddle. He tapped it lightly against the arch of my left foot several times and I sighed. The sensation was firm and pleasant. Then he brought the paddle back a few inches and struck, hard and sharp. The pain surged through my foot and up my leg. He followed it by another strike and I screamed. This was intense, unlike any other strike I had felt. There was no pleasurable warmth to follow the strike, only the pain, sharp and harsh. He struck me three more times and I opened my mouth to utter my safe word.

Before I could, he shifted, moving to my other foot. I closed my mouth and felt the sharp pain begin to spread and dull. Now, the warmth came, easing into my arch like an old friend. He tapped my right food lightly, several times again and I understood the purpose. It was to warm up my foot, to excite the nerve endings and relax the muscles. When he struck, I screamed again. The pain was intense. I imagined that he was pulling back to his shoulder, but when I opened my eyes, I saw again he was only pulling back a few inches.

He struck again and I saw that the darkness had overtaken his eyes. I cried out as the struck three more times. Again, I opened my mouth to speak, but he was already lowering the paddle. He dropped it onto the bed and took my feet into his hands, rubbing over the point of impact gently, easing the warmth into the rest of my foot. I looked up into his eyes to see the darkness easing.

Henry gently set my feet down. They felt sore and warm from his strikes and the gentle rub that followed. I watched him remove his clothing and open the small foil packet. I hated that thing. I wanted to feel him, bare inside me. I thought of how he felt on my tongue and closed my eyes. The condom was just another barrier, like the silence he kept about himself.

However, those barriers were breaking. Tonight he had brought me into his world. He shared it with me and this, I understood, was his expression of gratitude that I took part in it. He took hold of the spreader bar and raised up my legs, pushing them toward my body, bending my knees, so that I was exposed to him. He entered me fast and hard, and I cried out again for the pleasure of it. He was hard and fast as he pulled out and entered. I gave over to the feeling, letting my cries and shouts ring out, savoring each push into my body. I tightened around him and felt the rush of pleasure up my body with his thrusts and brushing out, forming goose bumps on my skin. Each thrust pushed more of it through me until I felt him pulse inside me. He held himself inside of me and shook, his body trembling from his effort and pleasure.

Slowly Henry pulled out of me and lay down beside me. He breathed heavily and when I looked over, I saw the darkness settled and the green of his eyes turning bright once again. He turned to look at me and kissed me, softly on the lips. When he pulled away, I licked my lips to still taste him there.

I stretched my legs out and relaxed in my bonds, letting my mind float on the pain and pleasure of my evening. When I turned again to look at him, he stared at the ceiling, his hands folded over his chest. He looked like he was contemplating and I wondered if his mind went through a period of processing, the way that mine did.

"Why didn't you use your safe word?" He turned to look at me. His eyes were clear, serious, and full of concern.

"Why did you stop before I needed to use it?" I kept my eyes focused on his.

He turned and looked back up to the ceiling. I wished that he would not, but I thought he needed to. He was reaching down into himself, understanding me, understanding us. I waited patiently for him to speak. "I didn't need more."

I thought of the pain I endured on my feet. He could have delivered so much more.

"I could do more, but the feeling changes and turns. It's not what I want. Where you carry me, it brings me to that edge. I feel alive and on fire." He turned to look at me again. "I'm afraid that I'm hurting you."

I pulled at my bonds. I wanted to bring my hands down to him and could not. Henry smiled. A little of the darkness stirred and then calmed. His dragon was sated, it seemed. "It hurts, but you don't hurt me. Sometimes I think I could take more. Not tonight. I was about to call out red when you switched feet and stopped. But sometimes."

Henry sat up and began to unfasten my cuffs. He freed my wrists and my ankles. I twisted and turned everything to loosen them. My feet still hurt, but the pain was a light throb now. By morning, it would be gone. Henry stepped out of the room to his bathroom and then back in again, that cursed sheath gone. I still wanted to feel just him, but resigned myself to acceptance. One day, perhaps.

Henry pulled the bedspread down under me and brought it and the sheets over our bodies. He reached out to the bedside table and pushed the button on the remote. Slowly the lights began to dim. He pulled me to him, and

I rolled over to snuggle against his body. I closed my eyes and listened to the sound of Henry's breathing as sleep slowly overtook me.

FIVE

On Monday, the party still spun through my mind. It was an amazing place, strange in its formality and display. As my mind processed the weekend, I felt like Alice through the looking glass. It had seemed so perfect there, but I knew that his world could have a dark underside, just like any. I wondered if Mistress Aevia was part of that. I doubted it. If she had trained Henry, she could not be so bad. It was my jealousy, perhaps.

I focused on work and watched my day speed by. There would be no time with Henry tonight. He would be seeing Mistress Aevia. I tried to keep my jealousy down with the thought that I would be spending Wednesday and Thursday both with him. Instead, I would use tonight to do the things that I neglected over the weekend: grocery shopping and laundry.

After work, I stopped by the market near my apartment. As I picked over tomatoes, I heard a familiar voice behind me.

"Small world."

I turned and smiled to see Michael. I was still too elated from my weekend to let complications bother me. He had a basket with a selection of produce. "Shopping too, I see."

"A few extras on the way home. I happened to see you and thought I would come over." He ran his finger over the bell peppers and picked one out. "Are you doing anything Friday night? I thought I might take you to dinner and a movie."

A date? The complications decided to rear their heads whether I cared about them or not. I offered Michael another smile and shook my head. "That sounds nice, but I really can't."

He frowned deeply. "Henry?"

I nodded and picked out my tomatoes.

"I'd heard rumors," he said. "Is it official then?"

I moved on to avocadoes. I thought of our talk about collars and shrugged my shoulders. "Not really, but I don't like to complicate things."

Michael picked out a tomato. "Do you think he has the same concerns?"

I thought about Mistress Aevia. Would they be playing a game of who could whip harder? Perhaps they took turns giving over to each other, or they just enjoyed rough sex. I pushed those though from my mind. Thinking about her was going to do me no good. I had not asked Henry for exclusivity, so I certainly had no right to expect it or be jealous if he took advantage of an evening with an old flame. Besides, Michael was not trying to ask Henry out, he was trying to ask me out. I didn't want to complicate my emotional life any more than it was. Henry could run his how he saw fit.

"I'm sorry, that wasn't fair." Michael leaned against the produce counter. "I just worry about you. How long do you think this thing with you and Henry will last? A few weeks, a few months?"

"I don't know." I turned to face Michael. "I'm not asking that question right now. That's not the point anyway. I only want to focus my energy on one person, and that's him."

Michael nodded. "I have to respect that, I suppose." He stood back up straight. "I have to go, but remember. When he finally breaks your heart, I'm right here."

Michael left before I could say anything else. I didn't want to know that he was waiting there in the wings. I didn't need him there. I just wanted him to be a friend, and I wondered if he would be satisfied with that.

Slowly, life began to settle into a kind of normalcy. I had my nights with Henry, which were becoming wonderful sensual explorations. One night, he would have some new sensation, not for pain but to delight me. He showed me the tool in his trunk that I had taken for a screwdriver. He called it a violet wand and it reminded me of the static electricity balls I would see in stores at the mall growing up. This ran static electricity up a glass tube. When he touched it to my body, everything came to life. I shivered and moaned as he found different places to touch and test.

Other nights, we would explore pain. Often it would be new modes of impact play. Other times it would be finding new ways to clamp and pinch my skin. He would fold open my labia with clamps, which was excruciating and delicious at once. He showed me his collection of needles, and to that I had to say no. Not a permanent no, but I was not ready for that yet. He had taken me to another event, this one demonstrating needle and knife play. It looked fascinating, but I saw something between the performers. I could not touch on it, but I sensed a deeper level of intimacy. As deep of a bond as I felt myself forming with Henry, I knew we were not there yet.

There was still so much about him I did not know or understand. As much as we explored sensations, we did not deepen the Dominance and submission side of our relationship. Sometimes I wondered if we would, or if this was the level that it would stay. My attraction for him stretched outside of my submission. If my submission could not deepen, what would that mean for the rest of our relationship?

Henry took me to another party and Mistress Aevia was there. She did not hesitate to hide her displeasure, and Henry bristled under her disapproval of me. I placed my hand in his to keep him calm, to reassure him that it was okay. His was the only approval I needed. I did not have to prove myself to anyone else. Other submissives, who had caught onto her coldness around me, had been sure to remind me of that fact. I did not belong to her; I belonged to him. At the end of the day, he was the only one I had to please.

It all seemed so much to manage, this new world with him. Somehow, I found myself learning. I felt relieved that other submissives were eager to offer advice and tips. I helped me manage my nervousness and navigate this strange place.

I had a routine with work as well. My relationship with Henry had not taken away the focus with which I threw myself into projects, and my team quickly adapted to how I worked, tossing ideas around me when I threw myself into creating a layout, so that I picked them up and implemented them as I could. Karla matched pace with me and the two of us became the drawing boards for everyone's ideas. It created a unique energy and flow that I enjoyed immensely. Nora was pleased, as even our toughest client had been impressed with our work.

Michael finally seemed to fill a niche in my life as well. He made no other overtures since our conversation at the grocery store. He had said his piece and seemed content to wait and let the chips fall where they may. We were friends. That was enough for me, and he seemed to accept that that would be all he would have. We enjoyed coffee on the weekends, usually on Sundays, where we talked about our week.

Only my friends from college caused me real worry. We would get together either Friday or Saturday night to wander the clubs. I had begun noticing friends drifting away a few weeks ago and the trend was still continuing. Their lives were pulling them away as they started careers and chased after people to start families with. We were all growing up, and that meant growing apart as well, it seemed.

SIX

I sat in my apartment, resting from another busy week of work and submissive training and reflected on everything. I was tired, but it was a good tired. We had another project under our belts. Henry and I had found a new level to impact play. I still had a welt on my thigh from his new flogger and I kept ointment on it as he instructed. The device was a mean one, its tails made of thinner and heavier strips. The welt it left was healing, but I thought I might have a light scar. The idea sent a thrill up and down my spine.

I still did not have the full emotional connection that I wanted with him yet. I had tried to probe, to get him to open up about some aspect of his life, perhaps what had drawn him into the BDSM lifestyle. His eyes would grow dark and he would turn the conversation around again to me or to something else. I knew that I needed that deeper connection with him, but I was unsure how to tell him. I was afraid of seeming clingy or making him think he was inadequate as a Dominant. I did not feel that way at all.

I was beginning to understand why we were in a holding pattern. I was still becoming accustomed to his control. I knew he did not want to move into another level until I was ready. I thought that I might be the one to ask. He had mentioned that I might want to, and it occurred to me that he was waiting to see if I would.

I liked that idea. He told me that control was not taken by the Dominant. It was given by the submissive and then wielded. It would make sense then, that I would be the one to ask, at least at first. Later, when he understood how I transitioned, he might bring up the subject. The only thing that I was not sure of is what control I wanted to give to him next.

A horn sounded outside of my apartment. I recognized the sound of Lewis' car. I stood up and grabbed my keys. I had my clubbing wallet stuffed into my back pocket with my ID, one credit card, and some emergency cash. I locked the door and stuffed the keys into the pocket of my jeans. I waved to the car and headed down. Trin, who had been my roommate in college, opened the back door and I climbed inside. Six of us total were piled into Lewis' car. When we arrived at the midtown strip, Jake's car, with five more, joined us.

The clubs were busy tonight, more so than usual. I found it curious, but crowds fluctuated sometimes. Most likely one had some live show to draw out the extra crowds. We made our way into one, ordering drinks and then invading the dance floor, letting our bodies move to the sounds of a techno-mixed pop beat. I could not name the song and did not even care. I let it carry me as I danced and enjoyed the revelry with my friends.

Trin pulled me to the restrooms after we finished a dance. She primped in front of the mirror and waited for people to clear out of stalls. I knew her well enough to know that this was Trin-speak for "I want to talk to you." The last stall cleared out. When no one else came in, she turned to me.

"Henry Lennox?"

I smiled in spite of myself. Trin's mouth dropped open and she turned from side to side. I laughed at her schoolgirl excitement, but I understood where it came from. To her, he was some figure on high. He was not like the rest of us. To me, he was my boss, the man down the hall from my office.

And something more that I was still trying to fully define.

"They let you out of college and you turn into a vixen," Trin said. I rolled my eyes. "Everyone wants to know who you are. Your face was all over the news for weeks. I didn't recognize you, I mean," she paused and gestured over my clubbing choice of jean and a t-shirt. "You looked glamorous, hello."

I laughed.

"Then my mom is on the phone talking to your mom, and she says something weird. I'm thinking to myself, no way."

I froze. "My mom is talking to people about my love life?"

Trin shrugged her shoulders. The weight of the situation did not seem to affect her at all. "To my mom, but they were roommates when they were in college. Anyway, I went and pulled up one of those pictures online and I'm like 'damn.' Why didn't you tell me you were dating a billionaire?"

Someone came in and headed to the stalls. I leaned against the counter and sighed. I was going to have to talk to my mother. I thought she had the good sense to not talk about this to everyone she knew. I hoped that Trin's mother was just an exception.

"It's complicated," I said.

"I'll say. So, what's he like in bed? I was reading up on him, and apparently he likes the rough stuff."

I shook my head. "You know I don't talk about that."

Trin frowned. She took my hands and led me back out to the club. We danced for another song and then headed out to the next club on the strip. As we went in, a thick techno beat, devoid of any pop, sounded. Nina, Jake's girlfriend, began to bounce happily as we paid our cover and made our way past the bouncers.

The music thumped and black light dominated the club. I looked around for some clue as to what was taking place tonight. This was certainly different. Usually this club was brighter and the music was loud, but more subdued with a light pop beat. Our group pushed through the crowd and Trin frowned when we found the dance floor roped off. Jake muscled through and found us a couple of high tables near the bar to gather around. He and Lewis left for drinks while the rest of us took our place on stools or standing.

From here, we had a reasonable view of the dance floor. Slowly the boys came back with drinks and we each took ours. Rum and coke. I thought to myself that the boys were going all out tonight.

"The bartender said there's some kind of fetish show," Jake said over the sound of German lyrics on an industrial beat.

My friends shrugged, but I was intrigued. I indicated that I wanted to wait and everyone nodded or shrugged their acquiescence. After another song, the music volume decreased and two people walked out onto the dance floor. A woman in stiletto boots led a man on a leash. Around us, people whistled. I tried to focus on them.

The woman stopped and barked an order that I could not hear over the crowd. That he could amazed me. Perhaps the routine was rehearsed, orders memorized like lines. He lowered himself to his hands and knees. The woman raised her leg and placed her foot on his ass, letting the heel dig into the vinyl pants he wore. She held up a flogger, presenting it to the crowd, who cheered for her to smack him. She brought it down swiftly on his ass, and the snap of the tails reverberated over the crowd.

"Now that's what I call pussy whipped," Lewis said. He laughed as Jake shoved his shoulder for the awful joke.

I just rolled my eyes. Around me, my friends cracked jokes about the show. I was entranced with the artful way the Dominatrix moved. She stepped around her submissive in careful steps, striking at his buttocks and thighs. When she was done with the flogger, she pulled his hair, forcing his mouth open. She placed the handle in his mouth and let him go. She pulled another whip from her belt, this a two-pronged beast that made me flinch to see it. When she struck him with it, his grunt through the handle of the flogger was loud enough for me to hear.

Jake made another joke, this one getting louder laughs. I thought about who was missing from our crowd tonight. I had been agonizing over how my friends were drifting away into new lives. I realized now that I was drifting too. Listening to them crack jokes and jeer, I understood what I did not want to admit before. I did not tell my friends about Henry and me. It was not because of how complicated the relationship was. It was simply because I knew that they would not understand. None of us got into kink in college. The closest we got was body shots in Panama City.

I was entering a world that they did not understand or respect. It bothered me and I did my best to mask the effect of their jeers. These people were professionals, opening a part of themselves to the general public. My friends mocked this, not knowing that in a way, they mocked me as well.

After the show ended, the dance floor was cleared of sweat and opened. We danced for a couple of songs, but I was not feeling it. I wanted to get out of the club. I started out and my friends followed, probably assuming it was just time to move to the next. We squeezed through the crowd and out to the street.

"Hey, it's the freak show," Lewis pointed up the sidewalk.

I turned to see the fetishists loading equipment into a van. They must have just finished unwinding. I wondered if they would be moving on to another club or retiring for the evening.

"Hey, sweetie," Lewis called out to the Dominatrix as she walked to the van. She leaned in next to another woman who was testing equipment and deposited a small crate. "Come here if you want to see a real man."

"Can it, Lewis," I said. I was growing impatient with his immaturity. "You don't get it. Just deal and move on."

The woman testing equipment turned and my blood froze. I had not seen her in the demonstration or in the club. Had she been in the background or simply somewhere else? She put down the rope she was inspecting and walked toward us. Lewis backed away. Even he could sense that she was not someone to be trifled with.

"I suppose that you do get it then, Miss Stacy?" Mistress Aevia's voice was cool, even and full of mockery.

"Yes, I do." I turned to my friends. "Go on to the next club. I'll catch up."

Reluctantly, they turned and walked on. They could sense drama, but I did not want them to witness this. I turned back to Mistress Aevia and met her gaze. We were not at a party or an event. Here, she was a person, just like me.

"What is your problem with me?" I asked, doing my best to keep my gaze steady. She was an intimidating and imposing woman.

"You are trouble," Mistress Aevia said. "Plain and simple and trouble. I have seen a hundred women like you come through the scene in the past few years. I call you Midnight Submissives. You are oh so willing to do anything under the covers and behind closed doors, but to you it's just a game. You are not serious about your submission, you don't understand what is behind it. You are fake."

I gritted my teeth. I wondered how much of this poison she fed to Henry and wondered if it was beginning to sink in to him. Was that, then, why he didn't push for more, or why he still kept me at arm's length in some ways? Were her words starting to get to him?

"You know nothing about me," I said. "And it doesn't matter. *You* don't matter." Her eyes darkened. I steeled myself and continued. "The only person who matters is Henry."

"Nice words. They convinced him. They don't convince me. You waltzed into his life with your baggage. You started trouble and you will waltz back out again." Mistress Aevia stepped closer to me, so that I had to tilt my head to look up at her. From the corner of my eye, I could see the others and thought I saw sympathy there. "Henry can handle a lawsuit. He can probably even come out of it all with his reputation in tact. He won't be so lucky when you show your true colors. He will finally see you for what you are, and once again, he is going to be left heartbroken and bleeding. Another pretender, thinking she can be a submissive. Do you know who will be there to pick up the pieces and put him back together again? I will."

I kept myself steady, but questions began to flood my mind. I started to wonder if my assumption that Mistress Aevia was his obsession was actually true. If that obsession had been a submissive, one he trained and collared, who was only playing at her submission before turning and walking out, then so much about him made sense.

I averted my eyes as I thought and realized my mistake too late. When I looked back, Mistress Aevia was leaning closer, mistaking my action for deception.

"This time," she said. "This time I will make sure Henry sees you for what you are. I will not let another little bitch break his heart."

Mistress Aevia turned and walked away. I stared after her, seeing the sympathetic looks from the others, but not really processing them. I backed away slowly, my mind spinning with thoughts. Was this all just a game after all? No, I knew better. I felt the depth of my submission already. I knew I craved to give him more. I thought about Michael and how I was managing, barely, to keep him at arm's length. How did that look? How much had Mistress Aevia already poisoned Henry's mind with her assumptions about me? How much had I contributed to it, not even realizing what I was doing?

I turned and walked down the strip to the next club. My mind burned with questions, and I no longer wanted to be here. I thought of strong arms, ropes around my wrists, and thought that I had never wanted to be with Henry as badly as I wanted to now.

THE END

Thanks for Reading!

I hope you enjoyed reading Broken Purity. ☺

Make sure you get a copy of the next book in
the Alpha Billionaire Series Book 3: Broken
Chasity

BROKEN CHASITY BOOK THREE

ONE

I hung up the telephone feeling torn and full of angst. Conversations with my mother could do that. Some – most of them if I had to be honest – were light and pleasant conversations. She would catch me up on what was happening back home and talk about Dad's latest adventure with the lawnmower. He bought a brand new one last year, a nice fancy riding one so that he wouldn't have to worry about throwing his back out doing yard work. I never understood why he didn't just pay someone else to do it. We had any number of companies vying for the opportunity take on the mess of weeds and grass. Our neighbors also seemed to have no end to the ability to produce teenage offspring who needed spending money.

Dad was a do-it-yourself type, though. If he could not do it, it probably never got finished, which explained our garage full of half-finished projects. If a hobby existed, he attempted it and left the remains sitting along the wall and workbench to collect dust. I liked to think that his inability to finish anything was what drove me to see through to the end of a project. I remember going out to the garage and looking at projects, unfinished, never to be picked up. They looked like discarded toys and always made me feel sad.

Today's conversation was about me and my relationship with Henry. I found it hard to talk to her about much of anything. So much of what we did was tied to the Dominant/submissive dynamic. The thought of describing that to my mother terrified me. What if she tried to make me see a psychiatrist? What if she decided it was not consensual and called the police to report abuse?

Talking to my mother, it struck me just how serious the whole thing really was. I fumbled through the conversation and I could hear that she did not completely believe everything I told her.

"Are you happy, dear? That's all I really want to know. Rich men can be so thoughtless sometimes and I want to know that he's treating you well." Mom had sounded so sincere and concerned.

"Yes, Mom. I'm happy and Henry is wonderful," I had told her.

I wanted to be able to ask for her advice and knew that I couldn't.

How do I give him more power? I wished that I knew the answer to it. I wrestled with trying to find some aspect of myself to hand over to him and somehow it alluded me. When we talked about it starting out, the idea had seemed so simple. I would just pick something and say, "Let's do this." Only I couldn't seem to pick those things out. It was like there was something in it all that I couldn't quite see.

I sighed as I looked at my phone. It shook along the counter to tell me I received a text message. I swiped the screen, expecting to see a worried note from my mother. Instead, it was a message from Henry. I smiled and some of the angst eased.

Plane taking off. No time to call. Party on Friday.

A party on Friday would be one of *his* parties. I remembered my first party with him; he had played with me as he spoke to someone else. I had been embarrassed and excited at the same time by his demonstration of power over me. The memory still tightened my stomach. I reached my hand between my legs without thinking about it. I wanted him so badly.

I sent a text back to him quickly. *Looking forward to it.* Phone in hand, I walked to my bedroom and lay down, placing the phone on my nightstand. I wanted Henry so badly and I knew I would not see him before Wednesday.

This trip would not have him returning until late Tuesday night. I unbuttoned my jeans and slid them down my thighs, my mind filling with the things Henry would want to do to me. I slipped my hand beneath my panties, finding myself wet and waiting. In my mind, I saw only Henry's eyes and the delicious darkness that I loved. I pressed my finger into my clit and rolled it around, imagining the feel of his flogger against my thighs and back. I wondered if I would be able to sit down on Thursday without wincing and as I brought myself off, I hoped not.

I wanted to savor as much of the delicious pain as he could give me.

Monday was a flurry of activity at Lenox Advertising. As soon as I stepped off the elevator, I heard the buzz. Another promotion had taken place. I walked up the stairs and down the hall to my team's office, picking up snippets of conversation. When I walked in, everyone was excited, sharing the news that Karla received a promotion and was moving to another team. She would be a team supervisor and liaison, taking on the role that Nora had left behind to become our manager.

I was as excited as the rest of the team. This was a big step for her and in just my few months with the company, I knew Karla deserved it. Nora spent most of her day out of the office conducting interviews. When she was in, I could plainly see the conflict on her face. She was proud of Karla. She was also annoyed at losing Karla. We had three projects lined up and without Karla, we could easily fall behind. It was the worst time to have to bring in someone new to train and acclimate to the team.

I thought about my own first days here. The team had been open and inviting, but I had an advantage. They needed a certain mindset for the team and I fulfilled that need. We needed someone to take Karla's place, and unless they brought in someone experienced from another company, that was not going to happen with someone new. We would be shuffling around to fulfill Karla's role while welcoming in new talent.

Whoever the new girl turned out to be – I had little doubt I would see anyone but a woman – it would be hard. I resolved that I would be as open and welcoming to her as everyone else had been to me. I thought it was the best way to show what a difference they had made in my first days here.

That afternoon after work, we adjourned downstairs at the Bluepointe to enjoy appetizers and drinks. Tomorrow, Karla would be off with her new team and they would be the ones enjoying this custom with her, or one similar. We filled our last hurrah together with stories of Karla's early days on the team and teasing about the ways Henry would flirt with her in the office.

"I really didn't know what to do with him." Karla sipped her drink and offered me a smile. "I admire you being able to keep up with him. It has to be exhausting."

Giggles resounded around the table. I offered Karla a shy smile in return but said nothing. I still didn't like the idea of discussing my sex life with my teammates, even though they were so open, at least with their affairs with Henry.

"No blushing?" Wendy leaned her shoulder into me with a laugh. "That's a change."

I blinked at Wendy.

"She's right," Lillian tilted her head to one side. "You're still coy, but you're not as timid. Henry must really be making an impression on you."

I was at a loss for words. Tina started to probe, looking for what kind of relationship would be bringing me out of my proverbial shell. I did not know what to say. All of these women knew about Henry's proclivities. It would be nothing to talk about being tied up, flogged, or even shocked with his violet wand. I did not know how to explain the rest to them, and I was certainly not ready for the knowledge that it was somehow changing me, turning me into a different person.

Michelle, blessed Michelle, caught on quickly to my discomfort. She turned attention back to Karla and her promotion, allowing me to breathe without the pressure of answering questions I had no idea how to answer. I continued to listen as everyone shared their favorite Karla stories and wondered what it would be like when I eventually left the team. Would I be smiling and laughing as graciously as Karla did, or would I be wondering who she was that took up so much of the conversation?

On my drive home, my mind began turning over Wendy and Lillian's observations. My relationship with Henry was intense. It was something I had never felt before – something I had never imagined I would feel. I thought about the way that I craved his strikes and how I wanted to be on my knees before him. It was new and strange to me. It was also merely what he and I did together, how we expressed and shared ourselves with each other.

I was not sure how I felt about the idea of it actually turning me into something new. I was not just his submissive. I was becoming something else outside of that. I realized that I did not want to change Henry. All of that darkness was entrancing and I enjoyed the fear and security that I felt all at once within it. I did not like the idea that Henry was somehow changing me. I wondered if he knew and what he thought of it.

My night did little to pull me away from my thoughts and worries. I wondered how to talk to Henry about it, or if I should. I found myself once again wishing that I were under Henry's flogger and bound to his bed. I found myself thinking that it might not be such a good place to be, not if it was having such a deep internal effect on me. When I turned to the internet to look up BDSM and changes, I found little that comforted me. BDSM, it seemed, had a transformative effect on many of the people who participated in it. They seemed to revel in the idea of change.

I wondered if I was alone in thinking otherwise.

Tuesday night, Henry arrived into town too late for me to receive a message from him. Instead, I woke Wednesday morning to a text of *Good morning. Come to my office after work.* I dressed, excited at the prospect of seeing him. The simple request erased doubts of Monday from my mind.

Or was it a command?

I reminded myself that he only dominated me at certain times with ritual and preparation. Still, the idea that he had meant it that way excited me.

Nora was missing from the office when I arrived at work. I suspected she was off on yet more interviews and no one else had information to the contrary. We set about our work, our morning focused on one project. Our day was divided into three parts now to keep the different projects organized and on track. At eleven, as we were wrapping up one project and moving onto the next, Nora arrived with a young woman following behind her.

The young woman was beautiful, as stunning in her own way as everyone else in the office. She had a slender body that her white dress fit over easily. Her blonde hair rested in large, natural curls around her face and shoulders and her wide blue eyes sparkled in a face with a soft, clear complexion. I thought that she looked like a delicate doll and wondered how she would manage the quick pace of an advertising office. This one, at least, was not brutal with its employees. The clients could be, though, and I wondered how she would manage with some of our worst.

"Everyone," Nora walked up to the table. "I want you to meet Bethany Lewis. She is the newest addition to Lennox Advertising."

Bethany stepped up to the table and offered us a large and infectious smile. The doll-like face came to life with color. "It's so nice to meet you all. Nora has told me so much about you."

We each took turns introducing ourselves around the table as Nora walked back to her desk. Bethany repeated each of our names as she offered her hand for a gentle shake. It was an odd habit, but one I had seen before. It was common for people who had trouble remembering names, a trick to train the mind to associate name and face instantly. We turned our attention to the second project of the day and introduced Bethany to it. We caught her up on the proposal and our progress so far.

Bethany's questions left me doubting her fit with the team. She seemed slow to understand some of the concepts we showed her. I kept quiet, unsure just how to respond to clarify without seeming condescending. Michelle clarified an idea and a light came on in Bethany's eyes, bringing new life and color to her face. She pulled over a blank piece of paper and picked up a pencil.

Her hand moved quickly over the page, producing lines and curves, shading and darkening areas. Before my mind could process what I saw, she had created half of a scene, displaying what Michelle had described to her in simple terms, the way we saw it in complex ones. I felt my concern about her place on the team melt away. She would not have Karla's ability to take lead with part of a project, but she would be able to match me in drawing up concepts. I had new appreciation for Nora's abilities as a manager. She had managed to find the perfect person to come into the team, to balance what we needed with what we could already handle.

Henry came by in the early part of the afternoon as we moved from the planning table to our desks. I gave him a small smile that he returned casually. He walked down to Bethany's desk to introduce himself and welcome her. I focused on my own work, but didn't miss the flirtations that came from him or the giggles that made up Bethany's response. I glanced around and saw no expressions of worry or disapproval on the faces of my other teammates. This was nothing more than Henry Lennox being Henry Lennox. I did my best to check my own jealousy over the flirting. As I watched Henry leave, I felt my heart sink a little.

I threw myself into my work for the rest of the afternoon. The team wanted to take Bethany down to the Bluepointe for drinks after work. When I messaged Henry, he told me to come back up to the office after.

With a sense of dread, I followed everyone downstairs to the Bluepointe once more, this time to welcome our new member with drinks and appetizers. As we sat around a large high top, the busy restaurant all around us, Bethany gushed with questions about the team and the project. Her blend of curiosity and simple joy at everything set me at ease after the afternoon. I remembered my resolution from that morning and decided to keep it. I did not want to be the person turning a dark glance to the new girl or making her feel unwelcomed, not with how everyone else had made me feel.

Bethany's questions eventually turned to Henry and they wowed her with their own stories of affairs with Mr. Lennox. I kept my own to myself, thankful for once that I was already in the habit of not sharing my own exploits with the team. No one thought twice about it and with no questioning glances from the others, Bethany felt no need to ask if I had ridden that particular train. After our drinks and appetizer were finished, we each paid our portion of the tab, splitting Bethany's drink cost amongst ourselves as a welcome and slowly made our own ways out to the parking deck or to the front of the building to wait for rides.

As I walked to the elevators to go back up to the office, the flutter of heels on tile caused me to turn my head. Bethany rushed up to me.

Her face was a mix of what I was coming to understand was her normal cheerfulness and something a little more serious.

"Michelle told me that you're seeing Mr. Lennox," Bethany said. "I hope I didn't step on your toes with my questions."

If Michelle mentioned it, Bethany had probably asked. Once again, I had underestimated her abilities. I shook my head and offered her a real and natural smile. I remembered Henry telling me how carefully Ana screened applicants before accepting them for hire. It would be so like Ana to hire a girl to my team who would be concerned about how Henry's flirting would make me feel.

"You didn't," I said. I struggled with how to explain things to Bethany in a way that she would feel comfortable and realized I really didn't have an explanation for myself. "We have our thing and Henry does his thing."

I felt like I had said nothing at all, but Bethany's eyes deepened with understanding. I suddenly felt jealous of this girl and it had nothing to do with Henry at all. Behind the bubbly personality and need for simple explanations of advertising concepts lay worldly knowledge and experience that I simply did not have.

"That's why you weren't upset about everyone talking about him." Bethany nodded as though she had uncovered all the wisdom of this world that was somehow eluding me. "This whole place is amazing. If that conversation had happened at my sorority house, daggers would be flying."

I laughed as I pressed the button to go up. It was a relief to know that I was not the only one surprised by the strange open acceptance in this office. We chatted lightly for a few more minutes as I waited for the elevator. When the doors finally opened, Bethany turned to walk out to the parking decks. I stepped into the car, deciding that I liked Bethany, genuinely and truly. I knew that it would only be a matter of time before she said yes to the flirting and advances. I hoped silently that he did not keep flirting around me and that I was able to remain as calm when Bethany talked about her night with him as I was when the rest of the team did.

Was this, though, a sign of the limit of our relationship together? Was it only going to be the Dominance and submission without any growth of a romance? I wanted more with Henry, but as I thought about his continued office affairs, I wondered if I was the only one who wanted that. How long would I be satisfied with things as they were, and when would I feel the need to move on?

The elevator opened at the Lennox Advertising suite. I stepped out and walked up to Henry's office. Hillary was gone for the day, so I let myself in with a timid knock. Henry sat behind his desk, his attention on his computer as he waved me in. I set my purse on the couch and walked up to his desk, waiting patiently for him to finish whatever he was working on.

"Have you had a chance to take in the view from up here?" Henry asked as he continued to click away at his keyboard, his face a twist of expressions.

"Not yet," I said.

"You should." His voice sounded less like a recommendation and more like a command. "I'm almost finished with this."

I walked around his desk and up to his window. Below, the city spread out in an ocean of lights. The expressway looked like a current snaking through, its direction marked by red or white. I wondered how many of my teammates were trapped in that flow trying to reach the suburbs and how many elected for in town apartments.

Henry pressed his body against me, startling me from the thoughts. I had not even registered him standing. I could feel him hard as he wrapped his hands around my waist and my heartbeat quickened as warmth grew between my legs.

"This breaks protocol a little," Henry whispered in my ear. "I hope that you'll forgive me."

I could not speak; I could only breathe out. His hands slid down and began to pull my skirt up my thighs. I trembled as my mind screamed *no* and my body cried *yes*. I knew that no one would see us this high above the city, and yet I felt like he was exposing me, inch by inch. It was exciting and terrifying. Somehow, amazing myself, I uttered no protest or safe word.

"The party Friday night." Henry's voice was full of the darkness that I longed for. He raised my skirt above my hips and pulled down my panties, letting them fall to the floor. I gasped as he reached between my legs and began fondling me there. "It has an ownership theme and I wanted to make sure you would be able to handle it."

"An ownership theme?" Curiosity found my voice. I breathed deeply as his fingers worked into me, heightening my arousal, and urging on my pleasure for him.

"It is a play party, a place for Dominants to display their submissives and slaves. It will be high protocol, with hands off even one's own property. To attend, you will be wearing something very revealing so that I can appropriately show what is mine."

The thought of being mostly naked around people who were almost complete strangers terrified me. With that terror, my pleasure spiked, riding my fear through an orgasm as I cried out. Henry's arms tightened around me and I felt safe, even as my fear stayed, quivering through my body after the spasms of my pleasure subsided.

"The idea of it turns you on," Henry said. He pulled his fingers from me and brought them to his mouth. I closed my eyes, hoping my futile gesture would hide my embarrassment. He was right.

Henry kissed the side of my cheek and down to my neck. I wanted to feel him inside of me and did not care that I was exposed to the world through his window. Instead, he pulled down my skirt and backed away so that I could pull up my panties and straighten myself. When I looked at him, I saw that darkness swirling in his eyes and knew that he had more planned for the night.

"Do you think that you can handle a party like that?" Henry suppressed the darkness as we walked around his desk and I took my purse.

"I can." I had no doubt and that terrified me more than the prospect of the party. I thought again of how I was changing and realized just how deeply that was taking place. A few months ago, I would have balked at being exposed to a room full of people. Now, I was willingly walking into that situation.

"Good. Follow me to my apartment. We will have a light dinner and then I would like to make up for being away."

My heart leapt in my chest. I followed Henry to his personal elevator down to the parking deck, leaving him to walk to my own car. Once more, doubts and worries were pushed from my mind. On the drive up town, I could only marvel at the changes and wonder at them. I was too caught up in the moment to question anything else.

TWO

I held the light coat around my body as we walked through the hotel lobby and to the elevators. I tried my best to hide my embarrassment and kept my eyes focused on Henry instead. Tonight's party was taking place in a large suite on the hotel's top floor. As we waited for the elevator, my mind turned with questions. Was I pretty enough? What if someone was not disciplined and broke protocol?

The thought of someone groping me uninvited revolted me. Knowing how Henry would respond to such a person terrified me. Tonight I was his property and while my mind tried to reason with me that it was demeaning and degrading, I could not deny the arousal it sparked in me.

The elevator opened and we stepped inside. Henry offered me words of encouragement as we slowly ascended. I suddenly missed the turbo elevators of the Lennox Building. I took in his words, letting them build and bolster my confidence. When the elevator dinged for the top floor, I remembered how to breathe and stepped out of the car behind Henry.

A young man greeted us when Henry knocked on the door to the suite. He was dressed very conservatively in a tuxedo and pants. I felt very self-conscious as I walked in behind Henry and the young man gestured me to a small alcove. There, with Henry watching, I slowly began to unwrap the coat around me. The young man turned and I widened my eyes. The backside of his outfit was only a few straps, meant to hold everything in place. All of him was exposed. I could see the metal of a cock cage between his legs as he walked and a thin metal bar that traced to his ass, where I assumed a plug was in place.

I took off my coat and hung it on one of the hangers in the alcove. I still felt exposed, but a little more confident now. I wore a short dress that hugged my thighs. It was open in the front and back, to expose me. I was clean-shaven tonight and thankfully free of any plugs. The dress opened at my breasts, where two X's coyly covered my nipples, leaving the rest exposed. I still wore no collar and the dress trailed up as a halter behind my neck. I had pulled my hair back tonight in barrettes, leaving it down in the back the way that I knew Henry liked.

"You look beautiful," Henry said and I glowed under the compliment. He offered me his arm and I took it, keeping my head turned slightly down and my eyes averted so that I did not offend any of the other Dominants here.

Around me I saw male and female submissives, some thin, some curvy, and some full-bodied. Each was in some way exposed, in whatever manner his or her Dominant saw fit. I thought they were all beautiful in the simple way they carried themselves. Some blushed profusely, their shame and humiliation evident. Others beamed coyly under the attention they received. All of them seemed taken by the theme of this party. We were all on display, willingly handing ourselves over to our Masters and Mistresses to be owned and used.

This party was vastly different from others that I had attended before. When Henry had warned me that it was high protocol, I realized I had not really understood what that meant. The atmosphere was almost stifling with its formality and yet I felt a strange comfort in it. Even the gaze of the Dominants was regulated. They could look, but I noticed eyes pull themselves away from me and other submissives. They could not gawk. This was a place that I could allow Henry to push my boundaries of exposure. I was safe not just from groping but even from silent harassment.

The protocol also required that I stay with Henry at all times. If he had to excuse himself, I had the choice of waiting outside the door for him or going in to assist him. I did the former. Henry was a very private man about some things. Knowing some of the extreme fetishes out there, I was thankful for the fact. I did not have to opportunity to chat with other submissives, as I normally would, and I missed that. Dominants did, however, engage me in conversation more with Henry's permission of course.

The experience gave me a wider picture of just how varied Dominants were. Some spoke to me as an equal when asking my opinion on a subject or asking me something about myself. Others spoke down to me, as though being a submissive made me beneath them. Those were few here and Henry did not stay around them long. Most of the Dominants carried themselves with clear confidence, but one surprised me. He was shy. I could tell by the slow and deliberate way that he spoke that he had overcome some kind of speech impediment. He was not what I would have pictured a Dominant to be, yet Henry treated him as he would any other Dominant he respected.

I followed Henry around the party, listening and participating in conversations as he gave permission. Mistress Aevia was absent form this party, and my confidence grew. A few casual questions revealed that she was travelling with her show right now. She would be in Philadelphia this weekend and Boston next week. It was a relief not to have her present and I hoped that her appearances would prove to be rare. I could handle the animosity between us if I was not exposed to it too much.

As the night progressed, Henry's desire became more evident. I could feel it in the weight of his hand at my back, or how it would begin to trail downward and stop. His want felt wonderful, and I wondered what things he would do later to show me how strong that lust was.

It was not just his lust that I detected. I saw it in others as well, men and women who gazed on me and other submissives. If allowed, they would have been happy to touch any of us. As I began to feel comfortable under their gazes, I wondered if I would turn away the advances. They wanted to touch and fondle me and I wanted them to, even as my mind tried to protest against the idea, to remind me that I was just a simple girl underneath this veneer of a submissive.

We wandered the party until guests began slowly to trickle out. He led me to the alcove where I collected my coat and wrapped it around my body. I did not feel as self-conscious now, not after wandering under the eyes of strange men and women the whole night. I followed him to his car and we drove back to his condo. My mind turned over the night, the party, and what I felt there.

"You're quiet," Henry said as he parked the car and cut the engine. He turned in his seat to look at me. I could not see his eyes in the dark, but imagined by the sound of his voice that they were even and concerned. "Did you enjoy the party?"

I was afraid to answer him. I did enjoy the party, in ways that I could not understand. I thought of the men and women gazing at me, wanting me, and I loved it. I was afraid, but I knew that I should answer him. The party was like any session and he always wanted me to talk to him about how I felt during one.

"Can we talk about it upstairs?" I thought there I might feel more comfortable.

"We can do that." Henry opened his door and stepped out of the car. I waited for him to walk around and open the door for me as well. I had never questioned the courteous gesture, but now I marveled at it. He was doing a service for his submissive and I wondered if it were proper.

We walked up to his condo in silence as I continued to contemplate the night. When he opened the door for us, he took my coat and I took off the dress and heels. Henry took them to the small laundry room adjacent to his kitchen and returned, considering the X tape over my nipples.

"Are you ready to talk about the party?" Henry asked.

I nodded.

"We can sit down if you want. You can relax to talk to me."

I shook my head. I thought if I tried to relax and to be just Stacy, that I would not be able to tell him. I felt something else as well, another need in this that I could not understand.

Henry studied me carefully as I stood waiting for him to speak again. "I want you to look in my eyes then as you talk to me."

I raised my head and my eyes to meet his. Beneath the bright green, I saw that dark shadow swirl and my unspeakable need rose up. I wanted to cry out, to beg for something, and I realized I had no idea what I wanted. Instead, I focused on my feelings about the party, how confused and conflicted I was about my reaction to everything.

"I enjoyed the party," I said. "I was nervous at first. It was reassuring having you there beside me, and everyone was polite and respectful. It made it easier to be exposed around them."

Henry brought a hand up to my cheek and touched it softly. "But?"

"I started noticing that you wanted to touch me and break the rules of the party. I noticed others wanted to as well."

Henry cupped my cheek in his hand. "That made you uncomfortable."

I took in a deep breath and tried my best to control my emotions. I could feel the tears swelling at the corners of my eyes and did not want to cry. "No, it didn't. I liked it. I –" I broke off, unable to finish my sentence. A warm tear rolled out of my eye. He lifted it away with his finger.

"You wanted them to touch you." The darkness swelled in Henry's eyes and again I felt my unspeakable need. I wished I knew what to ask for. "You think it's wrong for you to feel that way."

I closed my eyes, unable to continue looking into his. It was all too overwhelming.

"I did not say you could close your eyes." Henry's voice was gentle but stern. I opened my eyes again to see his look, heavy and dark.

He wanted to show me something and I wanted to see it. I thought of our first party and the night after, when he punished me for allowing him to play with me. That was his need to punish me, and it had excited me that night. Now I understood what I was feeling. *I* needed it this time. I needed him to punish me for what I wanted at the party.

"That's better." Henry's eyes were dark and somehow gentle. I had not seen this aspect of his darkness before and I felt strange and curious. Part of my mind screamed. I thought of a fly on the edge of a pitcher plant, the sweet sap and water tempting it inside. I knew what I saw there could be a ruse, a way to sway me, but I wanted to be swayed. I wanted to see that gentleness suddenly give way to aggression. "You were perfect at the party, everything I asked you to be and, as you have shown me now, more. I can punish you as much as you need, but I want you to understand how pleased I am with you first."

In my mind, the fly fell in, willingly accepting its twisted fate. I wanted nothing else except to be that fly, drowning in the pool of Henry's darkness. I could say nothing. I could not even move. I could only look into his eyes. Finally, I managed to nod or I thought I did. Whatever I had done, it was enough. He took my hand, his eyes becoming a deep, swirling, dark green and led me back to his bedroom.

I stood under the eyehook, looking on at the iron frame bed as he walked to his chest of toys and opened it. My eyes traced the design of the iron frame of the bed as I saw him lean over the chest and search for what things he would use tonight. He returned with cuffs and rope. He placed the cuffs around my wrists and I savored the warm, soft faux fur inside. He threaded the rope through the links of the cuffs and brought it through the eyehook above me.

He pulled and brought my hands above my head. I expected him to tie the rope off on the iron bed frame and realized it was too short for that. Instead, he looped it back through the cuff links and the eyehook again. Gently he spread my legs until they were shoulder width apart and pulled until I stood on the balls of my feet. I watched him tie off the rope in a simple knot and he returned to the chest.

"You enjoy impact," Henry said, "so that will be your punishment tonight."

Henry brought a blindfold to me and placed it around my eyes, tying it firmly at the side of my head. My sight gone, my ears and skin came to life. I was acutely aware of each motion he made around me and of each sound his body made moving across his carpeted floor. I listened to the rustle of toys in the chest and felt the air around me warm as he came closer again.

I had no idea what implement he would use. Would it be the flogger or the crop tonight? Would he bring out the leather paddle or something else, something crueler?

A dozen thick tails struck between my legs and I gasped. The impact was solid and full. It sent signals of pleasure and pain across my body. I wanted to feel it there again. Instead, I felt the impact at my thigh, harder as the tips of the tails stung me. I sensed Henry move and he struck again, across my right thigh this time, the tails stinging my buttocks.

He moved around me again, and I knew that Henry was in front of me. He touched my breast, picking at the tape that covered the nipple. Slowly he eased the end up and the tape pulled my skin up, clinging as he removed it from my body. He removed the tape from my other breast and both felt raw and tender. He kissed each softly and then I felt the sting of impact across them. I screamed and he struck again, no harder than before, but hard enough for the ends of the tails to sting the fresh and sensitive skin.

Henry moved away and returned. I readied myself for another strike at my breasts and felt it between my legs instead, hard, and swift. He struck again, too quickly for his arm to reposition and aim. He delivered a quick succession of strikes, one and then the other, pressing hard between my legs and stinging the skin between my ass and my sex. I cried out again, feeling my pleasure build with each strike, hearing myself beg for more with each scream and groan until I could not utter words, only sounds.

He struck between my legs and then my thigh, alternating this strikes on each leg and between them. I pictured him holding two floggers. That was all that made sense with how quickly he struck. The wanton abandon that I imagined in his eyes overtook me. My swirling pleasure built to a crescendo and when he struck between my legs again, he pushed my orgasm through my body on a wave of intense pain. I screamed as loudly as I could. He continued to strike, driving my pleasure with pain until my voice faded and my mind began to spin.

The strikes stopped and Henry moved away. I waited for his return and he carefully loosened the rope above me. I stood on unsteady feet and he propped me up, leading me to the bed so that I could lay down. I breathed slowly as he removed the cuffs and tossed them aside. He removed the blindfold last, and my first sight was of his eyes and the sated darkness there.

Something warm and soothing touched between my legs and the throbbing and burning pain eased. He spread it to my thighs and I sighed at the relief.

"You take your punishment very well." Henry moved away again as I lay, my lids heavy as I looked up at the ceiling. I heard the rip of foil and eased my legs apart. I wanted to feel him there. He rolled back and over me, parting my legs further and bringing himself between them, pushing into me slowly. I trailed my hands up his arms, savoring the smoothness of his skin and marveling at how sensitive all touch still felt.

He thrust hard now and I cried out. Everything between my legs erupted to life again and each stroke and thrust as he entered and pulled back was fire and wonder. He drew my eyes to his and I lay transfixed, moving my hips up to meet his thrusts and grunting at the force with which he pushed himself into me. I drew my hands along his body, testing and learning it, as though I had never touched him before.

As he came, pulsing into the sheath between us, he pressed hard against my body. Then he pulled out and rolled off me, spent and satisfied.

My mind swam in my pleasure and pain, processing my night slowly. Henry moved away to dispose of the condom and returned, pulling the covers under and over me before slipping in to join me. He pulled me close to him and I brought my arm over his body and curled my legs into his. Exhaustion over took me as I heard him whisper about beauty and pain. His words became color and color became darkness.

THREE

I spent my Saturday resting from my night with Henry and cleaning. My mind still tried to process through everything. His lifestyle confused me so much sometimes. He delighted in my want of other people, perhaps because he knew that I could not have them. That did not seem right and I could not understand what it was he had enjoyed. Perhaps, I thought, it was just that it gave him the opportunity to punish me again.

Even that did not seem quite right.

I could not understand my own thoughts and desires any better. I could not feel shame over what had happened at the party. That, I thought, he had managed to beat out of me with his floggers. Instead, I felt a strange calm and confidence about the party and myself. It seemed alien to me. I thought about how this lifestyle was changing me. It would do me no good to talk to Henry about it, or ask him why he felt the need to change me. It was not him, not completely. I was bringing it upon myself.

For that, I felt at a loss. I did not want what I did to turn me into someone else, but I did not want to stop either. I enjoyed the sensuality of the party. I enjoyed the pain and pleasure that Henry inflicted upon me afterward. As much as I chafed at the changes in myself and as confused as I was over where I stood with Henry otherwise, I enjoyed being his submissive. I enjoyed each moment and I wondered what it ultimately meant about me and for me.

I thought about my own doubts and needs. I wanted something more from Henry. I needed it. When I finally understood that I would not get it, would I have the strength to turn and walk away or would I accept for the sake of the carnal pleasures that I could not seem to get enough of?

On Sunday, I finished housework and drove to meet Michael for lunch. We sat on the patio of a small restaurant in town and talked about our respective weeks. Michael seemed to be getting along very well at Lellman& White. He had found a pleasant pace for work. I was happy for him in that. It relaxed him, which it turned out meant no more hitting on me or asking uncomfortable questions about my relationship with Henry.

It was nice to just sit and be friends. We sipped tea and were simply ourselves. By the time lunch was over, I discovered I did not want our afternoon to end yet. I ordered a slice of cheesecake that I knew I did not need just to spend a little more time with him.

The day seemed uncomplicated. I could be me without the need to process my thoughts and actions through pain. I did not need to be punished over friendly conversation and dessert. It was all straightforward and simple, and I loved every moment of it. I wondered at my own feelings, if I was starting to develop something stronger for Michael than just friendship. Once again, I could see it. I could see exactly why a girl like me would fall for a man like him. I wondered how much it would complicate things if I did.

My week was a flurry of activity in the office. Bethany was quickly adapting to the team, which made work easy to manage. We shuffled our projects and rushed to complete work. We had a two-week deadline for two of the projects and by the middle of the week, I wondered if we would meet them.

My evenings with Henry were more explorations into submission. I practiced kneeling positions with him and he demonstrated how I could please him there. I also practiced ways to stand and be available for him to tease and explore. In that, I had to practice being still, no matter what he did to me. I had started it confident, remembering my first party. I realized quickly that pressure was a large part of my performance there. Here, with just the two of us, I had only my self-discipline to depend on, and it was not enough to keep from squirming, panting, or moaning when his ministrations became intense.

"You have to be focused," Henry said to me as I recovered and returned to my standing position, feet apart with my hands held behind my back. "I want to take this to something more, but you must be able to focus through what I am doing when it is just the two of us. You can feel pleasure. You can even come, but you must be disciplined enough to be still through it."

When I tried to ask what he wanted to take it to, he would not tell me. He assured me it was nothing that would break my limits or was outside of the bounds of my submission to him so far. It was simply another expression of my submission and his Dominance. The sincerity in his voice told me that he was being honest and I found myself excited at the prospect of something new to try together. I did not push anymore to know and focused as best as I could on the lessons he was teaching me.

On Saturday evening, Henry took me to another lifestyle event. This was not a formal party. He called it a "play dungeon." I was curious and nervous about the prospect, unsure what to expect. We arrived to a small club downtown that was closed to the public for the event. Henry presented our invitations at the door and I followed him inside.

Tonight I wore a slender black dress and low-rise heels. I thought I was modestly dressed for something called a play dungeon. Admittedly, I did not really know what to expect, but I thought it would be a more hands-on version of the last party we had attended.

What I saw instead was an incredibly organized showing. The club's dance floor and bar area were cleared of tables, chairs, speakers, and anything else that might take up room or block access. Fetishists set up discreet areas displaying tools and providing room for participants to learn and experience. I saw several people that I recognized from other parties wandering from area to area. Some were dressed in leather, others in little clothing at all. A few were dressed the way that Henry and I were, as though they could easily be at any club or simply out for the evening.

"I want you to feel free to experience anything that you want." Henry leaned close to me to speak. The music that played was not loud, but the din of voices around us filled my ears with a cacophony. "You can read about different kinks and fetishes, but this is the best way to learn about them. Each person running a booth has years of experience, and I trust each and every one of them to be careful."

Everything that I saw awed me. I watched a couple approach a man holding a violet wand.

He assisted the woman in sitting down and proceeded to demonstrate the different attachments for the wand. Another fetishist demonstrated the use of a riding crop as he prepared to use it on a young man as his partner secured him to a bondage horse.

"Will you stay with me?" I looked up at Henry. I did not like the idea of wandering around here alone. I did not care how much Henry trusted the people in charge of demonstrations. I needed him there to know I was safe.

Henry gave me a smile and nodded. "I can stay with you." He gestured to men and women who stood around the different area displays, wearing only black pants and t-shirts. "Those are Dungeon Masters. Each one is responsible for watching the different play areas and stepping in if something looks dangerous or if anyone calls for assistance. They will also make sure you are okay."

"If the fetishists are so experienced, why do you need the Dungeon Masters?" I felt a little less sure now, even with Henry there.

"The fetishists also let new and inexperienced Dominants and Tops try out tools and techniques." Henry's confidence did not waiver, and I felt my own returning. "The Dungeon Masters make sure that those people do not harm anyone. Sometime accidents can happen as well and they step in in that case."

I took hold of Henry's hand and he squeezed mine reassuringly. He led me around, giving me time to see the different activities that we had not tried before, to see what I might enjoy. I watched a woman cry out as a cane struck her. At another, a woman grimaced as a woman drove needles through the outer skin of her breasts. I did my best not to cringe. Another area was partially blocked off for privacy. There a man urinated on his partner's naked chest. I shivered and turned away, unsure what bothered me more, the open display of such a basic, and private, physical need – or the look of ecstasy on the woman's face.

I stopped at the suspension display, transfixed by what I saw there. A young woman hung by ropes tied at various points along her body. She wore a tight-fitting body suit over which the white ropes stood out brightly. She looked like a fly caught in a spider web, and I thought that I had never seen anything so beautiful, not at one of these events at least.

As the fetishist carefully lowered her, Henry leaned in close to me. "Do you want to try?"

My excitement rose and I knew that I wanted very much to try it. I waited patiently as Henry spoke to the man who led the demonstration. He was older with greying hair along his temples. His hands looked strong and calloused from years of handling rope. I started to feel reassured, though I did not want Henry to leave me.

"Enjoying a little rope play, I see." Mistress Aevia stopped to stand next to me. I did not look at her and only kept my eyes focused on the man and Henry. "Suspension is simple. Oh it is beautiful and it takes a lot of talent on the part of the person doing the rope work." I did not miss the hint of admiration that she put into her voice for the man in charge of the ropes here. "For the person on the other end, it is just a matter of lying there and letting the other person work. Nothing like needles, which require you to stay focused. I suppose this would be perfect for someone like you."

I did not miss the derision in her voice. I kept myself steady and calm. Mistress Aevia did not have Henry's permission to address me. I was not going to make it worse by responding back to her, not when her taunts were so obvious.

Henry nodded and thanked the man. He returned, giving Mistress Aevia a smile, unaware she had broken his rule. "Mistress Aevia, it is wonderful to see you. I didn't think you were due back in town yet."

"We had to cancel our last shows. One of my performers caught a cold. It is always a pleasure to see you, Henry." Mistress Aevia offered him her hand and he kissed the back gently.

Henry turned his attention to me. "Frank is ready to show you suspension if you are."

The thought of not having to stand next to Mistress Aevia was a relief. I nodded and Henry led me over to Frank.

"I'm placing my submissive in your careful care," Henry said and he placed by hands in the thick calloused ones Frank offered.

Frank gave a bow of his head to Henry and then to me. His eyes were soft and gentle and I could not help but smile up at them. "Have you been suspended before?"

"No. Bondage, but not suspension."

Frank released my hands and led me to stand in the suspension frame. "I need to ask if you can remove your dress."

I felt suddenly very insecure. I was wearing nothing under the dress at Henry's insistence. I looked back at Henry and could see want and darkness stirring in his eyes. He would like nothing more than to see me naked and displayed here. It would not be any different, I supposed, then the party last week, but I was still unsure. "Why?" I asked the question timidly and expected Frank to chide me. I could see Mistress Aevia's mouth turn down.

"That's a fair question." The calm and direct response surprised me. "The ropes could slip on your dress, and you might get hurt. I could just pull up the skirt, but that could get uncomfortable at your waist with the material gathered there, and it will make it difficult to work around that area."

The answer satisfied me about the need. I looked to Henry again with a questioning glance this time. He gave me a patient nod. I took in a deep breath, took hold of the hem of my dress, and pulled it over my body. When I handed my dress to Frank, he looked apologetic.

"I didn't realize that you would be completely nude now." Frank set the dress carefully on a chair. "I have a cloth I can use to cover you if you want."

"That won't be necessary," Henry spoke up. I felt myself flush, but nodded to Frank in agreement all the same. My body, while I was with Henry, belonged to him and he wanted to display it.

"Well then, let's get started." Frank began to tie cuffs around my wrists and ankles.

I recognized the technique. Henry had used this as well, so that the ropes would hold me securely without tightening. Frank guided me to lay down on the floor and I did so as he began to tie additional cuffs up my arms and legs. Each cuff left a long strand of rope behind, and I wondered how everything would come together.

Frank kept my attention, even as I heard Henry and Mistress Aevia talking next to the frame. He worked carefully and quickly, and I was amazed at how expertly he manipulated the rope. I had thought Henry was good and realized that compared to this man, he was merely an amateur.

"How many years have you done this?" I could not hold back my curiosity anymore.

Frank smiled and I realized I had done something good in engaging him in conversation. He liked to talk about this as much as doing it. "I've been playing with rope for about twenty-five years in the lifestyle anyway. I grew up around boats, so I've been tying sailor knots and such since I was a child."

I could see that history in his work. Suddenly I felt less like a person and more like the sail of a ship being raised. That imagery calmed my nerves further and I watched as he threaded the ends of the ropes through the frame, bringing them together in order to pull me up. The strain was unlike anything else I had felt, as the tension of the rope pulled at my body in different places. It was only uncomfortable until I relaxed and let my weight distribute along my body.

Once I was in the air, he brought more ropes around, threading them between my legs and along my back to my shoulders. I felt as though I were hanging in some strange cot, unable to release myself. I was scared and elated at once, and the thrill of my predicament moved through my body, warm and tingling.

"What all is suspension used for?" I thought more questions would help me to stay focused.

"Sometimes it is just to display you. I can spread your legs open and position them any way that I want. Some Dominants like to use suspension as another mode for access. Others enjoy flogging or paddling submissives that they suspend. It heightens the bondage by making you more vulnerable."

I could see that and wondered if Henry would be doing any of this with me in the future. I turned my head to see his face. He was studying everything carefully and I thought it was very likely.

"Suspension is also good for sensation play," Frank continued. "You can turn your head side to side, but if you try to look behind you, the ropes pull uncomfortably and you feel like you are going to fall."

I tested my side-to-side motion, but decided not to test looking behind me. I was not terribly fond of heights, and though I was little more than a few feet off the ground, I did not want to chance panic at the sensation of slipping or falling.

"I have some things if you want to see what sensation is like when you are suspended." Frank's offer sounded very nice and I nodded my head, looking to Henry to ensure his approval. Next to him, Mistress Aevia's face was a cold and unreadable mask. "Are there any sensations you do not want to feel?"

Mistress Aevia's eyes narrowed and I felt suddenly nervous answering his question. She was waiting for the list of limits and provisions. I remembered articles I read about submissives who "topped from the bottom" and did not want her seeing me that way. Worse, I did not want her interpreting anything that I said or did to Henry that way.

Henry trusted this man enough to bind me in these ropes; I would trust him as well.

"Whatever you have will be fine."

I looked up at the ceiling of the club and prepared my mind for the sensations I would experience, bound here and helpless beyond anything I had experienced before. A light feathery sensation touched my back and I sighed. Smooth leather followed. He traced his fingers along my back and I could sense the rise of each callous. Something prickly and soft rolled across my back, alternating the feel of fur and the pinch of tiny, sharp needles.

My mind was beginning to soften and I felt strange. I knew this place. I went there so many times with Henry when the pain and sensations that he delivered would begin to take over my senses. Sometimes it would happen simply by being in his presence, following his commands and pleasuring him. I was not prepared for the idea that anyone else could take me there as well, and yet here I was, slipping into that mental space as one sensation after another, some repeated, others new, ignited my body.

Something cool, long, and thin touched my back and my mind drew back from that space. I could feel the sharp edge and as it turned, the tip began to touch my flesh. I struggled and tried to rise away from it, only to find the ropes holding me. My skin opened in a sharp, thick eruption of pain. Metal fell to the floor and my own scream filled my ears, punctuated by Henry calling my name.

My heart raced and my world was black highlighted by a red line of pain along by shoulder. I heard words and worry as hands touched by body, but could not make out anything said around me. Arms wrapped around my body and something soft pressed into my back. In my ear, I heard Henry cooing and calling my name while somewhere above me Frank repeated apologies.

"I'm taking you home," Henry moved hair out of my face as I opened my eyes. I was crouched on my knees with Henry kneeling in front of me. His eyes were bright, but heavy with worry.

I tried to move my arms and winced at the pain in my shoulder. Other hands pressed something into me and I turned my head to see one of the Dungeon Masters behind me.

"You might have to take her to the ER," he said.

"I don't want to go to the hospital." I felt panicked. With the lawsuit happening, the last thing that Henry needed was to be spotted at the ER with the girl at the heart of it. It did not matter what we managed to tell the doctors there about the cut on my back. The media speculation would be everywhere.

The Dungeon Master waved someone over to us and I saw an emergency bag drop on the ground next to me.

"I can suture it. It will close the wound." The man behind me pulled the cloth away from my body and looked past me to Henry. I turned to face him as well, to study his face. "It isn't too deep. She won't have to go to the hospital unless the wound starts to swell or redden. You will need to watch her."

Henry nodded and I could see he was not sure about the solution. "Thank you," I said. My own relief seemed to provide him some.

I winced as the Dungeon Master cleaned the cut and placed sutures through the skin. I realized by the way that he worked he was trained in this and wondered if he were a nurse or an EMT. Frank carefully cleaned the small knife he had been using in his sensation demonstration. It was no larger than his hand, yet it had felt enormous against my skin. As I watched another Dungeon Master help him begin packing the suspension display, I felt terrible.

When Dungeon Master finished dressing my wound, placing a large bandage over it, Henry helped me stand and carefully slid my dress over my body. The Dungeon Master handed me several more bandages and cleaning pads for the wound, giving me instructions on how often to clean it and when to have Henry remove the sutures. I listened carefully as I watched Henry walk up to Frank to speak to him. I was afraid of seeing anger and was relieved that he seemed to be offering him reassurance instead.

As the Dungeon Master packed up the emergency kit and walked away, I heard Mistress Aevia give a task next to me. Before I could wonder what she was going to say, Henry was at my side, saying his goodnights to her and leading me away. Around us, the rest of the play dungeon continued on, as though nothing had happened. Only a few worried and sympathetic glances betrayed that anyone else had been aware of my accident.

On the drive back uptown, Henry was silent. I tried to study his face, only to find it a mask of worry and other emotions. I realized that I had disappointed him and turned my attention to the road. When we arrived to his building, I followed him upstairs quietly and undressed in his condo. He examined my cut carefully and satisfied that it was properly tended, replaced the bandage over it. He led me to the couch to sit down, and I waited for the condemnation about how foolish I had been.

"What were you thinking?" Henry asked.

I was not sure what part I was not thinking about. I could not look up at him and instead looked down at my hands.

"Stacy, you should have told him that sharp objects were a no for you." Henry's voice was even and calm. "What was going through your mind?"

I played through everything again. Henry was right. I had seen the needles and I knew about knife play. I was a novice, but I was not completely naïve. "Mistress Aevia –"

Henry put his hands on mine and I looked up at him. His eyes were even and held mine in place. "Mistress Aevia is not your Dominant. I am. You do not have to impress her. I am the only one you should be worried about impressing."

I wanted to look away, but couldn't. "I'm sorry."

I could not bring myself to tell him about my troubles with Mistress Aevia. They were my own to handle.

"I was afraid you had been hurt." Henry placed a hand on my cheek and I tilted my head into it. He felt so warm and secure right now and with all of my doubts about everything else, I did not want to let this moment go. "I am responsible for you. You are responsible for you too. At a play party or dungeon, you have to communicate your limits to people. Do not expect them to guess. It does more than keep you safe. It keeps them safe as well."

I thought about Frank, and how upset he had become when he cut me. "Is Frank okay?"

"Frank will be fine. You're not the first emergency that he's had. Suspension can be very risky. He was more worried about you and I assured him everything would be fine. Promise me you won't do that again, that you will think before you answer someone about what they can do to you."

"I promise."

Henry's eyes released me and I closed mine. He pulled me close, holding me gently for the cut on my back. Henry felt safe, but I realized for the first time just how dangerous his lifestyle could be.

FOUR

I was surprised at how quickly the cut on my back healed. I spent the weekend in Henry's care so that he could monitor the cut for any sign of infection. By Monday most of the pain was gone and by Tuesday, I could move my shoulder normally without the need to wince. Henry didn't remove the sutures until Wednesday. He followed up that careful procedure with tenderness rather than a rough session of play.

I could not escape the feeling that I had disappointed him, his reassurances aside. I had failed him, and even though failure was to be expected – I was only learning – it seemed to me to be a big failure. As a way to make up for it, I threw myself into work to ensure that my part of the project did not fall behind. I wanted us to meet our Friday deadlines and we did that easily.

My cut managed, my work well under control, it seemed that the only thing for me to worry about was my complicated love life. I still did not understand where things were headed for Henry and myself. All of his tenderness and concern about the injury at the play dungeon could have been deeper feelings – or concern of a Dominant for his submissive. It could go either way, and with Henry, I had nothing by which to gauge his emotions. He didn't talk to me about his feelings. As usual, if I tried to engage him, he became silent and deflective.

He did not like talking about his emotional life, and I suspected it had everything to do with whomever it was that had broken his heart before. I thought of Mistress Aevia's misgivings about me and what had happened at the dungeon. I found myself again wondering how far off her assessment was. What if my submission to him was just to win his heart? Would I continue to submit when I had it?

My own self-doubts piled up in my mind, clouding my ability to reason through them.

On Sunday, I enjoyed a nice lunch with Michael. I apologized for having to miss our lunch last weekend. I had made an excuse that I was just feeling ill and he understood. Today, his attention was focused on making sure that I felt better and asking about my week. We talked about music and books, and I realized that I spent so much time reading about BDSM that I had missed new releases that I was looking forward to reading.

We spent the afternoon browsing through the bookstore so that I could pick up a few titles and catch up to him. The day was once again relaxing. I felt neither pressure nor complication from Michael. I found myself contrasting this weekend with my last one with Henry. In one world, dangers lay hidden beneath a thin film of ritual and protocol. In the other, life was the only danger. No knives lay hidden, waiting to come out to tempt or threaten me. There were no surprises. Everything was as I saw it.

With that came a simple thing that I had to acknowledge. Michael was being exactly what I had asked him to be, and nothing more. He was being my friend. That he could so quickly and easily accept that role in my life, without question or argument, awed me. With Henry, each step was either a fight with doubt or a dance with rules. Here it was a simple yes or no.

I mattered to Michael, enough for him to put his own ambitions for my affection aside and simply be what I needed, no stipulations, no rules, and no hiding. I felt my own emotional connection to him growing and my feelings deepening with it. Once more I wondered, what was next for us and what would that mean for Henry and me.

Life at work the following week did nothing to calm my doubts and conflict. Walking down the hall, I heard a giggle and Henry's voice. I turned a corner, not wanting my presence to make him or the girl uncomfortable. Snippets of rumors floating in the office later told me that Henry had found another one-night conquest, this one a young woman on the production team.

I reminded myself that I knew our relationship was not monogamous. I had not made that demand. I asked myself why I had not broached the subject and only Michael came to my mind and my confusing feelings for him. I did not know if I was falling in love or only infatuated. I knew that I enjoyed getting to see him. Just as I thought Henry must enjoy the flirting, I was enjoying my inner conflict. I was confused, but I also felt alive.

If we were not monogamous because I was not broaching that subject, then what did I actually want out of the relationship? Once again, I felt conflicted, but the realization that I felt alive remained. I had no idea just what to do, so I resolved that I would simply carry along, to let this play unfold around me.

On Saturday, I helped Henry prepare to host his own party. There was little work for me to do, so I mostly waited. Henry did not have me undress, which was unusual. Staff came into the apartment to see to their work, cleaning and dusting the few surfaces in the wide-open room. Caterers brought up trays and narrow tables to serve hors d'oeuvres. Their presence told me why I was still dressed. They were not building staff.

The condo felt welcoming. The windows looked out over the city. The end of the hall outside his door was open to the roof, where guests could enjoy the evening air on the veranda there.

I had never seen Henry's home so open and pleasant. It was a strange transformation. Henry himself was as cool as he ever was. This party, he told me, would be like most with standard protocols for Dominants and submissives. No Dominant could speak to me without his permission, though I could freely mingle with any other submissive. It was not a play party, so there would be no demonstrations of his control of me. I would simply be at his side unless engaged with other submissives.

As guests arrived, I assumed my role beside and behind Henry, helping him to welcome guests, opening to door for him as people arrived, and either taking coats or directing other submissives where to place them. I felt natural and at ease in this role, and my own confidence was returning. My doubts about the lifestyle and its changes upon me eased. While it was a strange and dangerous place, in so many ways it was familiar and comfortable as well.

Mistress Aevia arrived with two submissives at either side of her. Henry welcomed her warmly and I decided I would take coats for all three of them, rather than directing her submissives where to go. I thought since Henry showed her deference, that the show of respect from me for her submissives might be appreciated as well. Her submissives both thanked me shyly, but Mistress Aevia only gave me a cold stare.

She said nothing, however, which was a change for her. I wondered if Henry had spoken to her about that. Had he heard her after all and just not wanted to confront her publicly, or had she said something to him after the dungeon fiasco? Either one did not matter. I could ignore her glares much more easily than I could ignore her words.

Frank arrived a short time later and I was happy to see him at the party. I was worried that my foolishness might cause him problems, but no one seemed surprised or taken aback that he was there. He came with no one and when I took his coat, he whispered to me, asking if I was okay.

"I'm fine. I am so sorry about what happened," I whispered back, feeling both guilty and elated that I was breaking a rule, but wanting very much to apologize to him.

Frank gave me a smile and I thought that he appreciated the apology. I put his coat away and Henry greeted him. I looked back to see Henry wink and knew that he had heard my whispered conversation. I sensed that his wink was an indication that he understood my rule breaking. I wondered if I would still be punished later and hid my smile at the thought.

Henry had yet to give me a punishment that was not in some way pleasurable to me. I knew that some submissives were subject to anything from writing sentences to kneeling on rice for disobeying their Dominants. I supposed that such activities could instill discipline or help one grow. I was thankful that Henry did not feel the need to take those kinds of actions with me, even if I might deserve them sometimes.

I realized, however, that such punishments were not something we had talked about before. I would have to ask him about that. Did he believe in giving me actual punishments for disobedience, or did he simply expect that he could address something and I would learn? I thought about the dungeon. What had taken place was enough for me not to repeat my mistake again. I supposed that I did not need any additional punishment for it.

In thinking about it, I did not want to push the idea of being punished simply by acting out. It would be interesting to discuss it with Henry, to learn why he did not want to punish me for disobedience.

Guests wandered the room, talking in small groups. Others moved back out into the hall to go up to the veranda above. I followed Henry as he moved from group to group, listening to the conversations and answering when permission was given. When he finally made his way to Mistress Aevia, I steadied my breathing and waited. She would say something unkind and I did not want to give her the satisfaction of seeing my reaction.

"How are you this evening?" Henry took Mistress Aevia's hand and kissed it.

"Well enough. Your apartment is lovely as always." Mistress Aevia's tone sounded light. Perhaps, in Henry's own home she would mind her manner then. I thought about her use of terms. I could not bring myself to think of this place as an apartment. Where I lived was an apartment. This was far nicer. "I see your pet is not getting others into trouble this evening. That's a relief."

Her tone remained light, but her words stung nonetheless. I bristled but kept my breathing calm and my face as expressionless as I could.

"It's good to see that Frank can still show his face in public. That kind of carelessness can ruin reputations," Mistress Aevia continued.

"Enough," Henry's voice was even, and I felt reassured by his defense of me. "Accidents happen, especially when you are new. If you'll remember I was foolish at my first play dungeon too."

Well, somewhat reassured. I could have done without being called foolish. I glanced up to meet the eyes of one of Mistress Aevia's submissives. He gestured and I followed him away to let the Dominants talk. I thought if I were not present, Henry would not need to make his feeble attempts to defend me.

"You shouldn't let her get to you," the young man said when we were well out of their earshot. We walked to the hors d'oeuvres table and picked out a few bites of finger food. I took a small glass of wine as well. The alcohol would be nice to calm my nerves.

"I can't help it." I wished I could say more, but I knew better than to speak badly of a Dominant to her submissive. He was being kind enough to show me sympathy and I didn't doubt it would cost him later. I was not going to repay that with disrespect.

"I know, she's mean," he said as we walked away with our pickings. I glanced at him and he smiled. "I'm Allen, by the way."

"Stacy," I said and felt silly. Of course, he would know my name.

"It's a pleasure to actually get to speak to you. I saw you at the club with your friends and I appreciated you speaking up. Most people wouldn't do that around vanillas."

I shrugged and realized I had not actually been out clubbing with my friends in weeks. I spoke to Trin and one or two other friends on the phone from time to time. I did not miss going clubbing with them, especially after the scene with Mistress Aevia, and I wondered if that made me a bad person. I did not blame them for what happened. She was looking for a time and place to belittle me. It was not their fault that she took advantage of opportunity.

"I just hate it when people are rude and stupid," I said. "They really were out of line."

"It's not the worst that I've heard. People outside of the lifestyle don't understand male submissives." Allen shrugged and leaned against the wall. "Hell, sometimes people in the lifestyle don't understand us. We're weak and unmanly."

I looked to Henry and Mistress Aevia as they talked. She laughed at something he said. "Not weak. Not if we can handle what our Dominants put us through."

"Amen." Allen took a bite of wrapped sausage. After he swallowed it, he looked at me. "She will get over it, you know. Mistress is mean; believe me I know. But she is fair. She just has to accept that Henry's a big boy now. He doesn't need her to watch over him anymore."

I thought about my mother and how protective she could be, and how caring and protective Henry was of me after the dungeon. I could see a Dominant taking on a mother-like instinct for her submissive. We depended on them for so much. We depended on them to heed our limits and safe words. We depended on them to watch over us at events.

"If she's being a mother hen," I said, "I doubt it. Mothers don't let go of sons easily."

"No, they don't. I don't think I've ever seen anyone look after another Dom the way she does after Henry, though." Allen gave me an apologetic look that I found touching. "She's not in love with him or anything like that. She took him under her wing to train him when he came into the lifestyle and she just feels responsible for him I guess."

"People don't really train like that anymore, do they?" Allen seemed to know a lot about the lifestyle, which was not surprising given his Mistress. I might dislike her, but I understood she had a wealth of knowledge and experience.

"Not really. I wish they did sometimes. The first Dominant I had was self-taught and a downright prick. I would say that he was abusive, but I don't think he really understood he was hurting me. He just didn't know any better."

I thought about mine and Henry's activities, and how they could go if he were not trained on how to do them, if he were just learning as he went along or assuming expertise because he read a book. I shuddered and offered Allen a gentle smile.

We talked more about the lifestyle and he shared with me his own experience among others like Mistress Aevia, who were trained under what he referred to as the Old Guard method. I thought I understood a little more of Mistress Aevia's harshness and why Allen was not afraid or ashamed to admit that she was mean. The Old Guard used to never accept women into the ranks of the BDSM community. When Mistress Aevia, who I was surprised to learn was about ten years Henry's senior, had entered the lifestyle, she would have had to go above and beyond to prove herself. I thought of women breaking into the upper echelons of business and the reputations they would receive as being hard and cold. It would have been no different.

Nothing I learned surprised me, but I was not sure how it was going to help me either. I did not doubt for an instant that she would continue poisoning Henry's mind and I knew I had to find a way to resolve the situation. She held an important place in his life. I would demand that he stop sleeping around the office before I even considered telling him to block her out of it. I also suspected that Mistress Aevia wanted that to be an end game. I knew how it would end, and Henry would be in the right.

The party continued through most of the night. When guests finally began to trickle out, I was relieved. I was tired and ready to spend the evening with Henry alone. Mistress Aevia and her submissives were the last of the guests to leave. I gathered the three coats, handing Mistress Aevia hers first before handing her submissives their coats.

"I would have thought you would have corrected her on protocol," Mistress Aevia said to Henry, and I could hear the glare in her voice. "A submissive treating submissives like Dominants."

Mistress Aevia walked out to a silent Henry. I looked at Allen who mouthed a silent *thank you* to me as he and her other submissive left behind her. Henry closed the door and I walked to one of the stools at the kitchen bar and sat down. I was exhausted now and the lack of defense from Henry did not help it at all.

"I'm sorry," Henry came up and sat down on the stool beside me. He leaned against the bar and looked at me. I draped my arms across the counter and leaned my head on them. "I should have said something to her."

"What would you have said?" My tone was exasperated, but I did not care. I had enjoyed so much of my night, Henry's other conversations, getting to know Allen.

"That you were showing an instinctive awareness of community protocol that she should have been honored by." I could feel Henry looking at me, but I did not want to meet his eyes right now. "You recognize that she is respected in the community, more than I am. You were showing her respect by treating her submissives the way you did."

Henry let out a deep sigh and turned. I glanced from the corner of my eye to see him staring off into his kitchen. "She has some kind of imagined grudge against you, otherwise she would have thanked you for the show of respect. I don't know why she dislikes you so much –"

"She hates me." I saw no reason not to interrupt and correct him.

Henry turned around and took my shoulders. He turned me to face him and brought my head up by the chin so that I had to look in his eyes. I fought the temptation to avert my own.

"I don't know why, but I'm sorry. I don't defend you like I should and that is wrong of me. She attacks you when she knows that protocol keeps you from speaking up for yourself; and I shouldn't let her do that."

Henry's sincerity touched me and my heart leapt into my throat. He should be able to defend me better, but he couldn't. It wouldn't do any good. She would simply declare it a sign of my unworthiness. I was so weak I depended on him to speak up for me. I had no idea how to solve my problems with her, but I understood more than ever how hard it was for him to balance it all. He was caught in between by her designs and protocol.

I took Henry's hand from my chin and held it in my own, kissing the fingers softly. I felt every emotion well up that I was afraid to share, afraid to hear him turn away and not reciprocate. I closed my eyes, took in a deep breath and pushed them down. The whole situation was complicated enough for him. I did not need to add that into it all.

"You don't punish me." I had no idea why the thought popped into my head so randomly or why I had spoken it aloud. I looked up at Henry to see him confused by the statement. "I mean when I actually do something to disobey you."

"No." Henry was silent and I could see him thinking, debating something within his mind. He took his hand from mine and stood, guiding me down from the stool as well. As he spoke again, he began removing my clothing. "Mistress Aevia would as part of my training. If I did something wrong, if I disobeyed her, even if she just felt something I did was not satisfactory, I would be punished. Not in the way I punish you because you are daring at a party. This would be completely unpleasant. I hated it. By the time she was ready to punish me, I already understood what I had done wrong. I was not repeating offenses and I had already resolved not to repeat the mistakes I made.

"It was her way of instilling and keeping discipline, though. She had not just me to train, but her own submissives as well. I had tried it with my first submissive and just could not feel it. Like me, she was not repeating mistakes. They were just mistakes or errors she happened to make. So, I decided that I would have my rules and rituals, that I would set a rigid discipline of what was expected. I would rather be obeyed because you want to obey me, not because you want to avoid punishment."

I smiled, understanding. With understanding came warmth. I no longer worried about the feelings I was afraid to express to Henry. He undressed me and inspected me carefully. The door opened and one of the building staff entered as I stood there naked, his hands lifting my breasts and opening my labia and buttocks. She ignored us as she began cleaning and I did my best to control the flush that moved over my body.

When he finished my inspection, Henry led me to the bedroom. I paused under the eyehook, but he led me to the bed instead, drawing down the sheets and laying me down. The soft cotton felt cool under my skin and I was aware of my mostly healed cut along my shoulder and adjusted myself on the bed so that I would not aggravate it.

Henry opened his chest and brought out a Wartenberg wheel. He took off his clothes and lay down beside me. "Be still or I will stop."

He moved the wheel lightly along my arms and down my torso and legs. The prickling sensation of the pins brought my skin to life and I sighed, controlling my urge to shiver or move. He brought it between my legs and ran it over my labia. I gasped at the sensation and moaned, wanting to feel more – more than the wheel.

I wanted his pain, but he gave me tender sensations instead. It felt wonderful, the gentle prickling on my skin as he moved the wheel along my body. When he finally stopped to enter me, sheathed as always, he was slow and gentle. Every sensation felt wonderful, but my body craved the darker, harder side of him. When I urged him to go harder, he only shushed me and continued slow and easy. I met his eyes, expecting to see his darkness tormenting me, but he held it back. There was only tenderness as he brought me to orgasm and achieved his own.

I lay next to him, my body draped over his, listening to the sound of his breathing as sleep overtook him. I felt satisfied and confused at the same time. Why did he withhold that darkness from me, knowing that I craved it? Why was he not even taking pleasure from the torment of withholding it from me? I knew that I should ask him, but I did not know how. I fell asleep there, wrapped in his arms as my mind spun with questions I could neither answer nor ask.

FIVE

Monday was a more relaxed day at work. Two of our projects were down and everything else was on schedule. I enjoyed an easy day of working and planning with my team with an extended lunch tossed in the middle where we all talked about our weekends. I mentioned attending a party with Henry, but not the details of it. That I offered any hint at all about my romance was enough for the girls and I felt a deeper sense of inclusion with them.

I was becoming friends with them and it felt good. I realized that my new life was replacing my old. My teammates were slowly becoming the ones I talked to about my love life, even if only in small snippets. My time away from work with Michael and Henry was becoming my social life, and I found myself valuing my alone time in between as a way to process my nights with Henry and try to prioritize between him and my growing feelings for Michael.

That afternoon, I received a surprising email. Ana invited me for drinks downstairs after work. I had no plans. I would not be seeing Henry again until Wednesday due to various clients he had to meet with. I accepted her invitation happily and when five o'clock rolled around, I made my way down to the

Bluepointe to wait for her arrival. She joined me fifteen minutes later, looking relieved to be out of the office.

"How was work today?" I asked as she joined me at the small high top that I had chosen.

Ana stuck out her tongue in an amusingly immature gesture that I would not have expected from her. "If I have to speak to one more lawyer, I think I will start picking them off from the roof of the building."

I laughed as the bartender came by. He deposited a prepared drink in front of her.

"Thank you," Ana looked up at him. She looked back at me. "Hungry?"

I was not too hungry. Our extended lunch today brought with it extra food. "An appetizer is fine with me."

Ana nodded and looked back up to the bartender. "Can you bring us a sampler?"

"Sure thing." He turned and walked back to the bar to enter our order.

I looked at Ana's drink, something pink, grenadine perhaps, floating among liquor and mixer. "You always get the same thing then?"

"I like routine," Ana said. "It helps you manage the unpredictable parts of life."

That I could agree with. I sipped my own drink and wondered why Ana had invited me down. She seemed to like me well enough, but drinks were a new move I had not expected.

"So, I'm just going to come out and ask. Is everything okay with Henry and everything that's happening?"

Ana's question startled me. I didn't expect a personal talk. I thought it might be something about the case, but this caught me off guard. She offered me a smile. Her eyes were warm and friendly, and I relaxed.

"I know that you and Mistress Aevia have some – problems. I also know that Henry is an adjustment to make, especially when you're new to the lifestyle."

I let out the breath I was holding and nodded. "It's taken a lot to adjust to, and it confuses me sometimes. I'm sure you've heard about what happened at the play dungeon."

"I had. For what it's worth, no one is saying anything bad about you. Word about accidents get around and that is how everyone took it. An accident." Ana studied me carefully and I saw understanding come into her eyes. "It was more than that, though, wasn't it?"

"It was Mistress Aevia. Not that it was her fault; I made my own mistakes. She started taunting me about how suspension was perfect for someone like me. She doesn't think that I'm serious about being Henry's submissive, that it's just a game for me. When Frank asked if there were sensations that I didn't like, I could see it on her face. She was just looking for things to use to judge me. I could hear it in my head. 'A real submissive would be fine with that or this' or 'look how she tops from the bottom.' So, I told him whatever he had was fine and it was at first. I was even in that mental state, where your mind is just floating with the sensations."

Ana nodded with an understanding look that surprised me. I decided to file my question away and continue my story.

"Then I felt the knife and I freaked out. I'm lucky I didn't get stabbed or get Frank in trouble. I felt terrible and I know Henry was disappointed in me."

Ana shook her head. "I doubt he was disappointed. Worried, I'm sure. Concerned that you didn't state a limit, but not disappointed. You're still learning. You will make mistakes and yes, sometimes those mistakes can be dangerous. It is why it is important to learn quickly and learn how to apply lessons to other things."

"Right now, I'm trying to learn how to bury the hatchet with Mistress Aevia. She and I had words about a month ago, outside of a club where she and I happened to be. She's intent on proving that I'm bad for Henry, and there is no telling what she tells him." Ana gave me a nod and I could see that my worry there was not unfounded. "I know it's hard for Henry to be in the middle of it, and she chooses her battles very carefully to keep him there."

I took another sip of my drink. I decided if I was going to talk about Mistress Aevia, I could talk about more as well. Perhaps Ana might have some insight for me.

"Someone hurt Henry and Mistress Aevia still holds a grudge about it. I wish I knew who it was, so that I don't make the same mistakes. The thing is, though, I'm not even sure where he and I are romantically. I know he still has his office affairs, which I can accept, but I don't know what that means. Am I only his submissive, does he want something else with me? It doesn't interfere with the Dominant/submissive relationship, but it is still hard, especially since I know I want more."

"Have you told Henry what you want?" Ana looked up as the bartender dropped off our sampler plate and thanked him. When he walked away, she looked back at me, taking a piece of calamari and waiting for me to answer her.

"No. I don't know how to. When I try to ask Henry about his own feelings, he clams up and avoids my questions."

Ana took a deep breath in and out, and I knew I was about to be chided. "If you aren't communicating to Henry, then it is getting in the way of your dynamic with him. You can't just communicate what you want as his submissive. If you need something else from him, you have to tell him that too. If you don't, you will start withholding your needs as a submissive as well and that is bad."

She took another bite of calamari. I picked up a cheese stick and rolled it between my fingers.

"I know Henry can be hard to talk to about those things," Ana continued. "He is not open emotionally, so it makes it hard to know if you'll be accepted or rejected. As you know from the continued office flings, he does not do monogamy well. I'm glad that you're not letting it interfere with work. That is beyond commendable. You need to make sure if you're going to accept that part of Henry and not ask him to stop, that you not let it affect your dynamic and relationship too."

"I wish I knew how to do that." I took a bite of my cheese stick.

"Maybe by understanding where it comes from," Ana said. Her face grew long and I sensed a confession coming. "I'm the one who hurt him."

That confession stunned me. I put my cheese stick on my plate and my hands in my lap.

"I met Henry through a mutual friend that we had. He was charming, if a little cool, and I could feel the power coming from him. I was new to the lifestyle and Mistress Aevia had just recently released him. He seemed like the perfect person for me to learn from and submit to. We had the talk and met several times before I finally offered and he accepted. Everything was great between us. I enjoyed giving over to him, and the highs and lows he would carry me through were amazing."

Ana's eyes filled with her memory and I thought about my own sessions with Henry. They were amazing. I wondered how in the world she turned from that to the person she was now.

"In the middle of our dynamic, we became emotionally involved – romantically. The blending of the two was incredible, and that I was in love just intensified everything I felt when we were doing a scene. He collared me and I felt like I was wearing a wedding ring. For a long time, I felt complete and wonderful.

"I don't really know what happened to cause it. I think that what I was doing was just growing. Some people come into the lifestyle knowing instantly what role they want like Henry did. Others don't. I thought I was submissive because that was how women were in my family. My mother was never abused or anything like that. My father loved her very much, but his word was law and he was the final word in the house. My brothers are the same way in their homes and my sisters married men like our father."

"I started to feel different, though. As I began to understand more about my submission, I began feeling other urges. I was not getting what I wanted out of submitting and I found myself wanting what Henry had – the power I was giving him. I became bratty and argumentative. Henry was new to being a Dominant, but he quickly understood what he was seeing. I think how Mistress Aevia trained him, making him be her submissive and working up to Dominant, helped him with that. I think what I was feeling was what he felt all through his training with her."

"He sat me down and we talked about what I was going through. He helped me understand that I was not a bad person, that I was just changing and growing. Some people stay with submission, others don't, and I was the latter. He released me and continued to mentor me, to help me take what I learned as a submissive and apply it to being a Dominant instead."

"When the dynamic ended, though, something fizzled in the romance between us. So much of our romantic lives were tied up in BDSM and our dynamic together. I think we forgot how to be a couple outside of it. People told me that it is just what happens, that two Dominants can't be together, but I know that's not true. You've met Dominants at the parties Henry goes to that are dating and married to other Dominants. You find other ways to connect together. Henry and I missed that chance, and our relationship ended too."

Ana paused to sip her drink as I took in the story she told me. I picked up my cheese stick again and ate it, out of duty more than anything. I didn't feel hungry.

"Henry does kink things with his flings sometimes, and I know that he's taken part in sessions and play parties and things like that.

You are the first submissive he has taken on since things ended between the two of us. I would imagine that he's afraid, on whatever level Henry Lennox feels fear, of the same thing happening again. I know that Mistress Aevia is waiting for it. That is why she treats you the way she does. She and I had our own scraps after our relationship ended and it took me a long time to prove to her that I was still for real, that I had merely changed. She doesn't think Henry is capable of finding a 'real submissive' and has tried to set him up several times. He refuses, and that is good on him. He has to choose a submissive for himself and she has to choose him for herself."

"Do you think that I'm a good submissive?" Ana's openness and honesty made me trust her and want her approval. If I could get it, I thought, I could be sure of everything.

"I don't see the two of you in session," Ana said. I felt my heart sink. "I know what I see of you. You've changed a lot since you and Henry started, and the changes I see I like. You have a new focus and a new openness to you that I didn't see before. I know that Henry has been happy with you. Those are both good signs to me. Ultimately, that is for you and Henry to decide. My approval or Mistress Aevia's approval means nothing. You have to approve of yourself and Henry has to approve of you. That's all."

Henry's heartbreak mystery was solved and more of him made sense. I wished that Henry had been the one to tell me all of this, but in a way, I was happy Ana had. I felt a new connection to her and as we shifted our conversation away from Henry and onto other things, I thought that was reciprocated. I had someone I could talk to about the lifestyle and myself on a regular basis and not just in snippets at parties. The idea was refreshing and relieving.

I thought I understood Henry's need to have his affairs still. They were not just pleasure; they were perspective. They kept him from becoming too emotionally invested in our dynamic. I was still not sure how to approach the subject with someone who kept himself closed emotionally, but at least I knew now that romance was not out of the question for us. I simply had to be patient, to let Henry find a way to that on his own.

I drove home later feeling calmer about my relationship with Henry and more understanding of Mistress Aevia's dislike of me. It was not personal at all. There was not something she saw in me that I had to doubt. It was something she would see in any woman. I had tried to tell myself that before, but Ana's story confirmed it. It was also refreshing to know that it was not just me. It was Henry as well. She was not protecting him. She didn't trust him to make his own decisions about taking on a submissive.

That knowledge, I thought, was the most valuable piece of information I had from our conversation. Mistress Aevia was setting up her own downfall in that war. While she continued to drag Henry between us, I would continue learning from him and growing as his submissive. Eventually, he would see that he could trust himself with me and he would see her lack of faith in him. I doubted that Mistress Aevia saw herself as not trusting Henry. She did not strike me as the kind of person who would. For her flaws, I thought that in her own mind, she probably saw herself as protecting him, the same as any mother who tries to control a son. When he hit her with his realization, it would probably be a wake-up call that ended all fights and arguments.

My thoughts surprised me. Six months ago, I would not have been thinking so long term about a struggle I was having with someone tied to a boyfriend or boyfriend-like person. I would have been looking for a direct way to deal with it now, rather than seeing how the situation would resolve itself in a much better way later. I thought about the changes that Ana described. She was right, just as my teammates were right. I was changing. I still didn't know how I felt about it, but I supposed not all of the changes were bad, not if I was learning to have patience with my problems.

SIX

The week brought a refreshing bit of news. The lawyers for Lennox Enterprise and Michael were meeting regularly now, trying to work through to a final settlement that both sides would find agreeable. A settlement was good. The news would talk about it for a day, perhaps two, and then the whole thing would be forgotten.

Henry seemed more relaxed by the news. When we got together on Wednesday, he was cheerful and light. I had worried that the news was too much, that it had taken too much of a weight off him at once. When he bound me, bent over, to the foot of his bed and brought out his flogger, however, I knew better. His darkness swirled around me, as wild as ever, and I reveled in the pain it brought. I felt insane and it felt nice.

Friday brought us another party, this one different that the others Henry typically took me to. When I arrived to his office, another nice dress waited for me, black with lace sleeves. It was conservative and classy and I wondered where we would be going this evening. Henry had only told me that he wanted to take me to an important function, not a party, but nothing else.

I changed in his office and he drove us down town. We arrived at the Plaza Hotel to cameras flashing as the valet took Henry's car. I stayed close to him and avoided looking directly at the cameras. I did not care how much Henry's lifestyle was changing me, I still felt strange and shy around the media and the memory of the news reports with my face splashed on the screen from the opera haunted me.

We walked into a charity event and I found myself awed by the number of celebrities that I saw around me. I held tightly onto Henry's arm as he led me around, introducing me to people that I only saw on screen. He spoke to them like familiar friends. I felt like Cinderella come to the ball and realized very quickly that I was out of my element. There was no strict protocol here, no way to know who to approach and who to avoid. I felt strange, shy, and so very terrified.

So much for the positive changes the lifestyle made on me.

Henry wanted to go and speak to someone else, but I felt overwhelmed. He brought me to a table to sit and I urged him on to his conversation. He did not need to be held down by my shyness. I sipped punch and smiled at people as they passed.

"Fancy seeing you here."

The voice caught me off guard. I looked up to see Michael. He sat down in front of me and sipped his glass of wine.

"Henry brought me," I said. "It's incredible the people I've seen."

Michael nodded. "That is Henry, always out to impress a beautiful woman."

I smiled at the compliment, but he moved the conversation before it could linger or become uncomfortable. With another familiar face, someone I could relate to, I felt more comfortable. Michael was as relieved to see me, as I was to see him. He had come at the insistence of Mr. Lellman. They were considering him for a promotion, and something like this would be important for him to attend.

Even though Henry had mentioned nothing about the cost of tickets to attend this event, I knew from my mother going on about celebrity charity functions how many thousands of dollar entrance typically cost. If Mr. Lellman was insisting that he come, then it had to be a serious promotion. I congratulated Michael on his prospects and we enjoyed people watching, wondering what conversations were happening out of earshot.

Henry returned and I felt suddenly self-conscious of Michael being there. I realized that my hand would linger on his from time to time and that my growing attraction was showing. Henry greeted him pleasantly enough, though, and Michael returned the greeting with equal civility. I forced myself to relax. If the two men at the eye of the lawsuit storm could be calm and gracious, then there was no reason to be nervous. When I looked in Henry's eyes, however, I saw something different.

I spent the rest of the night with my attention pulled between both men. I would follow Henry until the pressure of the social setting weighed upon me and Michael would be there to relieve me and help me relax. I was an emotional yoyo, a Ping-Pong ball moving between both men. By the time Henry and I finally left, my mind was spinning and even though I had no alcohol to drink, I felt tipsy and light.

We arrived to his condo and I stripped once we were inside, waiting for his command as always. Henry did not wait to inspect me. He led me to his room and I saw the darkness heavy in his eyes. I felt excited and terrified, ready to feel whatever he had for me.

He bound my hands with rope, tight and secure behind my back. He laced the rope up my arms and then around my torso, under my breasts. I could not move without straining my arms or restricting my breathing, though if I were still and calm, all was fine. This was the most intense that Henry had bound me before. Even with my hands behind my back and bent, I still had the relief of my feet to help hold my weight. Here, I felt helpless to move. The sensation of my bondage overcame me quickly and before he brought the flogger to my buttocks, I was swimming in his dominion over me.

Each motion of his flogger claimed my body as his. I screamed as he struck hard, feeling the pain turn over into pleasure as my body processed it. He laid me on the bed when his strikes were through and entered me from behind. Even sheathed, I could feel the desire in him and my body screamed for him to own it. I reveled in each thrust as he pushed hard into me and when I came, I cried out loudly, offering it up to him.

When he finished, he untied me and gently rubbed the places where he had struck hard, soothing them with soft lotion. He lay next to me in his bed, cooing softly and guiding me into sleep. My body belonged to him and there I felt warm and safe.

The next morning, I could not remember my dreams, but I still felt the mood of them. I was troubled by the night and as I sat quietly and ate breakfast with Henry in his kitchen, still naked as I was always to be in his condo, I understood why. I thought about Ana's warnings that I had to communicate with him. If I let my fears block it, then our dynamic would be hurt. I did not want that, but I was scared now.

"What's wrong?" Henry saw it too and his face drew down at the thoughts my expression conveyed.

"Last night," I said. "I need to talk to you about it."

"If it's about Michael –"

I held up my hand to cut him off. "It's only about Michael a little. It's more about what happened when we came back here. I enjoyed everything, but I should have stopped it and I'm sorry. I was not in the mind frame to. I should not have even let you session me. I was so tossed about and confused by my night that I couldn't think straight."

Henry started to say something, but I shook my head.

"You should have stopped too. Everything you did was about possessing me. I felt it and I reveled in it, but my mind was in space as soon as you tied me up. I like the idea of you possessing me, but Henry, you were acting out of jealousy over Michael and that was not right." I felt like I needed to explain more. I could see some understanding in his eyes, but he was not completely there with me. I thought of how else to express myself and remembered the dungeon party. "That night at the dungeon, when I was suspended, Mistress Aevia taunted me. She doesn't think I am a real submissive and she has told me so before. That's beside the point right now. I was not trying to impress her. I was trying to prove myself to her. I acted out of my fear that she would take anything I said about limits as proof I was fake and use it against me. I got hurt and I could have hurt Frank's reputation. I could have hurt him. He was holding a sharp knife when I panicked."

I placed my hand on Henry's, seeing more understanding in his eyes. "It was the same thing last night. You acted out of jealousy. It isn't a reputation that could have been hurt, though. It was me."

Henry moved his hand over mine and squeezed it gently. "You're right, and I'm sorry. I won't do it again. If I'm feeling something negative like that, I will wait until it passes so that I am focused. I didn't mean to frighten you, not like this."

My heart felt full and I smiled. I wanted to say *I love you*, but the words would not come. Instead, I said, "I forgive you."

SEVEN

The party and our conversation were both revelations for Henry and me. Communicating with him helped me to feel that deeper connection that I needed and when we were together, he was as giving of his darkness as ever. I felt warm and happy with things, ready to wait out the emotional rollercoaster that was romance for us, confident that we would find a way to make that connection where he and Ana could not.

Michael invited me to dinner and a movie on Saturday and I accepted. I had no other plans for the weekend, save for my session with Henry on Friday night. It went as well as the rest of the week had and I walked into Saturday evening feeling light and easy. Even my growing feelings for Michael could not quench my elation. Everything seemed fine and right. Somehow, even Michael fit into everything. Life was a huge puzzle with all of the pieces in place. I just couldn't see the big picture.

We enjoyed dinner with our usual easy conversation and light banter. The movie was a romantic comedy that was corny, but had us both laughing anyway. When he took me home, he walked me to my door. I ignored the sounds of traffic, a car speeding away and horns blaring, and debated within myself what to do next.

I wanted to kiss Michael. The surety of that feeling was strange and empowering. I could not deny the attraction I felt for him and I no longer felt afraid of it. I wondered, though, how fair that would be. If I kissed him that could lead to other things. Even if I did not invite him in tonight, it would invite him to think and to hope. Everything was beginning to even out between Henry and myself.

Did I want to risk leading Michael on?

I opted instead to kiss him on the cheek and tell him goodnight. It was a gesture that could stay innocent or lead to more without expectation either way. Michael left and I walked inside, feeling my week was the best that I had in a long time.

I spent my Sunday with housework, looking forward to Monday, when I would see Henry again for another session. Over laundry, I wondered what delights and pain he would have for me and if he would try anything new.

Monday I walked into the office, still elated from my whole week, ready to take on a new project. We spent our day at the planning table, tossing ideas around until Nora was calling for us to go home. I felt energized and ready for my evening with Henry. I had in mind something that I wanted to ask him to do with me, a small way to hand him more power, one that would give me a way to feel his Dominance throughout the day.

I drove to his condo, my mind spinning over it and how to approach him with it. Would he think it was silly or would he like it? I was energized by how successful our conversation the previous weekend was and ready to take the chance and ask.

Henry was waiting upstairs to let me in. I started to take off my clothes, but he stopped me.

"I want to talk to you first." Henry guided me to the table and I followed. This would be easy, then, to introduce the topic of giving him more power. I could just make it part of the conversation he wanted to have. I sat down in a chair and waited for him to sit and speak. "I have to make a confession."

I thought it might be about his office affairs and offered him a gentle smile. Even the idea of him sleeping with my co-workers could not bother me right now. I thought he could even say he slept with Bethany and I would not mind.

"I've been following you around this weekend." Henry's voice was steady and calm. His eyes swirled and my mood dropped. "I could not help myself. All week I have kept myself checked, but this weekend, it was too much. I know that you had a date with Michael and I know he took you home."

My blood was cold in my body. I glanced at the door and back at him, wondering how quickly I could dash there before he caught me. I stilled my nerves. This was not some new relationship. This was Henry, my Dominant. It was not something new. He had done it before and I suspected that for at least a while he had people watching me in order to ensure reporters did not approach me. I would not freak out and run away. I would be mature and strong. I would explain again the limits and why it was unacceptable.

"It was wrong and I am sorry." His admission helped to calm me. "I can't handle you seeing Michael. It's all too complicated with him."

I stood up, feeling anger swell through my body. The suddenness caught me off guard and I could not hold back the flow of words that followed it. "You're trying to tell me who I can be friends with?"

Henry stood slowly and brought a hand up to my arm. I could see him struggling to find the right words and no longer cared. He was forty-four years old. He should not still be struggling with emotional connections now. "Stacy, you need to understand that –"

"No, you need to understand that there are limits to what you get ask for. I don't insist that you stop your little office affairs. They aren't part of what we have between us and I accept that. You don't get to dictate who my friends are."

The darkness in Henry's eyes stirred. "Maybe I should start doing just that. You can't seem to pick your friends better than Michael Cavanaugh."

I pushed Henry's hand away. "You will not get to dictate that. You told me from the beginning that you would not, and you will not start controlling my life that way now."

Henry's voice raised. "It's time to renegotiate a few things."

"If you think you can tell me who my friends are, then there is no dynamic between us. Period."

I walked past him to the door, relieved when he did not stop me. I was down the elevator when my phone buzzed. I saw that it was from him and swiped the call away. Not five minutes ago, I was considering negotiating new power to him, now he was trying to take what was not his right. I wondered at my foolishness and the man who seemed to think it was okay to stalk me and then apologize.

THE END

Thanks for Reading!

I hope you enjoyed reading Broken Chasity.
☺

Make sure you get a copy of the next book in the Alpha Billionaire Series Book 4: Broken Desires

BROKEN DESIRE BOOK FOUR

ONE

I liked Mondays. The expectation in the corporate world was to dread them. Monday was that thing that called you from your weekend. It dragged you screaming into the office and barricaded you inside, threatening not to let you leave until Friday – if you were lucky. My father would bemoan Monday morning. His eyelids would hang heavy on his face and he would barely muster a smile when I would skip down the stairs and up to the kitchen table with a cheerful "good morning."

Mondays were like a new door in that creepy old house you were always afraid to go into, but dared anyway. Anything could lie behind it, a dusty room, spiders, or finally the wicked old witch said to haunt the place. Of course, we all knew that the old witch was really just a kindly old woman, who lived alone because all of her kids and grandkids either moved away or were killed in some war overseas. She was shy; otherwise, she would have invited all the neighborhood children up for apple pie and ice cream.

Both were homemade and so tasty.

Stereotypical ideas of creepy old houses aside, I always saw Mondays as a birth of sorts. It was the birth of a new week with new experiences. That Henry was often part of those experiences only increased my love of the day. The heights of sensation he would carry me to and the chance to swim in his darkness were incredible to me. I was either in love with the man or the idea. I didn't know anymore and I did not care. I relished those nights as his submissive.

Today, I was not looking forward to Monday.

The last one had ended in a fight. Henry had tried to tell me that I could not see Michael any more, after admitting to stalking me the previous weekend. One or the other, I could have handled. Combined together, they were a sign of his inability to control his jealousy. Combined with his inability to be emotionally honest, it was not a good sign.

I had spent my week telling myself it was good that I walked out. Jealousy was not something I needed. I had worked hard with myself not to be jealous of his office affairs, even avoiding sight of him if I heard him coming down the hall flirting, just to avoid an awkward scene. It was only fair for me to expect the same kind of respect in return.

Convincing myself of this was another matter. Once again, I had found myself without Henry in my life and I was miserable. How I had managed to make it through the week without my teammates questioning me, I didn't know. I had no contact with Henry and I didn't see Michael over the weekend either. Instead, I visited my parents. It was over between Henry and me, and I did not want to use Michael to get over him.

All of that led me to Monday, and the first time I could remember dreading the day. I threw myself into my work, just as I had the week before, and kept myself focused. I dodged questions from my teammates as I moved through the day. They were curious and I knew they were worried. I also knew that I didn't want to talk about it. Everything about Henry and me was complicated. I did not want to make it even more so with my story.

No, Henry would move on with his affairs. I would get over him and perhaps move on with Michael. I did not want to think that far. As it was, I didn't want to think about things really being over. I wanted to feel the sting of his flogger and the weight of the rope around my wrists. I wondered if something were wrong with me for having those cravings. Would I be able to go into a normal relationship with someone like Michael after everything I'd experienced?

In the afternoon, I received an email from Henry. He wanted to me to come by his office after work. I was surprised by the message, and a little concerned. Would there be more fighting? I thought about my unique position in the office. I was not the only one here who was his former submissive, but as heartbreaking as Ana had been for him, the end of their relationship was mutual. I was the first one to just up and leave – twice.

What if Henry decided he could not handle me working in his office?

At five o'clock, I said my goodnights to everyone and walked to Henry's office. Each step felt heavy and every few I wanted to turn and walk the other way. I realized that I was not afraid of a fight, a reprimand, or even losing my job. I was just afraid of seeing him again. Would I break down and fall to my knees, or just start crying? I had no idea what I had walked away from, if it was just a Dominance/submission dynamic or a romantic relationship. I only knew that the whole thing left me torn up and heart broken.

Hillary sat at her desk and smiled as I walked up. She gestured to Henry's doors. "Mr. Lennox is waiting for you."

"Thank you." I walked up to the doors, pausing before opening the right one to enter his office.

Henry sat at his desk, this attention focused on his computer screen. He frowned deeply at something and let out a large sigh as I closed the door behind me. I stood there, too afraid to take another step. I remembered the last time I walked into his office with him working so intently. He had pushed me up against the window, exposed me, and fondled me. The memory made me warm and I longed for more of it.

With another sigh, he turned away from his computer and stood. He did not say a word to me. He only looked at me. From across the room, I could see the conflict in his eyes. The darkness that I always saw when he looked at me was there and it stirred wildly. Over it was something else, something emotional and careful.

He walked around his desk and up to me. When he brought up his hand, I wanted him to push me against the door, to hold me there. I wanted to feel him rough and domineering as he laid claim to what was his. Instead, he gently touched my cheek and brushed back a lock of hair that had fallen loose from my bun.

"Will you come and sit with me?" Henry stepped back and gestured to the couch that stood against one wall of his office.

I walked there and he followed, sitting after I did so. I looked up into his eyes and tried to discern what I saw there. I knew so little of the inner man. I could not place the emotions to match them with motives and reasons. I realized that I should be able to. I wondered if I had failed at being girlfriend or his submissive.

"I was wrong." Henry's voice was cool and even. He could have been telling me the time, except for his eyes. I thought I understood the emotions now. They were humility and contrition, something I doubted that Henry had to show often. I realized with more guilt, I should have recognized them. I had drawn them out before. "I tried to control an aspect of your life that was never given over to me and it was not my right to take it. You were right to walk out on me. I knew better, but I let my jealousy get the better of me, again."

I sat silently and listened to him. I was afraid to say a word. I didn't know who I was that Henry Lennox should be apologizing to me, but I didn't want to spoil this moment.

"You don't make any demands of me in my personal life," Henry said. "You have been patient with me and graceful. You have done everything that I have asked of you. I cannot dictate your personal life, and I won't. You walked out and you were completely within your right to do so. I've spent the last week thinking on what happened and how I would ask you to come back."

I thought about the last time that I had walked away from Henry. This was an improvement from spying on me outside of my apartment.

"No more jealousy?" I said.

Henry closed his eyes slowly and opened them again. The emotional conflict was calmer now. "I can't promise that I won't be jealous. I can only promise that I will try. I can promise that I won't attempt to control your personal life anymore. I won't tell you who you can and cannot see. I will show you the same respect you have shown me."

I moved to get on my knees and Henry stopped me. He leaned forward and kissed me. It was soft and gentle. His tongue pressed to my lips, asking for entry, and I parted them for it. When he pulled away, he moved to his knees in front of me. He pushed up my skirt and pulled down my panties, pulling my hips forward with them. He slid them down past my knees and brought his face between my thighs. I sighed to feel his lips there, his tongue gently seeking entrance.

I gave over to the emotions that flooded me, the pleasures that he filled me with. In that moment, I felt perfect, fulfilled and complete. I wanted nothing more than to stay this way. Knowing that it would end made my orgasm that much more intense, a promise of more to come.

I kept myself focused on my work, but I knew that I was showing a better mood. I felt it. Henry was part of my life again. Whatever that ultimately meant, whether he was my boyfriend, my Dominant, or some mixture of both, I felt whole again. The rest of my week flew by with work and seeing Henry. We spoke briefly about our dynamic to make sure we were both comfortable picking up where we had left off. My idea of some new power to give to him was forgotten; I was just happy to be able to continue as we were before.

When the weekend arrived, I was exhausted from my week. I rested on Saturday and put off as much of the housework and other chores as I could. I resolved to get my laundry out of the way Saturday evening, as I was too tired for clubbing. On Sunday, between bouts of cleaning, I met Michael for lunch.

We sat under the awning of our favorite park side restaurant as the rain played staccato beats above us. I listened as Michael talked about his week and his plans for a simple hiking trip next weekend. I tried to imagine Henry hiking and could not. I thought hiking with Michael, however, would be enjoyable and found my mind wandering to the things that a man and woman could get up to alone in the woods.

"What are you plans next weekend?" Michael laid down his fork and picked up his glass to sip his tea. His lunch was finished.

I shoved bits of my own lunch around on my plate. My thoughts had me confused and conflicted again, playing havoc with my appetite. Once again, though, I found myself not wanting to part company with Michael. I enjoyed our afternoons together and the simplicity that was developing between us.

"I'll probably go clubbing with friends, be a homebody, and clean on Sunday." I gave him a smile when I saw the inquiring look in his eye.

"I'm surprised you're not with Henry more on the weekends."

I shrugged my shoulders. "He has a lot of business trips that he takes on the weekends. It's a good time for him to meet with clients. I see him plenty during the week, though."

Michael gave a dismissive wave to my explanation. "I would think by now he would be taking you on some of these trips. It's good to let clients see an attractive woman on your arm. It shows stability."

I shook my head. "I don't think we're really to that point yet. Besides, I like having my weekends free to spend time with friends."

Michael returned my smile at the acknowledgement that I valued our time together. "If I were in his place, you would be with me every trip."

I took another bite of my food, hoping it would hide the blush I felt coming on at that. Michael must have caught on that I was feeling both flattered and shy. He moved the conversation to other topics. I wondered what it would be like to accompany Henry on a business trip. Would we have time to spend together, or would I feel like a third wheel as he discussed business? I was not sure that the answer mattered. That I was an important enough part of his life to be included on his trips would be a big change from what I had experienced with him so far.

TWO

I arrived at Henry's condominium, smiling to the attendant as he waved me through and into the parking deck. It felt strange to be such a regular sight at such a nice uptown high rise. I thought again about my conversation with Michael and pushed my own doubts from my mind. I wanted to focus on my night with Henry. He had a surprise for me this evening and I was looking forward to it. I did not want to spoil my mood or taint the evening

I rode up the elevator to the top floor. As I stepped off into the quiet hall, I remembered my first night here and the panic that I had felt. Henry owned all of the units on this floor and the one below. He had sound proofed them so that his activities would not disturb other residents. I had felt isolated, knowing that if something bad happened, I would have no way of being heard. Now, I felt safe. The only interruptions that would take place would be those already negotiated by Henry, such as the occasional cleaning staff, who always ignored what we did. I wondered how those conversations went as he interviewed them to work for him. While I was sure they were actually employees of the building, I never saw different individuals come up to clean his condo. He had specific people set up for the task.

Henry's door opened and I jumped, not expecting to see him peer out into the hallway. He gave me a smile and gestured for me to come up to him. "Larry called up from downstairs to tell me you arrived. Are you ready for our evening?"

I nodded, still recovering from being startled and unable to speak. To my surprise, he closed the door and led me down to another unit. Henry had told me to grab a bite to eat before coming up and I had opted for a fast, light salad at the Bluepointe. It was unusual for us not to have dinner together on these nights, but Henry had told me that he wanted to get started as soon as I arrived. I wondered about that now as he opened the door to the unused condo.

Henry turned on the lights and I stepped inside. I understood immediately the need for the new unit and what I saw amazed me. The unit was laid out as a mirror to his own condo, with a wide open main room and a hall leading off to the bedroom. The kitchen area was removed from this unit, except for a single counter along the right wall, and no furnishing were present, save for a plush leather sofa against the far left wall and a few chairs and stools situated around the room. Instead, a series of three frames dominated this room. I walked up to them to feel the cool, solid iron.

Memories of the play dungeon came back to me. I loved being suspended. The feeling of both helplessness and safety had been unmatched in any form of bondage that Henry and I had tried yet. It had also proven almost disastrous when I panicked at the feeling of a knife under me. I wanted very much to experience suspension again, but felt apprehension at the idea that something else might make me panic.

"Frank will be joining us this evening. He's arriving shortly. He has been training me in suspension bondage, but for the first few sessions we do this, I want to have him here to ensure your safety." Henry closed the door and stepped into the room.

My apprehension faded at the knowledge that Frank would be there. I was not sure if it was the presence of a third person and Henry's concern for my safety, or that Frank felt comfortable enough with me still to take part.

"I want to talk to you about limits before Frank arrives," Henry said. I turned to face him. His eyes were dark, but muted and controlled. "Frank's only job will be monitoring your suspension. I will be the one doing everything else. I would like play with your fear limits some, but I don't want to risk hurting you."

My stomach tightened with anticipation and my heart raced. Would he want to play with knives while I was suspended? The though horrified me. I held onto that fear and studied it. Was I just afraid or was there a reason behind it?

"No knives," I said. "It's not just being afraid of them. If I panic again, we can get hurt, you could get hurt, and you could end up in a lot of trouble on my account."

The darkness in Henry's eyes swirled and that fear of him that I enjoyed swimming in rose up in me. To my surprise, he nodded and smiled. Though his eyes remained dark and turbulent, I could see the smile touch them. Even his darker side appreciated my limit and admitting why. I did not understand and wondered if I ever would.

"I was not planning on using a knife or anything sharp." Henry led me to the counter where the kitchen once stood. A chest, similar to the one in his apartment sat here. He opened it to reveal various BDSM implements and toys. I thought he had simply moved the chest from his room until I studied the violet wand and realized it was brand new. "I want to play with thin metal, but I will use something dull and with no point, so that you cannot be cut or stabbed with it."

Henry pulled down the top panel of the chest. Several instruments sat in neat and careful pockets. He pulled out a thin, flat metal bar that was rounded on one end. He brought it to my arm and touched me. It felt smooth and cool. When he turned it on its edge, it felt dull and wide. I pictured myself suspended and thought it would feel thinner and sharper there.

"Would you be able to handle this, if I touched you with it while you were suspended?" Henry's voice was even, calm, and soothing.

It should have had a lulling effect, but instead my mind sharpened. Intellectually I would know that he was not holding a knife to me, but as I entered my mental space, that knowledge would not be forefront in my mind. "Can we take it slowly? I don't want to start struggling in the ropes while I'm suspended. Even if you are okay, I could get hurt."

Henry replaced the metal bar. "We can do that. I want you to explore everything in here. These tools are only for this room. Unless we discuss something, I won't be bringing in any other objects."

Slowly I pulled out items from their pockets, examining rods and glass tubes carefully. I recognized all of them on sight, as we had played with them before with Henry's other

304

violet wand. I noticed that the metal bar meant to simulate a knife could also be placed into the violet wand. That, I thought, would wait until I knew I could handle the touch of it on my skin. Satisfied that nothing here would surprise me, I closed the panel and examined the rest of the contents of the chest.

There, he had paddles of different widths, going from very thin to almost a quarter of an inch thick. He had a feather flogger and a short leather one. He also had other items designed to produce smooth, soft, and rough sensations along my skin. I felt comfortable with everything that I saw there. I closed the chest and looked at Henry, smiling to show my approval.

"I have ropes and harnesses here." Henry opened drawers and cabinets beneath the counter so that I could examine these as well. Harnesses were wide, padded, and made of strong leather with D-rings bolted to them. The rope was thicker than we used for our normal bondage sessions, soft but not smooth.

Henry closed the cabinets and a knock sounded at the door. He turned to me, his eyes dark and swirling. "Strip now. I am going to let Frank in and then I will inspect you."

As Henry turned to walk to the door, I took off my clothes, folding them neatly and setting them on the counter. I wanted to feel apprehension at the idea that Frank would see me naked again, but I couldn't bring up the feeling. I was becoming accustomed to the idea of Henry exposing me to others and wondered about myself. Once more, I was changing because of this lifestyle.

Henry stepped outside of the unit as I finished undressing. I looked at the three frames and wondered why all of them were set up here. Perhaps he intended on using this space for a play party. The thought of being suspended for guests to see me was both frightening and exciting. Again, I wondered at this change. I should turn away the idea, as the perversion that it was, not be aroused by it.

I took my place in the center of the room, standing with my legs shoulder width apart and my back and shoulders straight. I held my head even and averted my eyes down. Henry would signal me if he wanted me to look into his eyes. I faced the door, knowing that he would not want me to present myself in profile to him, no matter how many people came in with him. I brought my hands behind my back, resting them at the top of my butt, together with my palms facing out.

Henry opened the door and stepped in. Frank followed and closed the door behind him. Henry walked down the steps of the foyer to me, gesturing for me to look up at him. I met his eyes to see them full of darkness and approval. Behind him, Frank looked on as Henry began his inspection. I was ready for Henry to part me and examined thoroughly, but he simply looked me over before giving me his approval. I felt relieved and could see a similar look in Frank's eyes.

No one calls him Master Frank. Is he not a Dominant at all then? Henry certainly afforded him the same deference that he showed to other Dominants. I tried to imagine anyone in this lifestyle not calling himself or herself a Dominant or a submissive. Everything that I read focused in on that dynamic to the exclusion of anything else. I thought about it and realized I had seen other less formal dynamics hinted at, but never discussed. I decided it would be a question for another time.

Henry led me to the center suspension frame and walked back to the counter, returning with rope. He guided me to lie down as Frank moved a stool to the outside of the frame so that he could sit and observe. His face was a mask of calculation and concentration now. He was not here to enjoy the show that Henry was about to put on and I understood that Frank took his role in guarding my safety very seriously. It made me feel calm and I hoped that it would not spoil the fear play that Henry wanted to experiment with this evening.

I lay on the floor as Henry brought rope around my right wrist, creating a thick cuff as he had so many times before. He did the same with the left and then my ankles. He moved up my arms, testing them carefully before choosing a new place to create a cuff. As he did the same with my legs, placing cuffs along my calves and thighs, I had a new appreciation for the care and thoroughness that went into this. There was so much work that Henry did and yet I would be the one receiving the benefit. I experienced the sensations and the strange mental state that submission put me into.

When each cuff was in place, he threaded the ropes through the frame and brought them together into a firm square knot. He pulled gently and I adjusted so that my weight distributed through each limb of my body. As I lifted off the ground, my arms and legs parted at angles to my body. I could hear, in the silence of the room, the turning of wheels that guided the rope through the frame.

My mind began to hum. That mental state was close. Henry pulled until I was well off the ground. I could not look down and did not want to, but I was up to his chest when I looked over to him. He locked the ropes in place by fixing the knot to a solid hook. He walked away and returned with more rope, this time threading it under my body. I felt the tension on my arms ease, and with it, my breathing became easier.

"You should have all of your rope on hand with you." Frank's voice was even, but chiding. "Never turn your back on your suspended partner."

"Yes, sir." Henry sounded contrite and I saw a brief apology in his eyes when I looked at him. I gave him a gentle smile as I felt my mind begin to swim further into space.

I let my head fall back and the sensation of being suspended and weightless overcame me. I was aware of Frank giving Henry more cautions and Henry asking questions. I knew that I should be listening; they were discussing my safety. I didn't care. I liked this sensation and wanted to lose myself in it. My head rose and I realized that Henry was lifting it. When he let it drop back, it rested on something firm and wide.

"See." I became aware of Frank's voice and words again. "You will be able to provide sensations along the back of her neck now, but the strip will keep her head from falling back and there will be less risk of her passing out."

Henry responded, but I lost focused on their words. The sensation of floating overtook me again and sensations along my body moved like ripples across a still pond. Soft tails of feathers touched my stomach and breasts, and then my lower back and thighs. Warm and sultry leather traced over me before striking my buttocks, sending jolts of red pain through the serenity of my mind. I gasped and relished the pain in this space.

Various sensations moved through my body, pleasure alternating with pain in patterns that I could not keep up with or predict. The sensations began to build within me until I could feel them full and waiting to spill over. I was close to orgasm and wanted to come, to feel the height of that sensation pour through this ocean within my mind.

Fear flashed like lightening through my senses. I tensed as cool metal traced along my thigh. The swelling of sensations threatened to spill over at the shock and I fought the urge to struggle, whimpering and pleading in wordless syllables. The cool metal withdrew and I let out a sigh, feeling the swelling sensations calm and wait for their release.

It appeared again, cool and thin, tracing along my shoulder where a cut had healed into a light scar. I cried out and the swelling of sensation, reaching out to my fear, poured over me. I shuddered and screamed as my orgasm shook through my body. I felt elated and confused. The thin metal traced along my back, drawing the orgasm with it. I tried to recall the shape of the device Henry had shown me and could not. As my orgasm faded, my fear grew and I felt panic coming on.

"Red." I uttered the word I had not needed to use since our first session when he had told me about my isolation.

The metal withdrew from my body and Henry's hand was at my head, stroking my hair gently. Words floated into my ear, warm and reassuring. My panic subsided and the fear withdrew.

"That was very good." My mind could finally distinguish Henry's words now. I opened eyes I never realized that I had closed and turned my head to him. The darkness was still there, not yet sated, but held back due to my safe word. "Do you need me to let you down?"

"No." I had uttered the word without thought. Henry continued to study my face. I collected thoughts that were still scattered along the ocean in my mind. "I just need a minute to make sure the panic is gone."

"I'm going to put away the thin metal," Henry said. My lips turned down in a frown and he smiled at me before kissing me. "I'm going to bring out the wand."

I felt new excitement course through my body. Once again, Frank chided him about leaving me while I was suspended and Henry responded with the corrections he would make for the next session. I thought to myself that Henry needed a service submissive, someone to fetch tools and ropes for him.

"That's a good idea. Suspension is safest with a third person present," Frank responded and I realized with a flush that I had spoken the thought aloud.

"Would you share me with another submissive?" Henry asked from somewhere behind me. I could not answer his question. My thoughts were not collected enough. "That's something we can talk about some other time, when you're not still suspended and floating in sub-space."

Henry walked back up to me. My world became the gentle buzzing of the violet wand and I gasped as the light shock touched my shoulder and traced along my arm. It withdrew from my arm and touched my ankle, tracing along my leg and up to my inner thigh, teasing between them where I was still sensitive from the arousal of my orgasm.

He started to move the wand down and I let out a sigh. Henry brought it back then, shocking the delicate outer skin of my labia. I cried out and felt my arousal growing again. My body shook at the idea that he would use electrical stimulation to bring on an orgasm and he moved it down my other leg, letting it trail slowly along my skin.

Henry withdrew the wand and brought it back to my other shoulder this time. The shock was sharper now and I cried out again at the sensation. It sent signals of both pleasure and pain along my body and my mind twisted and spun in my mental ocean. I was not sure if I should moan or scream, but I did not want the sensation to stop. My senses became only the sharp, painful pleasure as it traced over my body.

Nothing else existed.

I slowly became aware of the sensation of lowering. My body was alive and tingling from the application of the wand and as I touched the soft, carpeted ground, I could feel every strand and fiber. I let out a moan and did not move. I could have. My body felt energized, but I didn't want to move. I was not sure if I didn't want to stop feeling the sensation, or if I was afraid of overload when the thousands of fibers moved over my body.

Rope snaked around my limbs and I moaned again at the touch of thousands upon thousands of fibers over my skin. When they were gone, I heard voices again, but I did not distinguish the words. I lay there, counting the fibers against my skin and marveling at the feel of them against my body. The floor beneath me shook and I counted Henry's footsteps as he moved. I heard more noise, familiar though I could not discern it in my current state. I ignored them and returned to reveling at the carpet beneath my skin.

Henry entered me and I gasped. I could feel every fiber of the smooth latex as he pushed gently deeper. I tried to raise up my hips, but Henry held me down, pushing me into the glorious carpet beneath me. I let out an elated cry as he withdrew and thrust, harder this time. My body moved along the carpet, my skin erupting in a symphony of sensation that overwhelmed me and made me scream. His hands, soft and strong, hooked over my shoulders and he thrust harder into me. I opened my eyes to look into Henry's. The darkness there greeted me and flooded over me, sating itself in his pleasure of my body.

THREE

The next morning, we discussed the session over breakfast. I felt alive and more aware than I had in a long time as I dug a spoon into my grapefruit. I was used to the violet wand making my skin more sensitive, but nothing like what I had experienced last night. Henry attributed it to the depth of my sub-space. He was pleased with me, that I was able to use my safe word before my panic became too much. He had been watching me closely and had been close to stopping with the thin bar anyway. That reassured me, but Henry emphasized to me how important it was that I had the presence of mind to use my safe word.

"Sub-space is risky sometimes," Henry cut into his omelet with his fork, "especially when you fall deep into it. Submissive sometimes don't use their safe word when they normally would. That's why I always make sure I am aware of your state when we play, but it is better that you can use your safe word as well."

I liked the praise. I thought of my resolution that I would focus on my training to be a good submissive to Henry as the best way to prove myself to Mistress Aevia. As we finished our breakfast, I thanked Henry for the session and sharing all of what he had learned from Frank with me. I saw something else in his eyes. It was not disappointment, but I understood that I had missed something. I played through the night in my mind, but could not think of what it was. I decided that next time I would pay more attention to the details to see what I had missed. I was still learning, after all.

Work that day was pleasant and easy. We were working under a looser deadline with our current project. My mind still felt sharp and hyperaware, driving me to work faster and more meticulously at the same time. I enjoyed the rush, and hoped that I would feel this each time we had a suspension session like the night before. My team seemed equally pleased with my work, and Lillian wondered aloud what I had gotten up to that I was so inspired. I was tempted to share, but found that I could not. I simply hinted that I had a good night with Henry. It was enough to get them playing the guessing games that they had so much fun with. I wondered if I would be able to tell my teammates one day about the different things that happened between Henry and me, and found myself very much wanting to.

It was another change that left me baffled and wondering.

I saw Henry again that night. He didn't have another suspension session planned, but he promised that it would happen again soon. We ate dinner together at his dining table and I shared with him the effects of our session on my day. He looked pleased and even shared a little of his own day. I was elated. Romance was stalled between us as I had to wait out his own conflict with his emotional demons. A discussion of his day was a start, at least.

"You got me thinking about something last night," Henry said after he wrapped up his brief recount of his day. "I've been wondering about this for a while, and I think it might be a good time to broach the subject."

I was curious now. I measured my own excitement. I did not dare hope for an emotional breakthrough this soon, and somehow I sensed that such a thing was not happening now anyway. "What is it?"

"I'm planning on bringing a woman from the office here next week, and I would like you here as well, to participate as my submissive."

I blinked my eyes and sat back, staring at my plate. Henry's suggestion sounded strange to my ears, but not as strange as my own feelings about it. I accepted that he had his office flings and hardly felt any jealousy now over the idea of him sleeping with another woman. He was not mine to lay claim to after all, not yet. I had thought about being with a woman before, I had even fantasized about it from time to time.

It was never something I felt a particular compulsion about, one way or the other. I realized I was simply indifferent to the idea.

"This is not something that I am commanding you to do," Henry said. "It is not something that we negotiated before, so you are free to refuse me. It is something I would like to share with you, though."

I looked from my plate to Henry. The sincerity in his eyes touched me and I wondered at this man sitting with me. It was important to him to be able to share this, but I could not articulate my question to learn why. Something in his eyes told me that even if I could ask, he could not articulate an answer, not in any way that I would understand. I thought about Ana's advice, about resolving my questions about our relationship.

This proposal, I thought, would help me put any reservations I still had about his flings to rest. If I could take part in one, then I would know that I would be comfortable with them in the future. It might also help me to resolve how I felt about the state of our relationship, which would help me keep my focus on our dynamic.

"I can do it," I said, "but I'm not really into women."

"If that's something you're averse to, you don't have to participate at all." I could see some disappointment in Henry's eyes, and that he kept it carefully measured and held back. I was touched by his consideration of limits.

"I'm not bothered by the thought of being with a woman; I've just never really felt the urge to do it. I can participate, as long as there is not the expectation that I have to do anything to her."

Henry gave me a broad smile and any disappointment faded from his eyes. "You can pleasure me then. I would like you to help me with a few things. She is into bondage and discipline as well, so I would like you to help me bind her and bring me tools to use, things like that."

That I could handle. We discussed limits around the evening. I would be there for his pleasure and to help him. If I felt that I wanted to do anything else, I could, but it would not be the expectation and he would not be disappointed in me if I did not.

The rest of my week was Henry-less. On Thursday afternoon, he flew to London to meet with a potential client. If that worked out, then within the next couple of months, he would have a trip to Paris to make as well. I remembered my conversation with Michael and thought that the trip to Paris would be the perfect one for Henry to ask me on. The city of love – of course, I wondered just what that would mean for us. Would we be seeking Parisian kink or would there be the opportunity for something else there?

I received a phone call from Michael during lunch on Thursday, asking if I would like to go on a date on Saturday night. I accepted without thought. With all of the wildness that came with being a submissive, it would be nice to have something simple to look forward to. It was about time that I decided how I would balance my feelings for Henry and Michael anyway, and I needed to know if what I felt for Michael was real or just infatuation.

In the afternoon, Trin messaged me, begging me to go out with her on Friday. I could tell, even through text message, that she was distressed so I agreed. I hoped that whatever was wrong was not too serious, but I could clearly sense that my friend needed me.

Friday ended my easy workweek and I met Trin downtown for drinks and dinner. She hugged me when she saw me. We followed the host to our table and ordered drinks and an appetizer. I decided that if whatever happened was this bad that dinner would be my treat and let the waiter know that early. Trin thanked me and did not fight, and I knew I made the right decision there.

"I'm sorry to be a downer on a Friday," Trin said after the waiter left our table. "I just couldn't face everyone for clubbing."

"What happened?" I was afraid it was something disastrous. If there had been a death in her family, I thought my mother would have called to notify me about it.

"I broke up with John."

I barely knew Trin's boyfriend. The two of them started dating towards the end of our junior year in college, and he never joined her for our group clubbing nights. I had met him on a handful of occasions and he seemed like a nice person. Trin was enamored with him. I placed my hand over hers. "What happened?"

"He was cheating on me," Trin said. She wiped away a tear that formed in the corner of her eye. "Everything was going so well. My lease is up in two months and we were going to move in together. Then I see where some girl has tagged him on Facebook. It was purely by chance, you know? I was at work and hardly ever check it there, but it was a slow day. When I went home, I checked out what she had tagged him for. It was some sexy selfie where she was asking him if he was 'hungry.'"

Trin sat back as the waiter returned with our drinks and appetizer. When he left, she continued her story. "I thought 'who is this bitch?' and started scrolling through her timeline. I thought I would give this girl a piece of my mind for targeting my boyfriend like that. I see where she liked a couple of pictures of him and started browsing her photos. Sure enough, she had pictures of the two of them buried in one of her photo albums. He was hugging on her; she was hanging on him. In one picture, they were kissing. These were recent, within the last four months or so."

"When I confronted John, he said it wasn't serious, that she was just someone he liked to have fun with, a good friend. He was all 'I love you and I want to spend my life with you.' I told him, if he really loved me, he would just be with me. I broke it up. It's fine to have a friend with benefits, but not when you have a girlfriend. That's just – I don't have words."

I did my best to comfort Trin over dinner. She alternated between tears and being fine. I felt terrible for her. I knew that she was in love with John, but I hadn't realized just how much hope she had placed in a future between them. Now, her trust was broken and that future was shattered. I did my best not to compare her situation to my own. Henry was at least open about the fact that we were not in any kind of monogamous relationship to the point of even asking me to join him for an encounter. I could not escape, however, the idea that when someone loves another person, he only wants to be with that person. It was an idea I had grown up with all my life. I did not know if Henry was challenging it, or if it were holding true.

The doubts that Trin's heartbreak brought up followed me into Saturday. I put aside the negative feelings as I prepared for my date with Michael. I wanted to focus on the evening and sorting out my own feelings. I would not be able to do that if I were wondering about just what was going on with Henry or fretting over Trin's failed relationship.

Michael picked me up at seven o'clock and we went for a simple dinner. We enjoyed our food over conversation about our respective weeks. I allowed my eyes to meet his on occasion, surprised by how relaxed I felt at the prospect of some romance between us. I didn't feel fretful. I still felt conflicted, but somewhere among that conflict was a surety.

I would continue to wonder about the unknown until I finally took a step forward.

The movie was another romantic comedy. It was not my first choice, as I didn't really care for the actors, but I enjoyed the company I was in. As we watched the male lead clumsily pursue the female lead, Michael placed his hand over mine. By the middle of the movie, when I had predicted the ending, I abandoned watching it altogether, turning to Michael and kissing him. He was surprised by the gesture, but his kiss was passionate and eager.

After the movie, Michael took me home. He walked me to my door, only this time, I did not simply give him a kiss on the cheek and watch him leave. I invited him inside under the pretenses of a drink. He followed me in and as I locked the door, he took my hand and drew me close to him.

"You are a beautiful woman," Michael said. "I don't think you recognize that sometimes, and it amazes me."

I smiled shyly under the compliment. He kissed me, his lips pressing firmly into mine, his tongue searching and yearning. I returned the kiss, wrapping my arms around him and setting aside all pretenses. His hands lifted my dress and my fingers worked the buttons of his shirt as we inched toward my bedroom, our passion taking up all of our senses.

Michael lifted my dress over my body and laid me down on the bed, unfastening and removing my bra as he did so. He kissed my breasts and wrapped his fingers in my panties, pulling them off and discarding them on the floor. As he moved down onto me, I tapped his shoulder and gestured to my dresser.

"The top drawer," I said. When he looked confused, I smiled at him. "Condoms."

"Oh, right." Michael stepped away from the bed and opened the drawer, pulling out a foil-wrapper and opening it. As he slipped on the latex sheath, I thought about how every encounter with Henry involved one, even now. I was touched by the seriousness of his desire, but I was not yet ready to take that step with him.

With the condom on, Michael returned to the bed, laying over me and brushing his fingers through my hair. I opened my legs for him and he entered, smoothly thanks to my arousal and want. I raised my hips to meet him as he pulled back and thrust gently. We set a smooth rhythm between us that slowly brought me to my climax. I gripped his arms and I came, happy to still feel him thrusting.

Being with Michael was simple and sweet with no need to name Dominants and submissives. We didn't need to set limits and safe words. I missed the ease with which a relationship could work, and as Michael continued to move with my body, I put all of it into my touch and reactions.

When he came, he rolled off me and lay beside me, still stroking my hair and breathing heavily against my shoulder. I turned onto my side and looked into his eyes, wondering what he was thinking, what would come next.

"I would like to do this again," Michael said. He tucked my hair behind my ear and kissed me softly on the lips.

"We can do that." I lay my head down on my arm.

"I want you to be mine." Michael's eyes grew dark and inside I shuddered at the intensity and sincerity of his words. I knew exactly what he meant by that.

"This is nice. I don't want it to be official yet." I struggled to find the right words. I didn't want to lead Michael on, but I wasn't ready to commit to him yet. I still didn't have my feelings sorted out yet, for him or for Henry. I knew that I enjoyed my dynamic with Henry, even without the advancing romance. I was not ready to give it up. "I need time for that."

Michael kissed me again. He slid his arm under my body and pulled me close to him. He felt warm and relaxed next to me. "I can wait, then."

I sighed and closed my eyes. The conflict that had seemed to be resolving rose up again. Michael was not just a possible suitor. He was a lover now.

I would have to find a way to resolve how I felt about both men.

FOUR

I stood naked and still as Henry examined me. He lifted my breasts carefully, examining the nipples and areola of each before releasing them. He ran his hands over my body, testing the smoothness of my skin and looking for any imperfection not yet detectcd. When he knelt down in front of me, he opened my labia, examining my sex carefully before moving around and doing the same with my buttocks.

Marie stood still, watching as Henry went through this intense and careful ritual. I was not used to having someone observe us. Her blonde hair fell below her shoulders and her blue eyes were full of curiosity and wonder as she watched Henry inspect each part of my body. It felt intimate and strange under her gaze. I kept my emotions and insecurities checked, however, so that I stayed looking ahead the whole time. I had told Henry that I would be able to do this tonight, to serve him as his submissive while he had sex with Marie. I was not going to falter in my service to him.

When Henry finished, he stood, giving me a nod of his approval. He walked up to Marie and took her hand, leading her to his couch. I followed, waiting for them to sit down. I took my place on the floor at Henry's feet and waited for my orders.

Henry placed his hand behind Marie's head and drew her to him, kissing her deeply. As he kissed her, he removed her shirt and lifted her skirt. I could see that she already wore no panties and felt myself grow warm between my legs, anticipating what was to follow. Henry brought her over him, so that he could place his head between her thighs. He gestured to his pants and I understood my order. Feeling my heart beat heavy in my chest, I unfastened his pants. He waited for me, hard and ready. I took him into my mouth, eager to taste him.

Above us, Marie moaned her pleasure. I sucked eagerly at Henry, wanting to taste him, to have it only for myself. I could feel him begin to pulse and each time I would hear his breathing steady. He denied me what I wanted to take in and taste. I felt humiliated and aroused at the same time by his withholding of himself.

He lifted Marie from his face and looked down at me. Darkness swirled in his eyes and I wanted him. I wanted to beg for him, but I knew what was coming, even before he gave me his order. "I have a condom in my pocket. Put it on me."

I slid my hand into his pocket and pulled out the foil wrapper. As I ripped it open, he brought her down over his face again, eliciting another gasp and more moans from Marie. I brought the condom over the head of his cock and rolled it down, covering it for someone who was not me. My face burned, matching the heat between my legs. I did not understand what I was feeling in all of this, but I knew I did not want to stop or turn away from it.

I also knew that I did not want to let him go. I kept my hand wrapped around him as he brought Marie off his face again. He looked down at me as he lowered her, and when my hand did not move from around him, the darkness engulfed his eyes. I swam there in it as he lowered her onto him and entered her. She pushed down against my hand, wet from his mouth and her arousal, driving me to the base of his shaft, where I continued to grip him, wanting to hold onto what was mine.

In Henry's eyes, I saw this was my punishment. I was attempting to be greedy, to lay claim to something that was not mine to claim. Henry had told me once that he did not like to punish, that he wanted obedience not from fear, but because I wanted to obey. There was another side to that as well, that he did not have to speak; I simply knew. He did not want me to refrain from what drove me to avoid punishment either. This was no different from me allowing him to play with me at a party or needing to be punished for enjoying lust and desire as others looked on my naked body.

For Henry, punishment was not merely an act of retribution. It was a consequence of actions. I wanted to grip him and therefore, I would touch Marie, whether I had wanted or intended to or not. I gripped him tighter and Henry moaned. Marie rocked over him, grinding against my hand as she did. When Henry came, I felt the pulse of his pleasure before it could enter her and smiled into the darkness of his eyes.

When he lifted Marie off his body, I carefully removed the condom and waited to follow him. I knew that he would not be through with her yet. He kissed Marie and stood, taking her by the hands and drawing her to her feet. As he walked to the bedroom, I stood to follow. He directed me to the bathroom, where I disposed of the condom and washed my hands, knowing I would be handling tools and rope next. I also took another condom to bring out with me. When he saw it, he smiled, the darkness still overtaking his eyes.

He guided Marie to the bed and laid her out on her stomach, naked now, and spread eagle. I walked to the chest and waited for his orders, bringing him rope when he asked for it, and helping him to thread it through the iron bed so that he could tie her securely down. Marie sighed happily at the feel of the ropes. I knew if I looked down at her, I would see the same look of pleasure that I had when I was tied up.

I could not. Henry's eyes held me in place and I could look nowhere else unless I was managing rope.

"Bring me my flogger." Henry's voice was heavy with his darkness as well. I knew the one he would want, the one he preferred to use on me. I brought it from the chest, holding it carefully, thinking of the pain and sting that it caused me. I laid it in his waiting hand and he turned his attention to Marie. Now I watched her, his eyes hidden to me, as he struck at her buttocks and thighs. She cried out, her face twisting in pain and then relaxing into ecstasy.

He struck her until her skin turned pink under the tails of the flogger. When he turned to hand me the tool again, I could see the darkness in his eyes fed, but not sated. I felt a swelling of pride, even in my humiliation and denial of the evening.

I left him sated.

I placed the flogger into the chest carefully and Henry commanded me to bring the condom. I opened the wrapper and knelt down so that I could ease it down his shaft. I kissed the tip of his cock softly before bringing the condom over it. I worked slowly and carefully, not feeling the need now to be selfish, only to please him. When I finished, Henry placed his hand on my head and I looked up at him. Within the darkness, I saw affection.

You did well, it said to me.

"That is very good. Sit on the bed with your legs spread and stay out of reach of Marie. I want to tease her with you."

From the bed, I heard Marie moan and felt new warmth move through my body. I was an object of want, a thing to possess, and again I felt the strange combination of humiliation and exaltation that it brought. I climbed onto the bed and positioned myself at the head, angling my body so that Marie would be able to see me. She struggled to reach me as I looked down at her, and I could feel Henry's pleasure and darkness at her denial as he moved over her and entered her.

"Touch yourself," Henry said. "Open yourself and play. Let her see what belongs to me that she cannot have."

I reached my fingers between my legs and touched myself, opening the gentle folds of skin as Henry bade me. Marie moaned and I watched Henry grasp her hips as he thrust into her, hard. My eyes ventured between their bodies and his eyes, and my arousal grew as I watched him take pleasure from her and from my tease of her. I gripped the iron bedpost as my orgasm shook through my body, but I did not stop playing with myself.

Henry had not commanded me to stop.

Henry pushed harder into Marie, as though he could push her up into me. Some part of me wanted him to and I did not know if it was my own desire for her or my desire to please him. In a strange part of myself, the part I knew was changing because of Henry and his lifestyle, I did not care. It did not matter why I wanted it, I only did.

When I looked into Henry's eyes again, I could see that he recognized my own want. My face burned with embarrassment as I felt another orgasm begin to push from my fingers through my body. I also felt the power of his denial to me. Neither he nor Marie would touch me tonight, and I understood that even if I had asked before, that would be the case. For him and Marie, tonight was about pleasure. For him and me, it was about our power exchange. By denying me, he wielded the power that he had over me, and as my humiliation flowed over me once more, I reveled in his control.

I was as conflicted over the experience with Henry and Marie as I was over my affair with Michael. He had a pair of drivers take Marie home when they were done, one to drive her car, the other to drive her. She could barely walk from the rough sex, but she looked elated and pleased. With Marie gone, Henry drew me close to him to lay in bed. He ran his hand over my hair and whispered soothing words to me.

"How was this experience for you?" he asked.

I had no idea how to answer him. I was still deciding what I thought of the whole thing. It had been strange and humiliating, even as it aroused and excited me. Small moments within it made me appreciate the dynamic that Henry and I had, and though that had thrilled me, it left me confused about what should come next. I thought of poor Trin and her ex-boyfriend. *If he really loved me, he would just be with me.*

Was that true for Henry as well? If so, then what did it mean that I could sate that darkness where Marie could not? I wanted to understand.

"I was afraid you were going to choose Bethany for this." I needed to say something.

Henry gave a small laugh, but I felt no mockery from it. "I would not do something like that to you. It could create drama. I'm sorry I did not tell you Marie's name before. She's part of Lennox News Online, so unless you happen to see her in the elevator, well. There is little room for embarrassment."

I appreciated the consideration. "It's okay." I lay against him and breathed slowly, letting my mind process through the evening as he stroked my hair gently. I had to admit to myself that I enjoyed the night. I was still not sure what that meant for me as a person, but I understood that while Henry could share this moment with his submissive, it was not something one did with a girlfriend.

FIVE

Neither days nor more sessions with Henry resolved how I felt about the night with Henry and Marie. When I heard the sound of giggles down the hall, and Henry's voice flirting with another woman, however, I felt no stir of jealousy or a need to avoid the scene. I simply carried on with my path and whatever I was doing. The night had given me one thing – a sense of peace about what the affairs meant for Henry and me. Without wondering constantly about what might happen romantically between us, I felt a new focus in my submission to him.

That relationship mattered between us.

On Thursday, he took me to hear the symphony orchestra perform Berlioz's *Symphonie Fantastique*. As with the opera and the charity ball, he bought me a new dress for the occasion, as well as a new diamond necklace and earrings to match. I felt like I belonged on his arm as we walked into the symphony hall and up to one of the balconies. This was not a private one for Henry alone, as we had at the opera. We shared this with others, these from Henry's elite, but otherwise mundane world.

Still, I could not help but lose myself in the enchantment of the evening, and when we returned to his condo and he tied me beneath the eyehook in his ceiling, I wandered into that mental space and swam in the darkness of his eyes. He had owned me tonight at the symphony as he owned me in his ropes. I could not distinguish the feelings between either one. I only knew that I was lost in them.

I contrasted the evening with my date with Michael on Saturday afternoon. He took me on a simple picnic in the park. We enjoyed the pleasant day and the simple food that I made for us to take – sandwiches and fruit. Where Henry did not dare to explore his emotions, Michael was very eager to discuss his own. He did not want to speak too loosely about his feelings, knowing that I was not ready to commit to any relationship yet, but he made them plain and clear.

He liked me, and the depth of emotion was as serious as it was reciprocated.

I was torn. I knew that I should be able to walk away from Henry to be with Michael and I could not, any more than I could turn Michael away for Henry. From Michael I had the simplicity and emotional connection that I needed in romance. In Henry, I had something deep and primal that touched my inner being enough to change me. I knew that Michael could see those changes as well, and I was comforted that he did not seem turned off by them.

I could not understand, though, why I had the depth of emotional attachment that I did with Henry. With Michael, I could see why I was falling in love. He was sweet when we were together. He engaged me intellectually and emotionally. We shared interests and met in a world we were both part of.

With Henry, I enjoyed a power exchange that was slowly growing deeper. I could understand why I might become obsessed with him, but the idea that I would fall in love through it was strange and frightening. I thought of Ana's confession to me and of Mistress Aevia's dislike and disapproval of me.

It was dangerous to fall in love with my Dominant, and yet there I was, caught between two men and emotions that I could not deny.

I carried that confusion with me through my week, finding it easy enough to place aside during my sessions with Henry, but it stayed with me any other time. How I managed to focus on my work with my turbulent emotional life, I had no idea. On Wednesday, when two sets of flowers arrived at my office, one from Henry and the other from Michael, though I did not tell my teammates that is who they were from, everyone gave their "oohs" and "ahhs."

For them, the flowers were a sign of deepening romance, and I wondered what they made of them with Henry's continued office affairs. Perhaps, I thought, it was just how they saw the world of Henry Lennox. He would be a playboy, even if he somehow managed to settle down with a simple girl like me.

On Friday, I joined Henry for another lifestyle party. This party was like the first I attended, where Dominants were free to demonstrate the power their submissives gave to them, and the experienced shared knowledge with the novices. I walked behind and to Henry's left, leaving him only when I went to join conversations with other submissives, allowing him to talk with the big boys.

As I left one conversation to rejoin him, Mistress Aevia crossed my path, stopping me. I did not raise my eyes to meet her gaze and did not want to stay around for whatever unpleasantness she had for me tonight. I stepped to move around her, so that she could continue walking.

"I have to give credit to Henry for being patient with you," Mistress Aevia said.

I said nothing. Speaking would only encourage her more and I wanted just to be away from her. I saw Henry finish a conversation and begin moving toward another group. I stepped forward when Mistress Aevia spoke again.

"I don't think I would tolerate my submissive playing around, especially if he were doing it in such a dangerous manner."

I paused, but didn't dare turn around. She knew about my affair with Michael. I didn't know if she was spying on me or if Henry had mentioned it to her. That didn't matter to me. I wanted her to get to the point and be done.

"A true submissive is faithful." With that, Mistress Aevia walked away. I gritted my teeth and breathed slowly, determined to keep my composure. It was bad enough for her to bring me down, but I didn't need her doing even more to make me doubt the dynamic that I had with Henry. I might not stand any place as his girlfriend, but I was at least his submissive.

I joined Henry as he began speaking to another couple. The woman was unfamiliar to me, but the man I recognized right away. Henry had spoken to him at the first party, while he played with me and brought me off. I flushed and kept my eyes averted, hoping to hide my embarrassment.

Henry and the woman did not seem to notice at all; they were wrapped up in the conversation that Henry began. I could feel the man's eyes on me, however, and it did not help my embarrassment.

"Henry," the man said during a brief lull in the conversation, "Do you mind if I speak with your submissive while you and Darla continue discussing advertising?"

"Are we boring you, dear?" I presumed the woman was Darla. She kept her head high and even, and I understood that she might be the man's partner, but she was not his submissive.

The man kissed Darla on the cheek and offered her a smile. "You know I love the business side of advertising, but I do like to leave work at the office once in a while."

Darla and Henry both laughed at that.

"Of course you can speak to her, Stuart," Henry said. He drew my eyes up to his own and focused his attention on me now. "If you don't mind, of course."

When Henry spoke the name, I realized why the man had seemed so familiar before and chided myself silently for not recognizing him immediately. He was Stuart Lellman, the son of the Lellman in Lellman& White. Darla

Penrose was his fiancée, though I supposed that by now she was Darla Lellman – I didn't really keep up with the high society pages.

"I don't mind," I said.

Henry's eyes released me and Stuart offered me his arm. I took it, and he led me away from their conversation, taking a drink for himself and offering one to me from a submissive who passed by with a tray. I thanked him and we walked outside to the balcony of the hotel suite that hosted the party this evening.

"I hope you don't mind me saying this," Stuart said. "I never really thought you were the submissive type – in BDSM anyway. You always seemed sweet and quiet."

I smiled and looked up at Stuart, though I knew I was not supposed to. He gave me an approving nod and I relaxed, knowing it was okay to meet his gaze. "I am still the sweet and quiet type."

Stuart shook his head. His eyes were bright and I tried to interpret what I saw there. "I mean the innocent type. I'm not sure how Henry managed to attract the attention of a girl like you."

I thought about that as I looked back inside where Henry and Darla still talked the business of advertising. How had Henry managed to get me? The question seemed strange, as though I were some kind of prize catch. I looked back at Stuart. "He showed me he was a real person."

The approval I saw in Stuart's eyes shocked me. "Most submissives when they start into this lifestyle don't know to look for that." Stuart gestured inside and to a young man. He wore a black suit and stood easily a head taller than anyone else around him. "Brock there. What do you think about him?"

I studied the young man, the way that he kept his shoulders back and how he seemed to affect a kind of detachment from those around him. He looked confident and calm, the way I came to expect most Dominants, with a few exceptions, to behave. "He looks like the kind of person who might be a good Dominant."

I looked back to Stuart, who nodded his head knowingly. "He is. That's not the point, he just makes a good illustration. You said the key word, 'might.' I've seen a lot of submissives come through who look at a man like him and think 'will' without bothering to get to know the person behind the façade."

I had read the horror stories of men and women finding what they termed 'plastic dominants' and understood Stuart's point.

Some of those stories just ended in annoyance. A few ended much worse.

"Those Dominants that just look good on the outside are nothing on the inside. Oh, some of them can play a good game, but eventually something leaks through. Sometimes a submissive sees it in time, but not always, and I have even seen a few that managed to work their charms, taking submissives away from good Dominants."

Stuart sipped his drink as I took in his words of wisdom.

"Not Brock, though. Brock is one of the good ones because he took the time to be mentored. He didn't come up through the lifestyle like Henry and I did, but mentorship is just as good, I think. You still get the chance to learn and benefit from someone else's experience."

"I guess most people go the mentor route now," I said.

Stuart laughed and shook his head. "We try to encourage it in our community, but we can't force it. I won't say that every self-taught Dominant is bad. After all, some Dominants look down on ones like Brock who seek a mentor rather than serve."

"Like Mistress Aevia." I had no idea why I knew that, but the look in Stuart's eyes told me I was right.

"You're good at figuring people out."

I was not sure that I believed that. "Mistress Aevia doesn't really make it hard to figure out where she stands on things. Did she train you as well?"

Stuart shook his head again and sipped his drink. "No, my Dominant was a little kinder and gentler than she is. She's not so bad. People like her that hold strongly to the Old Guard traditions are important in the community. Everything changes so fast around us. They help keep us grounded and remember the rules that have always kept our community and dynamics safe."

Stuart and I continued to talk as we sipped our drinks on the patio. Like Henry, he had many years of experience in the lifestyle and I absorbed I could learn from him. His Dominant had been less harsh than Mistress Aevia, but just as strict about protocols. She had also instilled in him a sense of respect for submissive that was reassuring to me. I realized that it was more than just showing me respect here.

For all of his talk about not thinking I was the kind of girl who would take part in something like this, I understood one thing very clearly. Stuart Lellman did not look down on me personally or professionally for what I was either.

SIX

After my encounter with Mistress Aevia, my conversation with Stuart was exactly what I needed to restore some of my own self-confidence. As I moved into my next week, I was no surer about how to handle my growing feelings for Michael and Henry. Somehow, things seemed to move into their places, and I felt as though my life was once more a complex puzzle with each piece in its place, waiting for me to pan out to see the larger picture.

The week passed and then the next. I drifted between work, my sessions with Henry, and my dates with Michael. Each aspect of life found its own little niche and somehow I managed to keep each one separate. Between work and my love triangle, I even managed find time to see Trin. We had not seen each other since she told me about her breakup with John and had only briefly spoken on the phone.

She was doing better now, ready to move on from her failed relationship and find greener pastures. We joined our friends for clubbing on Friday night. Henry was out of town for the weekend, so I would not be able to see him anyway. It was enjoyable, and devoid of obnoxious complications. We were simply young twenty-some things on the prowl in the city, moving between clubs, having fun without making too much of a nuisance of ourselves.

I liked seeing Trin laugh and have fun again. She even managed to flirt with one or two boys when we danced in the clubs.

On Saturday, I cooked and Michael and I stayed in. I was exhausted from my night of clubbing and just wanted a quiet evening. We watched movies on cable until they bored us and moved to my bedroom. Michael's touch was as soft and gentle as it ever was. I gently reminded him of a condom once again, but was touched by the seriousness that its lack implied. I wanted to feel him, flesh against flesh, and wondered at my inability to make that commitment to him.

Henry changed me in so many ways since this whirlwind started. I was changing and I was slowly coming to accept that was simply the price to pay for participating in Henry's dark world. I wondered, though, if I was becoming like Henry in some ways. Was I selfish, wanting both my romance and my submission, or was I afraid? I didn't know what I had to be afraid of. Michael's wants and intentions were plain, and as he trembled and pulsed inside me, I knew exactly where I stood with him.

I saw Henry for our next session together on Monday evening. He inspected me as he always did before our evenings began. As he lifted my breasts to inspect each carefully and parted my sex to examine it thoroughly, I felt both aroused and unsure. His actions were not merely to inspect me and show his Dominance over me. I sensed more of his jealousy as well. He knew about my affair with Michael, it was only natural that my friendship with him would progress after all. I understood that this act of inspection was as much about his jealousy as it was about his Dominance. When he finished, I watched him carefully to see if I would need to stop, if he would attempt once again to act out.

He did not. The ritual of inspection, I realized, was not just to help bring me into the mindset of being his submissive. It was also for him to shed any baggage from his day, including his jealousy over Michael. I did not like that Henry's jealousy was still showing itself, and I wondered if Mistress Aevia had said something to him, like what she said to me at the last party. I didn't doubt it. If he was able to leave it behind with the ritual of inspection, however, I thought that I could handle it.

What I could not handle, however, was the continuation of things as they were. Everything was fitting nicely into its place. I had my submission to Henry, my dates with

Michael on the weekends. Even my friends had their niche to fill in my life. That compartmentalization, however, did not stop my emotional turmoil and as everything continued its steady pace, neither relationship seemed capable of resolving itself. I had thought that when I took that step forward with Michael, that things would become clearer between Henry and myself, that I would be able to understand our relationship as just Dominant and submissive and set aside my emotions.

I only felt them growing. Even excepting Henry's display of jealousy, I felt it. As much as I was falling in love with Michael, I knew that I was in love with Henry. It was not just the passion of submission or the obsession over a Dominant. I felt deeply about him and my feelings for Michael were not enough to resolve it, block it, or take it away.

I was going to have to make a decision.

The following Monday brought news that I was unhappy to hear. It was on the radio, dominating the airwaves, and I knew that I would be speaking to Ana today. All attempts at reaching a settlement between Henry's lawyers and Michael's lawyers failed. A court date had been set on Friday. I wondered that neither Michael nor Henry had mentioned it to me. Henry was out of town for the weekend, so I supposed that he would not want to share that kind of news by text message or phone. Michael I had seen on Saturday, another date – dinner and a movie again.

Perhaps, I thought, he simply didn't want to spoil the mood with something that he would only have so much control over. After all, a settlement required compromise on both sides, and I didn't think that they were reached as easily as television dramas portrayed. According to the news, the court date was set for two weeks, and on every station, everyone wanted to speculate what the failed negotiations meant.

"For a while, we thought this whole sordid affair would die down. Now it looks like Henry Lennox's dirty laundry may finally be aired – in court," one radio announcer said before I change the channel in disgust.

While the office was buzzing about the pending court date, my team was quiet about it, though I could see it was on everyone's minds. We worked through another planning session until Ana called Nora to request that I come to her office. I left my team and steadied my breath. I knew what to expect.

This would be about the case.

I entered Ana's office and sat down across from her desk. She gave me a strained smile and waited for her secretary to bring us cups of hot tea.

"I'm going to guess you know why you're in here," Ana said as her secretary closed the door, leaving us alone to talk.

"I heard it on the news this morning. Settlement negotiations broke down." I took a sip of my tea and set the cup down.

Ana shook her head and frowned. "They didn't break down. Negotiations were going perfectly well on both sides. Michael pulled everything back and decided to move forward with the court case."

That news stunned me. Again, I wondered why he wouldn't tell me this, to give me some warning. I thought about everything that had built up between us from friendship to romance. If he was trying to protect me, hiding the information was a poor way to do it. I couldn't even get past being stunned to wonder why he would pull back from negotiations.

"I'm not surprised that Michael didn't tell you," Ana said. I looked at her, stunned again for a different reason. "Yes, I know about your relationship with Michael. I am not going to say I approve, but that's not my place anyway. It's going to make what happens next harder for you, though, so I want to make sure you're ready."

I supposed that it was possible Henry would tell her about my affair with Michael. If he was feeling jealous, I saw no reason why he would not seek Ana out as a confidant. She was not going to tell me how I should conduct my personal life, but her worry and disappointment about my choice in lovers was plain. "What happens next?"

"The case is on Judge Sterling's docket, and he has already stated that he does not want a media circus in his courtroom. You and I both know that is exactly what will happen. Before the judge will approve the date, he wants one last meeting. You, Henry, Michael, and the lawyers get to sit down and talk this out. They will either come to a settlement, or prove a settlement is not possible."

I took a deep breath and sipped my tea again, hoping it would calm my rising nerves. I liked nothing that I was hearing and could not see how this could be anything but bad.

"Why did Michael withdraw from negotiations?" I asked.

Ana shrugged her shoulders. "I wish I could tell you. No reasons were given. He pulled everything back and his lawyers submitted for a court date." Ana took a sip of her own tea. The worry and disapproval left her eyes, and I could see that for this part, at least, she was just my friend. "You're upset with Michael and that is understandable. It is also between the two of you. He could have pulled back from negotiations for any number of reasons. I will tell you this, until the meeting, do not talk to him. Don't call him, don't text him, don't email him, and whatever you do, don't see him. His lawyers want this in court because they know Sterling's record with harassment cases. Sterling is prejudiced toward the plaintiff and with good reason. Even the ones that get their case heard in court face an uphill battle. Michael is one in a hundred – one in a thousand when it comes to harassment cases. His lawyers have one simple job, and that is to make the case look favorable for Michael, and anything you do is up for grabs."

"Why do I have to go?" This case was between Michael and Henry. I was not named as a defendant in the case.

"Because you are a material witness and the catalyst at the heart of this whole thing."

"I signed a sworn statement already. There's nothing else they need from me."

Ana sat back in her chair. "The statement you signed was not for the lawyers. It was for the company and our insurance company. Legally, I can't hand it over to them, not without a court order, and Michael's lawyers are not going to subpoena the statement. They don't want to. Your statement is very plain, simple, and clear, and it will blow a hole in their case. You cannot cross examine a statement, but you can cross examine a person, and they will twist everything they can about you, about your personal life, your relationship with Henry, and your relationship with Michael."

I did not like this. I didn't like any of it. I felt like a bird about to let out of a coop for a hunt. "Henry can release it then."

Ana's lip curled up in a half smile and she sipped her tea. "I wish. If his lawyers put it on the table, Michael's will challenge its admissibility on the same grounds – they can't cross examine it. Only they will twist it around and say that it is prejudicial, that it is an internal document witnessed by someone with no reason to challenge it. A judge like Sterling, who likes to ensure plaintiffs in a harassment case have a fair chance, is more likely to buy it."

I was not going to get out of this. No matter what, I would have to sit in that room between

Henry and Michael. I was terrified and I could tell that Ana saw it as well.

"We have three days until you meet with the lawyers," Ana said. "You and I are going to go over everything that Michael's lawyers may bring up to discredit you. It means you are going to have to tell me things you may not want to, but don't pretend for a moment that what Michael's lawyers don't know they won't assume."

I resigned myself to my fate. I nodded and felt tears sting my eyes and roll down my cheeks.

"We'll get started this evening. I will make sure that you're ready, and by Thursday, nothing the lawyers can pull out will startle you or shock you."

I was grateful that Ana was willing to help me prepare. I was not sure what I would do without her. In truth, however, I was not worried about what Michael's lawyers would say about anything. They could show pictures taken by helicopter of me naked in Henry's apartment, giving him a blowjob while he went down on Marie.

That would not bother me.

I would be sitting with my lover and my Dominant, facing my conflicted emotions, fears, and worries in the worst way possible.

Ana worked with me for three days in the evening, helping to prepare me for the meeting with the lawyers. I told her details about my relationship with Michael, expecting to see more disappointment. I saw worry and concern reflected in her eyes, but judgment and disappointment were not present. I was relieved by that, but wondered at what was there. Why was my story so concerning to her? I supposed that it could be in relation to my dynamic with Henry.

She thought of any angle that Michael's lawyers might use to discredit me, and I found myself awed by her shrewdness. I caught a glimpse of what she must be like as a Dominant, and found myself envying whatever person she chose as a submissive – realizing that at the different parties she had attended, she always arrived alone.

By Thursday, I felt that I was ready to face the lawyers and whatever questions or accusations they might hurl my way. I could not imagine them coming up with anything Ana had not covered. She was focused on one simple thing – maintaining my innocence. Thinking about the parties with Henry and my night with him and Marie, I did not feel so innocent. I supposed that in the beginning, I was, and that was what she wanted me to remember. It did not matter what I learned about myself now. It only mattered what my mindset was the day that Michael had approached me.

She only had one question that I could not resolve, and I hoped that the lawyers would not bring it up. If Michael had put me in a situation that was so blatantly sexual harassment, why was I dating him now? I could not answer that. The Michael that I saw now seemed so different from the Michael who had been my manager, who told me that I needed to be a team player when Henry flirted with me.

I could not explain that difference, though, and I felt at a loss. My only hope was that Michael's lawyers would find such a question too clumsy, that it had too much of a risk of making him look bad, to ask it. Ana seemed to think it was possible for that to be the case, and I held onto that assessment.

After work, I drove to the courthouse, where a conference room was set aside for the meeting. Judge Sterling planned the evening meeting so that he would not have to reschedule cases on his docket that day. I was tired from a day of creative planning and implementation, and nervous about the prospect of sitting in a room with both Michael and Henry. I knew that

Henry was jealous of my relationship with Michael and I hoped that he would control it there.

When I arrived, the lawyers were in their seats around a long mahogany table, and a young woman whom I assumed to be Judge Sterling's clerk stood next to another door. Michael sat on one side of the table. A man stood and directed me to a seat on the other side, introducing himself as James Patterson, the lead lawyer for Henry. He shook my hand and offered me pleasantries. The other lawyer was Nathan Alexander. He was not nearly as polite as Mr. Patterson was, but I did not expect him to be. Ana had warned me that Michael's lawyer would make himself as distant as possible in order to put me off and make me uncomfortable.

If Mr. Alexander looked at me with contempt, Michael's look was unreadable. When he met my eyes, I did not see affection. They were blank pools, hiding any emotion or thought. I felt strange and alone in this room, and quiet whispers of reassurance from Mr. Patterson did not help my unease.

Henry was the last to arrive. He entered with a quick hello to Mr. Patterson and me. He said nothing to Michael or Mr. Alexander, and I could sense his unease and discomfort at the triangle present in the room. When he sat down, the clerk opened the door and stepped through. Moments later, a tall and distinguished man with short grey hair entered the room. He still wore his judge's robes. When we all went to stand, he placed up his hand.

"This is not my courtroom, this is an informal hearing," Judge Sterling said as he sat down. "This is very simple. You will discuss this case together and come to a settlement. If I see that a settlement is not possible, then I will allow the case to proceed. I do not want theatrics. We are all adults in this room and I expect reasoned discourse."

He met each of our eyes as he spoke, and when he met mine, I could see conflict in his. I did not belong in this, not on this side of the table anyway. I didn't imagine that he dealt with many cases of sexual harassment brought by male plaintiffs. I breathed slowly to control my own annoyance with Michael. This case was a sham and Michael knew it. Getting angry, however, would not help at all.

"Thank you, Your Honor," Mr. Alexander said. He looked from the judge to me as he spoke. "This is a complex case. Unfortunately, Ms. Caldwell's absence from all discussions and our inability to so much as speak to her has made it difficult to negotiate a reasonable settlement."

"You don't need to speak with her. The case is against me." Henry's voice was even and calm, but beneath it, I could hear that darkness and the protectiveness of my Dominant. My body fought between nervousness and relief to hear it.

"Mr. Lennox, you will refrain from interrupting," Judge Sterling said plainly. He was neither impressed nor intimidated by Henry's outburst, but then nothing that Henry said was directed at him.

Mr. Patterson patted Henry lightly on the arm and whispered something to him.

"I am sorry, Your Honor." Henry gave the judge a deep bow of his head.

Judge Sterling nodded. "While this is informal, I can hold you in contempt if I need to." He looked to Mr. Alexander once more. "You may continue."

"Thank you, Your Honor," Mr. Alexander looked from the judge to me again. "Would you explain why you have remained away from this case and elected not to speak to us at all?"

"No one said you wanted to speak to me," I offered. "I never received a phone call or a letter from your office."

"All of the times that you saw my client, he never mentioned it to you either?" Mr. Alexander sounded disbelieving of my answer, even before I could speak it.

"No." I didn't feel the need to elaborate. I remembered Ana's warning. Keep answers simple. The more words I used, the more chances he had to interrupt me, and the more tools he had to twist and use against me.

Mr. Alexander shrugged his shoulders. "I imagine that you kept him too busy to think about the case."

I did not miss the implication in Mr. Alexander's voice. On one side of me, Henry tensed and Mr. Patterson squeezed his arm. On the other, Judge Sterling frowned. He was also unhappy with what he heard. I thought of my delicate dance with Mistress Aevia and how she tried to keep Henry in the middle of our little war. I had to be calm and non-confrontational with her. I had to be the same way here.

Remember your innocence when Michael first approached you, Ana had said to me. I kept my breathing steady to maintain my calm. "He could have brought it up any time."

"You didn't approach Mr. Patterson either," Mr. Alexander said. "You spend a great deal of time in Mr. Lennox's company. I suppose you kept him too busy to bring up the necessity of talking to his lawyer about the case."

I didn't need to see Henry to know his reaction. I could feel the tension in the room build, centered on him. I also recognized the predicament that his question placed me in. I was either deceptive, or Henry was trying to keep a material witness away from the case. I felt terrible, but I knew how I needed to answer. It may not make Henry look good, but if I were to be any use to him as a witness, I had to maintain my innocence. "Henry was just protecting me from the controversy and media storm."

"It *is* easy to protect someone when she spends all of her time bound up in rope." Mr. Alexander's tone was cool and dismissive. Henry's chair thumped on the ground and Mr. Patterson pushed him back down into it, whispering to him harshly.

My face burned and I looked at Michael. His face was still stoic and unreadable. He could have been in a negotiation with a client. I supposed that he was in a negotiation of sorts now. He was negotiating this case into the courtroom, and to do that, I had to appear as a flimsy witness to his character. I only hoped that this display would work against him and remove Judge Sterling's prejudice to want to side with Michael.

"You approached Mr. Lennox to initiate an affair." Mr. Alexander changed the subject quickly and I felt off balance. I looked up at him, startled by the misconception of events that had taken place. "At what point did you urge him to have my client fired from Lennox Advertising?"

"I never did." My confusion kept my answers short and I was thankful for that. I couldn't think of anything else to say.

"You said nothing to Mr. Lennox that would have led to my client's termination?"

My mouth opened, but would not form words. I closed it and looked to Michael, who was still stoic and calm.

"Michael told me that he expected me to have an affair with Henry." I looked back at the lawyer.

"In those exact words?"

I clenched my fists. Oh everything was so clear that evening in the office, and I knew this man was going to twist what I said around. "He said that he would not tell me what to do with my personal life, but when it came to Henry, he wanted to make sure I was a team player."

Mr. Alexander nodded his head solemnly as he looked at me. His eyes softened and I saw pity there. I wanted to spit in them. "A team player. Isn't it true that he was only concerned because of the rude way you treated Mr. Lennox when he came to introduce himself?"

Henry again shifted in his seat, and Mr. Patterson held him down. I was trapped. I no longer wanted to spit in Mr. Alexander's eyes. I wanted to run, and knew that I couldn't. If I talked about Henry flirting with me, he would bring up the other affairs in the office. Ana had said that Michael's case centered on the notion that the affairs created a hostile work environment for him.

My mind was working again, but I did not like where it was going.

"If what you say is true," Mr. Alexander said casually, "then essentially, you would be saying that it was my client who was harassing you in the office, creating for you an environment where you felt you needed to exchange sexual favors in order to preserve your job."

"Yes." I kept my answer short and simple. I knew better than to hope that he would leave it at that.

"Why would you start a relationship with a man who was sexually harassing you in the office?"

Mr. Alexander's question was met only with my silence.

I still could not answer that question. I looked from him to Michael. He met my eyes, but I saw nothing there, no apology, no remorse that our feelings for each other were being brought up in such a way. I was standing in the office again, watching him dismiss my attraction and light flirting as he told me to invite Henry to my bed.

Only now, it was not light flirting that he dismissed. I thought of the kind words he said to me, of the gentle way that he would touch me, and every part of me felt dirty.

"Don't you think it's peculiar that a woman would so easily welcome a man like that into her bed?" Mr. Alexander pushed his advantage.

"That is enough." Henry was on his feet and shouting.

"Mr. Lennox, sit down." Judge Sterling's voice was calm and firm.

I only kept my eyes focused on Michael. I saw a reaction now. Light came to his eyes. He was pleased. This entire scene was playing out exactly the way that he wanted to. I wondered how far back his plan had gone. Was this a new development or had it occurred to him the first time I sent him a text message?

I wanted to die.

"I think it is important that we understand why an innocent young woman would pursue a relationship with someone who according to her acted in such a despicable manner." Mr. Alexander's voice was full of mockery.

"Because she is a forgiving person and Michael is slime," Henry shouted. "He is manipulative –"

"Mr. Lennox, please do not make me hold you in contempt. I know you can pay the fine a thousand fold, but my clerk would like to not file paperwork this evening." Judge Sterling's voice contained some levity. He was trying to diffuse the situation.

"He is deceitful and he is cowardly," Henry continued. "He doesn't deserve someone like Stacy forgiving him and he should be thankful that she even gave him the time of day to say hello."

"You make Ms. Caldwell sound like the perfect angel." Mr. Alexander's voice dripped mockery and venom.

I looked from Michael to Henry. There was no darkness in his eyes, only rage, directed at the lawyer and through him to Michael. My skin tingled at the realization. I was not looking at jealousy. It was indignation.

"Don't you dare make a mockery of her. She did nothing wrong. You and I both know it." Henry clenched his fists and I knew what would follow if Mr. Alexander dared to push any further.

"Mr. Lennox, I am going to tell you one more time to sit down." Any levity was gone from Judge Sterling's voice. "If you strike Mr. Alexander, as deserving as it may be, I will have no choice but to have my clerk bring in an officer. While I am sure an evening downtown will do wonders for your famous temper, I doubt you want a mugshot to be featured in tomorrow's papers."

Henry backed away from the table. I expected him to sit down. Instead, he looked around the room. He wanted to say something, but when his eyes met mine, any words stopped. His eyes held me. I could see all the rage he felt at Mr. Alexander trying to shame me, and I understood as I looked into them, that he was not merely a Dominant protecting his submissive. He was a man protecting the woman that he loved. My heart clenched in my chest. I wanted to cry, to throw my arms around him.

I had betrayed him.

Henry turned and walked away. He opened the door, ignoring Judge Sterling's protests and it closed behind him with a loud thud.

"You see why we cannot reach a settlement, Your Honor," Mr. Alexander said.

I studied Michael's face carefully, looking for any sign of remorse or contrition. He only looked pleased by the outcome and I could not stand to be in here anymore. I turned to Judge Sterling. "May I be excused, Your Honor?"

"I still have several more questions for Ms. Caldwell." Mr. Alexander sounded ravenous at the prospect of questioning me without my defender here.

"Your Honor, I think that before I say anything else to Mr. Alexander, I should speak to a lawyer of my own." It seemed late in the game to mention it, but it impressed upon Judge

Sterling just how out of my element I was in all of this. I needed that. I needed this conversation to end where it was, for the judge to see that this case was not as simple as I was sure Mr. Alexander had made it seem.

"You may be excused." The look of sympathy on Judge Sterling's face was more than I could handle. I stood and walked to the door, feeling the tears in my eyes.

I hoped that Henry would be in the hall outside of the conference room, but he was nowhere. I walked out alone to my car, tears blurring my eyes. I sat in my car for half an hour with no motion from the courthouse. The lawyers, Michael, and Judge Sterling would still be discussing the case then. I collected myself and drove home, feeling terrible about everything now.

I should never have messaged Michael. I should never have met with him.

I should not have been so stupid as to sleep with him.

SEVEN

I could not sleep that night and called into work sick the next day. I could not face the office and I could not face Henry. Every moment that we shared together played in my mind and I thought I could not have been a more foolish girl. He cared for me. Every sign I could have hoped to see was there, but I was too wrapped up in my own insecurities and my foolishness about Michael to see them.

I spent the day wondering what I could do to make this right. I would end things with Michael. That was not in doubt. I would try to find a way to pick things up with Henry, to make right what I had so foolishly screwed up. I resolved that I would not be another heartbreak for him, that I would do right by him somehow.

The mess with the case came first, however. I thought of the life around me and how everything fit into place like a puzzle. I tried to pan out to see what I could not grasp from my own little place in it. Every piece was perfect and I saw it. I saw the one thing that I had overlooked, the one gambit that had not yet been played because *I* was the one holding the card.

I called Michael and told him that I wanted to meet with him this afternoon. I let my excitement fill my voice. I could not wait for the evening. I had to see him now. Michael agreed to meet me for coffee. I went to the Starbucks where I had first met with him, when I was worried that Henry might try something drastic to put this whole case aside. I ordered my Chai Latte and found a table away from anyone else. I did not want people to be able to hear us, but I did want him to have incentive not to raise his voice, make a scene, or threaten me.

Michael arrived fifteen minutes later. He ordered his own drink and joined me.

"Are you okay?" he asked as he sat down. Care and worry were in his eyes now, and the emotion that I was used to seeing was present.

I held back my own revulsion and nodded before sipping my drink. "I didn't sleep at all, but I'll be okay."

"I am so sorry that you ended up in the middle of all of this. Nothing that happened last night went the way it should have, and when Henry exploded, he didn't help anything at all." Michael sounded so worried and sincere. "The judge realized there is no way to reach a settlement and decided the trial will go on in two weeks. I know it is not going to be easy, but I will be here for you, every step of the way."

I set my tea down and looked at Michael. "No, you won't. You will be out of my life, completely. I never want to see you again. I never want to talk to you again."

Michael was stunned. This was not what he expected, and I was glad for it.

"You will do one thing, though, on your way out of my life."

Michael blinked his eyes. "What's that?"

I kept my voice low to make sure that no one would hear us. "You will drop the case against Henry and his company. Completely. You will not say anything else about it. I will even let you walk away without a media statement about how horrible of a person you were to bring up a case of false harassment, when so many men and women struggle to get real cases heard and tried fairly."

Michael sat back and laughed. Things were over between us. His little game of playing with my heartstrings was done. The emotion was gone from his eyes. He was only cool now. He was so much like Henry in some ways, but only on the outside. I thought of Stuart talking about the plastic dominants who would lure submissives away from their true Doms.

"Why would I do that?" he asked. "I'm winning. Sure, you sealed your innocence in that room, but Henry looks like a bigger monster than I do. At the end of the case, Judge Sterling is going to do what he always does. He is going to side with the plaintiff because he does not want to be one of the judges who turns away a sexual harassment case, or finds for the defendant. He depends on feminist groups to ensure his election, and he will not risk their support, even for the likes of me and Henry Lennox."

Michael seemed sure of himself. I smiled. This was going to feel so incredibly nice.

"You will drop the lawsuit, completely, without a word and without a fuss. If you don't, then by Monday morning, you won't have a job." I let my own confidence fill my voice. I felt strange, as though someone else were in control of my body. I also felt sure. I knew exactly what I needed to say to make my case, and I did not doubt that I would be heard, listened to, and believed.

"How could you possibly affect my job?" Michael waved his hand dismissively and raised his cup to sip his drink. "You're a low-level creative consultant. At Lellman& White, you were nothing but an intern. There is nothing you have that could even make me worry."

"I have the ear of Stuart Lellman."

That gave Michael pause. He held his cup in the air and waited.

"It is amazing the people that you meet when a billionaire takes you to charity fundraisers, symphonies, operas, and high society parties on a regular basis. I mean, sure, I'm just the quiet girl on Henry's arm. What was it you said? 'It's good to let clients see an attractive woman on your arm. It shows stability.' You would be surprised how many people are actually impressed with that attractive woman."

Michael waved his hand dismissively again. "There is no way that Stuart Lellman would listen to you. You don't even know anything about him."

"I know that his wife enjoys talking business with Henry, even at social parties." I folded my arms and fixed Michael with my own cool gaze. "I also know that Judge Sterling is not the only feminist. So is Stuart. He is a very serious one who does not merely have to play to a voter base."

It was a guess, little more than a bluff. Thinking about our conversation, of the respectful way that he spoke to me and the obvious distaste that he had for plastic dominants and men like Michael, I thought it was a safe enough guess to keep my confidence. Michael blanched and I saw his confidence begin to wear away.

"I also know that Stuart likes me. I'm simple and I'm quiet, but I am also observant and I learn quickly. I know the kind of people that he likes and does not like, and he does not like men like you. When I tell him the conversation that you and I had, he is not going to see it the way your lawyer saw it. He is going to see it for what it was. And he is not going to like that he has someone like you working in his father's office. You are a threat to the very cultivated reputation that his father built."

From the look on Michael's face, I knew that I had him.

"You will lose your new promotion and your cushy job. This time, though, there won't be a very kind and generous recommendation like you received from Henry. You will be a pariah that no one will want to hire again."

Michael clenched his fists and realized his situation fully. We were in a public place. Anything that he did would have witnesses. It did not matter if it was an action or simply words. We were in broad daylight, so there would be no following me home, no second attempt at a confrontation to try to woo me or intimidate me.

I placed my phone on the table and brought the screen to life. "I even have him on speed dial."

"Fine." The calculations in Michael's head were clear. He could not diffuse it or fight it. I had him. "I will drop the case. No comment, nothing."

I smiled and sipped my tea. "See, it's great when we can have a simple and honest negotiation."

I left the Starbucks feeling elated. No, it was not elation. I felt powerful. I thought about everything that I had experienced these few months with Henry and I realized that I had not changed at all. Oh, I was willing to do a few things that I would not have dreamed about before, but that was not the core of who I was. The change, what everyone around me noticed – except for Michael it seemed, who had been quite surprised to see it – was not a change at all.

It was strength. The lifestyle and my submission to Henry had made me stronger that I ever thought I could be. I had power as a person. More than knowing I had it, I knew how to grasp it and use it. I could trace the different lines of my life to the people in it and understand how they could not just affect me and control me, but how they could help me. I had no doubt in my mind that if Michael had pushed it, that Stuart would react exactly as I said he would. I would not even have to draw the comparison between Michael and the plastic dominants. I thought about our conversation at the party. Everything he described to me, I realized, was Michael. I had just been too blind to see it. Stuart would see it too.

That was power, it was my power, and I knew exactly what I wanted to do with it. Everything was clear to me. I knew exactly how to make things right with Henry because I knew how to grasp my power and hand it to him. I knew how to give over everything of myself because I felt it so clearly. My insecurities be damned. I would humble myself completely, and there, I knew that Henry would be able to forgive me.

I messaged him to let him know that I wanted to see him. He responded that he was at his condo and told me to come by. I drove uptown and waved to the attendant as I entered the building's parking deck. Today, I did not feel strange. I finally felt like I belonged here. The elevator could not take me to the top floor quickly enough, and when Henry opened the door to answer my knock, I wanted nothing more than to be on my knees before him then.

"Are you okay?" Henry looked confused by my state and I did not blame him. I did not think that I had ever felt the way I did in this moment. It had to be a new expression that I wore.

I walked in as he gestured and took off my shirt. It was not proper for me to be wearing clothes in his presence and I did not want to. Henry placed his hands on my arms to stop me before I could toss my shirt aside.

"Stacy, what's wrong?" He was worried now, battling to keep down his darkness even as my submission called to it.

"Nothing. Nothing at all." I struggled to find the right words to explain everything that I was feeling. I did not want to say anything to Henry yet about my conversation with Michael, not until he made good on his end of the negotiations. "I finally understand my own personal power and I realized that it does not belong anywhere, except right here with you."

I broke free of his grasp and began to unbutton my pants. When I looked up at Henry, my blood ran cold. I knew the words that he was about to say, even before he uttered them, and

I wanted to stop him. For the second time in two days, I wanted to die.

"I cannot accept your submission."

THE END

Thanks for Reading!

I hope you enjoyed reading Broken Desires.

Make sure you get a copy of the next book in the Alpha Billionaire Series Book 5: Broken Lust

BROKEN LUST BOOK FIVE

ONE

"I cannot accept your submission."

I looked at Henry, stunned by his words. After every up and down that we had been through, it was coming to this. My heart crushed in on itself in my chest. I could feel the tears stinging my eyes. I understood; I finally saw what it was that I was handing to him, and now I was going to lose it all.

Henry shook his head and ran his fingers through his hair. "Why can I never seem to say what I mean to you?" He let out a deep sigh and placed his hands on my shoulders. He fixed me with his eyes. I wanted to see his darkness there, but I could only see confusion and turmoil. "I cannot accept your submission tonight. I told you that I would not have a session with you if I were not in control of my emotions. Right now, I'm not. I just need to get my head together, that's all."

The tears rolled down my face, but the clenching in my chest eased. He was not turning me away. Henry wiped my tears from my cheeks and kissed me softly on the lips.

"I broke my word to you," Henry said. "I said I wouldn't act out in jealousy and I did last night. I am so sorry. I am sorry for everything you had to go through in that room. It was unfair to you and I only made it worse."

I kissed him now. I knew that what I saw was not jealousy, but I also knew that I could not tell him that. Henry would have to see it on his own. It would be the only way he would be able to distinguish the emotions and control himself.

"What do you need me to do?" I asked when I broke the kiss. I loved this man. With all my heart, I knew I did. I would let him do anything to me, but right now, I only wanted to help ease his confusion.

"I just need a few days. I promise I will get together with you once I have time to sort my head. I lose control of myself when I'm with you sometimes, and I need to come to terms with that in my own way." Henry paused, his eyes becoming worried. "You're not in trouble. You've done nothing wrong. I'm not punishing you or anything like that. Okay?"

I smiled, putting as much assurance as I could into it. "Okay. You'll call me when you're ready."

"I will. I promise."

Henry kissed me again. I buttoned my pants and put my shirt back on. With one last kiss, I headed back down to my car. I didn't feel good. I would rather have been with Henry, but I understood his need for time and space to think about what was happening. For my own reasons, I had been in the same place. I drove home, unhappy, but at peace with what was taking place.

My worst fear, at least, had not happened. Henry was not turning me away.

I slept soundly, surprised the next morning to feel rested. I spent my weekend cleaning my apartment and letting my own nervous energy out. I wondered what would be different once Henry sorted out what he was feeling. I hoped that he would not try to hide from his emotions or mask them as being something else. I knew what I had seen in the judge's chambers. The emotion was not jealousy, and if Henry could not understand it or face it –

It was a chance I had to take. I had to trust him to learn the things only he could learn, just as I learned the things only I could.

On Monday, I returned to a normal workday. No one mentioned the case. I realized that I had not heard much about it on the weekend news, though I didn't pay much attention to the television. I spoke to Ana briefly, but she had no news about what was taking place. I considered telling her about my conversation with Michael, but decided against it. I did not want to get her hopes up; most especially given the amount of stress she was under constantly because of this case. If Michael came through on his end, then all would be well. If he did not, then I would go from there.

That afternoon, I received an email from Henry. I was elated to see that he wanted to see me in his office. That was a good sign, I decided. When I finished my work, I made my way there, saying hello to his secretary as I did.

Henry stood at his window, looking out over the city. I stood with my back to his doors and waited for him to turn. I was not nervous. I wanted to enjoy the sight of him there. He looked like a prince looking down on his domain. In a way, I supposed that he was. Men like him were the equivalent of royalty in America. Their domain was the corporation rather than a tract of land.

He turned and smiled at me, walking around his desk. I stepped into the room and as I saw the darkness there in his eyes, I turned my own down. It was good to feel it there; I would show it respect.

Henry walked up to me and gently lifted my chin, giving me permission to look into those eyes. I wanted to get lost in them, but I knew that we had things to talk about. I searched his eyes to see what emotion was there, but it was still blocked behind the darkness. It would wait, then. He was here, which meant that he had come to some place of peace with what took place on Thursday.

I held onto that.

"How was your weekend?" Henry asked.

"Quiet. I did housework. You?" I searched his eyes to see if they held an answer.

"I did a lot of thinking. Thank you for being understanding with me. I know that this has been a challenging road for you. There is nothing that I can do to express to you how much it means that you're here right now."

I wanted to kiss Henry, but I also wanted to feel that darkness in him envelope me. It was the call of his darkness that won out and I smiled at him, feeling suddenly shy and insecure.

"You could accept more power from me," I said.

Henry smiled and the darkness in those eyes swirled. "I suppose that I can start there. What did you have in mind?"

I felt elated by his acceptance and suddenly very self-conscious. What I wanted was a very simple thing. What if he did not think it to be special or important? I decided that I could only tell him and go from there.

"I want to feel your dominance in a tangible way when we're apart," I said. "I was thinking that you could control what I wear all the time. Give me wardrobe restrictions."

To my surprise, Henry's smile grew and the darkness seemed to cover his being. Clothing was not that big of a deal. It was just the covering we placed over our bodies to hide the shame of nakedness. I did not understand why it drew out of him so much, but I found that I loved it.

"That's very good," Henry said. "I accept."

Now I did kiss him. I couldn't do anything else. He gave a surprised grunt and returned the kiss, wrapping his arms around me and pulling me tight to his body. I felt good there in his arms, whole and warm.

When we broke the kiss, I followed him down to his car. Rather than go to his condominium, we opted instead for my apartment. He wanted to go through my wardrobe and decide what he approved of and what he did not. My stomach tightened with excitement. It felt powerful and releasing to hand this control over to him. Yes, I would be limited by his decisions and I would have to accept them. That I was willingly entering into that felt incredible to me.

That he was accepting it was beyond my ability to describe.

When we arrived, I was glad that I had taken the time to do extra cleaning. Everything in my room was organized. All of my clothes were put away. I watched as he moved through my closet. He pulled out a few items, old shirts that even I never bothered to wear anymore; I had just never decided to give them away. He also pulled out all of my jeans, though he left me skirts and slacks. My work clothes remained untouched.

After he was finished with my closet, he went through my drawers, pulling out a few items. When he reached my underwear drawer, he pulled it out completely, dumping it onto my bed. He replaced it and sorted my bras out of the pile, placing them back into the drawer. He told me to get two bags for the clothes and I did so.

He put the underwear into one bag and the rest of the clothes he sorted out into another. With the clothes sorted, he sat on the bed and looked up at me.

"Do you have any other clothes?" he asked.

"No. I washed everything this weekend. I only have the stuff I'm wearing."

Henry nodded. "Take off all of your clothes."

I took off my office clothes and laid them on the bed. He added my underwear to the bag of them and allowed me to put the rest of my clothes into my hamper. Thinking, I pulled the clothes from Sunday out of there and held them up for his inspection. He took yesterday's underwear but let me put everything else – a pair of sweat pants and a t-shirt – back into the hamper.

"You're not allowed to wear underwear. Bras are fine, but panties are not allowed. You cannot wear them at the office, jogging, going to the grocery store, when we go out on dates, nowhere. Do you understand?"

"Yes, Sir," I said.

"Good. If I find that you have underwear in your apartment or if I catch you wearing them, I have a humiliating punishment for you."

My torso tightened in anticipation. "What?"

"I'm going to make a collar of your underwear with a ring and everything – made of underwear of course. If you wear them or if you own them, then the next lifestyle event or party that I take you to, I will make you wear that collar."

I swallowed hard and blushed deeply at the idea of that. Somehow, that seemed worse to me than being naked around guests or him fondling me in front of others. This was the first punishment that Henry had threatened me with that I could think of. He preferred obedience out of the desire to serve, not out of fear of punishment. I was not sure what it meant then, that he was giving me a penalty for disobedience now. Was it that he was confident I would not disobey or was it that he found a punishment he would enjoy levying?

I nodded, my thoughts making me unable to speak. I poured through my mind to make sure I did not have any other pieces hidden anywhere. I would not enjoy the punishment and I wanted to obey him.

"I don't have anything against jeans," Henry said. "I took them out because you won't like wearing them without underwear. I'm going to buy you jeans you can wear, though. I will also buy you new clothes for the office. I want you to wear an outfit that I buy for you any day that we will be getting together that night. It can be an extra reminder."

"Yes sir." I regained my voice.

He patted the bed and I sat down beside him. He laid me down gently and ran his fingers over my body, from my chin, over my breasts, and down to my sex, where his fingers lingered and teased me. I tried to push my body down to him, but he kept his fingers moving in time with me, not letting me be satisfied. Hungry for his touch, I turned to look at him.

"Please," I said. I wanted to feel him so badly inside of me. This moment in my room he was controlling me in a place and in a way that he never had before. I needed to feel him to have my body pleasure him.

"Eager, aren't we?" Henry stopped and unfastened his pants. He brought his cock out, hard and erect. My desire grew and I looked up at him expectantly. "Pleasure me."

I moved to his cock, wrapping my lips around it and sucking gently, willing myself to take my time and provide him with enjoyable sensations. I teased the head of his cock with my tongue before moving down the shaft and taking him in deeper. I sucked on him, wanting to please him, to taste his pleasure in my mouth.

Henry took hold of my hair and gripped, pulling at the roots. I let out a moan and licked my tongue along his cock, savoring the taste of his skin and the pain and sensation of his pulling. I wrapped my lips tighter and gently he pushed my head down, not deep, but enough to show me that he was controlling me. My torso grew tight and a deep urgency swelled between my legs. He pulled my head back and pushed it down again. I sucked hard under his control.

Henry pulled back and pushed my head down again, this time holding me in place. He pulsed in my mouth and his pleasure spilled over my tongue. I swallowed with each pulse and moaned my satisfaction at taking him in. When he was finished, he pulled me back, allowing me time to lick him as I came off him.

He was still hard and when I looked up at him, I could tell that he was not sated. At his urging, I lay back and waited to see what he would have in store next.

Henry reached deep into the bad of underwear and brought out several pair. I watched as he looped them together. He brought my right hand up to my headboard and used them to bind me there. It was a loose binding, but it did not have to be tight. I felt odd bound this way, caught somewhere between comical and humiliating. He looped another group together and tethered my left arm to my headboard as well. He balled up the rest and placed them back into the bag.

I could see now that some of that darkness was sated. I watched him expectantly. He reached down to my sex and pinched the outer skin of one side hard. I winced and did my best to control the noise, remembering my thin walls. A wicked smile grew on his lips as he increased the pressure of his pinch. He was going to drive a scream from me.

I gritted my teeth, whimpering and fighting the urge to scream. I opened my mouth to cry out and somehow managed to stifle it. My safe word sat close to my lips when he finally eased the pressure. My skin throbbed where he had pinched and the rush of blood there felt warm under the sting of pain.

"That was impressive," he said. Then his eyes darkened again as he looked at me. "Or did it not hurt that badly?"

"It hurt," I said.

Before I could expand on that, he punched the outer skin on the other side, increasing the pressure of his pinch. I tried again to stifle my scream, the low whimpering sound slowly become louder. The pinch was agonizing pain, and I found my urgency swelling with each buildup of pressure. I thought of him doing this to my clitoris and let out a cry that I quickly stifled. He pinched a little harder than the first time and released it. Blood rushed there and warmth again grew under the pain.

"What made you cry out?" he asked.

I was afraid to answer, but his eyes demanded to know. I swallowed hard and built up the courage to admit it. "I thought of you pinching my clitoris that way."

He brought his thumb and forefinger there and I closed my eyes, steeling myself against the pain. He pinched and I pulled against my cotton bonds. It was all that I could do to keep from crying out; even as pleasure built up with the pain from the pressure, he placed there. He held my hips still so that I could not writhe and kept the pinch firm. I knew that it was not nearly as hard as the other pinches had been, and I realized it did not have to be. I gritted my teeth, uttering soft, deep guttural sounds as he continued to hold the pressure. Slowly the pleasure under the pain built to a crescendo and pushed an orgasm through my body. As it abated, the sensation become stronger and my safe word escaped my lips.

He released me immediately and when I opened my eyes, I could see the darkness held back by his concern.

"The orgasm made it more sensitive," I said. "I'm sorry."

Henry shook his head. "Never apologize for your safe word."

"Okay." I smiled at him. The pain was exhilarating and when his worry faded, I saw that his darkness was sated, at least enough for the night.

Henry pulled a condom from his pocket and slipped it onto his cock. I once again found myself cursing the existence of that sleeve, but I said nothing. It was something he was not ready for and I had to accept that, just as he accepted my limits. Sheathed, he slipped inside of me and I welcomed the feel of him, filling me. I thought of my nights with Michael and how sweet they had been.

As I met Henry's eyes, full of the darkness that I sated, I thought this was so much better.

****

On Thursday, I followed Henry back to his condominium from work. My day had been busy as my team finished up another project, but I was still elated to be with Henry, to be serving him. Nothing else mattered to me except for that. As I anticipated what activities he might have planned for the evening, my energy increased. I knew that it was adrenaline and that once it passed I would be exhausted. I did not care. I would ride that high with him and sleep the sleep of the submissive just.

When we arrived, we took the elevator up to the top floor and into his unit. Down the hall was the unit where he had the suspension frames set up. I wondered when we would be doing that again. Most likely, he would be waiting for Frank to be available to spot and assist. Henry was still learning the safe ways to manage suspension. While I wanted to do it again, I also knew that I needed to be patient. Safety meant more than just Henry being observant. It sometimes meant that I had to wait.

As I walked into Henry's condominium, I began to unbutton my shirt. He shook his head gently, but the look in his eye told me that I did not have to fear waiting this time. He had something to discuss with me. He led me to the table where a light dinner was already laid out for us. We each loaded our plates and enjoyed light conversation about our days. I waded through it happily, waiting for the discussion that Henry wanted to have.

"I would like to try something with you," Henry said as he finished the last of his meal. "You've never had anal sex, correct?"

I shook my head and my torso tightened. The idea of anything more than his finger going up where things ought to go out was erotic and frightening at once.

"I would like to do it. It's very pleasurable for me from both a physical and mental perspective. It can be for you as well," he said.

"It hurts, though." I had a friend in college who had tried it with her boyfriend. I enjoyed the pain I experienced with Henry, but nothing in my friend's stories was pleasant.

Henry gave a solemn nod. "Part of the enjoyment comes from the pain. It is just like anything else that I do to you that brings pain. I have to..." He paused and gave me a smile that I found warming in a very deep way. Maybe Henry had not come through all of what was keeping him from opening up to me, but he had come through some of it. "We have to be careful what that pain is. I want to begin training with you. It will involve using plugs on you that are successively larger until you are relaxed with something inside you that way. It will be painful, but the training means that your body is ready so that the pain is just that. It is pain, not injury."

As I listened to Henry, I realized I did not just love him, I trusted him. I had no doubt about the care he would show while he described this to me.

"We'll go slow?" I asked.

"As slow as you need to. I enjoy anal training, so you won't have to worry about rushing yourself just to please me."

I took in a deep breath and nodded my head. "I'll do it then."

The smile that moved over Henry's lips and the darkness that came into his eyes was all I needed. I stood and took off my clothing. He did not stop me. I neatly folded everything and took it into his laundry room. When I walked back out, he took my hand and led me back to his bedroom. I stood and waited patiently as he walked to the small chest that held his flogger and other items. He brought out cuffs attached to a thick chord and attached one to one side of the black iron headboard and the other to the same side of the footboard.

I was curious about what my position would be, until he led me to the opposite side of the bed. He bent me over the side and brought each cuff to my wrists, fastening them securely. I relaxed against the bed and listened as he shifted items around in the chest. My imagination worked with the possibilities and I wondered what would be the first thing that he would use on me.

"One of the flaws of my wardrobe restriction for you," Henry said, "is that it makes ordering you to wear a plug all the time difficult. I don't want to take the chance that it could slip out while you're in the office. That's not the kind of humiliation I want you to face."

My face burned at the idea and how the thought of it made my torso tighten. He was right, it was not really the kind of humiliation I wanted either. That did not change the fact that I found it arousing.

Henry's finger touched my sex and I let out a whimper. "Of course, you seem to like the idea. I must be having an effect on you."

"You arc," I said. My face burned hotter and as he slipped his finger inside me, my arousal grew.

"Good." He removed his finger and I heard something wet issue out of a tube.

He was preparing whatever device was going into me. I realized that I had not asked to see it and he had not offered. I tried to still my fears and remember that this was Henry. I trusted him. He said the plugs would get larger as we went along. That meant they had to start small.

How small was small when it came to an anal plug? I realized that I had no idea. My mind turned over thoughts, trying to imagine what would be small compared to the tight hole there.

"Do you want to see the plug before I get started?" His question halted the spinning thoughts and I realized that my fear was as arousing as the fantasy of my office humiliation had been. I did not want to see it. I wanted to fear it and at the same time trust him.

"No." My voice was low, but it was enough for him to hear.

Henry spread my buttocks with one hand and brought something wet and cold to the tender hole hidden there. He pressed it in slowly and I let out a small cry, surprised by the feeling of it penetrating me. It did not hurt. I only felt the smoothness slide along the sensitive nerves there. I remembered the night in my apartment, when his finger had slid there and how wonderful it felt. My fears were silly to me now.

The item widened and my fears did not seem so silly after all. As I stretched for the plug, the pain started, sharp and pulling, bringing me apart as this thing filled me. I let out another cry and Henry eased, pushing slower.

Somehow, moving slower did not help the pain. It made it easier to stretch around the plug as it continued to widen, but the stretching pain that accompanied it only lingered with each agonizing push. My arousal grew as I felt it fill me deeper and each cry led into a moan for my pleasure.

The stretching stopped. I tightened around the plug again, though wider than I normally would be. Henry thumped the base of the plug, sending the sensation through my body and I gasped. The pain from the stretching eased slowly and my mind contemplated this strange fullness in me.

"That was very good," Henry said. I heard the ripping of foil and then felt him there at the entrance of my sex. "This is going to feel very good."

He pushed into me and my eyes widened in surprise. I was tighter now, and as he pushed in, I could feel the pressure from the plug as it pushed him down, across that spot that sent shivers through my body. He pressed against my body, fully inside me and pulled back, thrusting harder now. The feeling of being penetrated in two ways made my head spin once again and that pleasant haze quickly took over. I grunted, cried out, and moaned as he pushed harder against my body, feeling so full of him, more than I had every felt before. I shivered with my orgasm as he drove it through my body and delighted when his own took over, driving him deep into me and holding him there.

When he pulled out of me, he released my cuffs and guided me to sit up. Moving with the plug was strange. It felt arousing and cumbersome at once. Henry spent the rest of the evening helping me to adjust to wearing it. I would wear one every night I was with him. He also guided me through my kneeling and standing positions, so that I could do them easily without the plug distracting me.

It was a wonderful night and I felt excited for my new adventure.

Two

The next day, I found myself missing the plug and wanting to be able to wear it in the office. I had enjoyed my first anal training session, more than I had realized last night and more than I ever thought I would have enjoyed it. I remembered my friend in college and the miserable time she had with anal. If Henry had trained her, I thought, she would not have had the complaints that she did.

The thought of bringing someone to Henry was enticing and strange. It brought to mind my conflicted feelings over the experience I had as his submissive during his fling with Marie. I thought to myself that I could not subject a friend to this lifestyle and then realized how unfair that thought was. I was enjoying it. I was gaining fulfillment from it in a way that I had never experienced in my life. I was also learning a new way to love someone. I did not just love the tender things. I loved the rougher, harder things as well, things that he would only subject me to if I said I wanted them.

It was an amazing feeling. While I would not bring someone like Trin into this, knowing that it was not something she would enjoy, if I had a friend who was curious or who hinted that she would like it, why would I deny her?

That question had other complications. Would I be able to introduce someone into my dynamic with Henry? I had no idea. I knew, though, that there would be other ways to introduce someone. I could simply talk to her, or talk to Henry about bringing her to an event or a party where it would be easy to introduce someone new.

It was only one of the many things that I pondered as my life returned to a normal routine. Each session with Henry brought the plug again. The first few times, it was the same one. Then he stepped up the size, increasing it slightly. The nights we continued my training, he asked if I wanted to see the plug and reveling in my fear, I said no. I finally admitted to him why, that I enjoyed feeling the fear that not knowing brought. To my delight, Henry had enjoyed that admission. After that, he stopped asking me and I enjoyed my fear more, allowing myself to express it for him.

Fear was a powerful thing. He told me when he first introduced submission to me that he wanted to try things if I was afraid of them. I was not afraid of anal training in and of itself, but I was afraid when I did not know what the plug looked like or what size it was. I wondered if there would be something that would scare me once I decided to let Henry try it. I was not sure. I was coming to trust him a lot, and that trust helped to remove the fear.

Being able to find a way to add it back in, however, seemed to be enjoyable for the both of us. I pondered this on my drive into work, thinking of the two weeks of anal training with Henry.

My thoughts were still with me as I came into the office. Nora quickly gathered us around the planning table so that we could go over details of a new project. As Nora debriefed us, I noticed looks from Lillian and Wendy. They had something on their minds, and I could only suppose that it had to do with Henry and me.

When Nora finished, both women moved around the table so that they were on either side of me. A conspiratorial look passed between them and I waited for the inevitable question.

"I don't think Henry's having as many office affairs," Lillian said softly.

The other girls at the table looked at me as well, hearing her. Nora did not seem to. She sat down at her desk and picked up her phone to make a call. I looked around at my teammates, surprised by the statement. I had not taken notice of the prevalence of the affairs. I was not sure if a few weeks were enough to set a pattern.

"Maybe he's not had enough time for them," I suggested.

I had only meant to throw some logic into the discussion, but it elicited around of "oohs" that drew Nora's attention. Everyone hushed. When she went back to the phone call, the conspiratorial whispers returned, wondering just how much time he and I were spending together.

"Maybe he is just too busy to set up a fling," I said.

Lillian shook her head. "He's not flirting as much either."

I looked around the table at my teammates. My eyes met Bethany's and I think she sensed my discomfort with the conversation. She quickly moved us onto our new contract.

Henry's office flings did not make me uncomfortable. I had grown used to them over the course of our own – defining what we had was still hard. I was seeing signs of Henry opening up and that made me hopeful. I loved the relationship we had, the Dominance and submission, but my heart was in this as much as my body was. I needed more, a depth to our relationship that moved beyond that.

I wanted him to love me as much as I was coming to love him. So many things were pointing in that direction. His outburst in the judge's chambers was one of them, but the smaller things I noticed warmed me as well. This could be another sign, but I wanted to be cautious. I did not want to become overly excited about the reduction in his affairs and assume a depth to our relationship that we had not reached yet. Likewise, I did not want to set up an expectation that Henry might not be able to meet.

Something else occurred to me as I continued to ponder this thought. I had met Henry because of his tendency to have these office flings. They were a part of who he was something that made him aloof and I had to admit, attractive as well. I had decided that I would not make the demand that he end them.

Now I was not sure how I felt about him ending them on his own, possibly for my sake.

That afternoon I received a message from Henry for us to meet at his condo after work. When I got into my car and started my drive uptown, my mind was on the affairs and what it would mean if Lillian were right. I turned on the radio to distract myself and I found success.

The new hour was dominated by the case Michael had brought against Henry and Lennox Enterprises. Only the tone and tenor of the conversation had changed. After delaying the court date, Michael's lawyers had announced today that they were dropping the case. No explanation was given. No mention of a settlement being reached was talked about.

The case was simply going away.

They played the statement by the lawyer over the air. I recognized Mr. Alexander's voice and I could hear the displeasure there. I could only imagine the conversation that the two men would have had, and I suspected that Mr. Alexander had tried to delay the announcement as long as he could, perhaps to change Michael's mind.

I remembered the look on Michael's face that day. There would be no changing his mind. He knew I could make good on my threat. I wondered how many hours Mr. Alexander spent trying to convince him not to drop the case. With a perverse feeling of pleasure, I found myself hoping that he billed Michael for every one of those hours.

When I reached Henry's condo, I could tell that he had heard the news as well. Had he heard it on the radio or from his lawyers earlier in the day? I thought the latter most likely. As I took off my clothes and folded them neatly, he walked up to me and kissed me gently on the lips.

"I have wonderful news." Henry's voice was light and cheerful, but I could see the confusion in his eyes.

"Is it about the case?" I asked.

Henry's smile broadened. "Michael decided to drop the case." I watched him as his expression changed and the confusion tried to take him over. We walked to the dinner table, where a light meal waited for us. "I don't know why, though. He was in a perfect position to carry it into court."

"His lawyers didn't say anything?" I asked.

Henry shook his head. "No. They contacted mine this morning to let them know. No explanation at all."

As we took our servings of dinner, sushi tonight, I contemplated how to tell Henry what happened.

"I know why," I said at last.

Henry gave me a curious look.

I took in a deep breath. I wanted to get this out before Henry's curiosity could become worry. Given the history that I had with Michael, there was no telling what he might imagine.

"I talked to Michael after we all met," I said. "He was pleased with himself about how everything went down and he was looking forward to going to court. I told him that I wanted him out of my life, but that he would be doing something first. I told him he was going to drop the court case."

"And he agreed just like that?" I could see in Henry's eyes that he was not sure what he doubted in the scenario.

"The last lifestyle party you took me to," I said. "I spent a lot of time talking to Stuart Lellman while you and his wife talked business. It was funny. The first time I saw him, I knew he was familiar, but my mind was not connecting the man I saw at the party to the man I saw a handful of times while I interned at Lellman& White. I remembered that day, though, and I got to know Stuart some, to understand who he was."

"I didn't mention the party to Michael or anything like that. I let him assume that I met Stuart at some other kind of function. I told Michael that if he continued forward with the case, that I was going to tell Stuart everything, including the conversation that Michael and I had, where he hinted that my job would be affected by how I responded to you."

Henry sat back, his eyes wide. "Stuart would not let Michael stay at the company. He takes sexual harassment very seriously. He used to lecture me about my affairs all the time. It's one of the reasons I'm so careful about how I treat them, actually."

"I had a feeling he wouldn't either. Michael felt the same way. He agreed to drop the case. I imagine his lawyers tried to change his mind, but I was hopeful. I didn't want to mention anything until they actually announced it, though. I didn't want to get everyone's hopes up and then Michael do something stupid."

Henry was silent. I could see as we ate our dinner that his mind was turning through everything, trying to make sense of what I told him. When we finished our dinner, he took my hand and brought me to my feet. I kept my eyes down, and he did not lift my head to look at him. I could feel his gaze on me, though, heavy and strong. His desire and his power filled the air, charging it.

"I would like to tie you up tonight," Henry said. "I'm going to continue your anal training, but I want you bound and at my mercy."

My body shivered. "Yes."

Henry led me to his bedroom and stood me under the eyehook in his ceiling. I waited as he brought over rope, tying rope cuffs around my wrists before looping them up through the hook. He did not tie it off to the bed. Instead, he brought my arms up and tied the rope off on itself. He brought out a bar with cuffs on either end and attached them to my ankles, forcing my legs apart. Now that I was bound, he brought a blindfold, putting it over my eyes.

Without sight, my senses awakened. The rope against my skin was luxurious. The cuffs at my ankles were soft, padded, and lined with satin. I was bound in comfort, but still bound. It occurred to me as I listened to Henry move about the room, that he did not stop to fit me with my plug first, something he normally did at the bed.

Henry's hands parted my buttocks and I felt the wet plug press against the tender hole there. I had no idea the size of it. I tried to relax, but standing, I could only release so much tension. As he slowly pushed it in, I stretched and cried out at the pain. I could relax enough to let it in, but not enough to relieve the intensity of the stretching. This one was larger than the last; it had to be for as much as it hurt.

Through each cry of my pain, Henry pushed and my arousal grew. My mind swirled and buzzed through each stretch of my skin. When it stopped and I relaxed around the plug, I breathed out a sigh of relief. Standing and receiving it was far more intense than when I was bent over the bed. I let my head hang forward and breathed slowly, feeling the plug inside of me, thick and solid. I thought of how tight it made me, and wanted to feel Henry between my legs.

The pain at my left buttock caught me off guard. The tails of the flogger left me and returned. I tensed as the strike landed, a crack against my flesh, and the plug pushed hard against my insides.

"Oh god!" I cried out.

Henry laughed and struck again, bringing the flogger hard against my right buttock now. I tensed again, feeling the fullness of the plug and the pain of his strikes. He struck again and I tensed. The plug inched as I tensed, centimeters in and out of me. It was enough to heighten my arousal and I moaned at the pain and pleasure I was experiencing. My mind began to swim in all of it until I was nothing but the strike of his lash.

Fire erupted between my legs as the tails of the flogger struck my sex. The pain, the pressure, and the fullness of the plug all blended. With each strike I screamed, the sound becoming thin and airy. My pleasure built and swirled with each strike, mingling with the pain and coursing through my body. The orgasm was powerful and carried through several more strikes before finally abating.

Henry stopped and I feared he would release me. I wanted more of this delicious pain. He moved close to me and I could feel his breath on my cheek. I wanted to feel him enter me. He grasped my breast and I felt a pinch at my right nipple. I thought at first it was his finger and let out a delighted moan. As the pressure increased, I realized it was not from his fingers at all. He had fixed a clamp there. He continued to tighten it and my cry grew deeper and more intense. The pressure hurt, even as it drove my arousal deeper.

"How is that?" His voice became the sea in which my mind swam.

"It hurts so badly," I said.

"Can you still use your safe word?" His question confused me as I drifted through the words. He repeated the question and it swelled through my mind like a wave. Why would I want to safe word for this? The pain was intense and delicious. I tensed my buttocks.

The fullness from the plug intensified the pain of the clips.

Somewhere logic stepped in. If I did not answer Henry this would stop. He needed to know I was safe. I focused on my thoughts. I did not want to say my safe word, but I needed him to know I would if I had to. "I can say it. I don't want to."

"Can I push you to it?" The darkness in his question made me shiver. I tightened around the plug again and let out a low moan.

"Yes. Please yes." Now I wanted to utter my word, but not until I was at the very edge. I wanted to feel as much of Henry's darkness as I could.

He removed my blindfold, his face even with mine. The darkness that swirled in his eyes was intoxicating and I let out a cry to see him, wanting it to spread over me. "Very good."

I looked down to see the clamp at my breast. A silver chain hung down with another clip at the end. He brought it to my sex and pulled up the outer skin, pinching hard. I delighted at the feeling. As I watched, he placed the clip over the pinched skin and tightened it. What was pleasant at first quickly became painful, and my skin throbbed around the clamp. I rolled my head back, letting that pain move through my body.

Henry placed another clip at my left nipple. Another clamp tightened down and I continued my swim through the pain. He pinched the outer skin of my sex again and tightened the clamp down. I moaned loudly and brought my head down, opening my eyes. The chains hung loosely now, and through the pain I felt the cool metal against my skin.

Henry took hold of both chains with this left hand. In the right, he held a thin paddle covered in black leather. He pulled the chains toward him gently, my nipples and the skin of my sex stretching. As he did, he slapped the paddle against my outer thigh.

The blend of pain was maddening. I felt the pull against my most delicate parts, the pinch of the clamps, and the sting of the thin paddle. He struck again, and I cried out. In response to my cry, he pulled harder. I looked up to his dark eyes and he held me there as he struck again, continuing to keep the tension in the chains.

His eyes engulfed me and he pulled harder. The strike of the paddle was sharper and I cried out. The pull at my breasts and my sex grew intense. He inched closer to me and pulled tighter. I clenched around the plug at the intensity of the pain and he struck, firmly along my buttocks, sharp and harder than he had struck before. The pressure reverberated through the plug and I let out a loud and guttural scream. He struck again and the pain swelled over in me, threatening to drown me. It was intense, but it was almost more than I could take.

"Red," I breathed the word.

The darkness in Henry's eyes eased. I swam through my pain and sensation as he removed each clamp slowly. It hurt as the clamps pulled away from my skin, and I shivered at the pain. With those removed, he unfastened the cuffs at my feet and untied the rope, gently easing it down. I found that standing was not an option and Henry guided me to his bed and laid me down. I swam in the sensations of our session as he gently released the ropes from my wrists.

When that was done, he rolled me onto my stomach and reached for the plug. I stretched as it widened from the base, and let out a small cry. Slowly my body closed as he slid the plug out of my body. At feeling it leave, my body shivered, a small orgasm pushing through into the waters in my mind. I smiled and relaxed there as Henry's hands moved over my body, soothing something cool into my thigh and buttocks where he struck me so hard.

I could not say if I had fallen asleep to his ministrations. My awareness did not return until I found myself draped over his body. He stroked my hair softly as he lay next to me as naked as I was. I wondered if we had made love, but I saw no condom on him and did not feel the sensation between my legs that indicated I had been penetrated.

No, he simply lay with me, skin to skin. It was warm and comforting.

"Did I fall asleep?" I asked.

"I don't think so," Henry said. "You were just very deep into sub-space."

Henry tilted my head up so I could look at him. "You were very wonderful tonight. Thank you so much."

The darkness in his eyes was strange. I had never seen it this way. It was more than sated. It was calm. I realized I was looking into his own internal sea, and I wondered if he had a place his mind drifted into the way I did. Did I allow him to go there? A chill moved over my body at the thought.

"Are you okay?" Henry asked.

"I am. It was incredible tonight." I breathed in slowly. My mind processed through everything backward and I wondered what had brought the session on. I could tell by the way that he had brought it up before that he had not planned it. I thought about my wardrobe restriction and the first punishment that Henry had threatened me with. Had he found another punishment that he enjoyed delivering? "Was I being punished for using my friendship with Stuart like I did?"

Henry smiled and kissed me. "No. I would never punish you for what you did there. You were brilliant." He paused and I could see him searching for words. "You were more than brilliant. When you told me what you had done, I saw a woman who had grasped her personal power and used it. As your Dominant, I want to feel the power that you give to me in the most real and tangible way I can. That is why bondage and the sadistic things that I do are so important. In that moment out there, I felt your power in a way I never had before. I needed to use it."

I understood. It was that way when I had come to Henry after talking to Michael, only I was needing to give it to him. Now, he had finally taken it. I kissed him and felt my exhaustion coming over me.

"We should get to sleep," Henry said. He moved the covers beneath us and brought them over us to wrap us in their warmth.

I snuggled against him again and smiled, letting sleep take me over.

****

The next day at work flew by me in a haze. I realized that I was still in the high from my experience the night before. I had never drifted that far into Henry's darkness or into my space. I wanted to go there again, but I didn't think it was something that I could do every session. It was intense and exhausting. I thought it could easily become overwhelming. I understood for the first time that limits were not just about the things that I would not do. It was also about the structure in our relationship and our well-being as well. We could drown in ourselves if we did that every night. We needed the limits to keep us grounded.

That evening, Henry had me come to his office. As I entered, he invited me around his desk, where he was just finishing his work. He brought his hand up my skirt and fondled my sex, smiling at me with approval.

"I like to check once in a while to make sure I'm being obeyed," he said.

"Was that why you brought me here?" I smiled at him as his fingers slid into the delicate skin there. "To make sure I'm being a good girl."

Henry laughed. He removed his hand and gestured for me to follow him to the small couch in his office. We sat down together and he took one of my hands into his. "I wanted to talk to you about something."

His eyes were serious and I thought I detected something else as well in them, something a little fearful. He was about to open up to me, I realized. I made sure that my attention was only on him in this moment, pushing back any other thoughts.

"I know that you and Ana talked, and you know about what happened between the two of us," Henry said. I nodded and waited for him to continue. "I invested a lot of myself emotionally into Ana. She was the first person that I had ever taken on as a submissive. It was wonderful, but all of it was just the dynamic between us. I put everything there, expecting that she would stay the same and would not change. I gave us no time to build anything else.

"When she did change, when she no longer needed or wanted to submit to me, it was hard. I realized that I had no other way to connect to her. We had built up nothing else as a couple. I don't want that to happen with us. I don't want what we have to just be the sessions together."

"I enjoy them," I said. "They are all incredible ways for me to experience something else in myself and in you. I don't want that to stop."

Henry smiled at me. "I don't want them to stop either. I can't just assume that they will continue forever, though. Right now, you enjoy submission, but what if that changes? What if something else keeps us from being able to do them? I don't want you to be left wondering what your place is in my life. I'd like us to start working on other things in our relationship, the couple side of us."

"I like that.". "How do you want to start?"

"I was thinking that tonight, instead of a session, we could have a date."

My body shivered with excitement. "I like a date."

"There's a new movie that will be coming out next month," Henry said. "There is an exclusive premier this evening and I can get us into it."

I thought about that. The idea of seeing a movie a month before anyone else had its appeal, but something about it as a date did not seem right. As he talked about the movie and where he would take me for dinner before, I thought back over our relationship. We had several occasions together that did not feel like dates to me. I had never understood why until now. They were things that only Henry could do for me. What I had enjoyed so much about Michael was the simplicity of the things we did. They were things I could do with anyone, but I was doing them with Michael.

I wanted that now with Henry. I needed to be able to have it if our relationship as a couple was going to evolve. I held up my hand to stop the flow of words from Henry. He looked at me curiously and I gave him a gentle smile. "How about instead of an exclusive premier, we just do a normal movie?"

Henry tilted his head to one side. "Just a normal movie?"

I nodded. "A normal movie, maybe even a cheap dinner." I felt a jolt of something playful and wrinkled my nose. "Assuming your palate can handle normal food."

Something dark came into Henry's eyes as he narrowed them. I laughed and he returned it. "So, nothing fancy, just a normal dinner and a normal movie." He looked up to think and then back down to me. "I can do that. Any particular movie or restaurant?"

"There's a nice little Mexican place by the movie theatre. We can have something there and catch a movie. I'll let you pick since I'm picking dinner."

Henry blinked his eyes and I could see that he was experiencing something new. Every date we had was something purely of his choosing. While I liked giving power to him, there was something nice about planning a date together and splitting the decision-making. I thought ahead to the next time we would have a session and thought that I might find my submission more intense. As I watched Henry process our conversation, I thought he might be seeing that as well.

"So this is what a normal date is like?" he asked. He had a playful tone, and I could tell he was joking with me. I had no doubt that Henry had experienced normal dates in his life, at least before creating Lennox Enterprises. I also had no doubt that it had been a while.

The playful banter between us was nice, however. I was not just his submissive in this moment. I was his girlfriend as well. I had no doubt that my jab about his sensitive palate would come back to me in the form of pain another night. I also found that I had no problem with that.

Henry stood and brought me to my feet. I followed him out and we made our way down to his car. The drive through traffic and out to the theatre was not too bad this evening. We arrived to a busy restaurant, where we had a pleasant twenty-minute wait ahead of us. Henry looked back to me to make sure I was okay with that. I showed him the movie times and nodded. We would have plenty of time to eat and walk over to the theatre.

As we sat down, the restaurant manager, an older Hispanic man, walked up to us. He offered Henry his hand. "Mr. Lennox. It's an honor to have you dining at our restaurant, sir."

"It's a pleasure," Henry said. "You have a nice establishment and we had a craving for Mexican food tonight."

The manager looked behind him. I followed his gaze to see a busboy clearing a table and knew what was coming. "We just have a table opening now. I can escort you back."

I squeezed Henry's hand. I was sure the manager meant well, but I did not want the guilt of eating ahead of people who had already been here. Henry looked at me and I shook my head.

Henry turned his attention back to the manager. "Your hostess already put us on the list, so we're taken care of."

The manager started to say something. I watched Henry's expression change only slightly, but it was enough for the manager to understand. He thanked Henry and moved on to speaking to other waiting guests, assuring them about the wait and thanking them for their patience. I hoped for his sake that the other guests had not overheard the conversation.

"Thank you," I turned my attention back to Henry.

"You said you wanted a normal date. Waiting is part of a normal date."

I laughed. "Sometimes."

I thought that waiting was probably not something that Henry Lennox had to do often. We talked as we watched the guests before us go to their tables. When the hostess took us back to our own, Henry thanked her and held my chair for me to sit down before taking his own.

Dinner was pleasant. I enjoyed a nice, light taco salad while Henry decided to try their steak meal. It smelled wonderful, but I did not want to eat anything that heavy tonight. I still had a movie to see and whatever we decided to follow it up with later.

I enjoyed our conversation through dinner even more. Henry opened up to me about his life before Lennox Enterprises, and I realized we weren't from different worlds at all. He grew up in a suburban neighborhood, comfortable but ambitious. He enjoyed advertising and had dreams and aspirations to be on the creative side of it. His real acumen, however, was with the business side. I sensed some disappointment that he was not able to focus his attentions where his passion was, but I did not notice regret. Henry had built himself quite the legacy. He had a lot to be proud of.

The movie after was a light comedy. I watched Henry sit, very serious as he watched the movie. I finally leaned close to him to ask if he was enjoying it, worried that he was not having a good time. Dinner had gone so well, I did not want the evening to end on a sour note.

"The movie's funny," Henry said quietly. "I'm looking for the product placement that we negotiated for a client."

I narrowed my eyes and whispered to him. "You did not take me to see this just to check out another team's work."

He looked at me from the corner of his eye and winked. "I thought you might like comedies too."

I put my arm in his and leaned against him. As the plot of the movie began to twist, Henry started laughing at the funny scenes. Once the plot became predictable, we began analyzing the use of clichés and tropes. Henry pointed to the product placement to show that he really was looking for it, and I rolled my eyes, though it did not really bother me at all. Henry's business was a part of who he was. I had magazines at home just so that I had the print run of ads that the team and I had created for clients.

I understood where he was coming from.

After the movie, we drove to his condominium, talking about our take on the movie and wrapping up loose ends of conversations never quite finished through the night. It was a pleasant drive, and I found myself looking forward in a new way to arriving to his place and removing my clothing. I was not more eager for it, but I saw a new aspect to it now. I realized I was not looking at a compartmentalized relationship, where I was his submissive at this time and his girlfriend at that time. I was looking at different levels, where we opened up to each other in different ways.

Once we were inside, I removed my clothing and folded it neatly. Henry picked up my cue and had me stand still so that he could inspect me. He lifted each part of my body, my breasts, my hair, and my arms. He tested the firmness of my skin and checked me for blemishes and marks. He spread my legs, testing the muscles there before moving up to my sex, parting the folds of skin carefully to examine me. He moved to my ass last, parting my buttocks to see if he was satisfied.

I felt owned again, brought to that other level of myself.

Are you mine?

His question, asked in my bedroom the first night after we had gotten back together, when he, the case with Michael, and everything about the world he was exposing me to were new. I had wanted it then and I felt it now.

I was his.

"You're ready," Henry said as he stood and walked around to stand in front of me. "Tonight, I am going to be inside you in a new way."

I swallowed hard and felt my nervousness rise. He took my hand and led me back to his bedroom. He bid me to sit down on his bed and walked to his chest of delights. I wondered if I would be bound to the bed and how. When he came to the bed, however, it was not with cuffs or rope. He brought his lubricant and a pink dildo with various ribs and bumps along its surface.

"You're wondering what I'm doing." Henry sounded pleased with my curiosity and confusion.

He stripped and laid me down on the bed, opening my legs. He brought the dildo between them and brought it to life. It buzzed against my sex and I moaned. Not everything, I reminded myself, was about pain, and I enjoyed the pure pleasure that he brought me. He held it against my body until I shook with my orgasm. Then he brought it wet to my sex and pushed it inside me. The vibration of it moved through my body as he brought it in and out of me in steady motions.

"I am going to take you from here." Henry grasped my buttocks under me. "But tonight I will penetrate you in both places. Do you like this so far?"

"Yes," I said. My pleasure swelled around the buzzing device in my body and washed over me. I liked it very much.

Slowly Henry rolled me over, keeping the vibrating dildo inside of me, and brought my hips up. It was time, and in my pleasure, I was ready for him. I listened as he unwrapped his condom and waited for him to press against me. He opened my buttocks gently and his cock was there, hard, wet from the lubricant, and sheathed. As his toy buzzed inside of me he pushed into me, opening my tender hole wider than any of the trainers had so far. I cried out as he moved slow, allowing my body to ease around him. The vibration of the dildo helped that. He stretched me and filled me bit by bit, as he moved.

I continued my cry with each push in, savoring the pain, as I knew he was savoring my reaction to it. When he was inside of me completely, he pulled back, sliding out of me. The sensation of his leaving, gliding along those sensitive parts of me, collided with the vibration in my sex. My orgasm pushed through my body hard and thick, clouding my mind with my pleasure. I did not realize he had thrust into me again until he was against my body. Slowly he pulled back and pushed forward again. I growled and moaned, savoring the pleasure of him working in my body until he pushed hard into me and pulsed, grunting at his own orgasm and grasping my breasts to pull me up and close to him.

"You are a very, very beautiful woman, Stacy." Henry's voice sound both dark and satisfied. He released me and pulled out of me. I fell forward again, catching myself on my hands. He removed the dildo and I lay down on my stomach, letting the sensations in my body move through me. My ass hurt from the sex, but it felt full and pleasured as well. I could still feel the buzzing of the dildo in my bones.

When Henry returned, he moved the covers of the bed under me and climbed into bed next to me. As he brought the covers over us, I pulled myself up to him and he wrapped his arms around my body, holding me close. I looked up at him and he smiled, kissing me lightly on the lips.

"Was it good for you?" he asked.

"It was wonderful. The orgasm that you gave me was intense."

"I could tell." Henry kissed me again. "Do you hurt?"

I considered my pain. It was already beginning to subside, and by morning, I thought it would be gone. "Only a little. Is that okay?"

"As long as it's not an uncomfortable pain, yes." Henry ran his fingers through my hair. I closed my eyes and enjoyed the beautiful dichotomy of our evening.

THREE

The next morning Henry had a proposition that he wanted me to take time to consider before answering. He had a business dinner coming up that he would be hosting at his condo. His guests would all be in the lifestyle, and the topic of the evening was an upcoming fetish convention and the role that each of their companies would play in supporting or promoting it.

Henry wanted me to be present as his submissive. I would be naked as I always was in his home and I would be serving them. The prospect terrified me. These business associates could at any time become clients that I and my team had to complete a project for. Of course, any business owner or executive at the parties and events I attended with Henry could become that person. In that, this was no different.

Nakedness scared me. I would be exposed to strangers. I remembered my promise to Henry to submit if fear was my only obstacle. I also thought about the dinner itself, and what my submission would mean. It was carefully calculated by him, I was sure, a way to remind them throughout the discussion what it was they were taking part in. I thought of Henry's desire to have a creative role in advertising, not just a business one. I wondered if he saw the creativity, he had put into this meeting.

I decided I would not disappoint him. I gave Henry my answer when I saw him that evening. That night and over the next week, we focused on protocol, how I would address him and his guests, how I would stand, and where I would be at all times during the evening. It was a lot to remember, but as the date for his dinner approached, I found it all easy to manage. It was no different than putting together the storyboard for an ad campaign with the team. In a way, that was exactly what I was doing, but it was BDSM that I was selling, not fashion.

The Saturday night was upon us. I stood obediently next to the dining table, my hands behind my back so that my breasts were full in front of my body. Henry would greet his guests and bring them in, since they would be arriving together. My job was to be quiet, to only speak when spoken to, and to serve everyone the hors d'oeuvre and drinks as needed.

Henry's guests arrived promptly at eight o'clock. As they entered and walked to his living room to have their discussion, I felt their eyes on me, curious and lustful. I controlled my breathing and focused on my submission and obedience to Henry. I did not want to blush or do anything to reflect poorly on him.

I waited for Henry's signal and poured wine into four glasses. I handled the tray carefully, remembering to walk with even steps, and brought them over, offering to each guest first and Henry last. He accepted his drink.

His guests commented on my presence there and my obedience. As Henry spoke, I heard the pride in his voice and was uplifted. I waited for each signal from Henry or a direct request from a guest. Their looks did not change and I found the lustful glances at my body arousing. I imagined what it would be like if Henry had me come over to pleasure him, or decided to display his ownership of me by touching my body in front of his colleagues. My arousal grew as my imagination became wilder, imagining Henry giving me over to one of them, or to all of them.

Such a thing would be out of character for Henry. I belonged to him and to him alone. That made the fantasy even more enticing. It was lusting after a level of humiliation that I knew I would never have to face. It was something I could never have.

The evening passed slowly for me as I completed my service and listened to them discuss the event and their roles. Henry had not discussed with me his goals, but from the sound of his voice as they wrapped up, I knew that he was pleased. Each of them said good night to me. Since they were now addressing me directly, I offered a smile and a good night back as well. Henry saw them out and walked up to me once we were alone.

"You were splendid." Henry took my hands and led me to the bedroom. I was caught somewhere between elation for his praise and shame for my fantasies. As he pulled down the covers and laid me down on the bed, the shame faded.

He took off his clothes and I could see him hard and erect. I wanted him in every part of me, and when I looked up at the darkness in his eyes, I could not help but smile.

"Tonight, the eyes of five men got to objectify you. I know that you are mine, but right now, I need to reinforce that for myself as much as for you."

I swallowed hard. I needed to admit my fantasies. "I thought of you having me pleasure you in front of them." The smile on his face broadened. "I also thought of you handing me to them."

His eyes darkened but his smile did not fade. He was still pleased with me, even with my dirty mind. Henry sat on the bed. I moved to him and brought my lips around his cock, taking him into my mouth. He brought his hands to my hair, running them through gently and then pulling, alternating between the sensations.

"This belongs to me," Henry said. I sucked on him more eagerly. I wanted to taste him in my mouth, to have his pleasure spill into me, but even before I heard the tearing of foil and he pulled my head away, I understood that would not happen.

I lay back and Henry moved between my legs. I was wet from my fantasies of the evening and his acceptance of them. He slid into me easily, filling me. I moaned softly as he moved slowly, in and out of my body.

"This belongs to me." He brought his hands to my breasts and grasped them, pinching my nipples hard as he moved in me. "These belong to me too."

I felt good with him there, complete, but I knew that he had one more place to lay claim to once more. Henry pulled out of me and brought up my hips, parting my buttocks to allow him entrance. He pushed, sliding into me with my wetness. I let out a cry to feel him stretch me. He entered me fully and pulled back. My night, his claiming of me, and the pleasures of my body combined. As he pushed into me again, the orgasm that swelled broke over my body, a wave of cool and warm that brought a new cry from my lips. Henry pressed into my body and held himself there as he pulsed, his orgasm shaking his body.

He pulled out of me and I lay on the bed, allowing myself to revel in his ownership of my body as he took care of the condom. When he returned to the bed, he drew me close to him and brought the covers over our bodies. He kissed me softly on the forehead and I closed my eyes to the sound of his voice, gentle praises for my obedience and affirmations of the beauty of my submission to him.

****

I spent my next week with Henry, each of us reveling in each other's bodies and my submission to him. Except for Wednesday, when we decided to treat ourselves to another nice and relaxing date night. Both of us were tired from our day, so I introduced him to the concept of picking up take-out and renting movie from his cable box at home. As we ate our dinner and watched his service go through multiple updates, he admitted to almost never watching it. I wondered at how he could pay for something and never use it. Then I thought of the empty condo units below us. That was not unusual for Henry.

By the weekend, I realized that I had not seen my apartment in a week. Henry had a meeting Friday night and I decided that I would eat take-out at home and join my friends for clubbing. It was something that I had not done in a long time. I decided it would be fun and messaged Trin to let her know that I would be joining them. She messaged back that she was the designated driver for the night and that she would pick me up at ten.

I walked from my car to my apartment, my food in hand, and let myself in. As I looked around, I wondered when I would see my apartment again after tonight. Tomorrow I had a lifestyle party with Henry and knew that I would be spending the night with him. I might return on Sunday, but most of my week would be with him.

"Thank god I don't have a pet."

I ate my dinner and got ready for clubbing. I tossed skirts on my bed, understanding finally the predicament of my wardrobe. I was used to wearing jeans for club hopping, but that would not happen tonight. Henry had bought new jeans for me as promised, fine designer label ones that I was afraid of ruining with spilled drinks and sweat. I tried on different skirts, imagining my embarrassment if any of them rode up. I finally settled on a loose knee-length skirt and a black blouse to go over it. I put on my shoes and left my apartment, my important items in a small clutch purse that I could keep wrapped around my wrist.

We enjoyed the clubs together, taking time to be young and having fun. It was nice to be out with my friends, but I was beginning to feel my separation from them more. Our crowd had grown smaller again, and I understood that I would not be doing this much longer myself. It was a fun holdover from college, but we were all moving on into the rest of our lives now. I decided that I would find something else to do with Trin besides just the clubbing. I enjoyed spending time with her and did not want to lose that.

They dropped me off sometime after two in the morning. I waved to Trin from my building entrance and she drove away. As I entered the building, my blood turned cold and the enjoyment from my evening quickly faded. Michael stood with his back against the wall, next to my apartment door. He looked up as he heard me and smiled.

"It's good to see you," he said. He walked up to me. His eyes held sincerity that I no longer believed in. I had seen his true colors, and nothing that he could say or do would change those stripes. "I've been thinking a lot about what happened and I'm sorry. I was wrong to treat you the way I did. I want you back. I feel lost without you here."

My heart was racing, but not with excitement. This man was outside my apartment in the middle of the night. I didn't know if he had stalked me through the clubs and made it here before me as Trin began dropping people off, or if he had simply waited here all night upon seeing I was not home. I did not like either prospect.

"Go home, Michael," I said. "There's nothing for you here. Any chance you had is gone."

"I can't believe that. I know that Henry has you wooed right now, but I know him Stacy. He's a very dark man. If he does not just dump you aside, then he will corrupt you and turn you into something else. He will take the beautiful and sweet young woman you are, and he will twist it."

I shook my head. "You know nothing at all about the relationship Henry and I have."

"I know that it can't work. You're too different and from two different worlds. I know that you're caught up in this idea of the billionaire playboy rescuing the innocent young woman. The real world does not work like that. He is not good for you and I need you to see that before he hurts you."

I let out a deep sigh. "Michael, the only person who had hurt me here is you. You got close to me and played with me, all to give yourself leverage for your case. All of that is done now. It's over. I don't want you. I don't want you to be part of my life."

Michael moved closer to me and I pushed him away. I did not want him in my space. He moved again, more quickly this time and grabbed my arm. He moved in to kiss me. I brought my other arm up and slapped him, hard across the face. He backed away, holding his cheek, his eyes darkening. This was not like Henry's darkness; this was debasing. I threaded my keys between my fingers and held up my fist.

"If you come near me again," I said, "I will cut you. Now leave."

Michael's eyes considered me. The darkness faded and something else came into them. I did not know if it was resignation or horror at what his obsession had done to him. I did not care either way. He stepped wide around me. I turned to watch him leave, stepping up to the entrance of my building so that I could see him walk to the end of the parking lot, get into his car, and leave. Once he was gone, I ran to my apartment, opening the door quickly, and slamming it shut behind me, locking the door.

I did not get to sleep until dawn, worrying that each vehicle might be Michael's car or that each knock through the walls might be his footsteps outside. I had thought about calling Henry, but did not. I would have to sleep in my apartment at some point again. It was best if I rid myself of my fear. I knew that he would not be back. Whatever the look was in his eyes, by the time dawn arrived and sleep overtook me, I understood that last night would be our last encounter.

By the time Saturday night arrived, I was rested and ready for the party with Henry. He dressed me in a provocative dress that rode high on my hips and low over my breasts. If I had to bend over, I knew that I would be revealing myself to those around me. With a perverse tingle between my legs, I wondered if Henry would see to it that I did.

When we arrived to the hotel for the party, I was excited and checked myself constantly to ensure that I was not pulling on the hem of my skirt. We entered and I saw several submissives in varying modes of dress, all accompanies by their Dominants. I smiled to those that I knew and socialized with regularly at the parties, eventually joining them for conversation when the Dominants broke off into their groups to talk.

Of them, Lori was my favorite. Like me, she came from a simple suburban background. She was a graduate student and a submissive to a professor at the university – though not one that was part of her own discipline. She attended a rival college from my own, and we enjoyed playful banter about our college teams as we all spoke.

As we socialized, I watched the faces of my fellow submissives grow pale. I turned to see Mistress Aevia walking up to us. The others backed away when it was clear she was approaching me. I did not know if it was fear, respect of privacy, or both that guided them.

"Stacy, it is so nice to see you," Mistress Aevia said. Her voice dripped with her self-importance. "I'm glad that I'm able to speak to you."

"Mistress Aevia, you don't have permission to speak to me," I said, keeping my eyes down. "Henry has only given one-person blanket permission, and she is not you."

I glanced up through my eyelashes to see the look on her face. Mistress Aevia's eyes narrowed and she stepped back. Finally, she nodded and turned. I thought at first my encounter was done, until I saw her walk up to Henry. They spoke and I saw a strange look cross his face. From the distance, I could not tell if it was surprise or something else. Mistress Aevia walked back over with him and I steeled myself for a reprimand.

"Stacy," Henry said, his voice gentle. "Do you mind if Mistress Aevia speaks to you?"

I blinked and looked up at Henry. I remembered myself and looked down quickly. I saw only concern in his eyes. He understood the problems that I was having with her. "Yes, sir. With your permission, she may."

"Thank you." He turned to Mistress Aevia. "Mistress, you may now speak with my submissive."

He walked away. I could feel Mistress Aevia's eyes heavy on me. I kept my eyes averted respectfully and my back and shoulders straight.

"I have to admit that impressed me. I'm not sure which of the two of you impressed me more, but still." Mistress Aevia paused. "You may look up at me for this if you'd like."

I took the invitation to meet Mistress Aevia's eyes. I did not find reproach there, only a cool evenness.

"Michael approached you last night and you stood your ground."

"You've been having me followed?" I doubted that Mistress Aevia would have would have done it herself. I could see it being beneath her.

"Yes. If he had attacked you or tried anything else, you would have had help immediately. I have a vested interest in Henry's success and happiness in the lifestyle. I wanted to make sure that the submissive he chose this time would not hurt him. I will not have anyone following you around anymore. You have proven yourself to me."

I was stunned. I thought to be delighted, and a *thank you* started to form on my lips. Then I remembered what Henry had told me after the suspension incident in the dungeon. I did not have to have the approval of anyone except for him. She was not my Mistress, and that she acted as though she had some claim over me and Henry was not right. She may have owned him once to train him, but that was a long time ago.

He had earned his release many times over.

"No," I said.

Mistress Aevia tilted her head to one side. "Pardon me?"

"No," I repeated. "I don't owe anything to anyone in this room except myself and Henry.

I don't have to please you, and neither does he. You don't have any vested interest in him. You trained him, and I sincerely thank you for that training. He is a wonderful Dominant and a powerful sadist. Neither of us owes you more than that thanks. Now, it is his life, and choices and mistakes are his to make, just like my choices and mistakes are mine. You can take your approval of me, Mistress Aevia, and with all due respect, shove it."

Lori and the other submissives that I had been speaking to were just in earshot. I heard them gasp, but I did not let it change my posture or my expression. I did not have to impress them either, as much as I liked their company. This was between Mistress Aevia and me.

I waited for her reprimand or for her to storm off and retrieve Henry again.

Instead, she smiled. "I see why Henry likes you. You have a quiet demeanor, but when you find your power, you do know how to wield it." She paused and breathed slowly. I understood that I had wounded her pride with what I said, and I was seeing her self-control now. "You are right. You never had to impress me. I hope that you will at least allow me the flaw to be selfish and to take satisfaction in seeing that Henry has finally found *his* submissive."

Now I let myself feel delighted. I kept myself controlled and nodded. "Yes, Mistress Aevia. You can have that."

Her look was cool, but I could see she was still pleased. I remembered Allen telling me that Mistress Aevia was mean. This would be the most pleasant that she would be to me. I thought that I could accept it now. I knew that she respected me.

I averted my eyes once more to show my respect to her. "Is there anything else I can do for you, Mistress?"

"No. You do it already." With that, Mistress Aevia walked away.

Slowly the other submissives returned. I breathed slowly and quickly turned the conversation away from their shock and praise. I was proud of myself, but that did not mean that I wanted everyone at the party discussing the encounter.

I rejoined Henry as we prepared to leave. I was elated that my war with Mistress Aevia was over, and that Michael was out of my life for good now. As we drove home, I rode on that high, letting it carry me up to Henry's condominium and guide my hands as I removed my clothing.

Henry led me to the bedroom and laid me on the bed, sitting beside me. "I've been wanting to do something with you and I think we're ready for it."

"What is it?" I asked.

"I want to edge you." When I looked at Henry in confusion, he explained it to me. "I want to bring you to the brink of your orgasm and back you down from it, so that you cannot actually come. It's a form of control over your body."

I bit my lip, trying to imagine it and nodded my head.

"When you cannot take any more," Henry said, "I want you to beg me to let you come."

"Yes sir."

Henry parted my legs and brought his face between my thighs. His tongue was there at my sex, exploring it, teasing up to my clitoris and down again. My pleasure swelled as he teased and pleased my body. The experience was purely sensual, and on the heels of the last two nights, it was perfect. It built to a crescendo and he stopped. The feeling pulled back down and I sighed.

When he started again, everything built again around the touch of his tongue. My pleasure moved up between my legs, a pounding urge to sweep through my body. As it reached its tipping point, Henry stopped again, and it eased down.

He started again, building up my pleasure and pulling back. Each time I grew more anxious for my orgasm. My body began to ache for the need, the parts that he pleased with his tongue and then his fingers grew sensitive and sore. The need for my orgasm was maddening and I finally broke down.

"Please let me come," I said.

Henry's eyes were dark as he shook his head. "I'm not convinced yet."

He brought me close again and I moaned in misery for my fate. Would he never let me come again? What if he edged me all night and gave me no release?

"Please," I said. "I need to come so badly."

Henry brought me close and down again. I let out a deep, guttural noise and gripped at his sheets. How could he do this to me?

"Please sir, please."

Henry brought me close again. I agonized as I reached close to that peak, knowing that he would back down again. As he took me to that edge, I opened my eyes, pleading with him.

"Come," he said and continued his ministrations.

The release was deep and strong. I cried out loudly as my orgasm moved through my body, not a wave now, but a quake that moved through my core and out to every part of me. When it stopped, I lay still, unsure if I was breathing or my heart was beating. My mind floated in a sea of pleasure and Henry's control over me.

It was a wonderful experience and I wondered when he would do this again to me. Often, I hoped.

Henry lay next to me and brushed his fingers through my hair. "You did very well tonight. I want to ask you something, but I need you focused and with me. This is something you can say no to."

I held onto Henry's words like a life preserver in the sea that was my mind and turned my eyes to him. "What is it?"

"Do you masturbate when we're not together?" he asked.

"Sometimes."

Henry smiled. "I want to control your orgasms, not just when we're together, but when we're apart as well. I want to own every one of them. Unless I tell you that you can, I don't want you to masturbate and when we're together, I don't want you to come unless I command it. Sometimes I want to make you come so many times that you beg me to stop. Other times, I want to edge you the way I did tonight until you go mad. Can I do that?"

I considered his request carefully. He was asking for more control of me. I loved this experience, but how would I feel when I wanted to masturbate, when I needed to because he was out of town on business? Would I be able to handle that? I thought about the feeling of his control. It would be a delicious torture. I would want to touch myself and to come. I would know that I was not allowed and I would feel his control. I knew that the desire that would drive in me would only make me want it more.

"I will be nothing but a craven mess when we're apart and I can't relieve myself," I said.

The look in Henry's eyes stirred me. That was exactly what he wanted, and I knew. I wanted it too.

"Yes. Will you sometimes command me to masturbate as well?" I asked.

"Yes, that will be part of it too." Henry kissed me gently on the forehead.

Henry pulled down the covers beneath me. I watched him remove his clothing and he climbed into bed. I rolled over to cuddle him and I soon fell asleep to the sound of his breathing.

FOUR

I thought that edging would be easier to handle as it continued and I grew accustomed to it. I was foolish to think so. In our sessions, he would bring me to the brink of my orgasm, sometimes through sensual touch alone. Each time he backed down, I ached. It was worse when he used pain to heighten my pleasure. When he edged me with the combination of pain and sensual touch, I would scream as I backed down. The pain he caused would heighten, and when he drove me to the edge again, it would only grow worse. It was enough for me to call my safe word, even though I knew I had not reached my pain threshold.

The intensity was amazing, and he worked me through this on several nights, using his flogger or his paddle to drive me to the brink. The pain and the pleasure of his touch would mingle and I would be ready to lose myself in my orgasm, only to have it brought down again. My tolerance for the intensity and madness grew, and the orgasms once he allowed them, were deep and intense.

As maddening as the edging was, the forced orgasms were worse. After the first session, I dreaded them as much as I loved them. My first few orgasms were wonderful. That I could have my pleasure freely course through my body without being edged was a release. Then he would follow them up with more and more, not ceasing. He would not give me a chance to regroup myself or relax. Once my orgasm passed, he would continue to stimulate me until I came again and again.

I would end exhausted. He would ask me how many orgasms I had and I would be unable to tell him. Even when I tried to count them, constant pleasure drove the memory of the last number from my mind. It could have been ten or two hundred.

Once everything was through, I would look back on it, amazed at how he was controlling my body. I felt his ownership in yet another new way and it was amazing. I was in love with his power over me, and with the man that wielded it.

The next weekend took Henry out of town. I spent my Friday out with Lori and a few of the other submissives that I had been speaking to at the parties. We enjoyed drinks and a quiet night out, exchanging stories of our Dominants and our regular lives. It felt good to have them to talk to about all of my life about. I would be seeing Trin on Sunday, and I knew that she and I would enjoy our day together. I needed this so much, however. It allowed me someone to ask questions of and share experiences with.

I understood that I was not the only one to have doubts sometimes, to wonder what was going on in my Dominant's mind and heart, or to have these strange and dark revelations that seemed to light up my world.

I spent Saturday working on my apartment. Henry messaged me periodically through the day. As day moved to evening, I felt his absence more. I wanted him near me and each time I noticed myself without underwear, I remembered his control over me. I wanted more than his presence. I needed his body as well. I needed him to take me, to pleasure himself while he brought me to completion. The urge made me want to touch myself and I knew that I could not. As I feared, that realization only made me desire it more.

I tried to read to take my mind off my frustration, but it did little good. On television, I saw only women who were allowed their pleasure.

Around nine in the evening, Henry messaged me. *Are you being good?*

I responded back to him. *It's torture, but yes.*

I knew that he would want to know how it felt for me. That I was aching would be a pleasure to him. I felt warm, desirous, and frustrated all at once.

Beg.

I bit my lip. Would I be allowed to touch myself? I messaged him back, pleading with him to touch myself. I sent three more messages, quickly, so that he would see my urgency.

You may touch yourself and come, but you must record it and send it to me.

I did not even hesitate. I pushed down my sweat pants and lay back on my couch. I brought my phone between my legs, adjusting the camera so that it would pick up my actions. I brought my fingers down to my sex and eased them in. I was wet in my frustration and so eager. I moved my fingers along the gentle skin and up to my clitoris, where I circled and pressed.

My pleasure swirled into a tidal wave that broke over my body. I cried out loudly, forgetting about my thin walls and my neighbors. My orgasm was hard and long, and I felt warm and buzzed afterward. I brought my fingers to my lips and licked them, holding the camera up for Henry to see. I tasted like desire and submission, and I loved it.

I stopped the recording and sent the video to Henry. My frustration abated, I relaxed to read my book again. Henry messaged me back with a simple thank you, followed shortly by a good night. I smiled and decided to sleep myself. An early night would be good for me.

I enjoyed an afternoon of shopping with Trin on Saturday. We browsed through the lingerie section and she held up a cute pair of underwear for me to see. They were satin and lace with a thin strip thong.

"You should get these," she said. "I bet Henry would like them."

I grinned and shook my head. I leaned over the table and whispered to her. "I'm not allowed to wear underwear."

Trin's mouth dropped open and her eyes grew wide. "What?"

I blushed and breathed in slowly to control it. I shrugged my shoulders. "It's a thing we do. I let him control some things and that's one of the things he controls."

Trin stepped back and turned her head to the side, considering me carefully. She put the underwear down and nodded. "I always knew you were a little kinky."

I rolled my eyes. "No, not before anyway." I thought about it and smiled. "I guess I just needed someone to bring it out of me."

Trin took my arm and we moved to another area of the store. "So, is it getting serious? You guys have been going on for a while now."

I thought about that. Were Henry and I serious? I thought of the dates that we enjoyed together, nice and simple ones that allowed us to get to know each other better. I learned where his love of the opera came from. His grandmother had been a singer and he had discovered an old recording where she sang an aria. She died when he was fourteen and he listened to it for hours, picturing her not as the ailing woman who illness had overtaken, but as a young and vibrant singer at the height of her career.

"We're getting there," I said. "Henry likes to take things slow."

Trin bumped her shoulder into my side. "He gets to tell you not to wear underwear, but he's taking it slow?"

I laughed. "In some aspects, yes. Which is okay. I'm really getting to know him, and I know where I stand with him."

Trin stopped to admire a dress. As she checked the size, she looked over the dress at me. "So is he rough in bed?"

I rolled my eyes. Before I could protest the question, she moved onto another rack and a different track of conversation.

I enjoyed my day and when Henry returned home, telling me that he wanted me to come to his condominium, I was happy to oblige. It would be nice to see him and I wondered which he would have in store for me that night, edging or forced orgasms.

I arrived to his building that evening and made my way up to his unit. He greeted me with a kiss and I felt warm and off guard. I welcomed it, though. It was full of passion and desire, and it mirrored everything that I felt.

When he broke away, he guided me to the living room to sit with him before I could take off my clothes. That meant that he had a serious discussion. I wondered what it could be. I did not see the darkness in his eyes that indicated a desire to negotiate something new into our power exchange. I also did not see worry or concern that would indicate something was wrong.

I only saw the passion and emotion of his kiss. I felt wonderful and confused at the same time.

Henry breathed in slowly and took my hands in his. "Stacy, would you move in with me?"

I was not sure what to say to him. The question was far away from anything I would have expected him to ask.

He seemed to notice my confusion and touched my cheek gently. "I asked you to do something that we had not even negotiated. You did not question me. You just did it. I asked myself why. You always question something new. I realized, you did it because you wanted to and because you wanted to please me. You make a decision, continually, to submit to me. When you sent me the video I commanded, that was part of that continual decision. I need to make a decision too, continually, to commit to you. I want to do that. Not just as your Dominant, but as your partner."

My heart leapt and my brain stopped it. I had everything that I wanted now, but something was stopping me from accepting it. I studied myself carefully. I knew my feelings for Henry. I knew what I wanted with him. The threesome with Marie came to my mind and I understood now. I had felt this before when Lillian mentioned that Henry's flirting was becoming less frequent. She was right. It was fine for him to change an action, but I worried that he might be changing something fundamental in him.

"What's wrong?" Concern moved into Henry's eyes now.

I smiled and brought his hands to my lips to kiss them. "I was thinking about the night with Marie, and that you're not flirting in the office like you used to. I want that commitment with you, but I don't want to change who you are. I've fallen in love with Henry Lennox, with all of the darkness and affairs that come with it. If they're a meaningful part of you, then I don't want to change that. I don't want you to become someone you will be unhappy with."

Henry laughed and kissed me. When he pulled away, I saw understanding replacing the concern. "The affairs were just things to pass the time and have enjoyment with someone. I won't say that they don't matter, because those women are people who I always strived to make sure received something in the encounter. The need to have those affairs, though, is not some deep need in myself. I only continued them because I was unsure of where we were headed. Maybe I was afraid of making that commitment to you."

I nodded, understanding what he was saying. "What about the encounter with Marie?"

"I wasn't sure that you enjoyed it," Henry said. "I've not brought up doing it again because of that."

"It took me a while to process the experience," I said. "I did enjoy it. It affirmed our Dominance and submission in ways that nothing else has. I was there to serve you. Even when you denied me, I felt your dominance over me and my submission to you. I wanted Marie. I still don't know if I wanted her for me or to please you. I'm not sure that it really matters, though, not for that kind of situation. I would do it again if you asked me to. The only thing I've never been able to settle – I know it is something that you would do with your submissive. I don't know if it is something that you would do with your girlfriend."

Henry squeezed my hand and I saw both his darkness and something else, something tender. "It's something I would want to do with both. I don't need them, but I do enjoy my affairs, and sharing that night with you, it was more than just physical gratification. I wanted to share with you a part of myself. I wish I had known how to explain it to you because I think you would have enjoyed it more. I wanted you to be a part of that with me, not just as my submissive."

I leaned against the back cushion of the couch and looked at Henry. "I wish I had been more receptive to the signals you were putting out to me. I might have understood it even without the explanation."

Henry smiled again and leaned with me against the cushions. "I'm not going to keep up the affairs. I want to focus on us. I would like a threesome with you some time, like what we had with Marie. When we're ready for it together, we'll talk about it and choose someone we know, who we think will enjoy the experience with us. As a Dominant, it's an incredible scene. I know it's humiliating for you and I revel in bringing that. I know that it builds a lot of want and desire, and withholding from you in that is a powerful thing. I want to experience that again as your Dominant, but I want to make sure that as my girlfriend, you're not left wondering, hurt, or worried by the experience."

I could accept that.

Henry took my hand and led me to his bedroom. He removed my clothes and then his, letting them pile on the floor. He brought me down to his bed and kissed me. I reveled in that passion again and understood. This moment was not about my submission. It was about us. He moved his hand down my body, caressing my breasts and my stomach. He found my sex and brought his fingers there, gentle as he moved into the tender folds.

When he moved between my legs and brought himself to the opening of my sex, I started. I looked at Henry and he stopped as he was about to enter me.

"Is something wrong?" he asked.

"You're forgetting your condom," I said.

He smiled. "Do you need it?"

My body shivered. I did not need it, and I saw now that he did not either. "No."

Henry pushed into me. I felt the flesh of his body, moving inside me and closed my eyes, moaning in the ecstasy of him. I put my arms around his shoulders and grasped his hair as he moved, working in and out of me. I raised up my hips to meet him, enjoying the sensation of him there. He was warm and smooth. My arousal and pleasure swirled. As he thrust more urgently, it built into a crescendo and rushed over and through my body. He moaned and pressed tight, pushing himself deep into me and spilling his own pleasure into my body.

When his orgasm passed, he pulled out of me. We lay there together in the afterglow of our passion and talked about the logistics of moving me into his condo. I admitted that it was far too sparse for me to be comfortable living in every day. I needed something more full around me in my furniture and my rooms.

We talked about arranging another unit for a home, combining our decorating tastes and making it something that we shared. This unit we would save for parties and meetings that he needed to host, and of course, the one down the hall for when we did our suspension again.

I hoped that would be soon and Henry promised me it would.

We talked about Paris as well. His trip to London turned out to be fruitful after all, and he would need to go to Paris in two months. He wanted to take me with him. We would have more simple dates here at home, but in Paris, he wanted to show me all of the things that only he could show me. I liked that idea, and reminded him that he could do that here sometimes as well, just as long as he let us have something simple occasionally.

I felt whole and complete. Any doubts and any wondering about what the future had for me where Henry Lennox was concerned was gone.

I was truly his and I understood at least that he was truly mine.

FIVE

The collaring ceremony is a solemn and joyous thing in BDSM.

Ana had explained to me that it was akin to marriage. As I studied the ceremony to know my part, I understood that. Henry and I had not talked about marriage yet. We were still getting used to being in each other's space every day. As I learned my role in the ceremony, however, I understood that it was a conversation that would probably come soon.

I was not playing a part. I was making a firm commitment to be his. I thought about Ana, the last submissive that he had collared. She had changed within herself and had to give back that collar. She could not submit to him or to anyone any longer. I wondered if that would happen to me as well.

We talked about it, and Ana had explained a little more of what she experienced as she came into the lifestyle and developed a relationship with Henry. She had enjoyed the control at first, but she had always felt a pull, even when she did not recognize it and when she later tried to ignore it. Her desire to train to become a Dominant was not something new. It was not an epiphany. It was already a part of who she was; she had not been ready to express it yet.

I examined my own self as I prepared for the collaring ceremony. I was not someone who needed to be in charge or in control. I thoroughly enjoyed the power that I handed over to Henry. While I learned with Michael and Mistress Aevia to take my power and use it myself when I needed to, in both instances I was happy to then hand it to Henry after. It was more than that. I needed to hand that power to him. I needed it to belong somewhere, and I chose Henry to be that place where my power resided.

Confident in my submission, I felt confident to move forward and receive my collar from Henry.

I asked Ana to present me to Henry. Though she had not trained me, in a way, she was a mentor to me, though unofficially. She was honored by the request and accepted graciously. She and I talked at length about my experiences with Henry and how I viewed my submission to him. In seeing her reaction, I understood that there was something in what I felt and experienced that she did not have with him.

Mistress Aevia would stand with Henry for the ceremony. I was nervous to have her there, but I remembered how our last encounter ended. I had her respect now, and I truly felt that I could respect her in return. It was fitting for her to be present. She had trained Henry. Though she did not really have any stake in him now, a place at his side during the ceremony was something that she had earned.

I chose Allen and Lori to be my attendants for the ceremony, to help me prepare. I felt close to both of them in this world and it meant a lot to have them be a part of it.

The night of my collar ceremony arrived. We gathered on the rooftop patio of Henry's building. The air was cool on my naked skin. Henry had offered me clothing, but I refused. I was always naked in his presence at home and when I served him. I did not want that to be different now. The air was not cold, and as my excitement grew, I began to ignore the temperature.

Allen and Lori braided my hair and pulled it up into a neat bun so that Henry would be able to place my collar on me. He stood next to Mistress Aevia, watching as my fellow submissives prepared me. He looked handsome this evening in a black tuxedo. In my hands, I had a leash, a symbol of the control and power I was giving to him, and a corsage for his tuxedo, a symbol of my respect.

When my hair was done, Allen and Lori both walked up to sit before the area where I would stand and offer myself to Henry. Ana walked up to me and offered me her arm. "Are you ready?"

I put my arm in hers and nodded. "I'm ready."

Ana walked with me until I stood before Mistress Aevia and Henry. I kept my back and my shoulders straight. My head was even, but I kept my eyes turned downward to show my respect.

"I offer this submissive to receive her collar," Ana said. "She has grown very much since I first came to know her from an innocent young woman into a vibrant and powerful submissive. She has learned to understand how to recognize that power in herself and hand it to another to use. She understands the intricate balance that takes place, not just within the Dominant, but within the submissive as well, to understand limits and show discipline and where necessary restraint. She is ready to receive her collar, if you are ready to receive her."

Ana released me. She walked up to stand on the other side of Henry. I stepped forward and bowed first to Mistress Aevia and then to Ana. To Henry, I held out the leash and the red rose corsage.

"I offer this corsage to you, Master Henry, as a symbol of my love and respect for the man you are. I offer this leash as a symbol of the power I hand to the Dominant that I have chosen."

Henry took the corsage and handed it to Mistress Aevia. As she pinned it to his tuxedo, she spoke, her voice full of pride and a hint of playfulness. "You're a Master now, are you?"

Henry gave a nervous cough and I suppressed my smile. He turned to me and took the leash from my hand. I dropped my hands to my side and brought them behind my back, holding them together with my palms out. "I accept your rose and your leash. Will you kneel before me?"

I knelt down. "I kneel to you, Master Henry. My desire is to follow you and to submit to you. Where you lead, I will follow you."

Henry presented my collar to our guests and to me. My eyes widened to see it. It was black with three rings set into it, one in front, and one on each side. A thin silver chain ran between the rings. Roses on vines were embroidered into the leather and beneath the front ring was embroidered an *L*. Henry opened it and placed it around my neck. I sighed to feel the soft satin lining. This would be a collar I would enjoy wearing every day. The thought of taking it off for work made me sad. I knew that Henry would have a day collar for me, though, one that he would present to me in private later.

"This collar symbolizes my Dominance and your submission. It is also a symbol of my care and protection of you. I will guide you on your journey from this day forward."

"I accept this collar as a symbol of my submission and your Dominance," I said. "I will wear it as a you guide me, and I will walk with you, serving you and supporting you on your journey, from this day forward."

Henry placed the leash onto the front ring of the collar. "You are mine, and I am yours."

"I am yours, and you are mine."

Henry very gently tugged on the leash and I moved forward on my knees to him. "Demonstrate your submission to me."

I blushed deeply and obeyed him. I moved aside the tuxedo jacket and unfastened Henry's slacks. He was hard and waiting for me. I took him into my mouth as he let out a deep moan. The taste of his skin was salty but sweet to me this evening. I pressed my tongue against his shaft and sucked eager to taste my Master's pleasure. He placed his hand at the back of my head and pulsed, spilling into my mouth. I swallowed with each pulse and when he was finished, I pulled away and fastened his pants once again.

He lifted my chin so that I could look up into his eyes. "You please me."

The words felt warm inside me. He took my hand and brought me to my feet. When he turned me to our guests, he presented to them His submissive.

THE END

Thanks for Reading!

I hope you enjoyed my Alpha Billionaire Romance Entire Series (Books 1-5)!

23020823R00259

Made in the USA
Columbia, SC
03 August 2018